"MEN ARE SUCH SIMPLE CREATURES, REALLY, IF ONE KNOWS HOW TO HANDLE THEM PROPERLY."

"Is that a fact?" Cole drawled. "Tell me then, Devon, how would you handle me? What would you do?"

"This." She reached up and laid her hand on his rock-solid chest. She felt Cole's body tighten, watched a muscle leap along the side of his jaw. "And this." She reached up on tiptoe, curling her fingers around the base of his neck.

"What else?" he asked, in a voice that sounded strangely hoarse. "No kiss?"

"Kiss?"

"Surely no lesson in flirting would be complete without it." With that, he wrapped his arm around her waist, pulling her tightly against him as his mouth descended on hers . . .

Other **AVON ROMANCES**

CAPTURED

VICTORIA LYNNE

AVON BOOKS ◆ NEW YORK

CAPTURED is an original publication of Avon Books. This work has never before appeared in book form. This work is a novel. Any similarity to actual persons or events is purely coincidental.

AVON BOOKS
A division of
The Hearst Corporation
1350 Avenue of the Americas
New York, New York 10019

Copyright © 1995 by Victoria Joehnk
Inside cover author photo by Glamour Shots
Published by arrangement with the author
Library of Congress Catalog Card Number: 94-96778
ISBN: 0-380-78044-5

First Avon Books Printing: July 1995

AVON TRADEMARK REG. U.S. PAT. OFF. AND IN OTHER COUNTRIES, MARCA REGISTRADA, HECHO EN U.S.A.

Printed in the U.S.A.

RA 10 9 8 7 6 5 4 3 2 1

To Mom and Dad,
with love

Prologue

❦

April 1861
Charleston, South Carolina

"**I**'ve never done this before."

Maggie Spencer was pleased with how the words came out; soft and innocent, with just the right amount of nervous trepidation to her voice. Satisfied, she slowly raised her eyes to meet those of the man in whose lap she was snugly seated.

"Like hell," he answered, his deep voice equally soft.

Startled, Maggie searched his eyes. She found neither anger nor cynicism in their dark brown depths, merely amusement. As though he was fully aware of the game she was playing, yet quite content to let her continue. She did.

"I don't even know your name, sir."

Again that flash of amusement crossed his face. "Abe Lincoln."

Maggie formed her lips into a pretty pout. He wasn't cooperating, but she wasn't about to object. She had determined to have him the instant she saw him walk into the Black Swan, the dockside tavern where she worked. That had been at midnight, nearly four hours ago. Unlike her regular customers, who were openly appreciative of her dark good looks, ample curves, and relaxed virtue, this man seemed almost indifferent. In

1

fact, it had taken her this long just to maneuver herself into the position she was in now.

It wasn't merely the man's physical appeal that drew her, though Lord knew that was considerable. Her eyes raked hungrily over his tall, masculine physique, his thick mane of tawny-gold hair. But that alone hadn't been enough to set her pulse racing. Rather it was the way he carried himself, his movements conveying a combination of animal grace and reckless confidence, as if the rules that the rest of the world lived by somehow didn't apply to him. She heard it in his rich laughter, saw it in his cocky grin.

"Why, Mr. Lincoln," she purred, shifting her hips to press firmly against his groin, "I do believe you've got your hands up my skirt."

"Is that a fact?"

Her eyes locked on his.

Fortunately he took her words as the invitation they were meant to be. He set down the glass of whiskey he'd been nursing and reached beneath the table. Her petticoats rustled softly as he tucked them aside. She felt his fingers brush lightly over her ankles and continue to travel upward. She closed her eyes, barely suppressing a shudder of excitement. It wouldn't do. Not in the middle of a crowded tavern. But then, that's what made the game so exciting.

Maggie sucked in her breath as the rough calluses of his palms scraped gently over the silky skin of her inner thighs. She waited a few seconds, then felt his powerful frame stiffen. His hands stilled.

She smiled in secret triumph, pleased that she'd caught him off-guard. Apparently he hadn't anticipated that she'd be wearing nothing beneath her skirts. She fluttered her lashes and sent him a coquettish smile. "Goodness, Mr. Lincoln, whatever did you find?"

He grinned. "The true meaning of Southern hospitality."

Maggie leaned forward, crushing her breasts against his chest. "Let's go back to your ship," she murmured in a throaty whisper.

"I have a better idea," he replied. "Let's stay right here."

It took a moment for the full intent of his words to sink in. Shock coursed through her, along with a strange, forbidden thrill. Her stomach tightened as she considered his suggestion. Was it possible . . . ? Could they really . . . ? *Here?* She shook her head, almost dizzy with the rush of desire that surged through her. That was taking her little game further than she'd ever taken it in her life.

He watched her silently, his lips curved in a small, speculative smile.

"Why, Mr. Lincoln," she finally managed.

"Why, Miss Spencer," he returned, a subtle challenge ringing in his tone.

Maggie's eyes darted around the room. Fat Harry was busy behind the bar and hadn't seemed to notice her. The rest of the patrons were either minding their own business or too deep in their cups to pay her any attention. Normally the Black Swan would have closed hours ago, but these days men lingered endlessly over their drinks, crowding the tavern until the wee hours of the morning. Holding stupid, pointless debates about abolitionists and self-rule. Immersed, as they had been for months, in heated talk of war—a war that she knew as well as anyone would never happen. It had been that way ever since South Carolina seceded from the Union.

Tonight was the first real excitement she'd had in ages. She glanced down at her skirts, noting the way he'd arranged them to fall discreetly over his lap. Correctly interpreting her silence for assent, he began to move his hands once again. His heavy, sensual gaze focused on her as he explored the tender flesh beneath her skirt. He moved with slow, steady strokes that were both deliberate and arousing: caressing her thighs and the soft swelling of her hips, tracing the rounded curve of her buttocks. Shifting his knees, he rocked her in a subtle motion that likely was imperceptible to a casual observer, but that played havoc with her senses. She felt hot and tense; her breath came in faint, shallow pants. Before she could react, he brought his hand to the lush tangle of curls between her thighs, massaging and stroking with unerring expertise, then slipped one finger inside her.

Maggie choked back a gasp and gripped the edge of the table. She clenched her teeth, struggling to keep from giving herself away. From a nearby table, two men regarded them curiously, then shrugged and turned away. Rather than cooling her passion, the risk of exposure only heightened her excitement. She hoped her expression was outwardly composed, but was too far into their game to truly give a damn. This man—whoever he was—was Christmas come early as far as she was concerned. It was time to open her present. With trembling fingers, she reached for the buttons on his trousers.

The explosion of cannon fire shattered the stillness of the night.

Maggie emitted a startled cry and let her hand drop. All around her, the patrons of the tavern exhibited various degrees of stupefaction as the first explosion was followed by another. A few men, fuddled by drink, stumbled upright and gazed around in a dull stupor. Most, however, reacted just the opposite. They leaped to their feet in eager anticipation, as if the moment they'd been long awaiting had finally arrived.

A boy of about eighteen lunged through the tavern door. ''They're firing on the fort!'' he shouted, bursting with pride and excitement. ''They're gonna knock them damned Yanks outta Fort Sumter!''

A roar of approval went up in the tavern as the men poured out after the boy, racing down to the docks to witness the action for themselves. Even Fat Harry hustled out the door, leaving the bar untended—a move that was unprecedented in the three years that Maggie had been at the Black Swan. She stared after him, stunned speechless. Abruptly recalling herself, she turned back to the man in whose lap she remained seductively perched.

"Rotten timing," he said amiably.

Unwilling to accept that he could be fully aware of the gravity of the situation and remain so calm, she informed him, "They're firing on the fort."

"Yes, I heard."

She studied him, waiting for a reaction. When none came, she continued darkly, "But won't that mean—"

"War," he finished for her. He shrugged and removed his hands from beneath her skirts, smoothing the fabric across her lap in a gesture that was as offhand as his voice.

Shock coursed through her. "War," she echoed lamely.

He nodded in mock solemnity. "I suppose there's always the possibility that the North will interpret this as a gesture of goodwill, but I wouldn't bet on it."

"You're . . . joking, aren't you?" she ventured uncertainly.

His lips twitched, but he didn't bother to reply. He eased her off his lap and onto the chair beside him, his manner suddenly brisk and efficient. "I regret, Miss Spencer, that our time together has unexpectedly been cut short," he said, his tone carrying the same grave courtesy that one might bestow upon the finest of ladies.

She stared at him in undisguised dismay. "But . . . but what about . . ."

"Another time, love." He raised her hand and brushed the back of it with a gentle parting kiss. "I'm afraid I'm one of those damned Yanks you Southerners are so all-fired anxious to be rid of. I believe my welcome in this fair city has just expired.''

A Yank?! But he was so charming! Maggie reeled in surprise as she watched his long strides carry him swiftly out the door. She opened her mouth to call after him, then hesitated, swearing softly instead. She didn't even know his name.

A blast of cool air greeted Cole McRae as he stepped from the Black Swan and followed the sound of booming cannon down to the docks. It seemed the entire city of Charleston had come out to witness the attack on Fort Sumter. Men, women, and children swarmed all around him, more than a few roused from their beds and taking to the streets while still attired in their nightclothes, determined not to miss a minute of the momentous occasion.

Cole found a spot away from the bustling crowds and stopped, watching the bombardment from his own private vantage point. He propped his foot up on an empty crate and pulled a cheroot from his pocket. He lit the thin cigar and drew in deeply, enjoying both the flavor of the tobacco and the warmth it brought. His thoughts ran along a purely selfish vein: he was glad he'd already finished his business in town, selling his cargo and taking on fresh goods and supplies. Judging from the giddy pandemonium that surrounded him, it'd be hell trying to get any real work done now.

This would mean war, no doubt about it. President Lincoln had refused to make any aggressive moves, despite the fact that several Southern states had already declared themselves seceded from the Union. In fact, the president had taken pains to ensure that if the South was really determined to fight for its independence, it would have to begin by taking the first hostile action. Well, the hotheaded fools had finally done it.

Cole frowned as he reconsidered, wondering if that

might not be for the best after all. Let them blow off some steam. Tension had been escalating between the North and South for years; why not bring it out in the open? After a few months—six at the most—the war would be over and the conflict would finally be settled.

As dawn rose and the sky was infused with soft shades of pink and gold, the damage Fort Sumter had taken became clear. The walls were already beginning to crumble under the constant shelling. Cole felt a momentary pang of sympathy for the men charged with defending the fort, but the emotion quickly turned to envy. At least they were being challenged. Tested. His own life was disgustingly void of anything remotely akin to that experience.

He found himself growing increasingly restless, wanting more. The war might actually offer an interesting diversion from his normal routine, he thought, brightening a bit. He considered putting his ship, the *Islander*, out to sea, if for no other reason than to match his skill against that of some arrogant Southern captain.

The more he thought on it, the more he liked the idea. An excitement he hadn't felt in ages built slowly within him. Why not do it? He tossed down his cheroot and smiled as he stubbed it out, suddenly eager for thrill of the chase. Anxious for the taste of victory.

It didn't occur to him that there might be any other outcome.

Chapter 1

July 1862
Fort Monroe, Virginia

Strange how a man could die and no one would ever know. Especially if one only died on the inside.

With an effort, Cole McRae ignored the piercing stares that burned into his back. He focused instead on weaving his way through the crowded streets, his long strides carrying him swiftly to his destination. The stockades, nearly abandoned after the Revolutionary War, were once again brimming with men doing time for desertion, drunkenness on duty, and insubordination to a ranking officer.

Cole stepped inside, taking a moment to let his eyes adjust to the dimness of the interior. A young guard who looked no older than seventeen and supremely bored, shuffled over. ''Tell Sergeant Coombs that Captain McRae is here to pick up his prisoner,'' Cole ordered. The boy nodded and headed off into the dark recesses of the building.

''You McRae?'' came a gravelly voice from down the hall.

Cole peered into the darkness. ''Coombs?''

''Yup.'' It was more a belch than a reply. The sergeant stepped forward, his eyes bloodshot, his cheeks covered with a week's worth of dark stubble. A stunning assortment of stains blotched what could only loosely be called a uniform. He reached down, absently scratching the fat, hairy belly that protruded from his shirt. "Me 'n' the boys was just having a little drink. C'mon." He turned and stumbled back down the hall.

Cole frowned as he followed him into an office that reeked of cheap whiskey. Five men lounged about in chairs, looking as drunk and sluggish as Coombs himself. The sergeant took a seat behind a thick oak desk and reached for the bottle sitting atop it. He refilled his glass, then looked around for one for his guest. Spotting a mug that had rolled onto the floor, he picked it up and blew into it to rid the inside of dust. He filled it and set it in front of Cole, gesturing expansively to a wobbly chair with torn upholstery and a broken arm. "Have a seat, McRae."

Cole ignored both the chair and the filthy glass of whiskey. "I'm here for the woman. Where is she?"

His question drew a low round of laughter from the men in the room and a slow, lewd smile from Coombs. "Anxious for her, are ye?" He removed a thin cigar from his shirt pocket, clamped it between badly stained teeth, then took his time lighting it. The sour fumes from the cigar mixed with the stale odor of cheap liquor. Incredibly, the sergeant himself smelled even worse. "So was I," he continued. "She's a purty little thing, but she won't make it easy for you. It just takes a little manly persuasion, if you get my meaning."

Cole got his meaning. Revulsion swept over him as he took a menacing step closer to the sergeant. "Spare me the details, Coombs. Just bring her out here."

Anyone a little less drunk, a little less stupid, would have heard the threat implicit in Cole McRae's voice. The sergeant, however, was oblivious. He leaned back in his chair, locking his hands over his fat belly. "She's gonna hang anyway, right? So I figured, why waste it?" The loud guffaws from his men only served to encourage him. "She warmed up real quick though, once she got a good look at what I had to offer. I ain't never had no troubles with females, once they seen—''

"Save it, Coombs. I said I wasn't interested.''

The sergeant glared at Cole for interrupting, then took a deep swallow of his drink. He wiped his mouth with the back of his hand and nodded to his men. "She wanted it though, a man like me can always tell—''

Cole reached across the desk, watching the sergeant's chin drop with slack-jawed astonishment as he hauled him up by his grease-stained lapels. "All right, you want to talk," he said with a growl, "then let's talk. Let's talk about what I heard." He paused, pure disgust shining in his eyes. "I heard she got such a good look at what you had to offer that she left you tied to a tree, your drawers wrapped around your ankles and your bare ass a target for Reb sharpshooters. Then she ran so fast it took you and your men five days to find her.''

Coombs's eyes widened, then narrowed to thin, ugly slits. Unable to deny the truth of Cole's words, he struggled instead to release the iron grip the other man had on his clothing. But it wasn't until Cole chose to let him go, shoving him roughly back into his chair, that he was once again free. The sergeant's furious glare moved from McRae to his own men, who'd all come to their feet in a flash of drunken heat. But registering both the build and the dangerous air of the man before them, they backed down, soberly deciding they'd prefer to keep their teeth.

Realizing this, Coombs turned an even darker shade of crimson. "Harris!" he roared, "bring the little bitch out here. If the cap'n thinks he can do any better with her, let's let him try." His mouth worked in silent fury as he chewed the end of his cigar, then he turned and spat on the tattered carpet beside his desk. "I ain't never had no taste for Rebel whores no how.''

Cole ignored him and moved to stand by the window. Jesus, he was tired of filth like Coombs. Tired of men

like him who were almost certain to live through the
war, while every day good men died. He pushed the
thought from his mind. He wasn't going to think about
that now. He wasn't going to think about the raw, blistering burn of gunpowder. The anguished sobs of
wounded men. The hot, acrid scent of blood. God help
him, not now. Not now.

Finding the windowpane stuck, he used his shoulder
to push it open. The frame split like kindling, shattering
into pieces and falling on the street below. The effort
was not only excessive, but wasted. Like everything
else, the soft breeze that blew in from the harbor
seemed to die before it reached the sullen brick edifice
of the stockades. Cole was greeted by a blast of hot,
sticky air that did little to relieve the atmosphere in the
room. The men shifted uncomfortably in their seats behind him but said nothing.

The sound of shuffling feet in the hall outside drew
his attention back to the task at hand. He turned and
saw his prisoner for the first time. She was smaller than
he'd expected. That surprised him. He'd assumed that
a woman capable of twisting a knife into a man's back
would be larger, more threatening somehow.

She stood in the center of the room, her posture stiff
and erect. Her hair cascaded over her shoulders in a
thick sheet of dark mahogany. Her face was smudged
with dirt, as was her gown, but she showed little concern for her appearance. Instead she tilted back her
head and looked about the room, her gaze burning with
unveiled contempt.

When her eyes reached Cole, she stopped, as if registering his presence for the first time. He watched a brief
flicker of a question—hope perhaps—flash in her soft
green gaze, then the light was quickly extinguished.
Smart woman. But rather than turn away, she studied
him a second longer, coolly sizing him up.

Her stare traveled down his uniform, then back up

again. It wasn't a look he was used to receiving from women. It was the look of an opponent before a fight, probing for strengths, hunting for weaknesses. Her gaze rested briefly on his cheek, taking in the raw, ugly scar that marred his skin. For an incredible second, he felt the scar tingle, as if she'd run her fingers over the wound. The sensation vanished as quickly as it came, and she returned her eyes to his. "Are you the commanding officer here?"

Her voice was low and steady, the soft, husky tone almost incongruous for a woman her size. The hint of a British accent clung to her words. She waited, but when it became clear that Cole had no intention of answering, she squared her shoulders and continued, "There has been a terrible mistake. I insist on—"

"Where are her things?" Cole interrupted, directing his question at Coombs.

"She ain't got nothing. Her trunks was confiscated for the trial back at Charleston."

"Trial," the woman repeated acidly. "That proceeding was a mockery to anyone who—"

"Now, hold on there," Coombs cut in, lumbering to his feet. "I ain't gonna listen to you bad-mouthing the U.S. Army. You was found guilty fair and square. If they tried you again, they'd find you guilty again." His chest swelled with self-righteous pride as his gaze traveled back to his men, eager to restore his former status. "That proceeding," he mimicked haughtily, "was entirely legimit."

"I believe the word you mean, Sergeant," his prisoner informed him coldly, "is *legitimate*. Though I shouldn't wonder that the term would be entirely foreign to someone such as yourself."

"Why, you little—" Coombs sputtered, his face flaming once again. "Let's just see if a little time spent in that prison up in Washington don't bring you down a notch or two. Let's see how you like them rats and fleas and eatin' slop every day.''

"I can see that prison will have at least one distinct advantage," his captive shot back. "You, sir, will not be there.''

The sergeant lunged forward, but Cole caught him and tossed him back into his chair. "Sit down, Coombs," he ordered. "I don't believe it's possible for a man to look any more stupid, but if you open your mouth again, you might just prove me wrong. And I hate for anybody to prove me wrong.''

He fixed the sergeant with a dark glare, then turned to his prisoner, frowning as a startled whisper of a smile flashed across her face.

"Thank you," she said.

"Don't," Cole said. "You've nothing to thank me for, madame. I was not defending you, I was merely sickened by the sergeant here." If she had any ideas about his coming to her aid, now was as good a time as any to dispel them. "It is my misfortune to have been given the distasteful chore of bringing you to Washington. You'll make the journey easier for both of us if you learn to keep your mouth shut and do as I tell you. Do I make myself clear?''

He watched her face freeze, her eyes turn to glittering shards of crystal-green ice. She drew herself up to her full height, the top of her dark head barely reaching Cole's shoulder. "Perfectly," she answered regally. "I am now fully aware that you are every bit as contemptible as the sergeant himself. You may consider your mission accomplished.''

The woman obviously had more guts than common sense. And apparently she wasn't finished. "May I ask a question?" she inquired demurely.

Cole waited.

"Now that you've assaulted me verbally in a room full of people, shall I expect to be physically assaulted next? Or will you wait, as Sergeant Coombs did, until we're in private for that?''

"You wanted—'' Coombs cried.

"That's enough, Coombs,'' Cole said, his eyes never leaving his prisoner's face. He let her question hang in the air, escalating the tension in the room to a nerve-shattering pitch. Finally he broke the silence. "I have no desire to either touch you or speak to you, madame. I prefer that our journey, since it must be made, be short and uneventful. If you choose to provoke me and make it otherwise, you'll suffer the consequences wrought by your own actions.''

To his utter disbelief, his captive smiled.

The woman was clearly insane, that had to be it. In a fit of insanity, she'd knifed a man in the back. Rather than being terrified by Cole's vague threats, she merely looked amused.

"Well now, that is a difficult choice, isn't it?'' she said. "Allow myself to be passively taken to prison and locked away for a crime that I did not commit, or do everything within my power to escape and risk upsetting such a fine gentleman as yourself.'' She shook her head, wringing her hands in mock despair. "Dear me. Whatever shall I do?''

Snorts of appreciative laughter sounded from around the room as their audience cast admiring glances at the petite woman who'd stood up to the rugged captain in a way that none of them had dared. Sergeant Coombs joined in the laughter. "What'd I tell you, McRae? The woman's nothing but spit and fire. And now she's all yours.''

Cole had had more than enough of the stale room and its drunken occupants. He reached for his prisoner, intending to lead her away, then stopped, frowning at the thick iron shackles that bound her wrists. He turned back to Coombs. "Give me the key.''

The sergeant produced it from his pocket and passed

it over. He shook his head as he watched Cole reach for the prisoner's wrists. "I wouldn't do that if I were you, Cap'n. The woman's a natural-born thief as well as a murderer. You'd best leave those on, show her who's boss."

Cole grabbed her hands and pulled them up, surprised by the woman's sharp intake of breath. Good. Perhaps his warning had frightened her after all. He turned the key to strip the shackles from her wrists and froze. Her skin was bruised and swollen, rubbed raw in places from sharp, chafing contact with the coarse metal.

It was obvious what Coombs had done. He hadn't merely shackled his captive, but dragged her along by a rope attached to the heavy cuffs, like pulling a dog on a lead. Cole lifted his gaze from her wrists to her face, but the prisoner's expression betrayed nothing. She stared straight ahead, her slim shoulders thrown slightly back, her small chin tilted defiantly.

Either she was completely oblivious of the pain or she was one hell of an actress. Cole suspected that the truth fell somewhere in between. A grudging note of respect swept over him, but he pushed it away, refusing to let it take hold. Silently, he studied the shackles in his hand, then turned back to Coombs.

"That were the only way we could control her," the sergeant blustered gruffly as thin beads of sweat began to form on his upper lip. "It ain't like she didn't deserve it. Me and my men was real patient with her. She brung it on herself."

With every word, Cole moved closer. When he reached the sergeant's desk, he stopped, calmly setting down the shackles. "Stand up, Coombs."

The sergeant grinned nervously. "What?"

"Stand up."

"What do you want me to do that for—"

Cole was once again reduced to hauling the man up

by his greasy lapels. "Because I'm going to tell you something, Coombs, and it's real important. I want to make sure you can hear every word. Can you hear me, Coombs?"

The sergeant's head bobbed up and down.

"Good. Now listen. I left that port out there with a crew of one hundred men. I came back two weeks ago with less than twenty. Think about that, Coombs. Think real hard. That's how many men dead?"

"Eighty," the sergeant whispered hoarsely.

"That's right." Cole tightened his grip on the man. "Eighty men dead. You think it's going to matter to anybody if I kill one more?"

Coombs swallowed convulsively. He opened his mouth, but no sound came out.

"If I could kill my own crew, just imagine what I'll do to you if I ever see your ugly face again." Cole let that sink in, then abruptly released him. "Now get out of my sight."

The sergeant nodded feverishly. He inched sideways around the desk, his eyes never leaving Cole. Moving with a haste that was almost comical, he and his men scurried away, filing out the door in double-quick step.

Their abrupt exit left a heavy silence in the room. Cole turned back to his prisoner, expecting finally to see traces of fear on her face. Or, more likely, pure disgust. He found neither. She stood motionless in the center of the room, her features perfectly composed, her expressive eyes carefully blank. She lifted her chin and said in her soft, slightly husky voice, "My name is Devon Blake."

Cole studied the woman a minute longer, then shrugged. It didn't matter.

Devon Blake was in serious trouble. She'd known that from the first second she'd laid eyes on Captain Cole McRae. He hadn't said a single word to her since they'd left the stockades, nor did it look as though he intended to any time soon. But clearly he had not forgotten her. His hand was locked around her upper arm in a steel grip that defied resistance, forcing her into a near-run to keep pace with his swift, long-legged stride.

She risked another glance at her captor, searching for some sign of weakness in the man, but found none. He was hard and lean, with a body beneath his Union uniform that looked to be made of rock-solid muscle. He wore his hair slightly longer than most men, the thick, golden-blond length reaching just past his collar. His profile could have been carved in granite, so devoid was it of any expression. She noted once again the deep, jagged scar that ran from his left temple to the middle of his cheek, standing out against the tan of his skin. It was a frightening addition to his rugged features, giving him a wounded, slightly dangerous air.

The scar notwithstanding, the captain would probably still be considered an incredibly good-looking man. Except for one thing. His eyes. They were cold, flat, and showed absolutely no trace of mercy within their tawny-brown depths. Cole McRae had the eyes of a man who'd seen death too often. Who'd caused death too often. And who'd simply ceased to care.

Devon silently cursed her luck. Her two previous escorts, Sergeant Coombs and the man before him, had been crude, stupid men, easily duped. Marks she would have plucked cleaner than a Sunday chicken had she met them in Liverpool. She'd managed to escape twice, only to be apprehended later due to an unfortunate combination of bad timing and bad luck. But that had been child's play, she realized regretfully, compared to the work she had cut out for her now.

Devon knew how to lure a mark in, how to probe for weaknesses, how to maximize profit and minimize risk. But the man who walked beside her down the busy street, ignoring the fascinated stares of passersby, whose broad build and long gait spoke of complete self-assurance, was not a mark she would have chosen. In fact, just the opposite was true. Had the situation been reversed, where she was back in Liverpool, in her element, Cole McRae was a man she wouldn't have said so much as boo to, regardless of the money involved. But as the choice was not hers to make, the best she could do was to get away from him as quickly as possible.

To that end, she scanned the crowded streets, looking for an opportunity. Despite the oppressive heat, they were surrounded on all sides by a maelstrom of activity. Messengers raced by on hot, sweaty mounts, dodging wagons, mules, and soldiers. Troops drilled to the north, filling the air with the sharp rattle of musketry. Just ahead, crates of foodstuffs and other provisions were being unloaded and carried into the general store.

So immersed was she in taking in her surroundings that she paid no attention to their path until she felt a sharp rock cut between her toes. With a startled gasp, she came to an abrupt halt, despite the iron grip the captain still maintained on her arm. He stopped as well, scowling down at her. Devon ignored him and took another step, only to feel more sharp rocks sting the soles of her feet. Much to her dismay, she noted that the smooth clay pavement they'd been on had slowly given way to a rough, rocky road as they neared the docks.

Before she could move again, he grabbed a handful of her skirt and tugged it aside to reveal her filthy, bare feet and dirty ankles. Humiliation swept over her, along with a healthy dose of anger. She yanked the thin fabric of her gown out of his hands. "Just what do you think—"

"Where are your shoes?" he demanded. There was an unmistakable accusation to his tone, as if she'd deliberately chosen to shame and debase herself by running through the streets barefoot.

"Sergeant Coombs has doubtless sold them by now," Devon replied, bringing up her chin. "Apparently I'm considered far too grave a danger to the U.S. Army to be allowed the privilege of footwear."

"The only danger you pose, madame," he returned coolly, "is to yourself, unless you learn to control that tongue of yours."

"Oh, dear. Another threat. I suppose I shall have to begin writing them all down, lest I forget one." Pleased at having gotten the last word, she turned and started walking, refusing to show the slightest hint of discomfort as the brittle rocks and pebbles bit into the soles of her feet.

Unfortunately her show of stubborn bravado was wasted on Captain McRae. Before she could guess what he was about, he grabbed her around the knees and tossed her over his shoulder like so much unwanted baggage, not even breaking his stride. Devon made no attempt to silence her cry of outrage. She beat her fists furiously against his back, demanding he release her. When that failed, she squirmed sideways in his grasp, threatening to bite off half his ear.

Her struggles drew a crowd of amused onlookers, whose bawdy shouts merely increased her fury. "Put me down this instant," she hissed, her voice dripping venom, "or I swear I'll . . ." She paused, searching for another suitable threat, when a rough bellow from the crowd caught her attention.

"Here now, what's going on?"

Devon leveraged herself up as best she could, peering around the captain's shoulder. Her anger disappeared like gin at a drunkard's table, replaced by an overwhelming surge of giddy triumph. Her luck had finally changed.

The town blacksmith, drawn out of his shop by all

the commotion, stood squarely in front of them, blocking their path. The man's upper torso was naked beneath his apron, his huge body dripping with sweat from his labors. He held a twisted piece of iron in one hand and a heavy anvil in the other. Devon, glancing at the size of his thick arms, wondered if he bothered to work the metal over a fire, as most blacksmiths did, or simply bent it in half with his bare hands.

No matter. In either case, he was surely capable of knocking the stuffing out of the high-handed Captain McRae. The only pity was that she wasn't planning on staying around long enough to see it. Devon quickly arranged her expression into one of terror-stricken innocence. She even managed a few tears. "Please, sir," she choked out, "make him put me down. Please."

The blacksmith frowned at Cole. "Just what do you think you're doing?"

"I'm taking this woman—"

"Please, make him put me down," Devon wailed, cutting him off. "I have to get back home. My mother's ill, and she needs her medicine." A few more tears trickled down her nose. Her story was a bit trite, perhaps, but not bad for the spur of the moment. Besides, Captain McRae had been stupid enough to remove her shackles. Who would believe now that she was a convicted felon on her way to prison?

Not the blacksmith. "I think you ought to put the lady down," he said, his eyes locked on Cole.

Devon bit back a triumphant smile as her soft green eyes darted quickly around her. This was perfect, even better than she'd dared hoped. The streets were crowded and chaotic. It would take less than seconds for her to disappear into the thriving masses. The port was full of ships ready to sail; buggies and carriages waited at every corner to carry her out of town. Her mind was racing so swiftly ahead that she almost missed her captor's reply.

"No."

No? Did he say no?

Apparently no one else could believe it either. An expression of stunned surprise rolled through the crowd as it moved even closer in anticipation of witnessing the blows that were sure to follow. The blacksmith grinned and set down his iron and anvil. His hands formed thick, eager fists. He gave the captain one more warning. "I don't think the lady wants to go with you."

Cole McRae looked supremely unconcerned. "I'm sure she doesn't," he agreed easily.

A frown flashed across the blacksmith's face. He cocked his head, waiting.

"But I paid good money for one hour of the lady's time," Cole continued, "and I'm not about to let her run out on me after just ten minutes. A deal's a deal." As he spoke, he brought his hand up, letting it roam over Devon's backside in the most intimate of caresses.

Devon was too shocked by his touch to respond to his words. "Get your filthy hands off me, you obnoxious, bullying, blue-suited scum!" she shrieked, forgetting her helpless, tearful posture altogether. Abruptly recalling herself, she added, "He's lying!" But the words sounded like an afterthought even to her.

Her Uncle Monty had always warned her that her temper would get her into trouble, and it looked as if he was right once again. She listened to the awkward shuffling of feet as the crowd weighed her story against Captain McRae's, knowing she'd ruined whatever chance she might have had. Devon could almost feel their skeptical stares as they took in her bare feet, stockingless legs, dirty gown, and unbound hair.

The blacksmith was the first to make up his mind. "Bring her back here when you're done. I've got some money of my own saved up." After extracting Cole's promise to do exactly that, he stepped aside.

Devon was not used to defeat. Nor, since her very

life was on the line, did she take it well. As the captain strode purposefully toward the docks, she drove her fists once more against his broad back. "How dare you—"

Cole bounced her up on his shoulder, bringing her down sharply enough to cut off both her words and her breath. "One more word out of you," he swore, "and I'll see to it that you're bound and gagged all the way to Washington."

Devon fully intended to ignore this newest threat, but launching another verbal battle while slung upside-down was more than even she could manage. Besides, the position was making her decidedly light-headed. She hadn't eaten anything since the day before yesterday, as the greasy slop Sergeant Coombs offered her hadn't even been fit for dogs. She felt her stomach twist and she swallowed hard, fighting back a sudden wave of dizziness. She found herself dumped back onto her feet at nearly the same instant. Caught off-guard, she staggered back on shaky legs, pride and stubbornness alone preventing her from sprawling in an undignified heap at her captor's feet. She'd die before she'd give him that satisfaction.

They were on the deck of a Union gunboat. From what she'd heard, the journey to Old Capitol Prison in Washington—through the Chesapeake Bay, then up the Potomac River—would take less than three days. For the first time since her trial, real fear raced through Devon. The grim reality of her situation, inconceivable until this moment, suddenly struck her with frightening clarity. She might very likely spend the rest of her days rotting away in prison.

Devon scolded herself as she forced the thought away. Uncle Monty would be ashamed of her. Fear was a sign of weakness, and she had no time for that now. Besides, she'd been in worse spots than this before. All she needed was a clear, cool head and a plan of action.

She took a deep, calming breath, watching as a young sailor crossed the deck and moved toward them.

"Captain McRae here to see Captain Gregory," Cole said.

"I'm sorry, sir, the captain's gone ashore."

"When is he expected back?"

"Didn't say."

Annoyance flashed across her captor's face. "Your captain was to have prepared quarters for both the prisoner and myself. You may show me to them now."

The sailor nodded, automatically obeying the voice of authority, then the words sunk in and his eyes grew wide. He stared at Devon, then back at Cole. "The prisoner? You mean her? But she's a woman."

"I'm sure those keen eyes serve you well in battle, Ensign. Now show me to those quarters."

The boy stiffened. "Yes, sir. Right away, sir."

The tight, sparsely furnished cabin that Devon was to stay in during the journey offered her nothing in the way of encouragement. It contained only a low, narrow bed and a washstand with pitcher and basin. There was no window. Light and air entered the room by way of a skylight scuttle, cut through the ceiling to the deck above. The only exit was through the door they entered, which no doubt would be heavily guarded.

As if reading her thoughts, Captain McRae turned to the young sailor who stood waiting outside. "I want a guard posted here twenty-four hours a day. Nobody goes in, nobody goes out. Is that understood?"

"Yes, sir."

The captain turned back to her. A thick tension fell over the room as their gazes locked. "I trust you find the accommodations satisfactory," he said at last.

Devon tilted her chin. "Actually, I prefer satin linens on my bed to homespun cotton. Do see what you can arrange."

He regarded her in silence, then held out his hand. "I'm waiting."

Shock raced through Devon as she quickly arranged her features into a mask of bewildered innocence. "I'm sure I don't know what—"

"My wallet."

He couldn't have felt her lift it. She was too good. Not only that, she'd been pounding on his back and screaming in his ear at the time. Yet there he stood, his hand extended, his gaze flat and unyielding. Mustering as much dignity as she was able, Devon silently acknowledged her defeat. With a regal nod, she removed the slim leather case from the pocket of her skirt and passed it to him.

This was the second time he'd outmaneuvered her, and she was determined to make it the last. She merely had to keep testing him. Sooner or later, she'd find a vulnerability, a spot beneath his cold exterior where she could strike. As he turned to leave, she asked, "What would you have done if the blacksmith hadn't believed you?"

If he was at all surprised by her question, it didn't show. He shrugged. "I suppose it would have come to fisticuffs."

"That smith would have killed you."

A dark, shimmering brilliance entered his eyes. "He wouldn't have been the first to try."

Nor would he be the last, she vowed silently, watching his broad back as he turned and strode away. Captain Cole McRae might have won the first few skirmishes, but that was of little importance. The battle, after all, had just begun.

She waited a few minutes, making sure he wouldn't return. Satisfied he was gone, she reached into the folds of her bodice and retrieved a handsome gold pocket watch, inspecting it as best she could in the dim light of the room. *To Cole, With Love,* the inscription read.

A woman's name was engraved beneath that. His wife? Sweetheart? Very interesting. For a man who spoke so easily of killing and death, it seemed an awfully sentimental item to carry.

She lifted the watch in her palm, testing its weight. It was heavy. Good. It would bring a nice price. Devon tucked it back within the folds of her bodice and began planning her escape.

Chapter 2

Admiral Billings's office on the third floor of the Cotton Exchange Building was cramped and cluttered, an unlikely place for the commander of the blockade forces of the southeastern ports to spend his days. It did, however, have one singular advantage: a perfect view of the harbor. Cole McRae made use of this now, standing by the window as he waited for the admiral to return. His eyes moved from the gunboat where he'd left his prisoner a few hours ago to the charred body of a ship raised in dry dock. His ship, though the *Islander* was no longer recognizable.

The hull, once lean and solid, was now splintered and burned by explosion. Lead shot had ravaged the timber below the waterline. Of three masts, only one remained standing. The sails were shredded to mere rags. Fire had danced up the ship's rigging, the flame licking away at the newly tarred ropes until nothing was left but heat and ash.

The battle had taken place two weeks ago. Sometimes Cole evoked his memories of the encounter deliberately, a sort of self-inflicted pain. More often, however, the memories themselves chose when to appear, as if they were living, breathing things over which he had no control. They lurked in the dark shadows of his mind and haunted his dreams. They struck at will, provoked by the mere flash of metal in the sun or the feel of a hot breeze against his skin. There was no way to defend against them. No way to shut them out. Nothing he could do but relive the battle in his mind, over and over again.

One by one, the *Islander*'s cannons had been destroyed, either struck by incoming mortar or imploding upon themselves, unable to withstand the pressure of constant firing. In the end, the battle had drawn so close that Cole and his men fought it out with muskets and pistols. Some, lacking even that meager defense, hurled flaming chunks of wood at the enemy.

Out of habit, Cole raised his fingers to his cheek, tracing the jagged scar there. He would carry the harsh souvenir of battle always, vivid testimony to his failure as commander.

As the door opened behind him, he forced the brooding thoughts aside, straightened, and saluted his superior officer. Admiral Billings waved the formality away. The two men had been acquainted socially for years before the war; Cole had even briefly courted the admiral's daughter. But that seemed a lifetime ago now. He'd been a different man then, and the world had been a different place.

The admiral took a seat behind his desk, a stern frown on his face as his gaze traveled over Cole. "You look like hell, McRae," he said by way of greeting.

Cole didn't reply. None was necessary.

The older man studied him a minute longer, then gave a grunt of weary resignation. "Well, get on with it. Tell me what happened out there."

There was no question what he was asking. "My men and I were patrolling when we spied a runner heading out to sea," Cole answered. "She was listing to port and appeared to have taken some shots. We immediately set out to capture her. Despite her damage, she made good speed." Cole's stomach clenched. It was so obvious now. That should have warned him. He should have seen the trap.

"Were there any other signs that the ship was in distress?"

"No, sir."

The admiral's frown deepened. "Go on."

"We were about three miles offshore when the runner came about. Within minutes, she was joined by two warships, bearing down on us in attack."

Cole and his crew had been outgunned four to one. There had been no room to maneuver, no time to draw up a plan of defense or attempt an escape. The first shots had been lobbed immediately, solid hits that sent the deck of the *Islander* pitching, members of his crew scrambling to man their stations. The encounter that followed was better termed a slaughter than a battle.

"Did you consider surrender?" the admiral asked.

"That was not a choice. It was clear by their actions that the enemy was intent on destroying my ship, not capturing her."

"How many men did you lose?"

"Eighty, sir," Cole answered tightly. His emotions ricocheted wildly within him, soaring to a rage so complete it was nearly blinding, then plunging into bleak despair. He stared straight ahead, struggling to find the words to explain, despising himself for the cocky arrogance he'd shown in leading his men to battle. It simply had not occurred to him that he would lose. Or that he would lose so badly. "I accept full responsibility for each man's death," he managed at last. "Had they been led by a competent captain—"

"Sit down, Cole," Billings interrupted.

Cole stopped abruptly, his features tense and strained as he ignored the invitation.

"I know what happened," Admiral Billings said. "But you understand I had to get your official version of events." He paused, a fierce scowl on his craggy features. "I heard about what happened to Gideon too.

I'm sorry, Cole. There's just too many boys dying in this damned war.''

Cole nodded, his fists clenched against his sides. He'd learned to contain the fury that burned beneath his skin. He'd learned to live with the memories that assaulted him night and day. But he still didn't know how to handle the pain. His body broke out in a cold sweat, and his heart started racing. *Speak, dammit!* his brain commanded. *Say something!* He couldn't. Instead he stood there helpless and mute, as if someone were pouring lead down his throat and he just kept swallowing.

Billings studied him a moment longer. ''Sit down,'' he repeated, and waited pointedly for Cole to comply. Once he did, the admiral reached into a desk drawer and lifted a bottle of fine French brandy. ''Compliments of our friends the blockade runners,'' he said as he poured, then set a generous tumbler in front of Cole. ''We were able to stop this shipment. Mostly luck on our part. We're tightening the ports, but they're still getting through.'' He drank deeply. ''Good, isn't it?''

Cole said nothing. He took a long swallow of brandy, shamed by his inability to master the emotions that tore through him, and grateful for the opportunity his friend was giving him to bring himself back under control.

''We've been damned lucky so far,'' Billings continued. ''Most of the runners are more interested in profit than patriotism: bringing in lace, liquor, and perfume instead of bread and guns. But as you know, that's starting to change.'' He withdrew a faded portrait from a thick file and passed it across his desk.

Cole studied the image, guessing the man to be in his mid-thirties and, judging by his attire, fairly prosperous. He had thick, dark hair and a heavy mustache, both immaculately groomed. Despite the veneer of wealth, there was a coarseness about him, a cruelty that seemed to lurk just below the polished surface. "Who is he?"

"Jonas Sharpe. Captain of the runner you went after."

Cole's head snapped up, then his gaze returned to the portrait as fire pulsed through his veins. Jonas Sharpe. The man who'd nearly destroyed his ship, who'd attacked with such unrelenting savagery. The man answerable for the death of so many of his crew. For Gideon's death. Now he had a face. A name.

"We've lost five of our strongest blockaders," the admiral said. "All last seen in pursuit of a weak, badly damaged runner. Yours was not the first vessel to be lured out to sea, just the first to return."

Cole silently absorbed this information. Five other ships, their captains and crew all suffering the same violent fate.

Billings took another swallow of brandy, his stern frown back in place. "You realize, from a tactical standpoint, what Sharpe is doing makes no sense. The South is desperate for ships, yet he's destroying vessels he could easily capture and commandeer."

"He enjoys the kill." The words were out before Cole could stop them. But there was no denying the truth.

Cole was not naive enough to believe in civilized warfare. He'd been in battles before. He'd seen death and dying. But what he'd witnessed in that short, fierce encounter with Sharpe went beyond all bounds of what men could inflict on one another under the guise of military right or duty. Jonas Sharpe was a predator, a man who feasted on destruction. And the war gave him ample opportunity to indulge that appetite.

"Whatever his motive, he's cutting holes in our blockade," Admiral Billings said. "If any more of our ships fall prey to his trap, the blockade will mean less than nothing."

Cole nodded. "I understand." Ruthless determination filled his eyes. "The *Islander* won't be ready to sail for another thirty days. Give me a ship and enough time to gather a fresh crew. I'll leave with the tide at dawn."

The admiral tapped the file he held and shook his head. "I'm afraid there's more to it than just stopping Sharpe now." He withdrew a set of sketches and passed them across his desk. "I think you'll find these interesting. Tell me what you make of them."

Cole studied the sketches briefly. Whoever had executed them was highly skilled, tracing in even the most minor of details. "Warships," he said. "The harbor looks like Liverpool."

"Well, you're right about the harbor. But according to the Brits, those are merchant ships, properly ordered and deliverable to the Confederate States Navy."

"Merchant ships," Cole repeated in disgust. "With gunports cut into the sides, turrets for mounting the cannon, and sealed magazine chambers for powder and arms."

"Exactly. At our protest, their inspector went out to look at the ships. His report concluded that he found no warlike structures of any kind on the vessels."

"Was the man blind or just stupid?"

"Neither. He was interpreting British law to the letter. Their Foreign Enlistment Act prohibits the outfitting of warships in their ports but, interpreted narrowly, does not forbid the building of vessels that might become ships of war. Once they leave harbor, they simply dock at a non-British harbor for the addition of armament."

Cole threw the sketches down. "So much for British neutrality."

Admiral Billings sighed, peering into his empty glass of brandy. "The Brits are holding the cards right now, and they know it. They haven't openly come out in support of the Rebels, but they have no reason not to.

They have everything to gain if the South wins, after all. The word from our men in London is that they're playing it cautious right now, waiting.''

"Waiting for what?''

"For the next Southern victory. We've been hearing rumors that Lee is planning to invade the North. If he does, and he's successful, Lord Palmerston will waste no time in recognizing the Rebels.''

"Which will mean war with England,'' Cole predicted grimly.

Billings shook his head. "You know as well as I do that we can't go to war with England. Not now. Lincoln has enough on his hands trying to put down the rebellion. Palmerston knows it too, and that's why he's playing this little game, putting a face of neutrality on his actions while he continues to send ships and arms to the South.''

While the news wasn't surprising to Cole, it was still hard to accept. England was on the brink of recognizing the Rebels. According to rumor, so was France. McClellan's Peninsula campaign had resulted in a wave of inglorious defeat and bitter stalemate, until the Union commander finally found something he was good at. Retreat. He and his men were currently camped in the mud at Harrison's Landing, awaiting the platoon boats that would carry them back to Washington.

A heavy weight settled over Cole. Lee was on the offensive. Men like Sharpe were punching holes in the blockade. Lincoln was fumbling in the search for a commander capable of leading the U.S. armies. And the powers in Europe were one Rebel victory away from offering the South formal recognition. The future of the Union looked grim indeed.

"How is Sharpe connected to these ships?'' Cole asked.

"His agent was captured carrying these papers, as well as instructions for the network of blockade runners

Sharpe has in operation. The agent's mission, apparently, was to solicit the funds necessary for the completion of the ships. As you can see, four of the vessels won't be ready to sail for at least another six months. Those we can stop.''

"What are you planning?"

A glimpse of a smile broke across the admiral's craggy face. "We intend to start a different kind of war. A bidding war. Those ships are all being built by private firms. The South might have a preferred trading status with England, but the North has a deeper pocketbook. I've authorized my men in London to use whatever funds necessary to secure those vessels.''

"What about the fifth ship? The frigate?"

"Unfortunately we're too late to do anything about that one. Word is that she'll be ready to leave harbor any day.'' Billings cleared his throat and finished gruffly, "That's where you come in.''

Cole understood immediately. "If I find Sharpe, I find out where they'll be routing the ship.'' He thought for a moment. "What about Sharpe's agent? Any information there?"

The admiral shook his head. "Denies everything. Knowledge of the papers, working for Sharpe, even denies having murdered Lieutenant Prescott. We're getting nothing but lies.'' Billings paused, forming his fingers in a steeple over the sketches on his desk. "Any problems picking up the prisoner this morning?'' he asked.

Distaste rushed over Cole. "With all due respect, sir, surely there's someone else who's capable of escorting the woman to Washington. I would prefer to begin the hunt for Sharpe immediately.''

"I'm sure you would. And I would prefer you do your duty as assigned, Captain.''

Cole stiffened. The chore of escorting a prisoner was usually reserved for only the lowest of the low. But what had he expected after the debacle at sea, a medal? "Yes, sir." He came to his feet, standing rigidly at attention. "Anything else, sir?"

"Damm it, McRae, this isn't a punishment. What happened out there could have happened to anybody."

Cole clenched his fists at his sides, ignoring the obvious lie. What happened out there hadn't happened to anybody. It happened to him, to his men.

"There's a reason I picked you for this duty, Captain," Billings continued brusquely. "Your prisoner is not only dangerous, but devious. She's embarrassed us by escaping twice from her former guards. She'll lie, she'll steal, and she's not above using her charms as a woman to seduce her captors into releasing her. That's why I need you."

Cole found an almost grim humor in the turn the conversation had taken. "You believe I'm above seduction?"

"In this case, yes."

"Any particular reason I should inspire such unwarranted confidence?"

Rather than being irritated by his junior officer's impertinence, Admiral Billings settled back into his chair, looking supremely satisfied. "Devon Blake," he replied slowly, "is Jonas Sharpe's agent." He let that sink in, then lifted his gaze to Cole, all traces of levity gone from his face. "Now tell me, Captain, is there any reason I should doubt you'll do everything within your power to make sure she gets to Old Capitol?"

Devon Blake was Jonas Sharpe's agent. Cole felt his blood run cold as he absorbed the news, picturing the woman in his mind: petite, vulnerable, yet unafraid to show her scorn for the men who held her captive. The grudging respect he'd held for her turned instantly to seething contempt. Unfortunately a good deal of that contempt was directed at himself. Before he'd left the gunboat, he'd given one of the crewmen money and instructions to buy the woman a pair of shoes. He clenched his jaw in silent rage, sickened by the weakness he'd displayed in the gesture. That he should have been concerned about her bare feet when his men had been blown to bits so that there weren't even enough parts left for proper burial . . .

Damn her. *God damn her.* She would talk, he swore silently. She would tell him exactly where to find Sharpe. His eyes locked on the admiral's. "I'll take care of her myself," he said.

Devon jumped to her feet the instant she heard Captain McRae approach. She'd already taught herself to distinguish his brisk, purposeful tread from that of the other men who moved past her tiny chamber. Within seconds, the door flew open, causing her to blink against the bright glare of sunshine that flooded the room.

"I suppose it would be asking too much for you to knock before entering a lady's room," she said.

"Lady? You must mean yourself. What a novel interpretation of the word."

Devon hesitated uncertainly as a thick silence filled the chamber. The words he flung at her were undeniably hostile, yet the crewman who'd brought her the pair of dainty demi-boots she now wore had told her that Captain McRae was responsible for the gift. Even though she'd tried to hide it, he'd seen her abject humiliation at being forced to walk through the streets barefoot. Deciding that the gesture deserved to be acknowledged, she chose to ignore his verbal jab and focus instead on the small kindness he'd shown. She raised her filthy skirts, allowing the dark leather of the shoes to peek out from beneath the hem. "I wanted to thank you for . . ."

Her voice faded away as she glanced up at him, watching his expression darken as he stared at the boots, his face becoming a mask of cold fury. Obviously the footwear had been a mistake. Captain McRae loomed in the doorway, light bouncing off his broad shoulders and menace emanating from him. Confusion and fear raced through her as Devon struggled to understand why the sight of the shoes he'd bought her would make him so furious. As he moved forward into the cabin, she bravely held her ground. "What do you want?" she asked.

"Tell me where I can find Sharpe."

So that was it. Again. Devon had been through this exercise in futility so many times she'd lost count. If she was going to go through it once more, she might as well make herself comfortable. She let out a sigh, then turned and seated herself on the bed, taking her time in arranging her skirts. She folded her hands in her lap and daintily crossed her ankles. "I have no idea where to find Captain Jonas Sharpe. Shall I repeat that now, or do you prefer to ask the question over and over again first?"

When he didn't reply, Devon suggested, "I know, perhaps you can rephrase it in some clever way and trick me. How about, 'Where was Sharpe heading when you last saw him?' Or—"

"Do you deny that Sharpe arranged your passage from Liverpool?" Cole cut her off.

"No, I do not."

"Do you deny that you were carrying sketches of battleships being built for service against the United States?"

"How could I?" she asked reasonably. "They were found in my luggage, after all."

"And you were apprehended while still holding the knife that was used to murder Lieutenant Prescott."

"Yes, that was rather accommodating of me, wasn't it? Made the whole matter so easy to wrap up."

Her captor's eyes narrowed into dark, golden-brown

slits. "You appear to be taking this very lightly, Blake. That's a mistake. I doubt very much the guards at Old Capitol will prove as lenient an audience as I have been."

Devon didn't miss the insult: Blake, not *Miss* Blake, thereby implying that she was clearly unworthy of the courtesy of a title. She tilted her chin, unable to keep the challenge out of her voice. "Oh, but you're only telling half the story, *McRae*. Go ahead, tell it the way they did at my supposed trial. How I overwhelmed the lieutenant, a man nearly as big as you are, wrestled him to the ground, then tore the knife from his hand and stabbed him in the back. All without sustaining so much as a single bump or bruise myself. Amazing, isn't it? I'm surprised you're not quaking with fear at my sheer brute strength."

A look of annoyance flashed across his rugged features. "You're wasting my time with that pack of lies. If that were true, any competent solicitor could have—"

"Ah, yes, my valiant defender. He was either drunk or absent from court entirely. I spoke on my own behalf, of course, but the high-minded, noble men on the jury didn't believe a word I said."

"And you expect me to?"

Devon came to her feet, wishing for the hundredth time that God had seen fit to make her just a little taller. Standing before the captain in close quarters like this, with her neck craned back to meet his eyes, put her at a definite disadvantage. She pushed the idle thought away. As Uncle Monty had repeatedly told her, what she lacked in stature she more than made up for in spunk. She needed that now more than ever. Drawing on her calmest voice, she said, "I think it's only fair to warn you that I have no intention of spending the rest of my days locked away in some filthy prison."

His expression didn't change. "Is that so?"

She nodded. "Since my escape is inevitable, you might want to consider the options that remain available to you."

"Really. And what might those be?"

"I have an uncle in London who is extremely devoted to me. I can assure you that he will pay very handsomely for any assistance you might render in securing my freedom. You need only name your price."

That was a mistake. Devon realized it the second the words were out of her mouth. Her captor's jaw tightened until the scar that marred his cheek stood out in white relief against the deep golden tan of his skin. His eyes turned to dark, fiery orbs. He reached out, locking his fingers around her upper arm in an iron grip.

"After what Sharpe did to my men, you think you can buy me?" His voice was no more than a low, hoarse growl.

It took all of Devon's considerable willpower to keep from trembling. "What do you want, then?"

The captain's eyes bore into hers for seconds longer, then he abruptly released her, turning away in one swift motion. She studied his profile, watching as he dragged his fingers through his thick, tawny hair, then clenched reflexively at the knotted muscles at the nape of his neck. He drew in a deep breath, as though struggling to bring himself back under control. "I don't want your money," he said at last. He turned back to face her, his eyes traveling slowly over her with scathing contempt. "Nor am I interested in what's beneath your skirts. So you can spare us both the indignity of making that offer."

Devon bit down hard on her inner lip, forcing herself to ignore the crude gibe. "What do you want?" she repeated.

"Tell me where I can find Sharpe."

"I've told you already. I don't know."

Her words made no impact whatsoever. Like a cannon lobbing hot, explosive shells, he kept up the attack, firing away with dizzying speed. "How much was he paying you?"

"Nothing."

"You strike a poor bargain, Blake. Surely risking your life for the man was worth a shilling or two."

"I wasn't working for Captain Sharpe."

"Why did you murder Lieutenant Prescott?"

She grit her teeth. "He was already dead when I arrived."

He regarded her evenly. "Sharpe chose well. Lying comes very naturally to you, doesn't it?"

"I'm not—"

"Was Sharpe your lover?"

Devon sucked in her breath. "Insulting women comes very naturally to you, doesn't it?"

The captain lifted his broad shoulders. "Was that an insult? I wouldn't know, I've never met the man. Perhaps you should be flattered."

"Perhaps you should go straight to hell."

He made a *tsk*ing noise with his tongue. "And here all this time, I thought ladies didn't swear."

Before Devon could come up with a suitable reply, she felt a gentle jarring beneath her feet and was suddenly alerted to the shouts of the men on deck as the ship's engines rumbled to life. She glanced around the cabin, not even sure what she was looking for. Something to hold on to, something to stop this from happening. The ship was leaving—hours sooner than she'd anticipated. She took a deep breath, fighting a rising sense of panic. She could still get away. She had to.

She turned again to her captor, unnerved to find that his gaze had never left her. Her defenses shot back up, but she knew it was too late. A vague unease settled over her, leaving her feeling oddly vulnerable. Angry as well, as though he'd played some sort of dirty trick on her. For a fraction of a second, she'd let down her guard, and he'd been right there to see it.

Devon swore a silent oath, furious with herself. She'd lost control of the situation and given him an edge. There was absolutely no excuse for it. What was it about the man that turned her into a bumbling amateur? Even now, she could no more read the expression in his golden-brown eyes than she could snap her fingers and fly to China.

She gathered her dignity around her as best she could, determination stiffening her spine. "What happens now?" she inquired coolly.

He studied her for a moment longer, his rugged features locked in a mask of stern, silent appraisal. "That's up to you," he replied. "Tell me how to find Sharpe, and I'll do what I can to make Old Capitol more bearable for you."

Devon frowned. "Meaning?"

"Meaning linens without lice, food that doesn't slither away, fresh water once a week for bathing, and a guard who'll be paid regularly to assist you in warding off the unwelcome advances of other prisoners. As you might suspect, the inmates at Old Capitol are of less than sterling character. Hardly proper bedmates for a lady of your caliber."

Not bad, Devon thought. In one breath he had managed to capitalize on the fear he'd seen in her eyes, as well as slander her claim to the title *lady*. A worthy opponent indeed. "While I find your offer extremely generous," she replied, "and your concern for my well-being truly heartwarming, I'm afraid I must decline. Prison, you see, holds absolutely no appeal for—" she paused, smiling sweetly—"a lady of my caliber."

His expression didn't change. For all she knew, his features might have been carved in stone. He stepped toward the door, pausing with his hand on the dull brass knob. "I suggest you rethink that position, Blake."

"If I had all the time in the world, McRae—"

"You have three days."

She drew herself up to her full height, her slim shoulders thrown back, ready to do battle. "I suppose you think I should be frightened."

Cole McRae's fathomless gaze swept slowly over her. "What you should be," he finally replied, "is damned sorry you ever laid eyes on me."

The statement was startling, unexpected . . . and Devon couldn't have agreed more.

He waited, as if expecting her to say something. When she didn't, he stepped out of the room, throwing her tiny chamber into a haze of dusky shadows as he pulled the door shut behind him. Devon sank onto the bed, her mind reeling. She sat without moving, her body adjusting to the gentle swells and rolling rhythm of the bay. The men on deck serenaded one another with a bawdy ballad. Or perhaps the offensive lyrics were meant for her to hear. She couldn't say. The words drifted in and around her, then faded away.

The hopelessness of her situation settled over her like a thick, heavy fog. Her body suddenly ached with fatigue. A stinging sensation built behind her eyes, and she blinked rapidly, refusing to give in to tears. She tugged at the cotton string that hung around her neck, lifting it to reveal the thin gold wedding band she wore near her heart. Devon twisted the ring between her fingers as she struggled to rein in her fear. *What would Uncle Monty do?* She clung to the thought, repeating it over and over again in her head. *What would Uncle Monty do?*

After a few minutes, her courage returned. Well, she knew what Uncle Monty wouldn't do: he wouldn't sit here wringing his hands and waiting to be rescued, that much was certain. She gathered her wits and began to appraise her situation. As the blistering sun slowly sank, twilight descended over the ship. While the cooler air was a blessing, it would soon be impossible to see anything. Devon glanced around in vain for a lamp, not altogether surprised to find herself denied even that meager luxury.

In the encroaching darkness, a bit of ingrained wisdom from Uncle Monty slowly penetrated her mind: "Know your opponent, my girl. Know your mark better than you know yourself." To that end, she closed her eyes and focused on Captain Cole McRae, letting her thoughts drift randomly. But rather than a series of strengths and weaknesses that she might be able to use against him, an image rose to her mind that was far more confusing than it was enlightening. An image that ran contrary to everything she knew about the man, yet she couldn't seem to shake it.

She remembered a shaggy dog that she and her brother, Billy, had befriended back in Liverpool when they were children. One day when they went to pet him, the dog had snarled viciously, baring his teeth as they approached. As Devon protectively tugged her younger brother away, the dog backed off as well, dragging its hind legs behind it. It wasn't until that moment that she saw the poor animal was hurt, probably run over by a passing carriage. By the time she realized it, it was too late. The dog slunk off into an alley, and they never saw it again.

Devon frowned as she tried to mentally connect Captain McRae to that long-forgotten, wounded dog, then finally dismissed the attempt as absurd. She was absurd, she told herself sternly. And unless she relished the notion of spending the remainder of her days locked up in an eight-by-ten-foot cell, she had best quit thinking about Captain McRae and wounded dogs, and start planning her escape. *Now.*

Chapter 3

"**T**hat surely is a purty sight, ain't it, ma'am?"
From the deck of the gunboat, Devon glanced up at Justin Hartwood, the young ensign who'd showed her to her chamber when she'd first boarded. As he had also been assigned the duty of bringing her meals and fresh water for bathing, he was the only one with whom she had any sort of regular contact. She offered him a weak smile, then turned her attention back to the shore. Though she'd been staring intently at the thick groves of cedar and birch that lined the banks of the Potomac, she hadn't really seen them. She looked now, noticing the beauty of the river for the first time.

Golden waves of morning sunshine fell from a cloudless sky and verdant foliage hugged the white, sandy shore. Leaves filtered the brilliant light, creating pockets of cool, inviting shade. The musical whistles and chirps of birds filled the air. As the ship floated by, an occasional rabbit or squirrel darted down the bank, rewarding itself with a drink or a splash in the cool river.

Her brother, Billy, would have loved this. "It's very nice," she agreed flatly.

A deep furrow lined her brow as her mind automatically returned to her previous thoughts. Two days had passed. They would be in Washington by nightfall. She had to do something. Anything. But what?

"Ma'am?"

Devon stifled a sigh and turned back to Justin, hiding her impatience. If the boy would just leave her alone, she could think. Instead he seemed to be always dogging her heels, torn between the exaggerated sense of duty he felt was required in guarding a dangerous prisoner and a full-blown, smitten crush on that very prisoner. It was sweet, and just a trifle irritating. She regarded him levelly, waiting for him to speak.

"I, er, that is . . ." he stammered. A crimson flush stained his cheeks.

"Yes, Justin?" she prompted.

"I don't believe you killed that man," Justin blurted out.

"You don't?"

"No, ma'am, I surely don't."

"I see. And just how did you reach this conclusion?"

His cheeks turned an even deeper red as he gave her a sheepish grin. "Well, ma'am, seems to me that no one as fine a lady as you are—'sides how purty and tiny you are—could ever do something that mean."

Regret knifed through Devon. The boy had no idea of what she was capable. None of it had been her choice, of course, but still . . .

"That's the truth, ain't it, ma'am? You didn't kill that man?"

"That's the truth," she answered quietly. "I didn't kill that man."

Of all the crimes that could be levied against her, that was perhaps the only one to which she could justly proclaim her innocence. She supposed she should enjoy the bitter irony of the fact that it was the very crime which would see her locked up for the remainder of her days, but she just couldn't manage it. If only she'd never left England. If only Uncle Monty were here. Her stomach clenched in tight, nervous knots, and she fought to keep her hands from shaking. If only Billy hadn't died . . .

Justin cleared his throat, shooting a guilty glance around the deck. In a nervous, sotto whisper, he said, "If there's anything I can do to help you, ma'am, you just let me know."

Startled, Devon studied the boy. "You'd help me, Justin?"

Justin Hartwood nodded vigorously. "It ain't right, you going to prison. Not if you didn't kill that man."

"I—thank you."

Devon's mind raced as she surveyed the space around them, making sure they wouldn't be overheard. As usual, her captor was not far away. She'd yet to be permitted up on deck when he wasn't in attendance. And though the man never acknowledged her presence by either word or gesture, hadn't even spoken to her since his brief, stormy visit to her cabin two days ago, he was always there. Despite his casual posture, she knew he monitored her every move. Devon had tested her mettle against the finest shopkeepers and watchmen in London; she wasn't fooled by the likes of Captain McRae.

Cole stood alone, his forearms resting on the ship's rail, one booted foot propped up on a dense coil of rope. He was no longer in uniform, having abandoned the heavy blue jacket and pants for a white linen shirt and crisp navy slacks. A soft breeze messed his thick, tawny hair and tugged at his loose-fitting shirt, showing her a broad expanse of the deeply tanned skin of his chest. He stared at the passing scenery, seemingly lost in thought. She was struck again by what a magnificent-looking man he was—or rather, would be, if not for those cold, fathomless eyes.

During the course of their journey up the Potomac, she had considered calling him back to her cabin so that she might explain how she'd become tangled up with Jonas Sharpe. Maybe he would believe her. But it didn't take long for her to dismiss that fantasy. Cole

McRae had shown her nothing but scorn and contempt from the time he'd first laid eyes on her. He'd made it abundantly clear that he didn't believe a word she said.

Devon suppressed a shudder as she imagined what he'd do if he heard what she was about to say. Unwilling to chance it, she drew Justin closer. "I have an uncle in England. If I write him a letter, can you make sure he gets it?"

Justin looked supremely relieved. "Yes, ma'am," he answered quickly. He'd been fearing, no doubt, that she would ask him to help her escape. But Devon wasn't about to take advantage of the boy's youthful sense of gallantry. No sense putting them both in jeopardy. A letter would have to suffice.

She'd written two previous entreaties to Uncle Monty, but as she'd had to give them to her previous captors for posting, the chances of them actually having been sent were nil. More likely, they'd just been read for amusement among the men, then tossed away. Unless he received word from her soon, her uncle would assume that everything had gone exactly as planned. "I'll need paper and ink. Can you bring them to my quarters?"

"Anything else you need, ma'am?"

"I don't think so." Devon paused, thinking what would happen to the boy if he were caught with her letter on his person. She laid her hand on his sleeve and lifted her eyes to his, her soft green gaze full of understanding. "Are you sure you want to do this, Justin?"

He stared at her silently as the crimson flush stole back into his cheeks. "Yes, ma'am," he swore. "I'd do anything—"

"Hartwood!"

They both jumped at the sound of the deep voice behind them. Cole stood only inches away, a scowl marring his already stern features. He looked from one to the other, his dark eyes cool and appraising.

Justin came rigidly to attention, fear and guilt written all over his youthful face. "Sir?" he croaked.

"Far be it from me to interrupt such a tender scene," her captor drawled, "but I'd like a word with the prisoner."

"Yes, sir." Justin shot a meaningful glance at Devon, then turned to leave.

"Hartwood?"

The boy stiffened and turned back, his posture growing increasingly rigid as Captain McRae's glacial stare swept slowly over him. By the time Cole finally spoke, the boy looked stiff enough to snap in two.

"It appears that you and the prisoner have become rather friendly. Would you care to enlighten me as to the subject of your fervent discussion?"

"That's none of your business," Devon snapped.

Cole ignored her. "Hartwood?"

"Well, er—" Justin swallowed hard and stared straight ahead. "The weather, sir?"

"Are you asking me or telling me?"

"We were talking about the weather and the trees and the river, sir."

Cole gave a grunt of disgust. "Very good, Hartwood. The next time I need a nature tour, I'll know who to ask."

The boy flushed crimson from his neck to his ears. His eyes were suspiciously bright, glistening with both anger and embarrassment. His voice, however, remained admirably level. "Yes, sir."

"You are aware, I assume, that lying to a superior officer is a punishable offense." The words were spoken softly, just a hint of menace lying beneath the smooth, dark tone.

Justin didn't flinch. "Yes, sir."

Cole studied the boy a minute longer. "I believe

Captain Gregory assigned you below decks this morning. I suggest you see to your duties.''

"Yes, sir. I was just getting to—''

"Now.''

Justin saluted smartly, then spun about, leaving without another word. But Devon read clearly in his stiff gait the blow his pride had taken. Her heart instantly went out to him. She turned toward Cole, sparks of pure fury shooting from her eyes.

"You must be very proud of yourself,'' she hissed. "Humiliating that poor boy. It must make you feel like a big man, doesn't it, attacking someone who can't fight back—''

"That's enough,'' Cole swore. "Go after me if you like, Blake, but stay away from Hartwood.''

"Go after? I don't know what you're talking about. That poor boy was simply—''

"That 'poor boy' happens to be an ensign with the U.S. Navy. Because of you, that 'poor boy' just lied to and disobeyed a commanding officer.''

"And that justifies humiliating him like that?''

"If that's what it takes to see to it that he never does it again, then yes.''

Devon drew herself up, her delicate features frozen with scorn. "How very noble,'' she replied acidly. "I suppose next you're going to tell me that that was for his own good.'' She gathered her skirts and turned to go, but Cole caught her roughly by the arm and held fast.

"Obviously you don't give a damn about anybody but yourself,'' he ground out. "But you're going to listen to this anyway.''

Devon tried in vain to release his grasp. Failing miserably, she clenched her teeth, her eyes glittering green ice against her pale skin. She inclined her head, her hair a cascading curtain of dark mahogany around her shoulders. "It appears I have no choice. Pray continue, McRae."

Her sarcasm did little to dim the fury in his eyes. "A team of men working together in battle has a chance to get away alive. A group of men fighting to save their own skins has none. If Hartwood wants to live long enough to see the end of this war, he's got to learn to take orders the second they're issued. Not when and if he damned well feels like it. If he's smart enough to learn that, then he just may stay alive. That is, if someone like you doesn't put it into his fool head that he can do whatever he pleases and get away with it."

Pangs of guilt assailed Devon. Though she knew nothing about battles, there was an undeniable ring of truth to his words. Young, headstrong, impetuous—those had to be dangerous qualities to encourage in a boy heading off to war. And she was using Justin, if only to get a letter out. Perhaps even that one small act of defiance was too great a risk to ask him to take.

"There's one other thing you should know," Cole continued ruthlessly. "If Hartwood tries in any way to assist you in escape, I'll see to it that he spends the remainder of his days in the stockades. I won't like it, but I swear I'll do it."

One look at his harsh, chiseled features told her he wasn't bluffing. "I see," she replied coolly.

Cole dropped her arm. "Good."

"If you've finished your speech, I believe I'll retire to my chamber. I find the air up here has suddenly turned foul."

Devon swept up her skirts and turned away, but her regal exit wasn't meant to be. The deck suddenly gave way beneath her, and a horrid grinding roar filled in her ears. She fell hard, landing on her hands and knees. Behind her, Cole stumbled as well, but quickly righted himself. He peered over the side of the rail and let loose a string of expletives.

Stunned, Devon came awkwardly to her knees. She glanced around, watching as crewmen staggered up and rushed off to various positions on the ship. Urgent shouts filled the air. From the corner of her eye, she saw Cole's hand reach out to assist her, but she impatiently brushed it away. "What happened?" she asked, rising on her own.

"We've hit a shoal." He leaned against the rail, his arms crossed over his broad chest, looking both irritated and resigned at the same time. "We're stuck here until the current lifts us, or until the captain organizes a party of men to hook up ropes and try to pull us out."

Devon swiftly digested that bit of information. They could be trapped in the middle of the river for hours. It was a reprieve of sorts, if only she could figure how to turn it to her advantage. She stood beside Cole in silence, watching the pandemonium that surrounded them.

After a few minutes, a chagrined-looking Captain Gregory appeared. "It looks as though we're in a bit of a mess, doesn't it?" he said.

Devon listened as the two men discussed the situation. While Captain Gregory was older and held superior rank, he spoke to Cole almost deferentially, as though eager for his approval. Cole McRae had that effect on people, she noted. Men seemed to either leave him alone or bend and scrape just to please him. To his credit, McRae seemed to prefer the former to the latter.

"You know, I recall this very thing happened back in April," Captain Gregory was saying, "when Lincoln himself was traveling down the Potomac to visit General McClellan. Ship hit a shoal, just like this one. And you know what Old Abe did? Why, he borrowed the captain's bathing trunks and went for a swim. Right there in the middle of the Potomac. Don't that beat all?"

As far as Devon was concerned, the president's response was eminently sensible. Now that the gunboat had come to a dead stop, they'd lost what little breeze they'd enjoyed earlier. The sun was suddenly a scorching, burning force, the air thick and heavy with humidity. Perspiration gathered on her skin, leaving her longing for a cool dip in the river's gently flowing currents.

She glanced at her captor, noting the way his shirt had begun to cling to his broad, powerful chest. Obviously he was feeling the effects of the weather as well. She considered suggesting that they follow Lincoln's sage example, but quickly dismissed the idea. The thought of Cole frolicking in the water was too absurd for words. She doubted the man ever did anything simply because it felt good.

Devon frowned as she considered the heat. If it was this bad after only ten minutes, how would they tolerate it if they were stuck like this for ten hours?

As it turned out, she needn't have worried.

A loud, booming roar shattered the silence. The first roar was followed by another, then a shrill, piercing whine filled the air. Devon instinctively lifted her hands to cover her ears, a position that left her entirely unprepared for what happened next. Cole flung his body over hers, hitting her from behind in a rough tackle that brought them both crashing down. "Don't move," he grunted.

Move? With the weight of his body, two hundred pounds of rock-solid muscle, pressing her flat against the deck? She could barely breathe.

An explosion rocked the ship. Devon gasped, stifling the urge to scream. The shrill whine was louder now, coming directly at them. She felt Cole's body tense on top of her. He pulled her arms down to her sides, covering her completely with himself.

The second explosion was deafening. The shell discharged only scant feet away, driving through the deck and spewing up red-hot timber in its wake. She heard a man shriek with pain, followed by the heavy sound of a body falling. Her heart came to a stop, then slammed against her chest, beating at three times its normal speed. The sharp, tinny rattle of musket fire rang out from all around them. Above her, Cole's deep voice roared in her ears as he shouted out a command, but she couldn't make out his words. There was movement, however, as men rushed to obey.

"Get ready," Cole said, his breath fanning her neck.

Ready for what? She didn't have time to ask. Devon felt his arm slide beneath her, locking around her waist. A cannon roared again, this time closer. It was one of the ship's own, firing at the battery of Confederates who attacked from shore. She found herself lifted the instant the cannon went off and half-carried, half-dragged across the deck, Cole's body the only shield between her and the Rebel artillery.

Miraculously they managed to get across. Still dragging and carrying her, Cole made his way down the narrow stairs that led to her chamber. He flung her inside. "Stay here," he ordered, then he slammed the door shut behind him and was gone.

Devon sunk slowly onto her bed, too shocked to even think of disobeying. Though no more than thirty seconds had gone by from the time she heard the first shell fire and explode, it seemed a lifetime had passed.

Maybe it had. Her hands began to shake. Captain Gregory had been standing right beside them when the shell detonated. Was it his cry of pain she'd heard, his body that had fallen? And what about Justin? Where was he?

She even found herself worrying about her captor. Cole McRae was big, and likely the sort of man who would put himself in the middle of the fight. Wouldn't that make him an easy target? Devon felt her stomach twist painfully at the thought, but didn't bother to dissect her emotions. It didn't matter why that image upset her, only that it did.

She listened to the clamor on deck, frantic to know what was happening. The men shouted to one another above the roar of battle. Commands were tossed back and forth. Minie balls and grapeshot pelted the outer walls, striking so rapidly it sounded more like fierce rain than artillery fire. She felt the engines grumble and strain beneath her feet, struggling in a desperate attempt to free the ship and gain maneuverability. It didn't work. They were stuck, trapped in the middle of the river, a perfect target.

A new sound reached her ears. It took her a moment to recognize the heavy, dull rumble. The men must be dragging the guns from the starboard side to the port, where they could be put into play against the Rebs. No sooner had she identified the noise than a fierce blast rocked the ship, sending her flying against the wall. The explosion must have knocked the crewmen off-balance as well. The massive cannon they were pulling came loose, the wheels screeching as it careened across the deck. Devon heard it rumble back and forth until another blast knocked her flat once more.

She listened in horror as the huge cannon crashed down the narrow flight of stairs that led from the deck to her chamber, sounding as though it was taking half the ship with it in its mad descent. Devon pressed herself flat against the far wall, the only position that might save her from being crushed by the deadly weight of the huge gun if it were to smash into her cabin. She squeezed her eyes shut and muttered a little prayer as the cannon plunged and skidded. *Bless us O Lord for these thy gifts which we are about to receive* ... Inappropriate maybe, but it was the only one she remembered.

The cannon lunged off the last step and came to a bone-jarring stop, slamming sideways against the thick door frame. Still shaking, Devon waited. Nothing happened. She slowly let out her breath. The battle raged on above her, but the cannon wasn't moving. She crept cautiously toward the door and tried to edge it open, but the portal wouldn't budge. The gun was lodged firmly sideways, blocking it. While the position had prevented the cannon from smashing through the entry, it also rendered her a virtual prisoner in her chamber until it was removed.

As she considered this fact, another blast rocked the hull, louder still than all previous explosions. A keen silence followed, then the desperate cry reached her ears, "Abandon ship!"

More shouts echoed the first. Devon listened to the sound of furious footsteps rushing back and forth and boats being lowered off the starboard side.

"Wait! Wait, I'm trapped!" she shouted through the overhead scuttle, knowing even as she did that her cries were useless. If the shouts of the men didn't drown out her voice, the constant explosions would. They grew louder and more violent, culminating with a blast that knocked her off her feet once again and was followed by a piercing, screeching hiss. A shell had detonated, destroying the boiler. The impact knocked the ship sideways, finally freeing the hull, but it was too late. In a matter of minutes, maybe only seconds, the entire ship would go up in flames.

Devon threw herself against the door, pounding furiously. "Help! Someone! Let me out!" She lifted the small washbasin and threw it at the door. It crashed, then fell back, breaking in two. The door didn't budge. "Help—"

"Blake!"

McRae. He'd come back for her. Relief nearly sent her to her knees. "I'm in here!" she screamed. "I can't get out!"

"Wait there!"

Hysterical laughter bubbled up within her. Where was she going to go? She listened, but couldn't hear him. Panic choked her voice. "Don't leave me! Please!"

He returned within seconds. "Get away from the door. Get down," he shouted.

She flung herself to the farthest corner of the room, curling up in a tight ball. He drove hard against the door, battering it with a thick wooden beam. The portal finally gave and shattered open above the body of the cannon.

Her captor was filthy. His clothing was torn, streaked with smoke, sweat making it cling to his body. A dark stain—blood?—seeped over his left thigh. His expression was fierce, his rugged features absolutely frightening. Devon had never been so glad to see anybody in her life.

She gave a cry of relief and raced unhesitatingly toward him. Cole pulled her into his strong arms and tossed her over the cannon. He was beside her instantly, wordlessly taking her hand in his and pulling her with him through a maze of dark passageways. The crewmen had completely vanished, but signs of the battle were all around. The ship tilted wildly, leaning dangerously to port. The air was thick with heat and smoke, choking her lungs and burning her eyes.

She didn't understand how Cole managed to see anything, but somehow he did. He tugged her along, not slowing for an instant. When they reached the ship's rail, Devon peered over the side and gasped. All the boats had been taken. She turned to him, intending to ask what they would do now, but had no time to form the words. Cole McRae picked her up and threw her overboard.

The ship exploded before she hit the water.

Chapter 4

Blackness surrounded her. A sharp, throbbing pain started at the base of her spine and worked its way up. There was something else too. A noise. A voice, rather, one that was vaguely familiar and not at all welcome. It kept prodding her, insistent. Devon wanted to sleep, to make the pain and the voice go away, but she couldn't. Resigned, she slowly opened her eyes.

Cole McRae leaned over her, his expression, as always, grim. His hands were locked on either side of her head, one powerful knee lodged between her skirts. His clothing, like her own, was soaking wet. Small beads of water dripped from his hair and onto her face. She watched his broad chest heave as he dragged in deep, painful gulps of air.

"Are you all right?" he asked. He sounded irritated. Either because he'd had to repeat the question several times now, or because she might not be all right, and what an inconvenience that would be. Devon gritted her teeth as everything came rushing back. And to think she'd worried about him.

Her annoyance dissolved as a flash of alarm raced through her. The ring. She'd forgotten about the ring. Her hand flew to her chest, feeling beneath the soaked bodice of her dress. Please, she prayed, she couldn't have lost that. It was all she had left. The gold band was still there, tied securely with a bit of string and hanging from her neck. She let out a low sigh of relief.

"Dammit, woman, say something! Are you hurt?"

She slowly returned her attention to her captor. She knew what she needed to say, but getting out the three little words proved more difficult than she'd imagined. Her throat was raw, and just summoning her breath was an effort. Finally, however, she managed.

"Get . . . off . . . me."

To her amazement, Cole's mouth twisted into what might have been termed a grin. His deep brown eyes sparkled with golden light, but it was gone as quickly as it came, replaced by the dark, haunted shadows that normally sheathed his gaze. He rolled off her with a grunt, sprawling out next to her on the coarse, sandy bank.

Devon leveraged herself up and studied him from beneath a sweep of lowered lashes. The man made no sense. He was a dark, brooding, miserable human being. But he'd spent his own money to buy her the finest pair of shoes she'd ever owned—much to his regret, apparently. He'd been furious with her for talking with Justin, but only because of the risk facing the boy if he aided her in escape. And finally, Cole had saved her life. He could have abandoned ship with the rest of the crew, but he didn't.

Unable to resolve the disparities in his character, and annoyed that she'd even bothered to try, Devon turned away from him. She reached beneath her and pulled out the sharp piece of driftwood that had been stabbing her in the spine, then surveyed the area around them. It looked as if they had floated downriver a bit, pushed south by the current. They'd washed up on a small, sheltered inlet banked by a grove of dense cedar. She tilted her head to one side and listened intently, but heard nothing save the occasional chirping and squawking of birds.

"Where is everyone?" she asked.

"Upriver."

He didn't so much as glance in her direction. She waited. When it became evident that no more information would be forthcoming, she asked, "Was anyone hurt?"

He turned to look at her now, his dark eyes intense. "Bloodthirsty little thing, aren't you?"

Devon tightened her lips, refusing to give rein to her anger. "Just tell me. Please," she added, proud of herself for getting the word out without choking.

Their gazes locked and held. Just when she'd about given up hope for getting an answer, he spoke. "No one was hurt," he said at last. "Not seriously."

"I'm glad." Her captor gave an inelegant snort at that, clearly expressing his disbelief. Devon ignored it. "I thought, in a battle that fierce—"

"That wasn't a battle," he interrupted curtly. "More like an abandon-ship drill gone awry. We were barely able to answer their fire before deserting."

Devon didn't know what to reply to that, so she let silence fall between them once again. Cole shifted beside her. She heard his slight intake of breath as he stretched out his long legs. She glanced over, noting the deep crimson stain on his left thigh. "Is it bad?"

"No."

She bit back a sigh of frustration. Even if he was bleeding to death, she doubted he'd admit it. He probably considered that a sign of weakness. She moved toward him before he could protest, gently pulling the torn fabric apart. "Here, let me see." As her fingers lightly probed the injury, she realized that he was right. It was merely a flesh wound. A bit sore, perhaps, but nothing too severe. Their recent dip in the Potomac had even served to give it a proper cleansing.

Satisfied, she patted the fabric back into place, laying her hands over the wound. She heard him give another sharp intake of breath, then his large hand slammed down, pinning hers beneath it. Her head immediately snapped up. Was she hurting him?

"What the hell do you think you're doing?" he snapped.

Taken completely off-guard, Devon could only stammer out a reply. "I—I thought I'd . . ." she began, but her voice trailed away. That strange, golden fire was back in his deep brown eyes, but it wasn't pain she read there. It was anger, and something else. Something stronger. Devon's breath caught in her throat, and her stomach twisted. Her senses were suddenly heightened, and she became aware of everything at once.

They were alone. Totally and completely alone. Common sense told her that she should be frightened, or at least nervous, but she wasn't. For the first time since she'd stepped off the boat from England and into the middle of this horrible war, she felt as though everything was exactly as it should be.

Cole's face was framed by a mass of tawny-blond hair, which somehow served to heighten his rugged appeal. His firm, sensual lips were slightly parted. The angry scar that split his cheek stood out in white relief against the deep tan of his skin. She felt the muscles of his thigh quiver and tense beneath her fingers, then felt herself tremble in response as a shiver of delicious anticipation raced down her spine. It occurred to her that she should protest, force herself away. But she couldn't move her hands. Nor did she truly want to. She swallowed hard and tried again. "I thought I'd—"

"I know what you thought." Cole moved slowly toward her, tracing his rough hand gently across her cheek. His body was only inches away, raw power and sensuality emanating from him like heat from a fire. Devon froze, captivated by his touch. His deep voice was soft, almost a whisper. "I'd be happy to oblige you, Devon Blake, but know this: nothing changes.

You're still going to prison, and Jonas Sharpe will die under my hand.''

Had he slapped her across the face, Devon could not have been more stunned. She jerked back, alarm and indignation flashing in her soft green eyes. "I wasn't offering—"

"The hell you weren't."

"I thought you might be hurt."

"Did you? And just where did you acquire your nursing skills, in a brothel?"

Devon drew in a sharp breath. "Obviously I made a mistake," she conceded regally. Determined to regain her dignity, she rose to her feet. "I should have let you bleed to death."

He grabbed her arm as she spun away from him. "Where do you think you're going?"

"I require a few moments' privacy. I have to . . . to attend to myself."

His eyes narrowed, but he let her go. "Two minutes."

Devon moved quickly away from him, skirting through a hedge of boxwood and into a dense grove of cedar. She saw to her needs, irritated to find that her hands were still shaking. Once again, she'd completely lost control of the situation. He'd gotten to her again, and she was furious with herself. She was also flustered, embarrassed, and thoroughly confused. Damn the man.

After years of being in complete control of whatever situation she found herself in, she found Cole McRae's ability to muddle her thinking entirely unprecedented. Not only was it dangerous, it was a shocking blow to her pride. She had to get away from him. No sooner had the thought flitted through her mind when the realization hit home that this was the perfect opportunity. Devon frowned. It couldn't possibly be this easy. And yet . . .

She lifted her head, listening. Her two minutes were

up, but she heard no sound of Cole coming after her. They were alone and on foot, she thought, weighing the odds. Ordinarily that would give Cole the advantage, but surely his leg wound would slow him down. Not only that, he'd let her wander out of his sight, so he'd have no idea in which direction she headed.

Devon lifted her sodden skirts and moved cautiously away from her captor. She set a brisk pace until she was confident he was out of earshot, then broke into an all-out run. She moved recklessly, dodging fallen logs and tree stumps, trampling shrubbery and leaves beneath her feet. Beads of sweat clung to her skin as the midday heat bore down on her, thick and heavy as a blast from a baker's oven. The muggy air made breathing almost impossible and turned her arms and legs to lead, but she refused to let it slow her down. Exhausted and exhilarated, driven by desperation, she kept moving.

After a few minutes, Devon risked a glance over her shoulder. Still nothing. Victory swelled in her chest. She'd done it. She'd escaped. It had been so simple, so easy. Now all she had to do was make her way back to the harbor and find Jonas Sharpe—

Suddenly Cole McRae stepped out from behind a tree directly in front of her.

''No!'' The word flew from her lips before she could stop it. She cut sharply to the right, narrowly avoiding flinging herself into his outstretched arms. She heard his dark curse as she sprinted past, felt his hands brush the fabric of her gown. He was on her heels in an instant. The sound of his heavy, booted tread roared like thunder in her ears. Devon panicked. Her heart pumping furiously, using every last bit of energy she possessed, she pushed herself to run faster than she ever had in her life.

It wasn't fast enough.

Cole neatly closed the gap between them and brought

Devon down with a flying tackle. With a strength born of terror, she twisted and rolled from beneath his grasp, scrambling onto all fours as she lurched away from him. "Dammit, Blake!" She heard his low growl, then felt his iron grip around her ankle as he pulled her down once again. Devon had never struck another human being in her life, but now her survival instincts surged to the surface. She turned and swung as she fell, her fist landing solidly against the side of Cole's head. His grip loosened for a fraction of a second, enough time for her to pull free and lunge down a grassy ravine.

He was right there after her, grabbing her about the hips this time. But the momentum of her lunge, combined with the sheer force of gravity, propelled them forward. They tumbled down the steep slope, their bodies locked together as they rolled and slid. When they finally lurched to a stop, Cole's body lay flat atop her own. Devon instantly renewed her attack. She pummeled her fists against his back and shoulders and bucked her hips in a desperate attempt to break free. When that didn't work, she twisted and squirmed beneath him, letting loose a string of curses. He pulled back so that he was straddling her, caught her wrists in one hand, and effortlessly pinned them above her head. "That's enough!" he snapped.

Devon drew in deep, heaving breaths, feeling as though all the air had been choked out of her lungs. It didn't help. Rather than cool air, she was engulfed instead by the heady, masculine scent of Cole's body. He leaned over her, his body locked against hers in a position that had originally been necessary to restrain her movements. Now it was undeniably sexual. All of her twisting and struggling beneath him affected her captor in a way she hadn't anticipated. Through the ineffectual barrier of their sodden garments, Devon felt his erection press firm and hard against her belly. Captain McRae seemed to become aware of it at the same instant. Their eyes locked, and they both went suddenly still.

It was an opportunity Devon couldn't afford to miss. The vulnerability of her position, combined with the overwhelming superiority of his strength and the utter uselessness of any attempt to resist him, was finally driven home. He had accused her only moments ago of trying to seduce him. She realized now she had nothing to lose by actually attempting it. Summoning all her courage, she arched her hips against his and smiled her most seductive smile, despite the fact that she was trembling inside. "I'll give you anything you want," she said. "I'll do anything you want. Just promise you'll let me go when you're done. That's all I ask." In desperation, she reached up and wrapped her arms around his neck. "Please," she choked out. "Anything you want. Just let me go."

When still he didn't reply, but continued to stare at her with his cold, fathomless eyes, panic and despair gripped her. It was suddenly all too much for her. Her arrest, her trial, the drunken insults of Sergeant Coombs, the icy contempt of Captain McRae, the ship explosion, her clumsy attempt at seduction . . . Her nerves were strained to the breaking point, and she simply couldn't take any more.

Her eyes blurred with tears as her body went limp. She dropped her arms from around his neck and did what she swore she'd never do: she threw away her last vestige of pride and pleaded for her life. "Please listen to me," she cried. "I didn't murder that man— he was already dead when I got there. I wasn't working for Captain Sharpe. I didn't know about the papers in my trunks until it was too late. I swear it. Please, listen to me."

Cole froze above her. For a fraction of a second, his rugged expression softened as her words seemed to penetrate his cool exterior. But the moment didn't last.

He rolled off her and studied her in a detached, contemplative silence, then finally spoke. "That was a pretty performance, Blake. But I suggest you save your maudlin outbursts and crude offers for the guards at Old Capitol. They'll have more time on their hands to enjoy them than I do."

Devon gasped as red-hot fury uncoiled within her. His words instantly renewed her fighting spirit. "You son-of-a-bitch!"

He shrugged and rose to his feet, calmly ignoring the insult. "By the way," he drawled, "if your flight was meant to prove to me that I cannot trust you, you've succeeded. If that was a sincere attempt at escape, it was merely foolish." Taking her arm in an iron grip, he pulled her to her feet.

Devon jerked out of his grasp, furious with herself for showing any weakness. She should have known he would simply throw her shattered pleas for help back in her face. Unwilling to let him believe he'd actually bested her, she glared at him, then pointedly shifted her gaze to the gun tucked in his belt. "I can only assume that you are out of ammunition, McRae."

He frowned. "Why would you think that?"

"I can't imagine what else would have prevented you from shooting an unarmed, defenseless woman in the back. Certainly not your high moral standards or your righteous code of honor, as you appear to be deplorably lacking on both counts." Having scored her point, she turned her attention away from him and busied herself with brushing clusters of grass and leaves from her skirt. A shot rang out directly above her head. Devon shrieked and whirled about, staring at her captor with wide-eyed fear.

Cole simply raised his brows and cocked his head toward the smoking revolver in his hand. "What do you know about that," he said. "Looks like it was loaded after all."

It took her a full minute to recover from her fright. Finally she found her voice. "You are the most contemptible, vile—"

He squatted down, stuck his hand beneath her skirts, and grabbed her ankle.

Shock coursed through her once again, leaving her temporarily stunned. She slammed her fists against his broad shoulders. "Don't you dare—get your hands off me! How dare you—"

He released her abruptly, leaving her free to stagger backward. Her movement was accompanied by a telltale ripping sound as her thin cotton petticoat, which had remained firmly in his grasp, was torn to shreds. Cole came to his feet and tested the cotton strip in his hands. Satisfied, he grabbed her wrist and tugged her toward a thick, sturdy oak.

Devon instantly realized his intent. Despite her vigorous kicking, scratching, and screaming every blue oath she'd ever heard, he subdued her with an ease that was embarrassing. He positioned her arms so that she was hugging the tree, then neatly secured her wrists on the other side.

She glared up at him, fear and fury shooting from her soft green eyes. "You're going to leave me here? You can't do this. What if something happens to you? How will anyone find me?"

He didn't reply.

"How do I know you'll come back?"

He stared her straight in the eye. "I guess you don't."

Her fear escalated. Images of bands of lawless guerrillas, outlaws and deserters who were known to prey on refugees, war widows, innocent travelers—and just about anybody else who had the misfortune to cross their path—flooded her mind. She remembered the vague rumors she'd heard in Charleston of the unspeakable acts the Rebel guerrillas perpetrated on their helpless victims. Cole McRae might be a devil, but at least he was a devil she knew. It was the unknown that terrified her. Her heart slammed against her chest as she watched him walk away. "What if I'm captured by outlaws?" she called.

"Pity the poor bastards," he said without even bothering to turn around.

Cole moved north, taking note of landmarks as he walked. He was in unfamiliar territory, and that didn't bode well. He knew they were on the Virginia side of the Potomac River, somewhere between Richmond and Washington, but that was all he knew. Whether the volatile area was now Union-held or Rebel-held, he had yet to discover.

He slowed his pace as he moved from beneath the dense cover the cedar had provided him. The trees grew increasingly sparse, leaving him vulnerable and exposed as he crossed a dry, barren field. He didn't like it, but he had no choice. He gave himself one hour to beg, borrow, or steal a horse for himself and another for his prisoner. He didn't trust the woman enough to be away from her for any longer than that.

The thought of his petite captive brought a dark frown to his brow. He knew what she was. Liar, thief, murderess. Devon Blake admitted it all. She was also probably more experienced than any street-corner harlot he'd ever come across. Yet as much as he tried to convince himself of that, every instinct he ever possessed refuted that conclusion.

If the woman was a harlot, she was doing a piss-poor job of it. Her attempt at seduction had been absurd. Her smile had been nothing but a tight grimace; her normally throaty voice high and strained. Rather than shining with lust, her soft green gaze held only fear and panic. She'd been clearly terrified that he would take her up on her offer, and perhaps equally terrified that he wouldn't. She'd pressed her body against his with a stiff awkwardness, a wooden ungainliness so completely in opposition to her goal of seduction that it would have been laughable had it not been so . . . disturbing. Disquieting. Desperate.

Cole tried to push the thoughts aside, sickened by the fact that his body had betrayed him by responding to the woman at all. That for one brief instant when he'd heard her impassioned claim of innocence he'd almost believed her. He'd seen the tears shimmering in her eyes and felt himself to be nothing but a heaving, hulking brute for having driven her to that point. Fortunately he'd come to his senses quickly enough. Devon Blake worked for Jonas Sharpe. Obviously she'd do or say anything to gain her freedom.

He shook his head, irritated by the train his thoughts had taken. He was making too much of what had happened. Or rather, what hadn't happened. It was just lust, pure and simple. Contemptible perhaps, but understandable. After all, they'd barely escaped the ship explosion with their lives, only to toss and tumble atop each other following her ridiculous attempt at escape. She had offered herself, and his body had responded. There was no more to it than that.

Having reached that decision, he came immediately to another: the sooner they reached Washington and he was rid of her, the better.

A movement in the bushes ahead caught his attention and chased all thoughts of his prisoner from his mind. Cole dropped flat on his stomach, cocked his revolver, and waited. A tattered-looking group of soldiers emerged and moved noisily through the brush. The sun shone directly in his eyes, making identification impossible, but he could see enough to count their numbers. Five against one. Not bad.

They were heading west. Cole decided to hold his fire, waiting to see if they would simply cross his path and keep moving. For a moment, it seemed they would. Then they came to an abrupt halt as an argument broke out between two of the men. He could almost hear their voices. One of them lifted his arm, pointing directly to where he lay. After heated deliberation, the men turned and began marching straight toward him.

Cole clenched his jaw. The damned fools. Now he had no choice but to kill them. He raised his gun and took aim. Just a little closer . . .

Justin Hartwood's face swam into focus. Cole muttered an oath and lurched to his feet. That was a mistake. The men were green, too nervous to think straight, and he should have known it. Bullets began to fly before he could get a word out. Cole hit the dirt once again and rolled onto his side. "Dammit, Hartwood, it's McRae!" he shouted.

A lead shot struck near his head. He ducked but was too late. The shot ricocheted off the ground, kicking up a small rock that tore open the skin beneath his eye. The cut stung like hell and sent fresh blood trickling over his newly healed scar. "Hartwood!" he roared. "Fire one more shot and I'll personally carve your ass with a paring knife."

The bullets slowed, then stopped altogether. "Captain McRae?" a high, thready voice called back.

Cole rose slowly to his feet and approached the men. As he neared, Justin Hartwood stared at the blood that streamed down his cheek and went pale. He pulled a dirty kerchief from his pocket and offered it to Cole as he stammered, "I'm sorry, sir. We didn't know it was you, sir."

"Is that a fact?" he replied, glaring at the boy. Judging from the looks of him, Hartwood would rather be facing down General Stonewall Jackson himself. Cole ignored the kerchief, wiped the blood from his cheek with his sleeve, and turned to a more senior officer. "What the hell are you men doing out here?"

He listened impatiently to the tale of how the men had come to be separated from Captain Gregory, then wasted even more time arbitrating the dispute they had been having when he found them.

They were looking for the home of a farmer named Williams, a man known to hold pro-Union sympathies, in hopes of acquiring horses. One crewman felt they should continue west, the other insisted the farm lay due south. Gut instinct told Cole west, and it was in that direction that he marched the men. They found Williams in a little over an hour; he did indeed have horses to sell. Scrawny, unfit beasts which looked as though they could barely support a saddle, let alone the weight of a grown man.

Cole wasted no time bartering. He paid Williams twice what the animals were worth and considered himself lucky to get them. By the time he'd arranged for the purchase of saddles, food, and other supplies, the one hour he had allotted himself had stretched into two. Moving at as brisk a trot as the animals were able, they took another thirty minutes to make their way back to Devon.

He found his captive exactly as he'd left her, slumped against the oak, her wrists still bound. Cole immediately dismounted, grabbed his canteen, and strode to her side. He untied her wrists, then lowered her to a sitting position on the ground. He knew she allowed him to help her only because she had no choice. Her limbs were probably numb by now.

Cole fought back the waves of guilt and regret that washed over him by reminding himself that she was Jonas Sharpe's agent, but it didn't help. He'd had no intention of leaving her for so long. Not alone, and not in this heat. Perhaps she'd even believed that he wasn't coming back, he thought, furious with himself for letting his anger get the best of him. "I'm sorry," he said gruffly, supporting her back as he held the canteen to her lips.

Devon drank greedily. When she finished, she pushed the water away and studied the men who'd returned with him. They remained in their saddles a few feet away, as ordered. "I see you brought back reinforcements," she said, ignoring his apology. "Do you think you'll be able to manage me now?"

In the space of mere seconds, she'd been able to gather herself enough to issue that cool, calculated challenge. Cole was both amazed and grudgingly impressed. "I never doubted it," he replied.

Her soft green eyes turned to ice. "Then you're a bigger fool than I thought."

Cole took her arm and pulled her to her feet. If his prisoner was strong enough to engage in verbal sparring, she was strong enough to ride. He led her to the small blond mare he'd purchased for her. Devon stared at the animal stonily, then looked at Cole. "Exactly what do you expect me to do?"

"We've a few hours until sundown. We ride until dusk."

"I don't think so."

The statement was made so politely, so matter-of-factly, it took a moment for her refusal to sink in. When it did, however, Cole's response was equally matter-of-fact. "I don't recall giving you a choice."

"You should have bought a buggy," she insisted stubbornly.

"We're wasting time. Saddle up."

"No."

"Yes." He grabbed the mare's bridle with one hand, then wrapped his remaining arm around Devon's waist, intending to lift her up and place her on the saddle.

She dug her heels into the dirt. "I don't know how to ride!"

That hadn't occurred to Cole. He stopped, momentarily nonplussed, then dismissed it as unimportant. "You'll learn."

He stepped forward to put her in the saddle. Devon clawed at his arm. Unable to release herself from his grasp, she lifted her legs, using her feet to push the horse away. The nervous mare whinnied and danced skittishly backward, moving as far as the length of the bridle would allow. "Dammit, Blake," Cole swore under his breath and tried again.

Devon answered with an oath of her own, demanding he put her down. They chased the nervous animal in a circle, Cole holding the mare with one hand, his captive aloft in the other while she pushed the horse away with her feet. He swore again. Devon swore even louder. The mare's eyes grew wild. It lifted its front legs, ready to bolt.

"Put your legs down," Cole growled.

"Put *me* down."

"Dammit, woman, I was talking to the horse."

"Oh."

They chased the mare in another circle as his men watched the spectacle silently, their eyes wide, their mouths agape. Cole supposed he could ask for their help, but hell if he was going to. Devon Blake was just one woman, after all, and a small one at that. How hard could she be to handle?

Five long minutes later, he was asking himself the same question. "Captain—" Justin called out tentatively.

"Not one word, Hartwood," Cole snapped, his jaw locked in grim determination. He knew he looked like a damned fool dog chasing its own tail, but he wasn't about to give up. Or give in. He would get her on that horse if it took until the end of the war to do it.

After a lengthy, heated struggle, he finally succeeded in placing her atop the mare. He adjusted her stirrups while she clutched the saddle horn with both hands. "What if I fall off?" she squeaked.

"Don't tempt me," he shot back. His long, angry strides carried him swiftly back to his own horse. He tied the mare's reins to his saddle, mounted, and gave his men the signal to move out.

He heard his captive's stifled gasp behind him but ignored it, setting the pace at a brisk canter. Since the gasp wasn't followed by a dull thump, he assumed she'd managed to stay seated. He glanced over his shoulder to make sure. Devon clutched the horn, her eyes locked on the mare's neck as she bounced up and down. Cole let out a breath as he shook his head. The woman was going to be sore as hell come morning.

Good.

He shook off the thought and turned his attention to more important matters. Though it was doubtful they would run into enemy troops in this area, he preferred to play it cautious. Their best bet was to stay off the main roads and follow the line of the Potomac due north, toward Aquia Creek. The last he'd heard, that position was strongly Union-held and with any luck, it still would be.

They rode well into the summer evening, stopping only when the lengthening twilight shadows made it difficult to see. His small band, more accustomed to a pitching deck beneath their feet than the rhythm of a saddle, dismounted wearily and set about making camp. Cole drew two men aside to send ahead as scouts. He'd just finished conferring with them when he turned back to find Justin Hartwood gazing adoringly up at Devon Blake, who had yet to dismount.

Anger surged through Cole. Neither his captive nor Hartwood had heeded his warning before, but they damned well would now. He had enough on his mind without worrying about how long it would take Devon to convince the love-smitten boy to hand over his money and gun, and ride escort with her all the way back to England.

"Hartwood!" he roared. "What the hell are you doing?"

Justin tensed and spun around. "Why, er, nothing," he stammered. "Just helping the lady—"

"The lady," Cole repeated, his voice dripping sarcasm, "does not require your gallant assistance. She taught herself to ride in one day, I'm sure she can teach herself to dismount as well."

Devon's eyes flashed fire. "Obviously," she replied, directing her remarks to Justin, "your brave leader here is disappointed that I didn't fall off my horse earlier. How ungracious of me to have managed so well. Perhaps I can oblige his evil nature and fall off in dismount." With that, she swung her left leg around, then hung on to the saddle horn as she slid off the mare on her belly.

With a satisfied smirk, she looked up at Cole, bringing her hand to rest briefly on her backside. "Sorry to disappoint you," she said. "Perhaps you'll feel better to know that I am rather sore. Does that help?"

Cole took a deep breath. "Push me a little more and I guarantee you'll have cause to regret it."

Her eyes widened in feigned shock. "Oh, dear. Not that. What would you do next, McRae? Beat me? Tie a rope around my neck and drag me behind you tomorrow? I can assure you that nothing could be worse than another minute spent upon that cursed animal's back."

Cole met her gaze for long, cool seconds, then he too directed his remarks to Justin. "Hartwood?"

"Sir?" the boy gulped.

"You said you wanted to help?" Cole asked, his voice a low growl, his golden-brown eyes never leaving his prisoner's face.

"Well, uh, that is, sir—"

Cole's arm sailed above Devon's head. Despite her

cool facade, she flinched as he reached for the saddle behind her. With a quick jerk of his wrist, he freed a length of rope and tossed it at Justin. "Tie her up," he commanded.

Justin blanched, looking at the rope in his hands as if he didn't quite understand the command. "Er, uh, you want me to—"

"Now."

Justin flushed once again, his ears turning pink with embarrassment as he reluctantly reached for Devon's wrists. "I'm sorry about this, ma'am," he muttered.

"Not another word, Hartwood," Cole warned, determined to drive the point home. "This woman is an enemy to the Union, and therefore an enemy to the United States. She is to be treated no differently than any other prisoner. Do you understand me?"

"Yes, sir."

"Good." Cole waited until the boy finished, then checked the ensign's work. Satisfied, he turned and strode away, feeling Devon's furious emerald glare burn into his back. He ignored it and kept walking, moving until the blackness of his thoughts melted into the blackness of the night, leaving him empty.

He was honest enough with himself to admit that it wasn't just Hartwood and his captive that caused the dull fury that had been raging within him since they'd left Fort Monroe. They were a simple enough matter. Devon Blake would be handled and sent to prison. Justin would either learn to do his duty or spend the rest of the war in the stockades. They could be controlled. No, they weren't the problem.

The problem was rooted deep within himself, festering away like a raw, ugly wound. He needed to drink until he passed out. He needed a good brawl—a couple of hard, solid blows, either dealt or received, it didn't matter. He needed to turn the clock back, turn the weeks back, then go even further back than that. Back to the days when he'd been so reckless and wild. When he'd been so arrogant, so cocky, so goddamned stupid. Cole stopped and propped his shoulder against a thick oak as he stared into the darkness, then he closed his eyes. Despite his casual posture, his body was racked with tension as he poured his soul into one silent, fervent plea. *Please, God, let me do it all over again. Please. Give me just one more chance.*

The night answered with silence.

Memories of the battle he'd lost encroached upon his thoughts. He clenched his fists and pushed them away as a cold sweat broke out on his brow. How the hell was he supposed to lead a troop of greenhorn sailors all the way to Washington? He wasn't capable. He couldn't do it, he'd only get them all killed.

A rustle of leaves startled him out of his dismal reflections. He had his gun cocked and ready before he realized it was merely a squirrel darting between trees. Cole holstered his revolver and hung his head, taking a couple of long, deep breaths to ease the panic that flooded through his body. *Very brave, McRae,* he thought in disgust. *Scared shitless by a hungry squirrel.* He raked his fingers through his hair and shook his head. If he managed to get his men anywhere near Washington, it'd be a goddamned miracle.

Chapter 5

Devon rolled onto her back and gazed up at the night sky. Judging from the shifting stars and the faint rose glow that beckoned to the east, it was probably about an hour before dawn. Unaccustomed to sleeping on the ground, she drew her arms above her head, stretching to relieve her cramped muscles, then craned her head around to ease her neck.

She stopped abruptly when she saw Cole.

He was sitting with his back to her a short distance away, staring off into the horizon. He wore no shirt, likely because of the muggy heat that even now clung to the air. His arm was flung casually over his knee. Devon wasn't fooled by the relaxed posture. She could see all too clearly the knots and tense muscles that rippled beneath his deep golden skin.

It had been a long, restless night. They'd come to a truce of sorts—if having to lie next to Captain McRae, with her hands bound by rope and tied securely to his belt—could be called a truce. Knowing that his loathsome presence was within arm's distance made falling asleep hard enough. Staying asleep had proved impossible.

It was a low moan that had disturbed her first. She had opened her eyes sleepily, not really sure she had heard anything, when the rope that bound her hands was suddenly wrenched, propelling her directly on top of her captor. Stunned, she had lain flat on top of him, her fingers splayed open across his broad, bare chest.

Amazingly the impact of her body landing hard on top of his had not been enough to wake him. He had tossed beneath her, calling out a name. Devon had tried to pull free and shake him awake. Nothing had worked. Finally, desperate to awaken him, she had lifted her hand and slapped him. Not hard, but none too softly either. When she had lifted her hand a second time, his eyes had flown open and he had caught her wrist, holding it in a painful grip.

For a moment, Cole had simply stared at her, a blank, lost look in his eyes. She had known the instant recognition set in, however, for his features had turned to granite and a contemptuous sneer had curved his lips. Moving with chilling silence, he had angrily shoved her off him, pulled the rope free from his belt and thrown it on the ground, then stormed over to where he sat now.

So the man had nightmares. Devon should be thrilled. But she wasn't. Despite repeatedly telling herself that she didn't care, she found herself tossing and turning, Captain McRae's silent, painful vigil was far more disturbing than his presence next to her had been. She stared at him now, wondering if he'd ever gone back to sleep or had simply sat where he was throughout the night.

"The sun will be up shortly," he said without turning around, startling her. "Since you're awake, you may as well get up."

Devon rose without a word and walked into the low bushes a few feet from their camp. There she recited the alphabet aloud in a dead monotone while she performed her morning duties, the only concession she'd managed to win. Her hands remained loosely bound, not enough to truly hamper her movements, but rather, she assumed, to serve as a pointed reminder of her state of captivity. Gaining her privacy was a small victory, but it wasn't nearly enough. One day had gone by. She estimated that in perhaps two or three more days, she'd lose her freedom forever.

The thought was not a cheery one. Neither was the sight that greeted her when she walked back to the glen. Operating with brisk military efficiency, the men were in the process of breaking camp, leaving little trace that they were ever there. The blankets they'd slept on were rolled and neatly packed, the horses saddled and ready. Cole stood waiting for her, his expression cool and unfathomable. He'd donned his white linen shirt, and looked as though he'd dragged his fingers through his thick, tawny-gold hair. He would almost be presentable, in fact, were it not for the dark stubble that shadowed his cheeks and chin.

Devon shuddered to imagine what she must look like. Puffy-eyed and pale, probably. She hadn't even bothered with her hair, but simply let it hang like a limp, tangled mess down her back. Well what did anyone expect, she thought irritably, after sleeping in the dirt all night?

Morning had never been her favorite time of day. She preferred to ease into the day slowly, and was quite content not to even look at another human being until noon. Since she and Uncle Monty did the vast majority of their business in the wee hours of the night, that was rarely a problem.

Now here she was, cranky and irritable, being forced onto the back of a horse before the sun had even risen. Too tired to even put up a decent fight as Cole lifted her and placed her in the saddle. She'd save fighting for a more respectable hour, she decided as she let out a weary sigh and closed her eyes.

"Blake."

Her eyes snapped open. Cole had remained right beside her, rather than moving to his own mount. For once, she was able to enjoy the advantage of superior height, and gazed down at him. He looked exhausted from lack of sleep, and decidedly unhappy about whatever he was about to say.

He gestured at her hands. "Don't grip the saddle horn like that," he said curtly. "Use your legs to hold on. That way you'll move with the horse, rather than against her. You won't be as sore."

Devon simply stared at him, not saying a word, then she understood. He'd interpreted her reaction when he placed her in the saddle as one of pain, rather than simple weariness. Apparently it had affected him enough to offer her advice on how to ride. Despite his endless threats, the man was obviously not interested in truly hurting her. Devon nodded, storing the information away for future use.

They rode in a staggered line throughout the morning, exchanging no words but the essentials. The sun never did come out. Instead the day remained gray and hazy, the heat even more unbearable than it had been the day before. By noon, Devon was utterly miserable and felt permanently attached to both the horse and the saddle.

When Cole signaled for them to stop, she didn't object. Nor did she protest when he lifted her down from the saddle. In fact, she was thankful for the support of his strong arms. Her knees buckled before she adjusted to the feel of solid ground beneath her feet. She swayed against him, her cheek brushing lightly against his chest. In that brief, awkward moment of contact, she became instantly aware of the heat of his body and the heady, thoroughly masculine scent of his skin.

Memories of the night before flooded through her. Not of Captain McRae's nightmare, but rather of the physical sensations that she'd relegated to the dark corners of her mind. Memories of tumbling, drowsy and confused, on top of the man. The feel of his hot, half-naked body beneath hers. Wrestling, twisting and turning, and then finally slapping him awake.

The burning contempt she had seen in his eyes once he recognized her.

Devon jerked out of his grasp and turned away, focusing all her attention on awkwardly brushing the dirt from her skirts. She breathed deeply of the thick, muggy air until she regained her balance, then moved stiffly down the sloping bank toward the shallow creek where they'd stopped. She seated herself on a blanket of lush summer grass and watched as Cole and his men tended to the horses. Given that they were unsaddling them, she presumed their break was going to be a long one.

Lord knew, she needed it. She turned toward the water, hoping to find a respite from the unmerciful heat. Nothing. The creek was a deep, dank green, the water absolutely still. Not even a breeze was stirring. Spying a thick oak with a limb extending out over the water, Devon removed her shoes and stockings, silently cursing the ropes that bound her wrists as she did, for it made the simple chore a cumbersome task. Finally finished, she stepped up onto the branch and settled herself there, leaning back against the sturdy trunk, her skirts bunched up around her knees, her feet dangling in the water.

The position was highly improper, but she couldn't quite summon the energy to care. For that matter, so was unbuttoning the top two buttons of her gown and letting the air fan her neck and skim the tops of her shoulders, but Devon did it anyway. She let out a blissful sigh. If she closed her eyes, she could almost imagine she felt a breeze.

After a few minutes, she felt someone join her, and knew without looking that it was Captain McRae. Something about his presence put a charge in the air which made her nerves react instinctively. A similar feeling, she presumed, to what a mouse must experience when a hungry cat creeps into the barn. Automatically preparing herself to do battle, she opened her eyes and turned toward him. If he was at all shocked by her unladylike pose, he didn't show it. Devon checked the thought. The man already believed her to be a cold-blooded murderess. Obviously it would take more than a petty breach of etiquette to crack his stony facade.

Her lips tightened as she saw that he carried two plates. So they were going to go through that again, were they? She watched him move toward her, coming to a stop near the trunk of the tree. He set his plate down, then offered another to her. Devon turned disdainfully away, saying, "A lady does not eat with her hands tied."

"What would you know about what a lady does?"

She stared straight ahead, ignoring both the insult and the offering. It was pointless, really, since they'd already gone through this last night. It wasn't that the ropes that bound her wrists hurt, or even restrained her in any way. For in truth, Justin had tied them so loosely she could probably twist out of them with minimal effort. It was more the principle of the thing. And since stubborn pride was about all she had left in the world, she'd have to be a damned sight hungrier than she was now before she gave in. She tilted her chin a notch higher and waited for Cole to leave.

He set her plate in her lap.

Devon flinched, then anger surged through her.

Cole caught her wrists, guessing her intent before she could knock the plate into the water. "Don't," he said.

"I will not eat with my hands tied," she repeated furiously, glaring up at him.

He stared back at her. Before she realized what he was about, he pulled a knife from his belt and with a quicksilver flash of steel, freed her hands. The rope fell limply to the ground. Startled, Devon tried to tug her wrists free from his grasp, but he wouldn't let go, instead he tightened his grip ever so slightly until she stopped struggling and lifted her eyes once again to his. Their gazes locked and held, as if he was waiting for her to say something, but she hadn't a clue as to what that might be.

Finally he let her know. "I believe a word of gratitude might be in order."

Her eyes narrowed. "It'll be a cold day in hell before—"

"Eat," he said, dropping her wrists and turning away.

Devon watched him warily as he seated himself on the grassy bank. He drew one knee up, resting his elbow atop it. The posture was one she'd come to recognize as uniquely Cole's own, a combination of indolent ease and barely constrained power. She sensed a simmering energy just below the surface, as though he was impatient to spring into action. With his thick golden hair and tawny eyes, he brought to mind images of a savage lion stalking its prey . . .

Obviously she was weaker from hunger than she thought. Devon turned her gaze from him and studied her plate instead. Thin slices of ham, a corn biscuit, and an apple. Better than she'd expected. She nibbled the food, letting a silence fall between them as they ate. When she finished, she leaned back against the thick oak trunk, her outlook considerably brightened. She'd eaten, her hands were free, and the heat no longer seemed quite so intense.

She glanced around for the rest of the men and found them lounging about in the shade near the horses. Her eyes went back to Cole. Normally he was occupied with his own thoughts, and rarely deigned to even notice her. Now, however, his gaze was focused entirely on her, as though she were a strange, foreign creature to be studied.

Devon found herself amused rather than irritated. She splashed the water with her feet, then turned to him, her soft green eyes mocking as she raised a dark brow. "Am I really so fascinating?"

He frowned. "You don't look like a criminal."

She shrugged. "That's generally how it works. One does a much better business that way."

"Nor do you speak like one," he said, as if voicing his thoughts aloud. "That tells me you must have had some kind of education, some sort of proper upbringing. It seems you were meant to be a lady, though clearly that's a goal you'll never attain."

Devon fanned herself with her hand. "Is that a fact?"

"So the question is," he continued, "what happened? What brought you to the point of relying on thievery and murder for your very existence?"

"Perhaps I enjoy it," she said, forcing a lightness into her tone that she didn't quite feel. "Perhaps it's the only thing I've ever been good at."

"I assume you had a mother, a father. What happened to them?"

"What business is that of yours?"

"I may be able to help you."

Devon laughed out loud. She couldn't help it. Obviously the captain had decided to switch tactics, employing friendliness now instead of intimidation. Did he really think she was stupid enough to fall for it? "You want to help me," she repeated, her voice rich with bitterness and barely bridled contempt. "Now why don't I believe that?"

"You have little choice," Cole replied coolly. "But I need to know everything. How you came to know Sharpe, how much he was paying you, where he is now, everything. Start at the very beginning."

"And if I say no?"

"That would be a mistake."

"I see." She fought to keep from clenching her fists. "How very generous of you, McRae. And all I have to do in return is divulge all the personal, intimate details of my background."

Cole simply stared at her, waiting.

Devon took a deep breath. Given her current circumstances, anger was a luxury she could little afford. No, for now she would do best to play it cautious. But that didn't mean she had to deny herself the fun of throwing her captor's despicable ultimatum back in his face.

She silently bowed her head, as though weighing her options. When she lifted her eyes to his, her features were drawn in a mask of lost, weary innocence. "I suppose you're right," she said softly. "I really don't have a choice."

"I'm glad you finally realize that."

Smug, arrogant, bastard. Devon smiled sweetly. "Do you promise you'll help me?"

"If I can."

"Of course." Devon gazed forlornly at the water. A small sigh escaped her lips. "My mother was an actress," she began. "A woman whose beauty and talent were renowned throughout Europe. My father, the French duke, fell in love with her the first time he saw her perform. He swore he'd give up all his estates just to be by her side. But he was married, of course, so the affair was doomed from the start . . ."

"Blake . . ." Cole said warningly.

She paused, blinking in mock surprise at his intense frown. "Isn't that what you wanted to hear?" she asked, thoroughly enjoying herself now. "Pity. That's always been one of my favorites. Oh well, perhaps you'll enjoy this. My mother was a savage Indian princess. She met my father, the sea captain, on a voyage to Africa. Their love was destined by the heavens, but alas, a deadly pox spread among the crew—"

"That's enough," Cole cut her off.

"My, there's just no pleasing you, is there?" She shook her head in mild reproof. "As to my background, I make it up as I go along. Which version would you like to hear?"

"The truth. That is, if you still remember it."

She turned away, her light mood instantly dissolved. "The truth is rarely interesting. It certainly isn't in my case."

"Why don't you let me be the judge of that?"

Devon hesitated. Ever since she'd lived her life "on the dodge," as Uncle Monty put it, her background had become amazingly fluid, not unlike the stories she'd just told, tailored to fit whatever situation she found herself in. She'd become adept at letting people see whatever they wanted to see, and letting them believe whatever they wanted to believe. Up until now, that had always suited her. She'd stayed alive, and that was all that counted. But the truth . . . that was another matter entirely. She turned back to Cole, noting that his eyes had never left her. He wanted the truth, did he? She thought it over, then shrugged inwardly. She had nothing left to lose.

"Very well," she answered briskly. "I was sent for as a mail-order bride. Jonas Sharpe was acting as intermediary, as my intended was a business associate of his. Sharpe must have planted the documents found in my trunks, for I had no idea they were there. Furthermore, I didn't murder anyone. I discovered the body in an abandoned warehouse, only seconds before the soldiers arrived and arrested me."

Because she had told her story so many times, her delivery was rather forced and detached. She frowned a bit at that, but dismissed the concern as unimportant. Her purpose had been to relate the events as they had occurred, not to entertain. As she finished and Captain McRae studied her in thoughtful silence, a tiny spark of hope was lit deep within her. Dare she believe she'd finally found someone who would actually listen to her?

"It appears I should have defined the word *truth* for you before we began, Blake, as its meaning seems to elude you."

Devon drew in a tight breath, valiantly maintaining her composure. It had been idiotic for her to hope. Cole's response was no different than anyone else's had been whenever she'd tried to explain her circumstances. They'd all asked her for the truth, then refused to listen when she told it. So be it. She wouldn't waste another ounce of precious energy trying to convince him.

"As you will not answer," he said, "you leave me no choice but to draw my own conclusions."

She let out an inelegant snort. "Yes, of course. Surely a man of your vast intellect has me all figured out by now."

He leaned back on his elbows, his long legs crossed at the ankles. "Would you care to hear?"

"Not particularly."

"I think you prefer lies to the truth, stealing to honest work," he said, ignoring her. "You're intelligent but greedy, and want more from life than is rightfully your due. You were given some advantages at birth, but obviously those weren't enough for you. You're used to getting whatever you want, regardless of the cost to anyone else."

Devon opened her mouth, then abruptly closed it, fighting back her anger. What did she care what the man thought of her? She'd chosen her path, and had no apologies to make to anyone. Except to her brother, Billy, maybe, and it was far too late for that. As a familiar, aching tightness choked her throat, she pushed the thought away and swallowed hard.

Feeling Cole's steady gaze focused intently on her, she forced herself to relax against the trunk of the tree, determined not to show the slightest weakness or vulnerability, knowing all too well he'd only use it against her. She arranged her features into a mask of bored condescension and fanned herself with her hand. "Is it always this hot?" she asked after a few minutes.

He studied her in silence. "No," he answered at last, "not in August."

Devon nodded and swatted away a fly.

"Then it's even hotter."

She swung her head around to look at him. Was that meant to be a joke? Surely not. There was no trace of levity on his rugged features, no glint of humor in his eyes. She doubted the man even knew how to smile.

His next words proved her right. "It's worse at Old Capitol. Washington was built on swampland, did you know that? The prisoners there die of malaria in the summer, pneumonia in the winter."

Devon twirled her toes in the tepid water, sending ripples echoing across the smooth surface. "I presume you're trying to frighten me."

"Educate you," Cole corrected. "And, God knows why, give you another chance at earning my help."

"I see. And exactly what would I have to do in order to *earn* that help?"

"Tell me where I can find Sharpe."

Devon swung her leg over the tree limb and jumped down. She picked up her shoes and stockings, but didn't bother to put them on. "You have me all figured out, don't you?" she said. "For the most part, your insight is remarkable. There's just one little thing you missed."

"Which is?"

Her eyes locked on his, her gaze cool and unflinching. "I wasn't working for Jonas Sharpe. I have no idea where to find him." She started to walk away, then stopped and turned slowly back. "Oh. There's one more thing you should know," she said. "I was telling the truth; I didn't kill that man. I've never killed anyone . . . yet."

Cole rose slowly to his feet, towering above her once again. His eyes darkened, but whatever comment he was about to make was lost as the sound of someone stumbling through the bushes distracted them both. Justin Hartwood emerged, brushing away the twigs and leaves that clung to his uniform.

"I thought I ordered you and the men to stay with the horses," Cole said.

"Yes, sir." Justin nodded and held up his canteen. "I was just gonna get a quick drink."

Cole's features turned to stone. "What were your orders, Hartwood?"

Justin came to a dead stop. He glanced at Devon, then quickly averted his eyes, staring at the ground near his feet instead. A deep red blush crept slowly up his neck. "I was ordered to stay with the horses, sir."

Cole responded with a tongue-lashing that seemed to Devon entirely inappropriate for the magnitude of the offense. It was hot, the boy was thirsty, and he wanted a drink. So what if he disobeyed an order? She watched in mounting fury as Justin silently endured the harsh reprimand, then turned and marched back to the rest of the men, his skinny shoulders stiff with unreleased anger and wounded pride.

Devon wasted no time in voicing her contempt for the way Cole had handled the boy. "I hope you enjoyed that," she said in disgust. "You've finally succeeded in making him hate you."

To her appalled disbelief, Cole nodded. He stared after Justin, his profile harsh and unyielding. "I hope so," he said. "I hope Hartwood hates me enough to never risk disobeying another order in his life. I hope he lives through this damned war, and then long enough to tell his grandchildren what a mean, ugly bastard I was."

That was the last thing in the world Devon expected to hear. It partly explained why her captor was so harsh with Justin, but it didn't explain enough. She watched as he absently traced the scar that ran the length of his cheek, then, with a flash of intuition, made a connection. "Who's Gideon?" she asked.

He jerked his head toward her, anger and remorse lurking in the dark shadows of his tawny eyes.

"Last night," she said, forging ahead with more courage than common sense, "you had a nightmare and you called out a name. Who's Gid—"

"We've wasted enough time here," Cole said, cutting her off. "It's getting late, and I'm tired of listening to your lies."

Devon stiffened in anger but didn't say a word. There was no reason to get upset, she told herself. So far, everything was working just the way she wanted. Cole McRae had been as easy to fool as the rest of her captors had been. In one critical area he'd believed her farce, and that was enough. He might have seen through all her little lies, but it was the big lie that mattered. And that, she thought smugly, was the one lie he'd missed. By this time tomorrow, if not sooner, she'd have made her escape.

Cole rode behind his prisoner, watching her as she continued to bob up and down in the saddle. The woman was probably the worst rider he'd ever seen, and because of that, they were losing time, moving at only half the pace he'd planned. He should be furious, but he wasn't. The slower pace gave him time to think, time to sort out the inconsistencies that had been bothering him for days.

Nothing about Devon Blake was as it should be. She was stubborn, willful, a consummate actress, and a talented thief. Yet she was also more than what she appeared. The woman was both infuriating and strangely compelling. She undermined his authority, disobeyed his orders, and ridiculed his commands. She worked for

Jonas Sharpe, and deserved his loathing just on that basis alone. But no matter how hard he tried, he couldn't bring himself to do it.

He watched her slim back, remembering what she'd looked like only an hour earlier with her skirts bunched up around her knees and her toes dangling in the stream beneath her. She'd been a picture of fetching innocence, and he'd sensed instinctively that the pose hadn't been contrived. For if it had been, wouldn't she have jumped on his offer to help her, rather than telling him in so many words to go to hell?

Instead she'd laughed at him. She'd sat there on the branch of that thick oak, her long, dark hair spilling over her shoulders, and laughed at him. Mocked him with her absurd tales and unending lies. And even more amazing was the fact that he'd let her. Cole had sensed clearly that it wasn't personal. She simply didn't trust him. He doubted she trusted anybody, and found himself wondering what had happened in her short life to make her so bitter, so cynical.

And so afraid.

He'd seen that too, despite how desperately she'd tried to hide it from him. The woman could control her expressions, moderate her tone of voice, and maintain a posture of haughty disdain no matter how difficult the circumstances. But she hadn't yet learned to school the emotions that flashed through her eyes.

Cole was profoundly grateful for that. He found himself watching her eyes, studying them the way a sailor studies the sky, looking for storms. He could see them clearly in his mind, even though her back was to him. Soft shimmering green, framed by long, thick, sooty lashes. Amazing eyes. Devon Blake had eyes that would make even a plain girl pretty. On her they were breathtaking.

He tightened his jaw. Christ, he was beginning to sound as smitten as Hartwood. The woman was no more than a nuisance, and a dangerous one at that. Obviously he'd been too soft on her. It was his duty to make her tell him where he could find Sharpe, and if he needed to handle her more roughly in order to get that information, he would. It was a shame it had to be that way, but he didn't care. He owed at least that much to the memory of his men.

That resolved, he turned his attention back to the trail. The path they followed was poorly groomed, little more than a shallow rut that meandered slowly northward. They traveled for miles beneath the cover of dense trees and overgrown shrubs. Eventually the trees began to thin and bright sunlight flooded the ground just ahead, indicating a clearing of some sort. Cole let out a low whistle, signaling his men to a stop. He spurred his mount forward, arriving at the edge of the clearing just as a piercing screech of metal reached his ears.

A train. The path ahead of them opened up to a low, empty field. A hundred yards ahead, a train wheezed to a stop. Cole swore silently as Rebel soldiers poured out of the forward coach, swarming over the open field like a plague of locusts. Straining his eyes, he saw bright glints of metal where the rails had been twisted off the track, most likely the work of roving Union scouts. Until the damage was repaired, the train was going nowhere. And neither were they.

Cursing his luck, he dismounted, motioning for his men to do the same. He reached for Devon. "Not one word," he growled as he pulled her from her mount.

She simply glared at him in response, then shifted her eyes to look beyond him, her gaze resting on the train and the field of fifty or so well-equipped Rebs. When she turned back to Cole, the mocking light of challenge danced in her eyes. She opened her mouth as if to scream.

Cole grabbed her by her arm and jerked her against

him. "Do it and I swear you'll be dead before we will."

The amusement he'd seen drained from her delicate features. For an instant, burning hatred flashed in her soft green eyes, then her countenance resumed its normal expression of cool disdain. "I understand," she answered.

Cole's eyes narrowed. That had been altogether too easy. His prisoner wasn't a woman easily intimidated by threats, even if the threats were against her very life. "I mean it."

"I know you do."

He studied her a second longer, then abruptly released her. She turned away from him, moving with the stiff, awkward gait of one entirely unused to spending days in the saddle. She sat a few feet away from the rest of the men, her back to both Cole and the train. He frowned. Devon Blake was not one to be submissive. She had to be planning something.

After a few minutes of watching her, however, he changed his mind, vaguely surprised that she was finally heeding his threats. Devon sat silently by herself, plucking absently at the thick grass surrounding her. When she became bored with that, she dragged her fingers through her hair and began arranging it in a loose braid. Cole surveyed the rest of the scene. The horses were slackly tethered and remained saddled, ready to go. His men were alert, their guns cocked and ready as they watched the Rebs.

Everything seemed all right, but it didn't feel that way. Cole glanced back at Devon. Apparently she'd finished her meager attempts at grooming, for now she was curled up in the grass, as though ready for a nap. He let her be, keeping a watchful eye on both her and the Rebs as they repaired the damage to the tracks.

It wasn't until the shrill whistle blew, signaling completion of the work, that he was able to relax. The enemy soldiers reboarded; steam poured from the stacks as the engines were stoked with coal and fired up. The train began to slowly rumble forward. His captive stood and stretched, looking sleepy-eyed and thoroughly mussed from her nap. Cole turned from her to address his men.

That was all the time Devon needed. Before he could guess what she was about, his captive flew past him and toward the horses, leaping into the saddle with an ease that left him temporarily stunned. He grabbed for the reins, but Devon was there first, jerking them free as she drove her heels into the animal's flanks and spurred her mount forward. She burst through the thick underbrush, racing at breakneck speed after the train.

Cole let loose a furious oath as he grabbed his horse, leaped into the saddle, and tore out after her. Devon had about a twenty-yard head start and was making the most of it. She moved at a reckless gallop, leaning over her mount's neck, pushing the animal even faster. The wind whipped through her hair, sending it billowing down her back like a dark cloud.

Cole grit his teeth. The woman could ride. Dammit to hell, she'd been able to ride all along.

Even so, he was better—not by much, he admitted grimly, but enough. He was able to close the gap between them, thundering up right behind her as she rode level beside a freight car. It was a moot point now in any case. The train was moving at full speed, the steel wheels grinding against the rails, chewing up and spitting out anything that fell between them. Any attempt to jump aboard now would be pure suicide. He knew it, and surely she did too. Cole strained forward to pull her away from the speeding train.

He realized his mistake too late. He couldn't reach her, nor could he stop her. Instead he'd moved in just close enough to panic her. Had he backed off, left a little more space between them, she would have seen the danger and moved away from the train on her own accord. But he'd left her no choice.

She stood in her stirrups and reached for the boxcar. Cole's heart slammed against his chest. "No!" he screamed.

He was too late.

Devon jumped.

Chapter 6

Cole watched in horror as Devon threw herself out of her saddle, her small body poised in midair above the grinding steel wheels for what seemed an eternity before she slammed against the broad freight door. She grabbed for the iron beam that bolted the door, but was unable to grasp it securely. Her right hand slipped away, leaving only her left holding the beam, and her body dangling precariously above the churning tracks.

Cole didn't hesitate. He leaped from his saddle, hurling himself toward the speeding train. He crashed against the boxcar and grabbed hold of a thin metal ladder that was bolted to the side. Finding the deep grooves that ran the length of the car, he dug his boots in, gaining a foothold as he stretched his body forward and reached for Devon. The wind whipped over him, roaring in his ears as he shouted her name.

She couldn't hear him, or couldn't turn if she did. He watched as she strained upward, trying to get a grip on the thick metal beam. It didn't work. Her right hand slipped away once again, and this time her left slipped with it. She gave a cry of stark terror as her body plummeted.

Cole lunged for her, catching her as she fell. He wrapped his arm around her waist, pulling her to him as Devon threw her arms around his neck. Their bodies locked together, hugging the freight door as the ground sped away beneath them. Their moment's relief at having narrowly escaped with their lives dissolved instantly as the thin ladder to which Cole clung suddenly bent under their weight, jarring them both.

"Reach for the door," he shouted in her ear. His own hands were occupied holding both her and the ladder, and he wasn't about to let go of either one.

She shook her head in mindless terror, her small hands digging into his shoulders. "No, I can't!" she cried.

"It's all right, I've got you, I won't let you fall."

"No!"

The ladder cracked again. A bolt sprang free from above their heads, releasing the upper portion of the ladder and sending them hovering out over the tracks before they crashed back against the boxcar.

"Dammit, Blake, do it! Open that door!"

This time Devon obeyed. She stretched away from Cole, her hands shaking as she reached for the heavy metal bar. Cole held his breath. If the door was locked . . .

It wasn't. Devon reached it and pulled back, slowly sliding it open. Cole felt another bolt give way, and didn't wait for her to finish. They had one chance, and one chance only. He hung on to the ladder as he used his feet to shove away from the boxcar, propelling them in a wide arc over the churning tracks, then back toward the train. As they hurled toward the boxcar, Cole released the ladder, praying the momentum of the wide, swinging arc would send them through the open door, rather than crashing against the side of the car.

They weren't going to make it. Cole realized that in a split second of awareness as they soared back toward the train. The opening wasn't wide enough, he hadn't pushed hard enough. Just as he braced himself for the inevitable, the train lunged uphill, and gravity completed what Devon had begun. The freight door slid wide open as they flew past and into the dark interior of the car.

They skidded across the hard wooden planks, their fall finally checked as their bodies slammed into a stack of rough crates. Cole shoved Devon beneath him as he braced his body for the impact. The crates teetered, then came crashing down on top of them, splitting open as they bounced off his back and tumbled across the floor. He felt Devon tense beneath him but didn't move, not until he was sure the worst was over.

When the last crate had fallen, and the only thing filling the silence was the steady hum of the train's steel wheels whirling beneath them, Cole groaned and rolled over. His back hurt like hell, which he supposed was a good sign. He was probably still alive.

Devon moved out from under him and slowly sat up, her face deathly pale, her eyes wide and glazed as she stared at the interior of the car, then at Cole. "We made it," she whispered hoarsely, her tone one of awed incredulity.

"Barely." He grunted and stared up at the ceiling, not yet ready to move.

She leaned over him, her brows knit with concern as she placed a delicate hand on his chest. "Are you hurt?"

Cole stared up into her soft green eyes and fought back the urge to shake her senseless. "Of all the stupid, reckless—" he began as Devon scrambled to her feet, glancing anxiously around for a way out.

Cole shot up, ignoring the pain in his back as he placed himself between her and the open door. "Don't even think about it," he snapped.

"Don't be absurd," she said. "I'm not about to leap from a speeding train."

"What the hell do you think you just did?!" he roared. "You damned near got us both killed."

Devon's mouth turned down in disapproval as her

small, stubborn chin came up. "If you hadn't been chasing me—"

"You would have been crushed beneath the train's wheels," he finished for her.

She stared at him in horrified disbelief. "Do you actually expect me to be grateful?"

"For saving your life, you're damned right I do."

"Oh, please," she answered contemptuously. "You didn't save me, you rescued your precious duty and honor. How embarrassing it would have been for you if your prisoner had been killed while trying to escape." She paced back and forth, working herself into a fury that matched his own. "That would have spoiled all the fun, wouldn't it? How inconsiderate of me to risk dying now, rather than waiting to rot away in prison. Forgive me for forgetting how important that is to you."

"Blake—"

"No one's ever going to lock me up again. Do you understand me? Never again."

Cole stared at her. So she'd been in prison before. While that certainly didn't surprise him, neither did he relish the thought of her in a dark, dank cell. Nor could he completely harden his heart against the fear and panic he read in those expressive eyes of hers as she stared up at him, struggling in vain to maintain her brave facade. Irritated by the turn the conversation had taken, he found that his next word came out sharper than he'd intended. "Move."

Devon made a face at his rudeness, but moved nonetheless. He turned his attention from her to the crates that filled the boxcar. Given that no soldiers had been posted to guard them, Cole doubted he'd find much of value. He broke them open and began pillaging anyway, finding his suspicions correct. The items the crates contained, though luxurious, were mostly worthless to a nation at war. Lace corsets, bottles of scent, boxes of hand-rolled cigars. Obviously the shipment was intended for the black market.

Cole shook his head in disgust, sickened by the greed. While men died on the battlefield for want of rifles and ammunition, blockade runners still put profit ahead of their supposedly glorious cause of liberating the South. Well, that was Jeff Davis's problem, not his.

"What are these?" Devon asked, interrupting his thoughts. He glanced behind him to see that she'd begun digging through the crates as well. Spread out before her was a group of lithographs depicting a big man with dark hair and muttonchop whiskers in a variety of ridiculous poses. In one he was shown in full battle gear, sitting astride a pig, in another he was dressed in a frilly smock, clutching a bouquet of daisies.

"Butler. General Benjamin Butler," Cole answered. Then, seeing her frown, he clarified in profound understatement, "Union general. Not very popular in the South."

Devon nodded and stacked the prints back inside the crates. "These seem like silly things to be transporting," she said. "I would have thought the crates should be full of food and clothing."

Cole's eyes darkened. That was exactly the sort of thing he needed to hear to put this all back in perspective. Thus far, Jonas Sharpe was one of the few blockade runners who, in addition to ruthlessly attacking Federal ships, was also dedicated to supplying the South with badly needed munitions. That was just one of the reasons the man had to be stopped. And the instincts he'd relied upon all his life told him that Devon Blake was the key to stopping him. "Fortunately for the North," he answered curtly, "most blockade runners are not as dedicated as your boss, Sharpe."

Her hands paused in mid-air, then she shrugged and continued packing away the crates. "I told you, he's not my boss."

Cole refused to be drawn back into the same tired argument. Instead he flipped over a crate and sat down, calmly studying her. "You should have just yelled when you had the chance, rather than try something so stupid as leaping onto a speeding train," he said at last. "You nearly cost us both our lives."

She turned toward him at that, her brows arched in cool, mocking challenge. "As I recall," she said, "you threatened to kill me if I did."

Cole frowned, wondering if she believed he was actually capable of doing such a thing, then wondering why it bothered him that she obviously did believe it. "Is that why you didn't scream?" he asked.

"No."

"Then why?"

Her lips curled into a small smile. "Are you offering me suggestions for how to escape, McRae?" He waited, refusing to rise to the bait. Devon shrugged and settled herself atop one of the wooden crates. "I thought about it, of course," she said, finally addressing his question, "but I figured there must be at least two hundred men on this train. Compared to your six, that hardly seemed a fair fight."

She hadn't screamed because she didn't want him or his men hurt? It took Cole no more than two seconds to dismiss that as the lie it surely was. "Do you actually expect me to believe that?"

She stared at him for a long moment, then quietly averted her eyes. "No," she said. "No, I suppose I don't."

Cole felt a pang of guilt, which he knew was absolutely ludicrous. There was no reason he should believe a single word that fell from those traitorous lips of hers. The woman was a liar, a thief, and a murderess. Why was it so hard for him to remember that? He searched for another reason to hold on to his anger and it didn't take him long to find one. "You're an excellent rider," he said.

"So I've been told."

"You're quite a little actress as well. I truly believed you'd never sat a horse before in your life."

"That was the plan."

Once again, Cole was torn between strangling her and applauding her performance. Then he remembered the scene she'd created when he'd first tried to put her in the saddle, and his anger surged anew. "You made me look like an ass in front of my men."

She shrugged lightly and brushed the dirt from her skirt. "It hardly seems fair for me to take full credit. I'd say you accomplished that pretty well by yourself."

"If that's your way of begging my forgiveness, I suggest you try again."

"And I suggest you—" She stopped abruptly, her eyes wide as she pressed her hand flat against her breast. "My ring," she gasped. "It's gone!" Before Cole could say a word, Devon flung herself down on all fours, moving her hands frantically over the rough wooden floor.

Cole watched her, then caught a glint of shiny gold near the crates where they'd tumbled to a stop. He stood and reached to pick it up, holding it between his fingers as he casually inspected it. It looked to be a wedding band, and one of rather poor quality at that. The gold was thin and rather scratched, the stones nothing but a few diamond chips. He turned toward her, holding the ring aloft. "If you're going to go to all the trouble to steal something, perhaps you should aim higher. This is hardly worth—"

She jumped up and lunged toward him. "Give it to me!"

He swung his arm back, holding the ring just out of reach. "I must admit, you're very resourceful. When did you find the time to steal it?"

Devon glared at him, balling her hands on her hips. "I didn't steal it. That belonged to my mother, and those are her initials engraved on the inside. ELB: Elizabeth Layton Blake. Now give it to me."

Cole glanced inside. "So they are. Tell me, which mother was that, the famous actress, or the Indian princess?"

"Neither." She held out her hand, her eyes locked on his. Cole took his time, thinking it over and enjoying holding the upper hand for once. With Devon Blake, that was a rare enough occurrence.

"Damn you, give me the ring!" Her voice shook. So did her hand as she held it out, palm up. Her soft green eyes were sparkling bright, either with anger or tears, he couldn't tell.

He carelessly flicked the ring at her. "I suggest you watch your language," he said coolly, then shrugged as his gaze moved appraisingly over her tattered gown, dirty face, and wild hair. "Then again, perhaps it doesn't matter. No one will ever accuse a little tart like you of being a lady."

He saw her flinch as pain streaked across her face. Cole had wanted to hurt her. He wanted his words to be cutting, mean. It was her fault that Justin Hartwood and the rest of his men were now wandering, alone and probably lost, through the backwoods of Virginia. It was her fault that the *Islander* had been destroyed and his crewmen slaughtered. If he harbored even the slightest ambition of tracking down Jonas Sharpe, it was absolutely essential that he stop Devon Blake from getting under his skin. That he treat her with the contempt that Sharpe's agent deserved. Finally she turned wordlessly away.

That was what he wanted, after all, so why did he suddenly feel so dirty, so obscene? Cole let out a ragged sigh as he watched her retreat across the boxcar to sit near the open door, with her back to him, hugging her knees against her chest as she stared out at the passing countryside. The breeze from the open door blew back her hair, sending it cascading over her shoulders like a wave of dark silk. She'd placed the ring on the third finger of her left hand, and now absently twisted it around and around.

His nerves stretched to the limit, Cole turned toward the stack of crates, wanting to release at least some of his frustration by driving his boots through the wooden frames, when a small, delicate sniff caught his attention. He whirled around, glaring at his prisoner's back. God help him, the woman wasn't going to start crying on him now, was she? Though her shoulders didn't move, he heard another small sniff.

Dammit to hell.

Fine. Let her cry. He wasn't about to let her manipulate him again. He was the one in control here, not her. Cole turned his back on her, reminding himself for the hundredth time that she was Jonas Sharpe's agent. That she was every bit as responsible as Sharpe for the destruction of his ship, for the death of so many of his crew. For Gideon.

It didn't work.

What he saw instead was an image of himself, an image of a man he never thought he'd be. He saw himself with jarring, crystal clarity: a failure at command, tired and defeated, and just out of control enough to bully one small, helpless woman to tears. As hard as it was to believe, he'd actually managed to sink to a new low. A fresh wave of self-loathing washed over him. What the hell was he doing? *What the hell was he doing?*

He heard another sniff and knew he couldn't stand it much longer. Grabbing what he'd been able to salvage from the crates, he walked over to his prisoner and squatted down beside her. "Would you like some candy?"

Devon wiped the back of her hand across her cheeks

and jerked her head around. "I'm not a child," she snapped, her gaze flashing from him to the box of fine imported chocolates he held.

"I didn't think you were," he countered smoothly, setting the candy and a bottle of French brandy between them.

"I wasn't crying."

Cole nodded in polite agreement, ignoring the fact that her eyes were glistening bright, her long, dark lashes spiky wet. "This is the only food I could find," he said. "Since our provisions remain strapped to the back of my saddle, I'm afraid this is dinner."

He settled in beside her and picked out a piece of chocolate. After a few moments' hesitation, his captive followed his lead. He opened the brandy, took a deep swallow, then passed it to her as well.

She shook her head. "Uncle Monty never allowed me to touch spirits. He said ladies don't—" Devon stopped abruptly, then reached for the bottle. "I suppose that doesn't matter anymore, now does it?"

Cole watched as she carefully wiped the lip of the bottle with her skirt, then tipped the brandy to her mouth and took a long, deep swallow. She abruptly began choking. "It's very strong," she gasped when she could finally speak.

"Smooth," he corrected, and took another drink. He passed the bottle back to her. Devon accepted it with a small frown and took another sip. This time she managed to swallow without choking, though he did see a slight shudder pass through her slender frame.

They sat together in silence, sharing the bottle. Outside a gusty wind was kicking up, and Cole noted dark clouds gathering to the west. The storm would reach them soon, perhaps in an hour, maybe two. For now he felt nothing but the hot breeze that blew in through the open door; the thick, sultry air fanning them both.

The countryside slowly disappeared as twilight descended into dusk, and then into night.

Cole hadn't planned on getting Devon drunk. But now that the opportunity presented itself, he wasn't about to let it pass him by. Not if it meant a way for him to learn more about Sharpe. After the first couple of swallows, he'd merely tipped the bottle to his lips without drinking. Devon apparently had learned to acquire a taste for it. The brandy, he noted, was more than half-gone.

He searched for an innocuous comment, something he could say that would reveal a bit about himself, and perhaps coax her into doing the same. "This reminds me of where I grew up," he finally remarked.

"You grew up in Virginia?" Her voice had a sing-song quality to it that he didn't recognize, and was probably the result of the strong drink.

"No. Outside of Philadelphia. But the countryside is similar, rolling green hills and all."

"Oh." She drew her dark brows together as though processing very difficult information. Cole considered that she might be feigning drunkenness, the same way she'd pretended she couldn't ride, but decided that was highly unlikely. Given the diminutive size of the woman, combined with the amount of alcohol she'd imbibed and the speed with which she'd downed it, she had to be feeling the effects. "Tell me something else about you," she said.

"Why?"

"I'd like to know something about the man who's going to kill me."

Cole jerked his head toward her. "What makes you think I'm going to kill you?"

"You're not going to let me escape, are you?"

"No."

"And I'm not going to let you lock me away." Devon let out a dramatic sigh and wrapped her hands around her knees, resting her chin atop them. "Killing me is the only option we have left." She tilted her head toward him, her eyes as frank and trusting as a newborn babe. "Your parents were very rich, weren't they?"

He blinked at the rapid-fire shift in conversation. "What makes you say that?"

"I can tell. I'm very good at sizing up a mark. It's the little things that give people away. Like your boots, for instance. Expensive. Definitely not government issue. I'm right, aren't I?"

"Yes. I bought my boots."

She shook her head. "I meant, I'm right about your parents, aren't I?"

"I suppose so," he answered.

"That must have been nice."

He shrugged. "Money isn't everything."

Devon stiffened beside him. "No, you're right. Food is everything. Warm clothes are everything. Having a safe place to sleep at night is everything. But that all takes money, doesn't it?" She took another swig of brandy, and he watched her shoulders visibly relax. "Tell me what it was like," she said.

Cole shifted, distinctly uncomfortable. Not only had he just received a royal and, unfortunately, richly earned setting-down, he was rapidly losing whatever control he thought he'd had over the conversation. "My father runs a factory outside of Philadelphia," he said. "He build wagons, buggies—"

"McRae Coaches?" Devon gasped. "That's you?"

"No," Cole said firmly, not at all surprised at how quickly she made the connection. To most people, the word *coach* followed McRae as naturally as night followed day. "That's my father and brother. They're the ones who run the company. It's theirs, not mine."

Devon made a noncommittal sound. "So tell me

what it was like for you growing up," she said. "Your house must have been very grand."

"It was huge," Cole admitted. He stretched out his legs, leaning back as the memories spilled over him. "More like an institution than a home," he continued, voicing his thoughts aloud. "Run by an endless parade of white-gloved, stiffly starched servants, who kept everything in absolute order—including the children. To my mother, there was no crime worse than using the wrong salad fork at dinner. And God forbid my brother or I received less than perfect marks in our lessons." He paused, shaking his head. "We practically walked around the house on tiptoe all the time. No laughter, no shouting, no noise of any kind. As if there was a body perpetually laid out in the front parlor."

Devon laughed at that, a soft, husky sound that Cole had never heard before. She gazed up at him, her eyes shining and two tiny dimples curving the corners of her lips. He stared at her mouth, astonished by the wayward path his thoughts had taken. Rather than focusing on their discussion, he found himself wondering what it would feel like to kiss those dimples. "So I take it you decided not to stick around and build coaches," she prompted.

Cole shook his head. "Hell, no. I left when I was seventeen, determined to make it on my own. I signed up with a ship sailing to Constantinople and loved every minute of it. The spray of salt air, the roll of the deck beneath my feet, the feel of freedom when a burst of wind fills the sails and you understand what it's like to fly. I knew then that I'd found what I wanted to do with my life. I saved my wages, learned everything I could about captaining a ship."

"And you went out and bought a ship of your own," she concluded.

He smiled ruefully. "Fifty-foot schooners don't exactly come cheap. As I was only twenty-one at the time, getting the money for a ship meant swallowing my pride and going back to my father for a loan. Fortunately he believed in me enough to give me the money." He paused, then shook his head as he reconsidered his words. "Truth is, he thought I was still a damned fool kid, but gave me the money anyway. Within three years, I was able to pay back the loan, plus a handsome profit."

Devon hiccupped. "Thank you for sharing that with me."

Cole turned to see her smiling at him in warm approval. He'd become so wrapped up in his own reminiscing that he'd nearly forgotten what he'd set out to do. He was supposed to be getting information from her, not the other way around. "Now it's your turn," he said.

Devon stiffened and turned away. She reached for the brandy bottle and took another sip. "I told you," she said after she swallowed, "I'm not that interesting of a person."

"Tell me about your parents," he said. "When did they die?"

She looked startled. "I never said my father was dead. I don't know for a fact one way or another, but I doubt he's dead."

He frowned. "You don't know? Did you run away from home?"

"Actually, it was more the other way around."

"I don't understand."

"I know."

"Then why don't you explain it to me?" When she stubbornly refused to reply, he tried another tack. "Tell me where you grew up."

"Fordsham. In England."

"Did you like it?"

He watched as Devon nodded and ran her hands over her skirts, smoothing them down, a gesture he'd come to recognize as one of nervous agitation. "We didn't have as fine a home as yours, of course," she said finally. "Just a simple cottage. But my mother liked to grow roses, and that made it pretty. And once I stitched red gingham curtains for the windows. They didn't last through the winter though, because the roof leaked and the water ruined them."

Cole pictured Devon growing up in a drafty cottage with a leaky roof. "Where was your father during all this?" he demanded abruptly.

She shrugged. "My father was in trade. He traveled all the time when I was growing up. He sold dress patterns, farm equipment, furniture from catalogs—always something different. I imagine he was fairly prosperous, for he sent enough money home for my mother, Billy, and me."

"Billy?"

"My younger brother."

She hesitated, staring blankly out at the darkened countryside. "My mother used to be so excited whenever my father came home from one of his trips. She would spend days fixing up the cottage, dressing up Billy and me so he would stay longer. Getting everything perfect for him. My father would bring us all presents, and for a few days it would be better than Christmas, better than anything." She paused, twisting the ring on her finger.

"But it never lasted long. Within a week, maybe two, nothing was good enough for him anymore. I talked too much, or got my dress dirty. My mother's biscuits were too dry. And Billy . . ." Her voice trailed off, then she looked up at Cole, a brilliant smile pasted on her face. "Billy was a beautiful child. And so smart, so bright . . . but he was born with a crooked back. He couldn't walk without crutches, and not very well even then. Sometimes I would catch my father watching him with this pained expression on his face, as if it hurt just to look at him, and I would get so mad . . .''

Cole waited as she lifted the bottle of brandy and stared at the label, as if it held the solutions to all the world's problems. He sensed he was finally getting closer to the answers he wanted, as long as he kept her talking. "Go on, Devon," he coaxed.

"When I was twelve and Billy six, our mother died. She'd been ill for a while, and Father had been home for the end of it. About a week after the funeral, he told Billy and me to get all of our things together, that we were going to go on a special trip with him."

She looked up at Cole, her eyes cloudy from the brandy, a wistful smile on her face. "This is going to sound awful, but even though I was sad that Mother had died, part of me wasn't so sad. I knew that Father could never leave us again. I'd make sure that Billy and I were always perfect, and that way he'd have to love us."

"So where did you go on this special trip?"

"We boarded a train for Liverpool, which was the nearest city. Billy and I were so excited, it was the first time we'd ever been on a train. At the first stop, my father got off to get us something to eat. I remember he kissed me on the cheek, told me to watch Billy, and said he'd be right back."

She stopped abruptly and took another swallow of brandy. The wind blew around her, stronger and cooler now, tossing her hair like dark flames around her face. Cole saw lightning flash in the distance and heard the low grumble of thunder, and knew that the storm was sweeping in. He felt suddenly tense, as if the weather was stirring his own blood. "What happened?" he asked.

"When the train pulled away from the station, my father wasn't on it. I screamed and cried, begging the conductor to wait for him, but he wouldn't. He handed me some meat pies he said my father had bought for us and just walked away. But I knew it was all a mistake. It had to be a mistake.''

Lightning streaked through the sky, illuminating the dark interior of the car. A crashing boom of thunder immediately followed. The sky split open and rain poured down, as though the black underbelly of the clouds had been slashed with a knife.

"Was it a mistake?'' he asked, though he already knew the answer.

"When we finally got to Liverpool, Mrs. Honeychurch, of the Lady of Mercy Orphans Asylum, was there to meet us. They tell me that I didn't speak for a month after that.''

Cole clenched his fists in his lap, thankful for the dark so she couldn't read the expression on his face.

"You know,'' she continued in a tone of forced brightness, "I've always thought that was a rather twisted bit of logic. When a parent abandons his children, why is it always the children who are locked up? Shouldn't it be the other way around?''

He ignored her feeble attempt at levity, realizing now what she'd meant when she said she'd never allow anybody to lock her up again. She'd been talking about the asylum, not prison. "Was it very bad?'' he asked.

"I suppose not. Not if you always listened, always obeyed, and always did whatever Mrs. Honeychurch told you to do. Not if you were very, very good.''

"And were you very good?''

He could feel, rather than see, Devon's soft smile in the darkness. "What do you think?''

"I think . . . not.''

She laughed. "I'm afraid Mrs. Honeychurch spent a lot of time beating me with her shoe.''

Cole found no humor in the statement. "How often—''

"It wasn't so bad,'' she reassured him.

He scowled. "Is that where you got that scar?" He reached over to touch a spot right above her shoulder blade. He'd noticed it before, along with one other, near the base of her throat. She jumped when his fingers brushed her skin. "Easy," he said, not moving his hand. "I'm not going to hurt you."

Devon stared up at him, her gaze soft and unwavering. "I know," she answered, with an expression of such complete trust that Cole felt strangely humbled.

A need to protect this woman surged over him. The feeling was not only inappropriate but inexcusable, considering their circumstances. Yet he couldn't seem to shake it. Nor could he prevent himself from touching the faded mark near the base of her throat. "What about this scar?" he asked.

Devon hiccupped, then giggled. "I think I like brandy."

"Where did you get the scar, Devon?"

"Oh, that." She made a dismissive motion with her hand. "Uncle Monty and I learned of a duke who had murdered his wife. We contacted him and told him that we specialized in dealings with the dead. When we told him that his wife was appearing before his servants and spreading incriminating rumors of her untimely death, the man was properly horrified. He hired us to stop his wife before the rumors reached his friends and business associates. We'd wait until he was well into his cups—usually after midnight—then I'd make an appearance gowned in gauzy white robes, white powder blotted over my face and hair, moaning that my husband had murdered me. Uncle Monty would promptly begin chanting spells to get rid of me. The duke, completely shaken, paid us handsomely for our performance—and for our vow of secrecy. We figured that after the fifth visit his wife's dearly departed soul could finally be laid to rest."

"What happened?"

"Unfortunately the duke was growing increasingly terrified of being found out. He lost faith in Uncle Monty's incantations and came to the conclusion that the best solution was to kill his wife all over again. So late one evening when I made my appearance, the duke pulled a gun and fired."

Cole's stomach tightened as he looked at the long, thin scar. "An inch to the right and you would have been killed," he said grimly.

She took another swig of brandy. "Admittedly it was not one of our finer moments."

"If you knew the man murdered his wife, why didn't you simply report him to the authorities?"

Devon stared at him as though that was the stupidest question she'd ever heard in her life. "Who do you think the authorities would have believed? The duke, a man with power, position, and sterling reputation; or two lifelong criminals like Uncle Monty and me?" She hiccupped again, then shrugged. "Besides, one doesn't make any money by simply reporting people to the authorities."

"I see."

"I'm not usually such a mess," she continued. "Those are the only two scars I have, and they're generally well-covered, so it really isn't too hideous, is it?"

His thoughts strayed to the deep gash that ran the length of his cheek. "I suppose that depends on who's looking," he answered.

Devon reached up and lightly ran her fingers over his cheek. "Uncle Monty says that everyone carries scars. Only they're not always where you can see them. Sometimes people are scarred on the inside, and those are the wounds that take the longest to heal."

Cole felt something twist deep inside him, stunned by her words and amazed at the jolt he'd felt at her light, casual touch. Still he managed to keep his voice level. "What else did he teach you?"

She smiled. "Oh, lots of things. How to deal an ace from the bottom of a deck. How to lift a purse without making a sound. Which spoon to use at tea in order to fool people into believing that I was a *proper* lady." She paused and her smile faded. "Only I never did fool you, did I?"

Cole flinched, neatly sidestepping the question. "He sounds like a remarkable man, your uncle."

Devon nodded, then hiccupped. "He is. Except, of course, he's not really my uncle."

"Of course," he agreed politely.

"He taught me all about men, as well."

As Cole had abandoned any hope of directing their rambling conversation, he decided this was too good an opportunity to simply let pass by. "Really? What valuable insight did he share with you on that subject?"

Devon frowned, looking vaguely displeased. "He said I should never believe a word a man says once he's taken off his pants." Her glance moved outrageously down to his trousers, as though checking to make sure they were still there. Satisfied, she continued. "He also said I should never believe a promise that's whispered in the dark. The two are connected somehow, but I haven't quite figured it out . . ."

Cole fought to keep from laughing. "Let me know when you do," he said, then gently pried the brandy bottle from her grasp. "I think you've had enough."

She frowned at that but reluctantly acquiesced. "Am I drunk?"

"Yes."

"Did you get me drunk on purpose?"

Cole hesitated. "Yes."

"To ask me questions about Captain Sharpe?"

God, she was quick. Even when she'd downed nearly an entire bottle of brandy, there was still no getting anything past her. "Yes," he admitted.

"I see." She attempted to sit up straight, but swayed

suddenly to the right instead. Cole caught her before she toppled over. "In that case," she said weakly, "I won't feel bad for getting sick all over you."

"What?!" he roared as he jumped back, then immediately reached forward again to prevent Devon from falling flat on her face against the rough wooden floor. "Why the hell didn't you tell me you were feeling ill?"

"I didn't know I was," she protested. "Not until two seconds ago when everything started to spin so horribly."

"All right," he soothed, collecting himself. "All right." He grabbed Devon by the shoulders and eased her onto her back, then snatched a porcelain vase from one of the crates and set it beside her. "Do you need to be sick now?"

"No ... *Yes!* ... No ..."

Cole helped her over onto her side, held her hair back with one hand, used his other to support her forehead, and waited patiently while she emptied her stomach. When she finished, he gently eased her down again and moved to stand up. Devon's eyes flew open and she grabbed at his sleeve. "Don't leave me!"

"Shhh. Just lie still, I'll be right back."

From another crate, he removed a china bowl and a bolt of rose brocade silk. He stood by the door and stuck the bowl outside, filled it with rainwater, then returned to Devon. He propped her up on his lap and lifted the bowl to her lips. She groaned and turned her head to the side, refusing it. "It's just water," he coaxed. "Take a sip to rinse your mouth."

After she obeyed, he set the bowl down. With the storm sweeping in, the temperature had dropped a good twenty degrees, giving a chill to the air. Cole pulled the thick silk from the bolt and draped it over Devon, then dipped his handkerchief in the rainwater and gently began bathing her face and shoulders. She lay absolutely still, her breathing shallow.

It wasn't as if he'd poured the stuff down her throat, he thought, fighting back his guilt over her condition. Nevertheless, he'd shown a colossal lack of judgment in not taking the brandy away sooner. He felt her stir in his arms, then her eyelids slowly flickered open. "Do you feel better now?" he asked.

"Hmmm . . . McRae?"

"What?"

"What's your favorite color?"

He sighed. She was still drunk. "Go to sleep."

"What color?"

"Blue," he answered, just to shut her up, and because that was the first color he could think of.

She smiled dreamily. "Mine too. McRae?"

"Go to sleep."

"McRae?"

"What?"

"I wasn't working for Sharpe. At least not the way you think I was." She looked up at him, and for a fraction of a second, the cloudiness cleared and her gaze shone with crystal-green clarity. "Do you believe me?" she asked.

Cole stared down at the woman curled up in his lap. Obviously his plan to get her drunk had been a miserable failure, managing only to get her sick and leaving him with more questions. He knew now that her mother was dead and her father was a low-life bastard, but that was about it. The important questions, like who "Uncle" Monty was, and how had she gotten tangled up with Jonas Sharpe, and what had happened to her brother, Billy, would have to wait.

He considered what he had learned. Devon called herself a lifelong criminal, and he didn't doubt for a moment that it was true. She could haunt a duke, pick a pocket, lift a purse; and that was probably just scratching the surface of her audacious, felonious past.

But nothing he'd seen in her indicated a willingness to hurt someone else—let alone kill a man in cold blood.

Devon studied him, then let out a sigh as a look of infinite sadness swept over her face, and she closed her eyes. "You don't believe me."

Cole leaned back against the crates, easing the tense muscles that knotted his spine. He shifted Devon into a more comfortable position in his lap and absently stroked her hair as he thought it over. He shouldn't believe her. It was a disgrace to the memory of his men to even consider believing her. But a stubborn, nagging doubt still persisted. What if this wasn't just another one of her elaborate cons? What if she really was innocent? The possibility was so remote that it didn't even bear contemplation. And yet . . . it was a possibility.

He glanced down at his lap. Devon Blake was fast asleep. There'd be no more answers tonight. Cole let out a ragged sigh as he considered his situation: he'd lost his men, lost his ship, and was currently hidden on a train that was racing behind enemy lines, his only company his drunken prisoner and two hundred Rebel soldiers.

Another sterling performance, McRae, he thought in disgust as he closed his eyes.

What the hell was going to go wrong next?

Chapter 7

～✦～

"**W**ake up. Blake, wake up."

Devon stifled a groan and slowly opened her eyelids, taking in her surroundings. She was lying on the floor of a dirty, dingy boxcar. Cole stared down at her, looking obscenely fresh and well-rested. His tawny-blond hair was caught in a loose ponytail at the base of his neck, and his shirt—likely one he'd stolen from the crates—was crisp and fresh. "How do you feel?" he asked in a gratingly cheerful voice.

She glared up at him. "My head is pounding and my mouth tastes as if something crawled into it and died during the night," she said, then mimicked his obnoxious grin. "Other than that, I'm fine." She moved to sit up, then fell back with a groan. "What did you beat me with?"

"A bottle of brandy."

Devon forced her eyes open and studied her captor. Something was definitely wrong. Cole was acting altogether too pleasant. While it was entirely plausible—highly likely, even—that he was simply enjoying her misery, her instincts told her that something else was afoot. But with her head aching so fiercely, she was in no shape to figure out what that might be. She rose slowly to her feet, then gasped and spun around, shielding her eyes. "What in God's name is that blinding glare?"

"Blinding glare?" he repeated, then amusement

crept back into his tone. "Ah. I believe that's known as the sun. It's been up for several hours now."

Her lips twisted into a grim parody of a smile. "My, aren't you clever."

"Clever enough not to try to drink an entire bottle of brandy in one sitting."

Her hand flew to her stomach. "Please," she groaned. "Don't remind me."

"I found a tin of tooth powder in one of the crates. There's also a pitcher of fresh rainwater and clean linens," Cole said, pointing toward the rear of the boxcar. "Or do you need to be sick first?"

Devon stiffened, ignoring the queasy rumbling in her stomach as she brought up her chin. "Of course I'm not going to be ill," she pronounced haughtily. "What sort of weak, pathetic creature do you take me for?"

No sooner had she gotten the words out than a blurry recollection shot through her mind of her being violently ill and lying curled up in Cole's lap as he bathed her face with a cool cloth. Embarrassment streaked through her. No, please, it couldn't have been, she thought in mortified disbelief. Looking into his eyes, she saw laughter glinting in their tawny-brown depths and knew without doubt that the memory was real. No wonder he was acting so smug and superior this morning.

Realizing there was nothing she could do about it now, Devon pushed the humiliating memory aside and moved across the boxcar with all the dignity she could summon. Fortunately he was no longer watching. Cole stood with his back to her, allowing her a modicum of privacy as she attended her toilette. Likely because he was more interested in the passing scenery than out of any courtesy he might wish to bestow on her, she decided grumpily.

Her tasks completed, she dragged her fingers through the ratty nest of tangles that was her hair, wishing for the umpteenth time that her trunks hadn't been confiscated. She glanced around disparagingly when it suddenly struck her that she hadn't fully explored the contents of the crates last night. Devon went to work and was rewarded in short order with a beautiful sterling silver brush, comb, and mirror, a set of tortoiseshell hairpins, a bonnet she rather fancied, and a lovely new bottle of scent. She found a sturdy carpetbag, emptied it of its prior contents, and refilled it with her newly acquired treasures.

"Finding everything you need?" Cole asked.

Devon looked up to see him calmly watching her. She heard no censure in his voice, only a trace of amusement. He sat on a stack of crates, his arms crossed over his broad chest, his long legs stretched out. The pose suited him. It was relaxed, rugged, and yet strangely appealing—in a rough, masculine sort of way. "You have absolutely no conscience, do you?" he asked.

She shrugged and returned to her looting. "Why should I? It's all contraband, isn't it?"

"True enough."

She resumed her task, only to be interrupted again five minutes later while she perused a box containing an assortment of cures and ointments. She picked up a bottle of cockle pills and studied the label. It sounded vaguely familiar, but she couldn't quite remember what they were for.

"You have trouble with your cockles?" Cole asked, sounding suspiciously amused.

Devon tossed the bottle into her bag and replied coolly, "From time to time."

He made a mock bow, his expression grave. "In that case, you have my deepest sympathy."

She paused, disconcerted by his sincerity and feeling even more strongly that he was laughing at her, when she suddenly remembered why the label sounded so

familiar. She'd seen the pills in an apothecary while
with her Uncle Monty. When she'd asked him what
they were for, he'd blustered something about ''reliev-
ing the pressure to a man's lower extremities'' and
hustled her out of the shop. Devon gritted her teeth,
refusing to meet Cole's eyes as rich heat once again
suffused her cheeks.

''Now what in the hell do you need that thing for?''
he demanded a few minutes later as she examined a
lacy pink corset.

''It's a corset.''

''I know what it is. What I don't understand is why
a woman your size, who clearly doesn't need it, would
willingly submit to having the breath strangled out of
her.''

The truth was that Devon rarely wore corsets, and
for exactly that reason. They made it difficult to
breathe, and consequently harder to run. And since running was tantamount to survival for her, it considerably
lessened the garment's appeal. Still, one never knew.
She folded it carefully and tucked it away in her bag.
''I am not in the habit of discussing my undergarments
with a perfect stranger,'' she said.

''I'm far from perfect, Blake.''

She snapped her head up at that, staring at Cole in
mute fascination as a slow grin transformed his rugged
features. Devon abruptly reversed her earlier conclusion. Not only did the man know how to smile, he was
damned good at it too. His teeth flashed even and white
against his deeply tanned skin; his tawny eyes glowed
with warm golden light. Her heart slammed against her
chest, then started beating again at double its normal
tempo.

She skillfully hid her reaction, merely arching one
dark brow at his words until she was certain she
wouldn't sound as breathless as she felt. ''It appears
we've at last found something upon which we can both

agree,'' she said coolly as she turned back to her bag and secured the leather straps. She felt the train lurch beneath her and glanced outside, noting that they had slowed to a near-crawl as they chugged up a steep, grassy slope.

"Finished?'' Cole asked. When she nodded, he moved toward her, hefted the bag up, and strode back to the open freight door. She smiled to herself, pleased. The big lug was actually going to carry it for her. It was about time he started treating her like a lady. Cole looked straight at her, politely inclined his head, then tossed her bag outside without a word.

Devon lurched to her feet and ran to his side, too shocked to form any coherent words. "What?! My bag! Why, you, you—''

He placed his hand at the small of her back. "You're next.''

"*What?!*''

"When you hit the ground, tuck in your body and roll. Chances are good you won't break anything that way.''

"*What?* You can't be serious!''

"Are you ready?''

"No!''

"Don't worry, I'll be right behind you.'' With those words, he gave her a firm push, sending her flying out of the car and over the tracks. When she hit the grassy bank, she automatically obeyed his instructions, tucking in her body as she tumbled down the hill. The train wasn't moving as fast as she'd feared, and the impact with the soft grass was painless, but the steep incline of the slope prevented her from checking her fall. She didn't stop until she reached the base of the hill and slid headfirst into a pit of mud and slime.

She sat up, sputtering mad and oozing filth, but otherwise unharmed, when she heard Captain McRae tumble to a stop a few feet away. He was on his feet and calling her name almost instantly. Devon opened her mouth, intending to singe his ears with a string of curses, then abruptly changed her mind. Uncle Monty had always told her she had a wee bit of the devil in her, and she was about to prove him right yet again.

Carefully arranging herself in the position in which she'd originally landed, she settled back into the mud and let out a low moan. Cole stomped right past her. Devon stifled a curse and moaned louder, adding just a hint of long-suffering agony to her cry of pain. This time it worked. She heard him hesitate, then the sound of his footsteps as he raced to her side. He let out a vicious oath and squatted down beside her. She forced her body to go limp as he hooked his hands beneath her and dragged her out of the mud. "Devon? Devon, can you hear me?" he asked as he brushed slimy reeds and thick sludge from her face and mouth. She answered with another moan and slowly opened her eyes, hoping her expression was sufficiently dazed. "Hurts," she whimpered.

Devon watched his face harden and grow grim, either with suppressed anger or regret, she couldn't tell. "Easy, now, easy. Tell me where," he crooned, and began to move his strong hands gently over her body. Soft, light strokes that moved slowly up her calves, over her thighs, skimmed across her hips and belly, then brushed her rib cage. Devon froze, forgetting where she was and what she was doing, aware of nothing but his touch. It was a disturbing sensation; frightening and yet strangely pleasant at the same time. He moved with incredible gentleness for such a large man, she thought, content to let him continue. His hands traveled up toward her breasts.

"No!" she gasped. Cole's head snapped up, his eyes focused intently on her face. Devon swallowed hard, abruptly recalling her purpose. "Hurts," she said.

"It hurts when I touch you?"

"Yes."

His scowl deepened. "Where? Where does it hurt?"

She parted her lips and whispered a word.

Cole leaned over her, tilting his head to one side. "I can't hear you. Say it again, Devon. Tell me where it hurts."

"Right . . . here!" She brought up her fist and slammed it as hard as she could against his jaw.

Granted, it was a sucker punch. But as far as sucker punches went, it was a pretty good one. Devon had the immense satisfaction of watching Cole's eyes widen in shock as the unexpected impact sent his head reeling backward. She pushed with all her might at the same instant, knocking him over, then rolled on top of him, leveraging herself so that she was sitting astride his chest. She leaned over him, her breath coming hard and fast, her eyes blazing with fury. "Don't you ever, *ever* push me out of a speeding train again! Do you understand me, McRae?"

Cole simply stared at her, then reached up and absently rubbed his jaw. "Not bad."

Devon studied him for a second, then an awful realization swept over her as she registered the sheer size of the man stretched out beneath her, the barely leashed tension and power in his tightly coiled mass of muscles. No matter how much force she thought she'd put into it, her puny little punch wouldn't have been enough to even make him blink. And she could just as easily topple an oak as she could knock him over.

Which meant only one thing. He'd known she'd been faking and had played right along with her. In fact, he'd done it even better. Feigning concern as he ran his hands all over her body. Whispering tender words in her ear. Furious, she lifted her fist again, but Cole caught it and held it easily. "Temper, Blake. Once was perhaps deserved. Twice—no."

"You are the lowest, most despicable—"

"I presume this means that you're not really hurt."

"I suppose it's too much to hope that you are?" she shot back.

"Sorry to disappoint you."

She shoved off him, her fury mounting as she examined her gown. Or rather what was left of it. Rags would probably be a more apt description. What hadn't been ripped, slashed, or split apart was now dripping slime and thick black ooze. She not only looked but also smelled like something that came out of the business end of a goose. "I don't suppose you could have waited for the train to come to a stop," she bit out.

Cole followed her gaze in the direction of her gown and coolly shrugged. "I'm afraid not," he answered, then went to collect her bag.

"Would you mind telling me why?" she demanded when he returned.

"If my guess is right, that train's headed for Richmond, which is in the exact opposite direction of where we need to travel. Nor did I want to wait until they stopped to refuel, which would likely have meant I'd have to kill whichever guard was unfortunate enough to be assigned the duty of checking on the cargo."

Devon opened her mouth, then abruptly closed it, realizing that arguing about it now was pointless anyway. Her gown was ruined, she was a sticky, muddy mess, and her head was throbbing from the effects of last night's brandy. To top it all off, Cole didn't seem the least bit repentant. She decided to save her energy for something useful, like devising a way to make him as miserable as she felt. If nothing else, at least she'd get some enjoyment out of that.

They hiked in silence, once again staying off the main roads. The heat and humidity hung in the air like thick, shimmering waves they had to battle their way through. After about an hour without a hat or parasol to shield her from the sun, Devon felt completely done in. She'd been trailing farther and farther behind Cole as they went along, but now she came to a complete stop and sagged against a tall pine. It took him a full minute before he noticed that she was no longer trudging along behind.

He stopped abruptly and turned back. "Blake?"

His shirt was damp with sweat and clung to his broad chest; a light sheen of perspiration showed on his forehead. Other than that, he looked entirely prepared to hike all day and well into the night if need be. "Are you all right?" he asked.

"Perfect," she answered weakly, then sank to the ground. Her legs folded beneath her as she braced her back against the trunk of the tree. "You go on ahead, McRae," she said with a wave of her hand. "I'll catch up with you at Old Capitol. I promise."

"Is the heat bothering you?"

She tilted her head back and closed her eyes, fanning her face with her hand. "I barely noticed it."

He frowned and set down her bag. "So I see."

"How does anyone manage to live in this?" she asked after a minute.

"You get used to it."

"No," Devon countered immediately. "Being burned at the stake I could get used to. At least that's dry heat. But this—this is awful."

"Do you want me to carry you?"

She smiled at that, opened her eyes, and looked at him, certain he was joking. There was no trace of levity on Cole's face. Instead he looked dead serious. "All the way to Washington?" she asked incredulously.

He shrugged. "If you need me to."

An image flashed across her mind: Cole marching across the countryside, with her bag tucked under one arm, and her tucked under the other. Too hot and tired to care, she didn't bother to restrain the giggle that welled up inside her. "Don't you think we'd look the tiniest bit ridiculous?"

Cole stared down at her for a second, then shrugged again. "Probably."

"Just give me a minute. I'll be—"

The low, rumbling sound of an approaching wagon cut off the rest of her words. "Stay here," Cole ordered curtly, and moved off through the brush in the direction of the road they'd been paralleling. Devon obeyed, but only because she was too exhausted to run. After a minute, he returned, and she soon found herself deposited in the back of a buckboard wagon, nestled between sacks of flour, canned goods, and various other sundries. It was better than walking, but not by much.

Cole sat in front next to the Union officer who drove the conveyance. Listening to the two men talk, she learned that the area was solidly Union-controlled, with the exception of a few roving bands of Rebel guerrillas who managed to stir up trouble from time to time. A Union cavalry company was encamped nearby, their headquarters having been established in the local town in order to keep the guerrillas and Rebel sympathizers in line. The driver had been on his way to the army hospital to deliver supplies when Cole stopped him.

Devon made herself as comfortable as possible and eavesdropped as the men turned to talk of the war. They discussed campaigns, strategies, and the men who were leading them. They were both disparaging of a general named Pope, a pompous braggart who had recently been given command. High praise was awarded, however, to a man named Robert Lee. So much so, in fact, that it took Devon a minute to realize that Pope was actually fighting for the Union, and General Lee was an officer of the Confederacy.

Bored by their discussion, she glanced around, her eyes lighting on a small farm as they rolled slowly past. A woman stood in the front yard, tossing handfuls of cornmeal at the hens scattered about her feet. She was tall and slender, with lovely dark skin and a dress that was in as poor shape as Devon's own. As if feeling her gaze, the woman looked up. Devon knew without asking that the woman was a slave. It occurred to her with some astonishment that although she'd always known slavery existed, she'd never in her life actually seen a slave.

She'd heard that slaves were crude and ignorant, that they were fit to be used by their masters. She'd also heard that slaves were like contented beasts, singing songs as they toiled in the fields. But one look at this woman disabused her of all those shameful tales and falsehoods. Devon saw nothing but shining intelligence in the other woman's eyes, quiet dignity in her proud carriage.

As Devon watched, the lady of the house stormed out, berating her servant for dallying and threatening to send her off without supper if the woman didn't see to her task. The slave accepted the tongue-lashing with perfect indifference, then with slow, deliberate motions, resumed scattering cornmeal for the hens. The wagon rolled away and the moment passed. But Devon, recalling Mrs. Honeychurch and the asylum, was left with a new and painful understanding of the slave's plight. Sometimes the need for dignity was greater than the need for food or water.

They rode on for another thirty minutes, then lumbered to a stop at a large, wood frame house. The yellow flag flying atop the structure indicated it was also used as a hospital. Crisp white tents were encamped on the front lawn and cooking fires smoked cozily in shallow pits. Devon counted about fifty Union soldiers in the yard, all in various stages of repose. "You'll be wantin' to talk to the general," the driver said.

She glanced over Cole's shoulder as he helped her

down from the wagon and saw four men poring over maps spread out over a thick oak table on the front porch. One of them straightened and frowned. He said a word to the others, then moved toward them. The first thing Devon noticed about the man was his size. He was one of the few men she'd seen who was actually bigger than Cole. He had a dark red beard, a ruddy complexion, and a thick pot belly. Cowboy boots—with spurs, no less—and a cowboy hat completed his uniform. Against regulations, perhaps, but judging from the size of the man, as well as the number of stars on his collar, she guessed he could probably do pretty much whatever he wanted. A fierce scowl darkened his features as he boomed out, ''Cole McRae!''

Devon jumped. Cole froze for an instant, then continued to reach for her bag, dropping it casually at her feet. He turned around slowly and offered a lazy salute. ''General Brader.''

''I thought I warned you what would happen if I ever saw your no-good, yellow-bellied, worthless hide around these parts again.''

Devon stared up at Cole, watching as his features turned slowly to granite. He leaned back against the wagon, his arms crossed loosely over his chest, a posture that was not only reckless, but coolly insubordinate as well. ''Guess I didn't listen,'' he answered.

Silent tension soared. The soldiers surrounding them went completely still. Beneath the brim of his hat, Devon could see the general's skin turn the same angry red shade as his beard. ''You didn't listen,'' he sputtered, his tone steadily growing to a near-roar. ''Well, by God, maybe I oughta just make you listen.''

''You can try. That is, if you've got enough breath left in that fat belly of yours.''

Devon stifled a gasp. Had Captain McRae completely lost his mind? Not only was he outranked, but he was completely outnumbered and outsized as well. ''You son-of-a-bitch!'' the general roared and lunged straight at Cole. But instead of knocking him flat, as she expected, he wrapped his beefy arms around Cole in a bear hug, slapping him on the back hard enough to leave bruises. When he pulled back, a big smile showed beneath his beard.

Devon reeled in shock, slowly assimilating the fact that what she'd witnessed had apparently been no more than some sort of absurd ritual between friends. She let out her breath and examined her feelings. Part relief, because it meant Cole hadn't truly lost his mind, and part irritation, because she'd just lost what might have been a good opportunity for escape.

"How's that mama and papa of yours?" General Brader demanded.

Cole grinned. "Still trying to recover from your visit two years ago."

The general's smile widened. "I reckon they didn't expect me to bring a travelin' companion. Still to this day don't know what your mama objected to most: Miss Lila's rouge, her colorful vocabulary, or how sweet that gal looked in her low-cut, red satin dress. And when your mama tried to serve her tea and Miss Lila asked for whiskey instead . . ." He paused and let out a deep guffaw. "Why, I thought your mama was going to faint dead away on the spot. Took to her bed the rest of our stay, complaining of the headache."

Devon had instinctively stepped behind Cole when the trouble started, and remained there now, content just to watch until she got a firmer grip on this loud-mouth, blustery general. It wasn't long, however, until the general took notice of her.

"Now who's this here little filly?" he asked.

Devon stepped forward, watching the general's eyes widen as he took in the sight of her. She waited for Cole to introduce her, but as usual, the captain denied her even that small courtesy. Very well. Putting aside any embarrassment she felt at her current state of dishevelment, she lifted her chin and announced with as much dignity as she could muster, "My name is Devon Blake, sir."

"Whew," the general replied, waving his hand in front of his face. "Little lady, I've stepped in piles of manure left behind by sick cattle and baked beneath a hot Texas sky that still smelled a damned sight better than you do."

"Coming from a man with the grace and manners of an flea-bitten sewer rat, you can imagine how it pains me to hear that," Devon shot back.

General Brader's eyes widened in shock, then he threw back his head and roared with laughter. "Feisty little thing, ain't she?" he said.

Cole shrugged. "That's one word for it."

Devon glared up at them, feeling both dwarfed and ridiculed by the two men towering above her. But before she could get another word out, a young, lanky boy with carrot-colored hair and dark freckles loped up to join them. "Cole, you remember my son, Emmett," the general said, pride clear in his tone.

Surprise flashed through Cole's eyes, then he nodded and shook the boy's hand. "Good to see you . . ." He paused and glanced at his sleeve. "Private Brader."

Emmett smiled sheepishly, blushing to the roots of his hair. "Howdy, Cole," he said, then turned to his father. "Pa, me and Jimmy Johnston was just wondering—"

"Dammit, son! How many times do I have to tell you? You call me General when I'm in uniform, you hear?"

Emmett nodded and studied the ground near his feet. "Yes, sir." He cleared his throat and tried again. "General Brader, sir, Private Johnston and me was wondering if we could go into town for a spell. We got our chores all done now."

"Your duties, Private. When you're in the army, you've got duties, not chores."

"Yes, sir. Well, sir, our duties are all done now."

"In that case, you can go. But I want you boys back here by twenty-one hundred."

Emmett stared up at him, a confused look on his face. "Twenty—?"

General Brader let out an exaggerated breath. "Nine o'clock, boy. And not a minute past."

"Yes, sir!" Emmett broke into a wide grin as he nodded and spun around. "Thanks, Pa, er, General!" he called over his shoulder. "Thanks a lot!"

The three watched Emmett run across camp, clamoring a spoon against a stew pot, leaping over a pile of hay, yelling for his friend Jimmy, and otherwise raising a ruckus. "The boy's grown up," Cole said.

"Could've fooled me." The general snorted.

"I didn't realize he was old enough to sign on."

"He's not. Won't be eighteen until October. But the young fool was threatening to run away and join the infantry if I didn't bring him with me. That boy's just stubborn enough and stupid enough to do it too." The general sighed and shook his head. "Hell, I figure at least this way I can keep my eye on him. There ain't much trouble he can get into around here. We got some boys inside that was wounded in a skirmish outside of Fredericksburg, but that's about it. Looks like the real fightin's gonna be down near Richmond."

"Stubborn and stupid, huh?" Cole said into the silence that followed. "Wonder where he gets that from?"

The general grinned. "Go to hell," he said cheerfully, then, "What're you doing traipsing through the country on foot, McRae? Last I heard, you were parading off the coast in that fancy boat of yours."

Devon felt Cole stiffen beside her. He reached down

and grabbed her bag. "No. The *Islander*'s in dry dock, awaiting repairs."

Devon watched General Brader as he silently studied Cole. In the awkward pause that followed, she saw a flash of wisdom and perception behind his gruff facade. She wondered if he could feel the tension that suddenly coursed through Cole as clearly as she could.

"I see," the general said simply, then let it go. "Well, what are we doing standing out here gabbing beneath this blasted sun?" he said as he motioned them toward the house. "I'm full up, so I can't offer you all a bed, but there's a boardinghouse in town that takes in strays." He paused before the front door. "Good news is, I've got whiskey inside and I can probably rustle up some tea for the little lady."

"I don't believe I care for any tea, thank you," Devon said, knowing instinctively what was coming next. Every time Cole McRae's damned ship was mentioned, she bore the brunt of his anger. And the last thing she was in the mood for right now was to sit in audience while Cole recited a long litany of all her supposed crimes. "I believe I prefer to just rest for a moment on this lovely little settee." She lifted her filthy skirts and moved as gracefully as she could across the porch, toward a grouping of rattan furniture.

As she passed one of the soldiers who stood near the thick oak table, she saw his eyes grow wide. He waved his hand in front of his face and abruptly started choking. Anger and embarrassment coursed through Devon in equal measure. It was all Cole's fault that she looked and smelled the way she did. It was also his fault that she was about to have to defend herself once again against charges of murder and espionage. How would he like it if people believed all sorts of vicious untruths about him? she wondered, and instantly decided to turn the tables. She wasn't going to simply wait and try to defend herself anymore. This time she was taking the offensive.

Devon turned toward the soldier who'd been choking and clucked her tongue in silent commiseration. "Yes, I'm afraid the scent is rather terrible, isn't it? Unless I'm mistaken, I believe I'm covered in goose droppings."

The soldier's eyes looked ready to pop out of his head. "Devon . . ." Cole warned.

She looked up at him, her dirty face shining with innocence, then back at the soldiers. "That's my captor," she informed them politely. "I don't believe Captain McRae meant to knock me into a slimy pond, not really. But he did toss me off a speeding train, that was certainly intentional. As was forcing me atop a horse that I was quite terrified of. And I really can't blame him for tying my hands so I couldn't eat. I suppose that left more food for him and his men."

"That's enough," Cole said.

"Though I still object to the way he woke me out of a sound sleep and pulled me on top of him—"

"Dammit, Blake!"

She jumped, her eyes wide and her slim shoulders quaking with fear. "Oh, dear," she wailed pitifully. "Now I've made him mad. Please, please don't leave me alone with him. I just couldn't bear it again. Not when he's angry like this."

The soldiers had shifted imperceptibly during her tale, to the point where they were now interposed between her and Cole, their hands on their guns as they glared at him. Even General Brader wasn't smiling anymore. He looked deadly serious, and maybe even a little angry. "All right, boy," he said to Cole. "Looks like it's time for the two of us to have ourselves a little talk."

Feeling smugly superior, Devon glanced over the general's shoulder to see Cole's reaction. Though his face remained a mask of cool aloofness, she watched as his tawny eyes changed from irritation to ... amusement. The man was actually trying not to laugh! Well, damned if that didn't take all the fun out of it. The least he could do was to get upset. Frustrated by Cole's lack of response, she fanned herself with her hand and turned her attention back to her guards. "If you gentlemen don't mind, may I have just one tiny little sip of water? I promise I won't be any trouble after that." The soldiers tripped over themselves in their haste to oblige.

Though it might have been immediately gratifying, her ruse not only failed to rankle Cole, it also proved to be of no use whatsoever as a long-term strategy. When he and the general emerged from their talk an hour later, Cole didn't so much as glance in her direction. He strode down the front steps, heading for a sorrel that was saddled and waiting for him. General Brader moved out onto the porch, rubbing his belly and smiling like the cat who just ate the canary. He took a Colt from one of the soldiers, spun the chamber to check the ammunition, then pointed it straight at her. Devon shrieked and shrank back against the settee.

"Want me to shoot her if she moves?" he called to Cole.

Cole swung into the saddle then edged the horse back toward the house, hesitating as he saw the gun pointed at her head. Devon's heart started beating again. Cole wouldn't let anything happen to her, he just wouldn't. Granted, he might threaten her, he might be furious with her, but he wouldn't let anybody hurt her. Her instincts had told her that from the very beginning, and her instincts were never wrong.

He scowled at the general, his gaze moving from her to the gun. "You weren't planning on leaving me with the paperwork, were you?"

Devon gasped, and the general made a choking noise. "No," he said.

Cole shrugged. "In that case, use your best judgment."

The general slapped his knee and let out a deep guffaw as he passed the gun back to the soldier. "Use my best judgment," he chortled.

Devon wasn't amused. But the stinging retort she'd been ready to toss back died on her lips as she watched Cole rein in his mount, spurring the sorrel into a fast trot across camp. She froze, suddenly icy-cold despite the heat of the day. He was leaving her. Cole McRae was leaving her, and he didn't even care enough to say good-bye. She'd been nothing but trouble, so now he was turning over the chore of escorting her to Old Capitol to General Brader.

She watched his broad back as he rode away and out of her life. A keen sense of abandonment shot through her, leaving her feeling completely lost and adrift. For some reason, she'd become used to having Cole around. More than that, she'd actually come to depend on him. She'd believed he'd be there for her if she ever needed him. Wrong, she realized, feeling as though she'd just been kicked in the gut. Wrong, wrong, wrong.

Well, good riddance, she declared silently. She could take care of herself. She certainly didn't need him. She should be happy to see him go. Should be—but she wasn't.

Forgetting both her pride and her audience, Devon lurched to her feet, clutching the porch rail in both hands as she screamed, "McRae!" Too late. He kept riding. "McRae!"

Her captor slowed, bringing his mount up short as he turned around. "Cole!" she screamed. He dug his heels in the sorrel's flanks and spurred back toward her. Devon lifted her skirts and flew down the steps to meet him. Almost at once, she was at his side. Or rather, beside his boot and stirrup, staring up at him as he sat in the saddle. Her breath came hard and fast, as though she'd been running a great length. The sorrel tossed its head and neighed, stepping back.

Cole controlled the horse with gentle pressure from his thighs. He searched her face, frowning as he looked down at her. "Devon, General Brader isn't really going to—"

"You're leaving me?" she asked, in a voice she didn't like at all. She'd wanted to sound cold and contemptuous, to let him know he was a snake for abandoning her. Instead her voice came out frightened and trembling, betraying everything she was struggling so hard to keep inside.

She watched something flash though his eyes, but the emotion was gone too quickly for her to read. "Yes," he answered.

Devon nodded and swallowed hard, not trusting herself to speak.

"For about an hour," he continued. "Just long enough to see about finding us a room for the night, some food, and clean clothes. A bath wouldn't be out of line either."

Relief coursed through her, stunning her in its intensity. It must have shown on her face, for Cole looked inordinately pleased and altogether smug. Devon caught her breath in giddy anticipation, waiting for him to speak. She felt certain that something had just shifted between them, and that nothing would ever be the same again. He smiled his heart-stopping grin and leaned slowly toward her, soft sentimental words forming on his lips. "You may not have noticed it," he whispered, "but you're starting to attract flies."

Devon jerked back, slapping his leg as hard as she could. "I hate you, McRae."

He reached down and grabbed her chin before she could spin away. He tipped her face up to his, intently searching her eyes. "Do you, Blake?" he asked quietly.

"Yes. I hate you, I loathe you, I despise you. You're crude, rude, vulgar—"

Cole scooped her up in his arms, holding her in front of him in the saddle as he nudged the sorrel back to the porch, then dumped her on the other side of the railing beside General Brader. "I've changed my mind," he said to his friend. "Don't shoot her."

The general looked disappointed. "What do you want me to do with her, then?"

"Hell, I don't know. Just see if you can keep her out of trouble for about an hour."

"I reckon that shouldn't be too difficult."

Cole let out a heartfelt sigh and shook his head, once again spurring his mount around. "You obviously don't know the lady."

Chapter 8

~~~~~∞∞~~~~~

Devon glanced around the boardinghouse room, looking for something to distract her from the wet, splashing sounds coming from the other side of the thin screen partition. Of course, Cole had insisted on bathing first, claiming that the water would be so filthy once she finished that there'd be nothing to do but throw it out. True enough, she admitted, but it was still horribly rude of him to make such a remark.

She'd already wasted a good twenty minutes searching for a means of escape. But the door was locked from the inside, and Cole had the key. The glass that had once been a window was gone, probably shattered by the reverberation of cannon fire from a recent battle. Like all the other windows she'd observed in this small town, it was boarded up, allowing only traces of light and air to seep in through the thick slats. Consequently the tiny room was both muggy and dark, despite the fact that both lamps were lit and burning brightly.

She heard another splashing sound, and her eyes were automatically drawn back to the partition. She had to get away from Captain McRae. Now. Tonight. She'd find Uncle Monty and go back into business. Lift a few gold watches, a few wallets, run a con or two. As a matter of fact, she still had Cole's watch, and that had to be worth something. She'd sell it and move on. Forget she'd ever dreamed of having more. Forget that she'd staked everything she had, only to have her past catch up with her and ruin it all.

The sound of Cole's voice calling for his towel interrupted her thoughts. Devon glanced at the washstand and saw two threadbare linen towels stacked above it. She frowned in irritation. What did he think she was, his personal valet? She grabbed a towel, bunched it into a tight ball, and sent it flying over the top of the partition. Two seconds later, she heard a splash, followed immediately by a dark oath. "Devon," Cole called, his voice strained with patience, "I seem to have dropped your towel in the water. Would you care to bring me mine, or shall I come get it?"

An image of Cole moving toward her, naked and dripping wet, did strange things to her pulse and sent her scurrying into action. "No!" she cried. "Don't move! I have it right here." She grabbed the towel and raced to the partition, thrusting her arm behind it. "Here."

"Sorry. Can't reach it."

She strained her arm further.

"No luck. I'm afraid you'll have to bring it to me."

"I'll just set it down here and you can—"

"Bring it to me, Devon."

She knew that tone. Arguing with him would be pointless now. If she didn't comply, he'd just do something that would embarrass her even more. Not that she could think of anything more embarrassing than seeing him naked, but doubtless he could. She edged slowly around the partition, her eyes squeezed shut and her arm outstretched. "Can you reach it now?"

"Not quite."

She sighed and inched forward, then stumbled as her toes knocked into something thick and hard. The tub. Her eyes flew open as she swayed forward, nearly tumbling into the water on top of Cole. He was sitting there as pretty as you please, and as naked as the day he was born. Not only did he look as though he was thoroughly enjoying himself, he was making no attempt whatsoever to reach for the towel. Irritation flared within her, then instantly dissolved, her attention entirely captured by this new and fascinating glimpse of her captor.

She stared at him in mute wonder, unable to stop herself as her gaze traveled slowly over him. Cole's hair was sleeked back against his scalp, making his chiseled features even more pronounced and compelling. Wet, creamy streaks of soap clung to his broad chest, a glistening white contrast to his dark bronze skin. His shoulders and arms were thickly corded with muscle, visible proof of the tightly leashed power within his body. Even his legs looked strong, though she couldn't see much of those. Just the tops of his golden kneecaps and a glimpse of masculine thighs before they disappeared back into the water.

Devon's mouth went dry as an odd sensation shot through her stomach, making her feel nervous and excited at the same time. Solid, hard, lean, big—the words flitted through her mind, but none of them quite seemed to capture the raw, masculine beauty of Cole McRae.

"I don't suppose you'd care to wash my back for me?" he drawled.

That snapped her out of her dazed stupor. Heat bloomed in her cheeks as she flung the towel at his face. "Go to blazes," she said, then spun around and marched away.

She'd barely made it across the room when she heard another splash, then, after a minute, the sound of his footsteps behind her. Devon turned cautiously around, relieved to see that he was at least dressed now. Well, sort of. He'd pulled on his pants and shirt, but left the shirt unbuttoned. Her eyes went directly to the light smattering of coarse blond hair that covered his chest, then to the rippling muscles that lined his stomach. She noticed that he was barefoot too. Somehow that made him seem less intimidating.

Devon abruptly curbed her wandering thoughts and summoned her most disdainful tone. "May I?" she asked, tilting her head toward the tub. "Or were you planning on making me wait until morning?"

"Lord, no. The sooner the better." Cole waved his hand in front of his face in a gesture she knew was meant to rile her. Stiffening her spine, she ignored the insult and made for the tub when he stopped her again. She turned to see him toss three soft bundles, all wrapped neatly in brown paper and tied with string, on the bed. "You'll probably be needing these," he said gruffly.

She stared blankly at the packages, then back at him. A fierce scowl lined his features, and his hands were jammed deep in his pockets. He looked desperately uncomfortable, a fact that was amazing for a man who was always so totally in control. She would have studied that more, but her curiosity got the better of her. "What is it?" she asked, not moving.

"Why don't you open them and find out?"

She did. The first contained a pale blue dressing gown, edged with touches of ivory lace at the collar and cuffs. The second package held sheer knit stockings, a camisole, drawers, and a petticoat, all made from soft white cotton and trimmed with tiny blue ribbons. The last bundle contained a brand new gown. It was a lovely sky-blue calico with delicate touches of lavender. Blue and ivory ribbons were woven tightly through the bodice and sleeves.

Devon stared at the gifts, completely overwhelmed. She'd been planning on washing her garments in the tub after she'd finished her bath and simply hoping for the best. When Cole had said he'd needed to find new clothes, she'd presumed he meant new clothes for him, not for her. And what with goods becoming increasingly scarce because of the war, he'd probably had to pay through the nose for them. She frowned, trying to make sense of his gesture.

"If you don't like them," Cole said quickly, "We can go back tomorrow—"

"No!" Devon snatched up the gown, as if afraid he'd take it away then and there. "They're lovely, truly. I just didn't expect—I didn't think—blue's my favorite color," she stammered awkwardly.

Cole studied her for a minute, as though trying to divine the truth of her words, then something that looked like relief washed over his rugged features. "I know." He reached forward, running his rough masculine hands lightly over the delicate white undergarments. "These had pink ribbons on them, but I told the woman you had to have blue."

Devon stared at him in amazement, trying to picture Cole in a lady's mercantile. He had probably scared the shop clerk half out of her wits, making her replace perfectly good pink ribbons because he thought she would like blue better. Just like a man. Give a man a little bit of information and he thought he knew everything.

She stared at the garments, her throat aching with the knowledge that he'd actually wanted to please her. He'd done more than that. Devon was stunned, amused, and absolutely thrilled. "They're perfect," she said sincerely.

He nodded. "The color's right, and they should fit too. You won't have to bother with that corset thing."

"No, I guess I won't." She smiled up at him. "They're lovely, Cole. Thank you."

"You're welcome."

She became suddenly aware of how close they were standing. Looking up into his eyes, she saw flecks of gold in their warm brown depths. A lock of damp blond hair fell across his forehead, giving him a boyishly appealing quality. It dimly occurred to her that she should question his motivation. He'd probably only bought her the garments as a way to make her let down her guard, or feel indebted to him. Devon resolutely pushed those cynical thoughts away, regardless of how true they might be. For now, she just wanted to revel in the unexpected joy of his gift.

Her largess evaporated as she watched him cross the room and ease his long frame into a weather-beaten armchair near what used to be the window. "What are you doing?" she demanded.

He shrugged and looked down at himself. "Looks like I'm sitting down."

"I can see that. *Why* are you sitting down?"

"You want me to stand?"

"Stand, sit, do whatever you want, just do it on the other side of the door so I can take my bath."

Comprehension slowly showed on his rugged features. He eased back into the chair, locked his hands behind his head, and propped up his bare feet on a scarred pine table. "I'm afraid not."

Devon's eyes widened. "You can't mean you intend to stay here while I bathe? In the same room? What about my privacy?" she sputtered.

He shrugged. "Consider that a privilege you have yet to earn."

Devon unleashed the full fury of her glare on him. "Well, at least you're consistent," she stormed. "Every time I begin to believe you might be a halfway decent human being, you do something else to prove me wrong." She stalked behind the screen. Seconds later, she was back, sweeping up the frilly new garments she'd inadvertently left on the bed. "You give me your word you won't . . . interfere with my bath?" she demanded.

"My solemn oath," he swore as he nodded soberly,

though Devon could swear she saw hints of laughter glinting in his eyes.

"Hmph. Your solemn oath," she repeated hotly. "That and a nickel still wouldn't be enough to buy a penny candy, now would it?"

She stormed back to the huge wooden tub, surprised to find that he'd left her two buckets of clean, warm water. She tossed the garments onto a nearby chair and added one bucket to the tub, saving the second for rinsing. A tremor of nervous apprehension raced through her as she started peeling open the buttons of her gown, knowing he was just on the other side of the screen. Since there was nothing she could do about it, however, she pushed the thought from her mind, tugged off the rest of her filthy clothes, and fairly leaped into the water.

It was a strange sensation to sit in the tub entirely naked, knowing that Cole had just shared the same water, but she refused to focus on that. Instead she concentrated her energies on finally getting clean. She scrubbed her body twice, then attacked her hair, working the soap into a frothy lather as she removed every trace of mud and filth from her person. When she finished, she stood and reached for the bucket she'd set aside. She poured that over her head, letting the water cascade down her body like warm flowing silk.

Devon heard a sound on the other side of the screen and turned sharply. It sounded as if Cole had made a noise, but she couldn't tell whether it was a word or a groan. She heard his feet hit the floor and the sound of his chair scuff back, telling her he had stood up. She froze as the water cascaded in thin rivulets down her body, bracing herself to see him come charging around the screen, but he didn't. There was stillness on the other side of the partition, and a tension she could feel but not identify.

Not about to take any further chances, she quickly

stepped from the tub, buffed her hair and body dry with Cole's damp towel, and wrapped herself up in the dressing gown he'd purchased for her. As she'd left her bag containing her brush, comb, and other personal items in the main room, there was nothing more she could do here. Devon tightened the belt around her waist, then moved hesitantly around the partition, her eyes immediately searching out her captor. He was standing with his back toward her, his hands braced on the mantel above the fireplace.

She moved wordlessly behind him and took a seat at the small dressing table beside the bed. The mirror that hung above it was cracked in two places, but it would do. She flipped open the straps of her tapestry bag and began spreading out the contents on the table before her. She reached for the comb first, tugging gently through the mass of tangles until her hair hung smoothly down her back. She fluffed it with her fingers in an attempt to help it dry, then left it alone. Next she opened the jar of lady's finishing cream that she'd confiscated and proceeded to lightly smooth it over her hands, face, and throat. Sweet-smelling dabs of scent followed, applied sparingly behind her ears and along her throat.

Devon would have dabbed it between her breasts as well, but Cole had turned around since she'd begun to primp, and was openly watching her every move. Though she tried to ignore him, she was painfully aware that her heart was beating faster and her hands shook slightly.

Uncomfortable having him watch her toilette and suddenly anxious to abandon the small, confined space of the room, she dragged her fingers once again through her hair, deciding she would style it now, still damp, rather than wait the extra thirty minutes or so required for it to dry. She pulled her hair back and twisted it into a thick chignon at the base of her neck. But the heavy, damp strands kept slipping through her fingers, making her feel clumsy and inept under Cole's steady gaze.

"Are you nearly finished?" he asked.

Her hairpins clattered to the ground. Devon glared at him, scooped up the pins, then twisted her hair into a tight knot and stabbed it in place. "Yes," she said. A few wispy strands immediately came loose, falling softly around her face, but she didn't care. She stepped behind the partition once again, hastily dressed, and met him at the door. "I believe you have the key."

Cole said nothing. His tawny eyes moved slowly over her, taking in everything from the tips of her boots to the top of her prim hairdo. She immediately started to lift her hand to tuck in the wayward strands, but checked the impulse, bringing it slowly back to her side. She suddenly felt absurd, standing there in the clothes he'd picked out, like a doll all dressed up for him. Though that was obviously the last of his intentions. More likely, Cole McRae had simply grown tired of her constant state of dishabille. The ladies in his life probably spent hours gussying up just for him, agonizing over which frilly gown would please him the most. The thought caused a peculiar, twisting ache in her stomach and brought a frown to her lips. Well, she thought crossly, the hell with them.

As a matter of fact, the hell with *him*.

She tilted her chin and demanded, "Are we planning on eating this evening? Or would you prefer to stand here and glare at one another all night long?"

Again, that faint glimmer of a smile, and then it was gone, making her wonder if she had even seen it at all. Cole pulled the key from his shirt pocket, unlocked the door, and ushered her through with a mock bow. "After you, my lady."

The dining room downstairs was deserted, the lamps cast down. Apparently the boardinghouse offered only rooms, not meals. They left and walked a few blocks through town. Unlike the bustling city of Fort Monroe, the streets here were quiet, almost subdued. Devon saw few civilians, though military personnel seemed to linger on nearly every corner.

They stopped in front of the town's only restaurant. Faded muslin curtains hung limply at the windows, a welcome change from the usual practice of simply boarding them up. Inside, large battered tables with hurricane lamps were set up, each table seating perhaps six to eight people. Swinging doors on the far right of the room led to what looked like a saloon. She heard a rousing tune played on an off-key piano and the sound of men who'd been drinking, which told her the place could get rowdy, and quick. As far as she was concerned, Cole couldn't have selected a better spot.

As the restaurant was crowded, they had to wait a few minutes to be seated. When two men left, the hostess hastily cleared their places and motioned for Cole and Devon to sit down. The four men who'd remained at the table sprang to their feet when they saw her approach. She sized them up quickly: mid-twenties, large and strapping, cavalry uniforms.

Feeling their eyes on her, she smiled and swung her hips as she moved, changing her walk to a seductive glide. She hadn't taken more than a few steps when she felt Cole's hands slide over her hips from behind, holding her steady. Devon abruptly froze. She looked over her shoulder and hissed, "Take your hands off me this instant!"

"Only trying to help. You appeared to be having trouble walking."

"Quite the contrary, McRae. I know exactly what I'm doing."

"So do I," he answered as he slowly slid his hands off her hips. "And I sincerely advise against it, Blake. This will be your only warning."

"In that case, I'll be sure to give your advice all the careful thought and consideration it deserves."

With that, she turned back toward the table, nodded to the men who were watching their conversation with open curiosity, and proceeded to move with an even more exaggerated sway in their direction. When she reached the table, she lowered her eyes demurely. "Gracious, gentlemen, please don't tire yourselves on my account. Do sit down."

The man on her right reached for her chair, but Cole was there first, pulling it out for her to sit down. Devon arched her brows in mild surprise. "Why, Captain McRae, how very gallant of you. And here all this time, I thought you didn't know a thing about manners."

She settled in and introductions were quickly made. Lieutenant Davis, the man on her right, was not only charming, she decided, but startlingly good-looking. He had a solid build—not quite as big as Cole, but big enough—rich chestnut hair, bright blue eyes, and a handsome mustache. "I couldn't help noticing your charming accent, ma'am," the lieutenant said after a few minutes. "If you don't mind my asking, where are you from originally?"

Beside her, Cole rolled his eyes. "France," he muttered.

Lieutenant Davis frowned, looking from Cole to Devon. "France? You don't sound French at all. I thought perhaps England—"

"You're quite right, Lieutenant. I am from England." Devon shot Cole a scalding look, then turned back to the lieutenant. She leaned forward and said in a stage whisper, "Never mind Captain McRae. He has such trouble remembering things. The poor dear was recently shot in the head, you know."

The four men stared at Cole, their expressions heavy with appalled sympathy. Cole swore under his breath. "That will do, Devon," he said.

"Why, Captain, it's nothing to be ashamed of. I'm sure these men understand that you were once quite . . . alert." She patted his hand encouragingly, her tone that of one talking to a none-too-bright child. "Perhaps you will be again one day."

The four cavalrymen instantly rushed to assure him that his dull dim-wittedness would soon pass. The awkward silence that followed was finally broken when the hostess came over and deposited a plate in front of each of them. Devon looked down in dismay at the unappetizing mess of boiled beef, mushy peas, and burned biscuits. "It's all we got left," the woman snapped. "Take it or leave it."

Beside her, Cole shrugged and lifted his fork. Devon attempted a smile as she looked up at the hostess. "I'm sure it tastes lovely," she offered.

"Hmph," the woman snorted, then spun around and stalked away. Devon stared after her in bewilderment.

"Don't mind her," Lieutenant Davis offered. "She's been doing all the cooking, serving, and cleaning by herself since noon. The two girls that normally help out refugeed to Richmond this morning."

"I see." Devon took a bite of beef and chewed. She dawdled over her meal, stretching it out long after Cole had finished. She ignored him and set about flirting, laughing, and captivating each of her dinner companions in turn. She hung on every word of their stories, telling them how brave and strong they were, how fierce and frightening were the ordeals they'd been through. Cole pushed his chair back, an expression of weary boredom on his face.

Lieutenant Davis finished his tale of a particularly rough battle during which his shoulder had been split open by a bayonet. Devon assumed an expression of heartfelt sorrow at the news. "Oh, how dreadful. Tell me, which shoulder was it?"

The lieutenant pointed to his right shoulder.

Devon leaned over and gently placed her small hand atop it. "Does it still hurt, Lieutenant?" she murmured sympathetically.

His eyes traveled slowly over her, taking in the soft curves beneath her gown, the shimmering innocence in her green eyes. He smiled at her. "With an angel's touch like yours, ma'am, how could it feel anything but heavenly?"

Devon fluttered her lashes. "Why, Lieutenant Davis—"

"That's it," Cole said, clamping his hand down on her elbow as he stood and pulled her to her feet. "We're leaving."

Lieutenant Davis stood as well. He spoke to Devon, but his eyes were focused solely on Cole, and he was no longer smiling. "Your friend's a mighty impatient man, isn't he, ma'am?"

"My friend?" Devon repeated, her brows drawn together in confusion, then she waved the remark away. "Oh, no, Captain McRae and I are barely acquainted. You see, he was assigned the duty of escorting me to Washington, and I'm afraid he finds it a most tiresome chore."

"In that case, ma'am, I'd be honored to—"

Cole's denial was swift and absolute. "No."

A dark shadow passed through the lieutenant's eyes. His voice dropped a notch lower. Again he spoke to Devon, though his eyes remained fastened on Cole. "Doesn't say much, does he? Though I suppose for a dullard, that's to be expected."

Devon drew in her breath and glanced at Cole, not at all surprised to see that his expression remained completely unmoved, to the point of looking a trifle bored. "That's right," he agreed coolly, his eyes locking on Lieutenant Davis. "Now if you gentlemen will excuse us . . ."

"Not so fast." The officer on Devon's right caught

her arm as he and the remaining cavalrymen rose to their feet. "Maybe the lady doesn't want to go with you."

The room, which had been loud and boisterous when they entered, was now completely silent as all eyes focused on their table. "Get your hands off her," Cole said.

Though he hadn't raised his voice, the cold fury in his tone was enough to make the cavalryman flinch. He swallowed hard and resolutely tightened his grip on Devon's arm, not about to back down in front of his friends. "Let's just ask the lady—"

"I said, get your hands off her," Cole repeated, carefully enunciating every word.

Lieutenant Davis and the two other officers edged forward, clearly anxious for a fight. Devon studied them warily. The cavalrymen were bigger than she'd thought, and there were four of them. She suddenly regretted what she'd started, though she knew it was far too late for her to alter her course now. Besides, if the situation were reversed and Cole were faced with spending the rest of his life in prison for a crime he didn't commit, wouldn't he do anything within his power to escape that fate?

"Please, gentlemen," she hedged, unconvinced by her own argument, "there's no need for this. Why don't we—"

"Wait just a damned minute," cried Lieutenant Davis, "somebody stole my wallet!"

There was no time for any more regret. As Uncle Monty was fond of saying, "The show was on." Years of training took over. "No!" she gasped. "Are you certain?"

"Of course I'm certain! It's gone!"

"Give it back, Devon," Cole said curtly. "You've caused enough trouble here."

"I beg your pardon!" she cried, lifting a delicate

hand to her chest as though she'd just been mortally insulted.

"Give him back his wallet."

"Me?! How dare you!"

"Grab him, boys!" shouted the lieutenant. Devon ducked neatly out of the way as fists started flying. In close quarters as they were, Cole didn't stand much of a chance against the four of them. Especially when the men from the adjoining table jumped into the brawl, pinning Cole to the floor. They dragged him up, two men on either side of him holding his arms back.

"You're going to regret this, Davis," he growled.

"Oh, I don't think so," the lieutenant countered. "If there's one thing in this world worse than a thief, it's a man who's cowardly enough to blame his thieving on a woman." He reached for Cole's vest, which had been partially split open during the fight, and plucked free his wallet. "If she's the thief, then how do you explain this, McRae?"

Devon watched as shock flashed through Cole's eyes, then he jerked his head toward her. Summoning every bit of courage she possessed, she lifted her finger and pointed it straight at him. "Captain McRae!" she cried in horror, "you're a thief!"

All hell broke loose then. Lieutenant Davis and two other men dived for Cole at once, burying him beneath a pile of bodies. Men poured in from the saloon, joining in the melee. Within seconds, the room was filled with grunts, groans, and the sound of flesh meeting flesh. Chairs flew about the room like kindling; glasses and dinnerware were knocked to the floor and shattered. Devon lifted her skirts and ran as fast as she could, ducking between flying bodies as she made her way out the door.

She paused outside the restaurant, guilt washing over her once again. Cole really wasn't going to be hurt, was he? All she wanted to do was escape, she truly hadn't meant to hurt him. She thought of him lying on the floor, bloody and weak, then firmly pushed the image away. Cole McRae could take care of himself. Or so she hoped.

Please, God, Devon silently pleaded as she hurried back to the boardinghouse, *don't let him really be hurt. Well, maybe just enough to slow him down. No, not even that. Don't let him be hurt at all. Just delay him for ten minutes, enough time for me to collect my things and steal a horse. That's all I ask, God. Don't let Cole be hurt, and help me steal a horse.* Realizing the impropriety of asking God to help her steal a horse, she abruptly negated that. *Never mind the horse, God. I'll take care of that myself. Just watch over Cole.*

Once inside their room, she lit a lamp, grabbed her tapestry bag, and began flinging items inside. She'd just finished and was securing the leather straps when she heard the door softly click shut behind her. Devon gasped and whirled about, stunned by the sight of Cole standing there, looking mussed and dirty, but otherwise unharmed. Relief coursed through her. "You're not hurt!"

"No, I'm not. I'm afraid I keep disappointing you there, don't I?" Before she could reply, his gaze shifted from her to the bag she was packing. "Taking everything, are you?"

She shook her head and pointed to the bottle sitting atop the dresser. "I was going to leave you the cockle pills."

"Ah. I see."

He sounded calm, far too calm considering the circumstances. Devon licked her suddenly dry lips as her pulse began to hammer through her veins. "How—how did you get away?"

"I'm a very determined man, Devon." Cole moved away from the door, taking a step forward.

She automatically took a step back, staring at him in total bewilderment. "Yes, but how—"

"It's easy to slip away from a raging brawl: too much going on to see who's there and who's not. Next time you want to lose a man, get him into a fight one-on-one. Your opponent tends to notice if you leave."

Now he was giving her instructions on how to escape? Something was dreadfully wrong. Cole should be angry, he should be yelling at her. But he wasn't. She smiled shakily, deciding to stall until she could figure it out. "Thank you, I'll try to remember that." She took a step back and then another, until she felt the wall bump up behind her, leaving her no more room to maneuver.

As Cole continued to edge toward her, she studied his face, and her illusion that he was taking her little trick rather well was promptly shattered. He wasn't calm at all. His eyes were shooting sparks of golden fire, and his jaw was tightly clenched. He was completely, absolutely, utterly furious. "Did you even consider the damage you might cause? Or the fact that innocent people might be hurt?"

She shook her head as her voice seemed to desert her. "No, I . . . I just thought—"

"You thought?" he snapped. "You actually thought before you decided to pull that asinine stunt? What in hell were you thinking?"

Anger flooded through her, replacing the nervous tension that had paralyzed her only moments ago. She ignored the fact that he was towering above her, twice her size and armed with a loaded revolver. "I was thinking I'd get the hell away from you, McRae! That's what I was thinking!"

"Well, forget it, Blake. You're mine, and you're not going anywhere."

"Yours? *Yours?!*" she sputtered, too shocked by the possessive, arrogant absurdity of his words to form a coherent reply. "Have you completely lost your mind?"

"Obviously. Otherwise I would have hauled you out of the restaurant the second you started swinging your stubborn little ass at that table of overbearing, idiotic cavalrymen."

Devon's jaw nearly dropped as shock coursed through her. Granted, Cole was upset that she'd framed him for stealing the wallet, as well as for the vicious brawl that followed. But what seemed to upset him the most was the way she'd flirted with the lieutenant and his friends. Which, as far as she was concerned, was the least of her crimes. "Oh, that," she replied. "That was nothing."

He stood only inches away now, one strong arm braced above her head. Her senses were spinning, over-whelmed by the heat of his body, the clean, masculine scent of his skin. "Really?" he said. "How remarkable. Is that something else your Uncle Monty taught you?"

"Uncle—? Oh, no. No, I suppose that's simply something I've known how to do all along." She was stammering and stuttering like a complete fool now, but she couldn't stop herself. Her knees felt like jelly, and her mind still couldn't seem to focus properly. She licked her parched lips, striving to regain control of herself. It didn't help seeing Cole's eyes follow the motion of her tongue, or the way his gaze moved from her lips to her eyes as she spoke. "Men are such simple creatures, really," she said shakily, "if one knows how to handle them properly."

"Is that a fact?" he drawled. "Tell me then, Blake, how would you handle me?"

"My first instinct would be to run," she blurted be-fore she could stop herself.

He smiled, then lifted his hand and brushed it softly over her cheek. A tremor shot through her, as if he'd just set every nerve in her body on fire. "Do you still want to escape me?'' he asked, his deep voice soft as his breath gently fanned her neck.

Yes! screamed her mind. *No!* answered her heart. Her confusion must have shown on her face, for Cole frowned and shook his head. ''It's too late for that in any case,'' he said firmly. ''Think of something else.''

Devon swallowed hard, knowing this was a game he was playing with her. She also knew she was headed for nothing but trouble, but she couldn't stop at that moment not even to save her life. That was just her nature, and she'd long since resigned herself to it. If she'd been Eve, she would have bitten the apple. As Pandora, she would have opened the box. And she knew without a doubt that she was about to get herself into as much trouble as her predecessors had.

''Tell me,'' Cole coaxed again, ''how would you handle me?''

''Well,'' she began hesitantly, her eyes locked on his, ''I suppose I'd begin by telling you what a fine figure of a man you are. How handsome—''

''Forget about my pretty face,'' he interrupted impatiently. ''What would you do?''

''This.'' She reached up and laid her hand gently on his rock-solid chest, amazed at her boldness, stunned by the feelings that coursed through her at just that slight contact. She felt Cole's body tighten beneath her hand, watched a muscle leap along the side of his jaw. ''And this.'' She reached up on tiptoe, curling her fingers around the base of his neck. His skin felt like hot, rough velvet, making her ache to explore more. His hair was softer than she'd imagined, thick golden strands that slipped smoothly through her fingers.

''What else?'' he asked, in a voice that sounded strangely hoarse.

Devon blinked, searching for words. ''Well, I, er, usually that's quite enough—''

''No kiss?''

Her heart slammed against her chest. "Kiss?"

He lifted his finger, tracing it lightly over the contours of her lips. "Surely no lesson in flirting would be complete without it."

"True," she agreed in a breathless whisper. This was crazy. Absolutely crazy. "You start."

His lips twitched slightly, as though he was fighting to hold back a smile. "Generally it's done together."

Her nerves, which had held up remarkably well until that point, suddenly seemed to fray apart at the seams. "What? Oh, yes, I see. That makes sense, doesn't it? After all, one could hardly—"

"Blake?"

"McRae?"

"Shut up and kiss me." With that, he wrapped his arm around her waist, pulling her tightly against him as his mouth descended on hers. They fit well together, Devon thought, somewhat surprised. Given how big Cole was, and how small she was, she would have expected this to be awkward. Instead her body molded itself instantly to the contours of his, as if that was exactly where she belonged.

She hadn't anticipated the gentleness of his kiss either. It was simple, soft and sweet, as though he was forcing himself to take his time. His strong hands moved over her body in light, loving strokes, giving her time to adjust to the feel of being in his arms. She was dimly aware of him removing the pins from her hair, weaving it through his hands as he let it cascade down her back.

But just as she was assimilating all that, the kiss changed. With a gentle pressure of his jaw, Cole parted her lips and swept his tongue inside her mouth. Devon stiffened in shock and would have pulled away, but he must have felt it, for his hands stroked her back in soft, soothing motions, calming her. As if he was silently asking her to let go, to trust him.

She did. Devon melted against Cole and let him lead her, guide her through to what he wanted. She was rewarded with a kiss so fierce, so tender, that it nearly stole her breath away. Once the shock wore off, she found herself responding to the sensuous rhythm he was creating. Fire danced through her veins, the world spun away beneath her feet, and her emotions soared out of control. She locked her arms around Cole's neck, demanding more.

The kiss soared to a new height. It was no longer gentle, but hot, passionate, demanding. Devon mimicked the play of his tongue, felt his body tense as the hunger grew within them both. He cupped her bottom, lifting her up tightly against him, their bodies locked together in primitive desire. Pure masculine need emanated through him, exciting her to a new level, amazing her that she could arouse him as he was arousing her. Devon found herself responding with pure abandon, wanting this to go on forever.

Then, as quickly as the thought flitted through her mind, it all came to an end. As if exerting a herculean effort, Cole pulled back from her, both emotionally and physically. Devon stared up at him, feeling strangely bereft and suddenly wondering if she'd done something wrong. Even in the dim light of the room, she could see the golden fire that lit his eyes as his gaze traveled over her face and down her body, as if taking new measure of her. He ran his hands over her upper arms, gently brushed her hair back over her shoulders.

She sensed that the motion, while lovely, was nothing but a bid for time while he gathered his thoughts. After a minute, his eyes locked on hers. She stiffened her spine, unconsciously holding her breath as she waited for him to speak.

Finally he did. "It's time for bed now."

Chapter 9

"What?!"

He'd shocked her. Cole could see that clearly in her magnificent soft green eyes. Eyes that only moments ago had glowed with hazy passion were now shimmering with righteous indignation. But that was the only part of her that had changed. Her face was still flushed from their kiss, her lips soft and rosy, slightly swollen now, but forming the same sweet pout that had enticed him for days. And made him want to pull her right back into his arms.

Dammit all, what the hell was the matter with him? It seemed he'd done nothing but think about all the reasons that he *shouldn't* kiss her. And Lord knew, he had plenty; to begin with, there was the fact that she was Sharpe's agent. There was also the fact that she'd lied to him, tricked him, and obviously wasn't above using her feminine wiles to manipulate him. But in the end, none of that mattered. In the end, there was nothing but the overpowering urge to take her into his arms, to crush her body against his, to see if her lips tasted as sweet as he'd imagined they would.

Staying in the room while she bathed hadn't helped matters much. As he'd listened to the soft splashing sounds coming from the other side of the screen, his brain kept conjuring up images of Devon on the other side, naked, wet, and soapy. Hell, he'd wanted the woman even when she was covered in goose shit. The thought of her soft body, clean and fresh, splashing in a tub only a few feet away had almost been too much for him to bear.

And then she'd stood, her body silhouetted against the screen in dark relief, framed by the golden glow of the lamp. Cole had simply stared in stunned awe, unable to tear his eyes away. He'd not given much thought to what lay beneath Devon's clothes. Some, of course, but not much. Then behind the screen, he saw what he'd only dimly imagined. Devon was a small woman, but every ounce of her was pure feminine perfection, from her delicate ankles and shapely legs, to the gentle flare of her hips and tiny waist. Her breasts were small, but firm and round, with nipples that tipped up toward the sky. Then she'd turned, giving him an outline of the graceful curve of her back, her delectable derriere.

And that wasn't even the worst of it. While he watched in stunned awe, in a move he was sure was nothing but pure, calculated torture on her part, Devon reached for a bucket of water and poured it over her head. He hadn't been able to stop the groan that tore from his lips at the sight of the water cascading like liquid silk over her glorious curves, dripping from her body in thin, wet rivulets that splashed softly back into the tub.

Yet when she poked her head around the screen a few minutes later, there was nothing in her expression to prove that it had all been deliberate. In fact, just the opposite was true. Her face showed nothing but wary innocence, her skin glowed fresh and rosy after her bath. Cole suddenly found himself wanting her even more.

Clutching her wrapper tightly around her throat, she padded lightly toward the small dressing table and began spreading out her assorted feminine wares. Jars of creams, bottles of scent, hairpins, items that had all heretofore seemed to him nothing but trivial wastes of time, were now fascinating necessities in Devon's hands. He watched her primp and smooth and pamper, saw her thick glossy hair slip through her fingers.

His gaze had even followed her when she stepped back behind the screen to dress. Unable to stop himself, he watched her silhouette as she wiggled into a camisole, pulled on her stockings and secured them at her thighs, tugged her petticoat over her hips and tied it at her waist. He found every movement incredibly erotic, and was stunned that he did. Cole was too experienced a lover to be aroused simply by the sight of a woman dressing. He consoled himself with the rationalization that he'd never before watched a woman put on her clothes unless he'd first helped to take them off.

She'd looked absolutely adorable when she'd finally emerged, prim and proper in the blue and lavender gown he'd bought her, buttoned all the way up to her pretty little throat. Her eyes were glistening bright, her skin dewy-soft, fresh and sweet-smelling. He couldn't help but stare in appreciative wonder.

Given his state of mind, it was no wonder he'd reacted the way he had when she'd begun flirting with every man at their table, damned near every man in the room. He figured he couldn't entirely blame her for the stunt she'd pulled with Lieutenant Davis's wallet. Had he been paying attention the way he should have been, he would have seen that coming. Instead he'd been too busy working himself into a quiet fury over the way the lieutenant's gaze traveled over Devon.

But all of that was neither here nor there. The question was what to do now. The more he knew about Devon, the less he understood. The woman was infuriating one minute, aloof and intriguing the next. He'd thought that one kiss would be sufficient to quench the fire that had been steadily building within him; instead just the opposite was true. She'd responded so completely, and with such an intoxicating mix of passion and innocence, that it had been nearly impossible for him to break away.

But he had. He wouldn't allow himself to go any further, not until he knew exactly how she was involved with Jonas Sharpe. He'd let things go too damned far already. Cole wasn't ordinarily a man to let lust interfere with his thinking, but then he'd never met a woman like Devon Blake before. Tomorrow he'd get all the answers he needed about Sharpe, then he would know how to proceed.

"I'm not going to bed with you," Devon said as she darted out from beneath his arms and skirted across the room to stand behind a chair. "I'd rather go straight to prison!"

Cole arched a tawny brow. "Apparently my kiss left much to be desired."

"I mean it!"

"I know you do," he said calmly. "But it's late, and I think we could both use the sleep."

Surprise and wary distrust flashed across her delicate features. "Sleep?"

"Sleep."

"You want to go to bed to ... to sleep?"

"That's usually where it's done."

"That's where quite a few other things are done as well," she snapped.

"True, but that's not what I had in mind."

"Why not?" she demanded, then bright spots of color stained her cheeks. "I mean, of course not! Of course it isn't! But ... but you kissed me."

"I seem to recall you kissed me back."

Her knuckles went white as she tightened her grip on the back of the chair. "I thought it only polite."

Cole bit back a grin. "How very obliging of you."

"Yes, wasn't it? So in light of that, perhaps you could oblige me in something."

He waited to see where the conversation was going, wondering if he would ever figure out how her mind worked.

Devon said, "Perhaps you'd like to sleep in the tub tonight."

"Not a chance."

"I see," she replied stiffly, her eyes sparkling with emerald fire. "In that case, I will."

He shook his head. "In the first place, the tub has already been removed, and is probably being used by one of the other boarders as we speak." He watched her eyes widen as she glanced about the room, absorbing the impact of his words. "In the second place, the bed is plenty large enough for two, and that is where I want you to be. I won't get any sleep if I have to lie awake listening for sounds of you picking your way out the door."

Devon looked insulted. "If I do decide to pick my way out the door, I guarantee you won't be able to hear me—whether you're asleep or not."

"How comforting. However, it doesn't change anything. We're both sleeping in that bed."

"But you kissed me!"

He wished she'd quit reminding him of that. It just made him want to do it all over again. "Devon, I give you my word, all I intend to do now is sleep."

She studied him through narrowed eyes. "No more kissing?" she demanded at last, her tone laced with suspicion.

"No." *Not tonight, anyway,* Cole amended silently.

"How do I know that once we're in bed you won't . . . won't . . ."

"Turn into a wild, rutting beast who's unable to control himself?" he supplied.

"Exactly," she breathed, looking supremely relieved that he'd said it and not she.

"That's very flattering, but I can assure you that

you're quite safe." He waited until he saw her relax to add casually, "That only happens when the moon is full."

She brought her chin up once again, her features stiff with anger and embarrassment. "You're teasing me now. You think I'm being silly."

"You're right, I do." Before she could protest, he continued, "Your kiss was nice, Devon. Quite nice, as a matter of fact, but that's all it was. And as to sharing the same bed, I don't know what else I can say to put you at ease. I give you my word not to touch you. I've never been accused of snoring, though I suppose I don't really know for a fact whether that's true or not. I don't toss and turn, and you're welcome to all the blankets. Now is there anything else that's bothering you?"

Devon stared at him for a long, silent moment. "You have bad dreams. About someone named Gideon."

Her words slashed through him like a knife. If she'd been looking for a way to ensure that the flames of lust had been thoroughly extinguished, she'd found it. Cole felt his muscles tense as every nerve in his body suddenly screamed to life. "I'll try not to disturb you," he managed to say evenly.

She shook her head. "You don't—"

"It's time for bed," he said, abruptly ending the conversation. This time Devon complied without argument. She stepped behind the screen, returning a few minutes later with her dressing gown wrapped tightly around her, and slipped into bed. Cole tugged off his boots, removed his shirt, and began to unbutton his pants. Devon's appalled gasp filled the air. He stopped abruptly, realizing only then that he'd been stripping down out of habit.

"Sorry," he muttered and buttoned his pants. She flipped over onto her side and pretended not to hear. Cole doused the light and slipped into bed beside her. They both lay absolutely still, their backs to each other.

Thick, palpable tension filled the empty space between them. After what seemed an eternity, Devon's breathing changed to a soft, steady pattern, telling Cole that she was asleep.

He sighed and shifted onto his back, exhausted but unable to rest. A thousand images flitted through his mind, keeping him awake. He saw his ship, the *Islander*, under attack, her sails aflame as the screams of his crew roared in his ears. Next he saw Jonas Sharpe in his mind. Though he'd been shown the man's portrait only once, the image had attached itself to his memory. Then Gideon. Of course, always Gideon.

Devon muttered a word in her sleep and rolled over. Her hands were clenched in delicate fists, her dark, glorious hair swept carelessly over her pillow. The soft, feminine scent of her drifted toward him. Cole pushed aside his immediate physical reaction, forcing himself to focus solely on the facts.

She'd had a trial and been found guilty. She'd been arrested with the knife in her hand, the body of the slain lieutenant lying on the ground next to her. Her suitcase had been full of documents detailing the sale of warships being built in England for the Confederacy. In the beginning, he'd accepted her guilt completely, without question. More than that, he'd wanted to believe it, because it made everything so much easier. He'd wanted to see her as nothing but a liar, a thief, a murderess. But as the days went by, that had proved an impossible task.

There was something about Devon that made him feel strangely protective toward her. He thought of her sitting on an old oak branch, twirling her toes in the stale creek water, a picture of complete, fetching innocence. She'd risked her own life in her attempt to escape, leaping aboard a speeding train rather than screaming and putting his men in jeopardy. She'd returned his kiss with an artless sensuality that had sent his pulse racing, a kiss that seemed to define the very essence of the woman: hot and sweet and totally giving.

Either Devon Blake was Jonas Sharpe's scheming accomplice—and a hell of a lot more gifted an actress than he'd ever given her credit for—or she was as guiltless as she'd claimed to be from the very beginning. They were two completely contrasting images, and only one of them would prove to be right. Tomorrow morning he'd find out which one.

But morning came and went without a resolution to Cole's dilemma. It seemed he'd just dropped off to sleep when a pounding on the door awakened them both. It was General Brader's adjutant, requesting an audience with the general posthaste. They dressed immediately and headed for camp, where Cole left Devon with a guard while he sought out Brader. Once there, he heard the disquieting rumor that Stonewall Jackson was moving his men up from Richmond to confront General Pope near Culpepper County. The action could be heating up around them at any time.

As Cole left the general's office, he noted the somber mood that hung over the entire camp. The men who only yesterday had been playing cards and writing letters home were now checking ammunition and testing their guns. But until he heard differently, Cole determined to treat the rumor as what it was: a rumor, one of hundreds that flew from camp to camp, with no more substance or weight than the wind that carried them.

Hearing Devon's soft laughter coming from the corral near where the horses were penned, Cole turned and headed in that direction. He stopped at the entrance to the barn. A shaft of golden sunlight showed Emmett lounging in a pile of hay, a long piece of straw stuck between his teeth, while Devon stood, a grooming brush in her hand as she tended a chestnut mare. Something about the intimacy of the scene made him hesitate at the door, feeling like an intruder.

"I got me a sweetheart back home," he heard Emmett confess.

Devon continued to stroke the mare as she glanced over her shoulder at the boy. "Do you?" she asked. "What's her name?"

"Sally Ann." He paused, digging his toe into the pile of hay. "I was gonna marry her, but Pa wouldn't let me."

"Why wouldn't he?"

"Aw, he sez me an Sally Ann are too young to get married up. I gave her a ring anyway, just to make sure she'd wait for me. Maybe it's best we wait till after the war. Seein' as how she's clear back in Texas, and I'm all the way out here. 'Sides, that way, after I whup me some Rebs, I can go back a genuine hero, and won't Pa or nobody be able to stop us then."

Devon simply nodded and continued to brush the horse.

Emmett looked down, a worried frown on his face. "The only trouble is, most of my friends back home done went Rebel on me. I know I should hate them now, on account of them being the enemy and all, but I don't. I don't want to kill them neither. It ain't like I'm a coward or nothing, but I don't think I could shoot none of them boys I grew up with. It don't seem like that'll solve nothing, killing off all my friends just 'cause they're on the wrong side of the war."

"Have you talked to your father about this?" Devon asked quietly.

"Hell—excuse me, ma'am—heck no! Pa already thinks I'm too young. If I told him that, he'd send me back for sure."

"I think he would understand."

Emmett looked panicked. "You ain't gonna tell him, are you, ma'am?"

Devon sighed. "No, I won't," she promised, then changed the subject. "Tell me about Sally Ann. What's she like?"

The boy fairly leaped to his feet. "I got me one of them miniatures of her, you want to see?" he asked, proudly shoving a worn leather case at Devon. "She ain't smiling there, which is too bad, 'cause she's got just about the prettiest smile in the whole world. She's a mighty fine cook too. Why, last summer at the county fair, her cherry pie took first prize. And that wasn't just among the cherry pies neither. She was competing against all them other fruits too. Apple, strawberry, rhubarb, you name it. She won the prize for best pie, period. Now ain't that something?"

Devon smiled and handed him back the miniature. "No wonder you want to marry her."

Emmett nodded happily and settled back into the hay. "It ain't just because of her looks or her cookin' neither. Sally Ann's a lady, through and through. Just like you, ma'am. A lady, through and through."

Cole saw Devon stiffen, regret flashing over her delicate features. "I don't think Sally Ann would appreciate the comparison."

"Why not? You're a fine lady, ma'am, one of the finest I've ever met. You don't put on airs the way some do, but I can see you're a lady, just the same."

Devon paused, then lifted the mare's dark tail, which she'd brushed to a high glossy sheen. "If you were to call a tail a leg, Emmett, how many legs would a horse have?"

Emmett frowned. "Well, if you call a tail a leg, then I reckon a horse would have five legs."

Devon shook her head. "Not true," she said, a slight hint of melancholy in her voice. "A horse only has four legs. Just because you call a tail a leg, it doesn't make it so."

Cole felt his chest tighten at her words. All her insistence at being called a lady was nothing but a cover for a vulnerability that he never would have suspected. A title that, no matter how much she fought for, she obviously didn't feel she deserved. And he'd done nothing but make it abundantly clear that he agreed.

Something must have given his presence away, for Devon straightened and turned, her soft green eyes locking on his. She murmured a few words to Emmett, set down the grooming brush, then moved directly toward Cole. "We need to talk," he said simply.

She nodded. Her gaze ran over his face, her eyes inquisitive, but she asked no questions. For the first time since he'd known her, the confrontational edge was missing, as if both had agreed to an unspoken truce. But there was still something in the air between them, a primitive tension that was part wary unease with the shift that had taken place in their relationship, part sensual undercurrent.

They walked out of the barn, away from the main house and toward a small fishing pond on the outer edge of the property. The grass surrounding it was tall, lush, and inviting, but they were both too restless to sit. Devon leaned back against a tree, watching the slaves who toiled in a nearby garden. "I'd never actually seen a slave before, not until yesterday," she mused. "It's awful, isn't it?"

"Yes."

"Are they free now, or does General Brader own them all?"

"No. The general never would. The ones that come to us are considered contraband, like any other property the Union Army confiscates."

She frowned. "Then they're still not free."

Cole shook his head. "We don't have that authority, Devon. There's talk that Lincoln is working on an emancipation act, but so far nothing's come of it. At this point, we're simply fighting to keep the Union together.''

A commotion in the yard of the main house caused them both to turn. General Brader stood out front, issuing orders to his men as they mounted up. The soldiers split into groups of five, gave a few rowdy war whoops, then took off, galloping in different directions. Scouting parties, Cole presumed, probably being sent out to nearby camps to validate the rumors that had been circulating since daybreak.

He turned back to Devon. Unable to devise a smooth way to ease into the topic that was foremost on his mind, he asked bluntly, ''How did you come to be involved with Jonas Sharpe? You said before that you weren't working for him directly. Was he blackmailing you somehow?''

''No, he wasn't.'' She must have anticipated the question, for she didn't appear the least bit surprised by it. ''Surely you of all people know how hard it is to force me into doing something against my will.''

''Then how—''

''I tried before to tell you what happened, but you didn't listen to me,'' she said. ''It's too late now to do anything about it in any case. There's no point in discussing it again.''

Cole silently studied her for a moment. She wasn't just being obstinate, he realized, cursing himself for the clumsy way he'd blundered into the topic. She was nervous, frightened, and doing everything she could to avoid any discussion of either herself or Jonas Sharpe. Just as she'd done from the very beginning. ''Devon,'' he said quietly, ''I'm sorry I didn't listen before, but I'm listening now. I can't help you until I know what happened.''

''You're right, you can't help me.''

Cole stepped forward, closing the distance between them. He placed his hands gently on her upper arms, waiting until she lifted her gaze to his to ask, "Do you trust me, Devon?"

She took a deep breath, looking as though that were the most complicated question in the world. "I don't know if I can," she finally admitted.

He frowned. Did she feel that he wasn't worthy of her trust? Or was she simply saying that she wasn't capable of trusting anyone? Either way, he didn't like her answer. "Will you try?"

"It would be easier on both of us if you just let me escape."

"Perhaps, but I've never been a man to do something just because it was easier."

"No, I suppose not," she said, sounding utterly defeated. She searched his face, then sighed. "You're a man who always likes to do what's right, what's honorable."

Cole stared at her, stunned by the reluctant compliment. If that were true, he thought in disgust, he would have listened to her days ago, rather than let himself be blinded by his thirst for revenge. If he were so damned honorable, he wouldn't be thinking right now about how much he'd like to take her into his arms and make love to her. How much he wanted to slowly undress her, lay her down in the soft grass, and spend the rest of the day getting to know every inch of her beautiful little body.

"Start at the beginning," he said, dropping her arms. "How did you go from living at the children's asylum to becoming involved with a man like Jonas Sharpe?"

Her eyes widened. "I told you about the asylum?"

"With a little coaxing from a bottle of brandy."

"What else did I say?"

Cole shrugged. "Not much. You told me that you have a brother named Billy. And that Uncle Monty isn't really your uncle."

Devon stared out over the pond as though lost in thought. "It's not a very interesting story," she warned.

"I'd like to hear it anyway."

She nodded. Slowly, as if resigning herself for the worst, she began, "When I was fifteen and Billy was nine, we ran away from the asylum. At first, everything was fine. It was springtime and the days and nights were warm, and we didn't need much to get by. We were actually happier than we'd ever been at the asylum."

"How did you live?"

"Oh, there are ways," she answered with a light shrug. "We assisted peddlers in the marketplace, and collected rags and bones to sell to the junkmen. We were pure finders as well."

"Pure finders?"

"We collected dog droppings," she explained matter-of-factly, without any hint of embarrassment or self-pity. "Once they dried, the tanneries used the alkaline they contained to cure skins."

Cole considered her bleak existence, amazed that out of that had emerged the proud, passionate woman that Devon Blake had become. "What happened?"

"Winter came."

"Where did you live then?"

She gave a vague shrug. "Nowhere and everywhere. I should have taken Billy back to Mrs. Honeychurch's, but I was too proud. And I didn't want Billy to be there. It wasn't a very ..." she hesitated, as though searching for the right word. "It wasn't a very nice place to be," she concluded, in what Cole imagined was a profound understatement.

Devon shook her head. "That was a mistake. The days grew so short, there wasn't much time to work. After a while, I quit even trying. I spent my time stealing food, blankets, wood for our fire. I did whatever I had to do to get by."

Devon glanced up at him, as though expecting to see cold disdain or silent condemnation. When she found neither, she shrugged and continued talking. She seemed strangely remote, as though she'd learned long ago to detach herself from the memories. "But in the end, Billy caught a fever, and he never got better. After he died, I couldn't think of what to do. You see, for so many years, if I got up on a bitterly cold morning, it was for Billy. If I went out to find, steal, or beg for food, it was for Billy. Finding a warm place to sleep at night was for Billy. When he died, none of it seemed to matter anymore. It didn't matter whether I got up, or whether I ate, or anything that happened to me. I remember just wandering the streets as people rushed by, hurrying to get out of the cold, like they couldn't even see me, like I didn't exist. That was the worst part, feeling so alone. Then one day I came to a river, its banks covered with ice and snow. I thought about just walking into it and letting it sweep me away, how cool and inviting it looked—"

Horror raced through Cole at the thought of Devon as a young girl staring into the icy banks of a river, contemplating ending her life.

"Then, the next thing I knew," she continued, "a great big bear of a man was there at my side. He began talking to me, very gently, about such silly things. What was my favorite flower? My favorite food? Did I know any songs? We stood there all afternoon, even after it began to snow, just talking. Like we had all the time in the world." She paused and looked up at him, her eyes shining with a soft light that held him enthralled. "Do you believe in angels, Cole?"

Cole started, so wrapped up in her story that her question caught him completely off-guard. "I—well, I suppose I've never thought about it."

"Hmmm." She nodded pensively, as if pondering his reply. "This will sound silly to you, then, but when

I was a little girl, my mother used to tell me stories about guardian angels. How each of us has an angel that protects us and watches over us. And for a minute, I thought that this man was mine. A great big, roly-poly guardian angel. He appeared out of nowhere and somehow kept me from walking into that river, as if he knew what I was thinking and was sent to stop me, to tell me that even though I'd lost Billy, there were other things ahead for me, other reasons to go on. Somehow he convinced me that laughter and love still existed in the world and that one day I'd be lucky enough to find them again. Isn't that exactly what an angel would do?''

It took Cole a minute to find his voice. ''Yes,'' he agreed hoarsely, suddenly aching to touch her, to pull her into his arms. ''That's exactly what an angel would do.''

Devon smiled, her face alight with a soft glow as she shook her head. ''I'm afraid it was purely fanciful thinking on my part, however, for there's absolutely nothing angelic about Uncle Monty.''

Once again, she'd managed to shock him to the soles of his boots. ''Your guardian angel was Uncle Monty?''

She nodded. ''He introduced himself, told me his name was Montgomery Persons, but that I could call him Uncle Monty. Then he asked me my name, and about the little boy he usually saw me with. When I told him that Billy had died, he just stared at me for the longest time, then he asked me if I wanted to come home with him. Just like that. I looked from him to the river, and suddenly the river didn't look like such a wonderful place to be anymore. Suddenly it just looked cold and dark. So I let him take my hand and lead me home.''

A feeling of dread crept over Cole as a dark suspicion attached itself to his mind. He wondered if Monty was in fact a man with a predilection for preying on young girls. "What happened once you arrived there?" he asked carefully, but Devon's next words immediately put him at ease.

"He sent a maid to give me a hot bath, fed me the best meal I'd had in years, then showed me to a warm bed to sleep in. The same thing happened the day after that, and the day after that. He'd talk with me about a book I was reading, or whatever I'd done that day, but that was it. He never demanded anything, or made me feel in any way uncomfortable. I don't think either of us expected it to last, but I suppose we enjoyed each other's company, for we settled into a sort of routine without even thinking about it. After a couple of weeks, he showed me a few card tricks, and then a few other tricks, and the next thing I knew, he and I were in business."

Cole let out his breath, feeling shaken, relieved, and a host of other emotions that rushed through him too quickly to even identify. Devon had been lucky. Damned lucky. He considered what could have happened to her, then quickly pushed the grim thought away. "I thought you said that wasn't a very interesting story."

"Well, perhaps interesting," she acknowledged with a shrug, "but it's certainly not flattering. At least not to me."

Cole studied the petite beauty standing next to him, thinking of the way she'd stood up to him from the very beginning, refusing to allow herself to be bullied or threatened. She'd wrestled with the difficulties life had thrown her, obstacles that would have sent grown men crashing to their knees. But not Devon. She'd fought back, and done it with an inner strength and conviction that amazed him. And after everything she'd been through, she still believed in love and laughter.

"There is a point to my telling you all this," Devon said. She looked determined to finish and get it over with, as though revealing this much about herself had been an incredibly distasteful chore.

"All right," Cole said slowly, watching her.

"The point is, everything you said about me before was true. I'll lie, cheat, steal, do whatever I have to do to get by—"

"Devon," he interrupted, hating himself for what he'd said, for how quick he'd been to judge and condemn her.

"No, let me finish. We both know that it's true, so there's no sense pretending we don't. That's what I am. But I wanted you to know why—not that it makes what's wrong, right. It doesn't." She paused, then drew herself up, tilting back her chin to look him straight in the eye. "I'm a crook, a liar, and a thief. But I'm not a murderer. I didn't kill that man."

Cole heard it again, that combination of fear and nervousness skimming just below the surface, belying the bravado of her words. Telling him there was still something he was missing, something he hadn't quite grasped. When it finally hit him, he was furious at himself for not having seen it sooner. "But you know who did, don't you?"

Devon stared at him for a long moment, something that looked like sadness or regret flashing through her beautiful green eyes. Finally she nodded. "Yes."

"Who?"

"My fiancé."

Chapter 10

~~~ᗞᗢᗣ~~~

Cole wasn't taking the news well at all. Which was too bad, considering how he'd been able to accept everything else she'd told him without too much difficulty. She'd been afraid she'd see scorn or contempt—or worse still, pity—etched on his rugged features as she revealed her past, but she hadn't. Instead he'd listened with a tolerance that amazed her, as if he truly understood. But this, the fact that her fiancé was a murderer, this seemed to bother him.

"Your fiancé?!" he repeated, in what sounded like a roar.

Devon nodded. "Boris Ogglesby."

"You have a fiancé?!" He was still yelling. "Why the hell didn't you tell me this sooner?"

"I did tell you. You just didn't believe me."

"When did you tell me?" he demanded.

"Days ago." She shrugged. "It doesn't matter now in any case, for I considered our engagement broken once he framed me for murder."

Cole stared at her as though she'd just sprouted a second head. "How very sensible of you."

"I thought so."

He sank down onto the grass, looking suddenly exhausted. "Don't ever do that to me again," he said.

She frowned. "Do what?"

"Never mind." He reached for her arm, gently

178

pulled her down beside him, and asked pleasantly, "So who was the son-of-a-bitch?"

"I told you, Boris Ogglesby."

Cole arched a tawny brow. "You were actually going to marry someone who answered to the name Boris Ogglesby?"

"I thought it sounded rather dignified," she replied stiffly.

"If you're a Saint Bernard, I suppose it is."

Anger surged through Devon. "Fine," she snapped, rising to her feet. "If all you want to do is make snide comments—"

He caught her arm and brought her back down beside him. "Devon, wait. I'm sorry. I'm listening, I promise. I just wasn't prepared to hear this." He studied her, then a dark shadow passed through his eyes. "Were you in love with him?"

"In love with him? Of course—"

"I don't want to hear it."

"But you just asked."

"Listen to me. You may think that you're in love with him, but you're not. Trust me, I know."

Of course she wasn't in love with Boris Ogglesby. But how the hell did he know that? "How the hell do you know that?"

With one deft move, he wrapped his arm around her waist and pulled her smoothly onto his lap. "Because if you were in love with another man," he murmured huskily, "would you let me do this?"

His mouth captured hers in a kiss that was completely different from their first. It wasn't tender, soft, or gentle. This kiss began right where the last had ended, full of unrestrained passion and fiery longing, igniting a heat deep within her that set every nerve in her body ablaze. Devon leaned into him, their bodies locked together as she eagerly sought the play of his tongue. Her hands moved with wanton abandon over his body, tracing the hot, rough velvet of his skin, the corded muscles of his back and thighs.

Cole let out a low groan and tore his mouth away from hers as he pressed her back into the soft grass. He leaned over her, trailing soft kisses down her throat as he gently unbuttoned the top of her gown. That accomplished, he slowly eased the garment past her shoulders and brushed light kisses over the tops of her breasts. Her camisole came next. Moving with an expertise that she didn't want to think about, Cole pulled the delicate ribbons free and removed the thin cotton barrier. He cupped her breasts in his palms, gently caressing them until her nipples tightened to firm, solid peaks that he teased with his tongue.

The tension Devon felt inside abruptly exploded into wonder. She dug her fingers into Cole's back and arched her hips against his as their mouths joined once again. Their kiss deepened, following the reckless motion of their bodies, gaining a momentum that seemed to carry them forward, awakening a primal hunger deep within her that she was only just beginning to understand.

She'd never been less in the mood for conversation in her life, but Cole seemed to have something on his mind. He pulled back and commanded huskily, "Tell me you don't love Boris."

It seemed a rather silly request, but she decided to comply anyway. "I don't love him."

Cole rewarded her by finding an unexplored spot on her throat to kiss, a spot just below her earlobe that was so sensitive, the touch of his lips sent shivers racing down her spine, despite the heat of the day. "And you never did," he said.

She smiled. "And I never did."

His tawny eyes flashed victory. "I knew it."

Devon pulled back, regarding him warily. She rolled

out from beneath his embrace and hastily rebuttoned her gown. "What do you mean, you knew it?"

Cole reached for her and gently smoothed back a lock of her hair. "You wouldn't have let me kiss you the way I did, either now or last night, if you were in love with another man."

"What a ridiculous thing to say!"

He shrugged. "Maybe, but it's the truth. Women are run by their emotions. They can't separate love and lust."

Devon felt her temper soar once again. "Oh? And I suppose men can?"

"Of course. Men are ruled by logic. That's why we're men."

"What you are, Cole McRae," she shot back, "is a horse's ass! But only half as intelligent, and not nearly as pleasant to look at."

"But I was right about this Boris . . . Boris . . ."

"Ogglesby."

"Whatever. You don't love him."

"Love him! You idiot, of course I don't love him. I've never even met the man!"

Cole stared at her for a long moment, then said carefully, "I thought you told me he was your fiancé."

"He was."

"But you've never met him."

"That's right."

He let out a deep sigh. "Devon, it's nearly noon now. I'd like to get to the end of this story by midnight if it's at all possible."

Her emerald eyes flashed fire. "Don't blame me. I'm trying to tell you, but you keep interrupting. Or I suppose kissing me was just the logical thing to do after I told you my fiancé was a murderer."

Cole opened his mouth, then abruptly closed it. He frowned, tugging his hand through his thick blond hair.

"You just let me worry about what's logical, all right?"

"Oh, fine, McRae. You're so good at it. I forgot, you're a man, aren't you?"

She could see him summoning his patience. He seemed to have to do that a lot—or at least whenever she was around. "All right," he said slowly. "Why don't we begin again, shall we? Tell me how you came to be involved with Jonas Sharpe. And why you think this Boris person, the fiancé you've never met, framed you for murder."

Devon frowned. It sounded absolutely ridiculous when he said it. And yet at the time, it had all made perfect sense. She hesitated, wondering where to begin, then slowly started, "It was my idea to get involved with Jonas Sharpe. You see, he and Uncle Monty had done business together in the past—"

"What sort of business?"

"Legitimate business. Shipping, investments, that sort of thing." At Cole's frown, she continued, "Just because Uncle Monty was a crook doesn't mean that every transaction he was involved in was crooked. In fact, just the opposite is true. The more successful he was, the more capital he accrued, and the more influential he became. Uncle Monty happens to have friends among judges, politicians, and prominent solicitors, as well as the average ruffian on the street. Every level of society. He's truly a remarkable man."

Cole nodded, apparently impatient to leave behind her glowing praise of her uncle. "So what happened? Did one of their deals go bad?"

"No, nothing like that. Jonas Sharpe mentioned to Uncle Monty that he had an associate in the States, a fellow Englishman who was looking for a good English wife. A lady. Someone of solid background, outstanding character and moral fiber, reasonably attractive, and young enough to bear children." She paused, acutely aware that the only one of those criteria she met was "young enough to bear children." Obviously Cole would be aware of this as well. Nevertheless she continued, determined to reveal the shameful nature of her misdeed. "So I suggested me. I thought that maybe I would be his wife."

Silence. Total silence. "Were you serious?" Cole finally asked.

"Yes."

"Why?"

Years of practice enabled her to come up with a casual smile, despite the havoc of her emotions. "At the time, it actually seemed a good idea," she answered with a light shrug, then stood and moved away from him. She paused beneath a tall fir, picking at the bark as if it were the most fascinating thing in the world.

She heard Cole rise, then felt him standing behind her. "Why, Devon?" he asked quietly. "What did you want so badly that you were willing to travel halfway around the world to marry a man you'd never before set eyes on?"

Devon took a deep breath, suddenly questioning the wisdom of telling him the truth. She should tell him that it was all a con, that she was trying to steal money from the man. That was something Cole could understand, likely what he expected to hear from her. She could confess to that, and he would probably even forgive her for it. It would be simple and neat, and they could get this over with quickly.

But it wasn't the truth.

Devon turned around, leaning back against the trunk of the tree, her hands tucked behind her. She stared up at Cole, lost in silent contemplation, wondering where to begin. She searched his rugged features, striving to find a similarity between her life and his, but there was nothing. No common ground, nothing she could point to that would make him understand what she'd felt.

Why she'd needed to run from England, from everything. Finally she answered his question with one of her own. "Do you have many friends?"

He frowned, but replied with a shrug, "Yes, I suppose so."

"I don't," she said simply. "As a matter of fact, I don't have any at all." She reached for a dry twig, poked it absently at the ground near her feet, then let it drop. "It's not Uncle Monty's fault. He would do anything in the world for me, but the way we lived, constantly on the dodge, moving from place to place, made things rather difficult. He had his cronies and his drinking pubs, but I'm hardly the sort that a respectable young lady my age would invite to tea. Or the sort that a respectable young man would want anything to do with. So when Uncle Monty was out, I simply stayed home by myself."

"And you thought this Boris person would be a friend?"

"No. I'd hoped we would learn to get along together, of course, but I wanted more than just that. I wanted a real home, a family, a chance to meet other people and truly belong. Somewhere where I would actually be accepted, where I wouldn't ever have to run again, or constantly look over my shoulder."

"If that's all you wanted, why didn't you simply choose a man in England and settle down there?"

Devon flinched inwardly at his description of "all" she wanted. He had no idea what an impossible dream that was for her. "You don't understand the way Uncle Monty and I lived. We would work our way into the upper echelons one week, dining at fancy dinner parties and drinking from fine crystal. And the next week we'd be squatting over an open fire in a dark alley with the most notorious burglar in the city. But there was no place we ever really fit in.

"Besides," she continued, "even if I could convince

someone that I truly was the lady I pretended to be, how could I ever relax in England? The specter of my past would always loom over me, the fear that one day I'd run into someone with whom Uncle Monty and I had had dealings. That would bring nothing but shame to my husband, destroy everything I'd worked so hard to build. And if there were children involved and my husband learned about my past and cast us out into the streets . . .'' Her words trailed off as a small shudder passed through her frame.

''Maybe your husband would understand,'' Cole suggested.

''He wouldn't,'' she countered swiftly. ''You don't know the way it works, but I do. Once people know, they never quite trust you again. Once you're branded a thief, you always remain a thief in their eyes. My only chance was to start over, to leave everything behind. And marrying Boris Ogglesby seemed the perfect opportunity.''

''I see.''

Devon stared at Cole, wondering if he really did see, or if this all sounded like just another one of her elaborate cons to him. She reminded herself firmly that it didn't matter what he thought of her, and continued. ''Since all of Uncle Monty's dealings with Sharpe in the past had been legitimate, I thought there was no way he would suspect. But he did.'' She reached for the branch beside her and began absently tugging the leaves and scattering them at her feet.

''What happened?''

''Sharpe saw through me immediately. Apparently I'm not half as good at pretending to be a lady as I think I am.'' She paused, lifting her shoulders in a light shrug. ''Or perhaps he'd known about my and Uncle Monty's reputation all along, and that's why he selected me.''

"Did you know that Jonas Sharpe was involved in the sale of warships to the Confederacy?"

"No. I knew he was involved in a variety of investments, and that he made money running the blockade, but I didn't look any closer than that. The truth is, I was too wrapped up in my own situation. Too excited, too nervous, too happy. And then later, too worried."

Cole frowned. "Why?"

"Well, the Jonas Sharpe I met in Liverpool was very smooth and sophisticated, the perfect gentleman. But once we were at sea, I began to see a different side of him. He could be absolutely charming one minute, then fly into rages the next. One never knew what would cause his explosions of temper, but the results were horrifying. He'd punish his crewmen so severely for the slightest infraction, as if he derived a sort of twisted satisfaction from it. It was truly awful." She pictured Sharpe vividly in her mind: immaculately dressed as he strutted around deck, the cloying scent of his spicy clove cologne drifting in his wake. She didn't think she could ever smell cloves again without thinking of the man.

"Did he ever hurt you, Devon? Or touch you at all?"

Devon looked up. She had heard Cole angry before. But never had she heard the cold fury that filled his tone as he asked those two simple questions.

"No," she answered.

"Are you certain?" He studied her intently, his expression grim.

"Quite certain. He never came near me. But then, I never gave him the opportunity either. Once I saw what the man was really like, I spent the remainder of the voyage locked away in my cabin. For those last three weeks, I told him I was too ill to come out. I told him it was my . . ." She paused, heat rushing to her cheeks as she finished in a rush, "I told him it was my woman's time."

Cole stared at her, then slowly grinned. She could feel the tension slowly draining from his body as he accepted the truth of her answer. He arched a brow and asked, "For three whole weeks?"

Devon nodded her head and studied the ground, mortified that they'd stumbled into such an intimate topic. "The week before I told him my nerves were overwrought, the week during was simply too unbearable, and of course I needed the week after to recover. Judging from the wide berth Captain Sharpe gave me after that, I believe my performance must have been quite convincing."

Cole reached out and gently tilted her chin, lifting her gaze to meet his. "Good girl," he said, his eyes glowing with both silent laughter and genuine admiration.

Devon felt a warm glow spread slowly through her, thrilled by his approval. "I think the man feared I might actually be contagious."

His grin broadened. "Tell me what happened next."

"Once we reached Bermuda, he arranged my passage on a blockade runner into Charleston."

"He didn't accompany you?"

Devon shook her head. "He said he had other business to attend in Bermuda. The runner made it into Charleston without difficulty, but Mr. Ogglesby never showed up to meet me. I waited a few hours, then decided to strike out on my own. I'd chanced to notice an address with my fiancé's name next to it when I was in Captain Sharpe's office, so I headed in that direction. But instead of finding a bank as I'd expected, the address led me to an old, abandoned warehouse. I was about to return to the docks when I saw Mr. Ogglesby and another gentleman enter the warehouse."

"Are you certain it was Ogglesby you saw?"

"Positive. Captain Sharpe had given me a framed tintype of the man. A sort of wedding gift, I suppose."

"So you followed them inside," Cole continued for her.

"No, not at first. I was anxious to make a good impression, and didn't want my fiancé to believe I was following him around town or skulking on street corners waiting for him. I determined to return to the docks and send a boy out with a message that I'd arrived, when I heard the sounds of a struggle coming from within the warehouse."

"At which point you should have run for your life."

"True." Devon smiled ruefully. "It may have escaped your notice, but I tend to be a bit impulsive at times."

Cole frowned. "I presume that's your way of telling me that you charged into the warehouse, determined to save your precious fiancé's life."

"I'm afraid so. I ran inside, but it seemed that Mr. Ogglesby and the other man had already left. There was nothing but darkness and absolute quiet. The interior was a mess, however, with broken crates and smashed furniture, as though a violent struggle had just taken place. I was about to leave when I tripped over something." She paused and took a deep breath, fighting back the sick churning of her stomach. "It was a man's arm. He was lying face down in a pool of blood, a knife dropped on the floor beside him."

Cole braced his hands on her shoulders in a gesture of comfort and support. "What did you do?"

"My first thought was that it was Mr. Ogglesby, and that he might still be alive and need my help. I dropped to my knees and managed to roll him over. But it wasn't him, it was the other man. I was so shocked, I couldn't think. I didn't think. When I heard a noise at the door I grabbed the knife to protect myself. But it wasn't whoever killed the lieutenant. It was Union soldiers and they immediately arrested me."

"Did you tell them what you've just told me?"

"Of course, but they didn't believe me. My gown was covered with blood, I was holding the knife in my hand, the body of the slain lieutenant lying next to me. They retrieved my trunks from the docks and found the papers Captain Sharpe had planted inside. The prosecutor cabled to England and received a wire back detailing my rather colorful background—Uncle Monty and I, though we were rather good, did run afoul of the law a time or two—and that was it. Nothing I said made any difference."

"What about Ogglesby?"

"I gave the authorities his name, of course, but they couldn't locate him. Or any record of him. Given the amount of evidence they had against me, I doubt they put much effort into the search." She took a step away from him and shrugged, striving to sound casual despite the fact that she was quaking inside.

"That's it," she finished. "Everything. The rest I believe you know. After my trial, the dubious honor of escorting me to Old Capitol was given first to a lieutenant named Kilgas, then Sergeant Coombs, and then you. And so . . . here we are."

Devon waited for Cole to speak, feeling suddenly shy and horribly vulnerable. She'd said too much, she realized. She should have just told him about the events leading up to the murder for which she'd been convicted. Instead she'd told him about Billy, about her Uncle Monty, her shady past, and all her hopes and dreams for the future.

"I'll find Sharpe and Ogglesby, Devon," Cole swore. "I'll bring them in and make them pay for what they've done."

Bitter disappointment stabbed through her. Finding them was the last thing in the world that she cared about. It wasn't until she heard Cole speak that she realized what she'd been hoping to hear him say. She wanted him to take her into his arms and tell her that her past didn't matter. That he understood who she was and what she'd done. That he would be different from everybody else she'd ever met and not condemn her for the mistakes she'd made. That she really could start all over again and build a new life. But apparently that dream was as unattainable as the rest of her fanciful hopes and wishes.

A puzzled frown crossed his face as he studied her. "I promise you, Devon," he repeated, "I'll find them both."

She forced a tight smile. "Good," she answered dully and moved past him, returning to the main house without looking back.

Cole stood in General Brader's study two hours later, paying only partial attention to the discussion under way. Instead his focus was on Devon. She was across the hall, moving among the wounded. The men had been brought downstairs where it was cooler and rested in cots in the front parlor. She had said last night that she'd always known how to handle men, and as he watched her move among them now, he saw that that hadn't been a vain boast.

Her presence brightened the room. She carried herself with natural ease and charm, as if there was no place in the world she'd rather be than in a stuffy sickroom full of wounded soldiers. Devon stopped here and there to chat, to offer a drink of cool water, to write a letter for a man whose hands were bandaged, then another for a man who simply had never learned to write. Occasionally someone called her over just to sit beside him for a few minutes, and even that simple act was enough to brighten the soldier's eyes.

She was every inch a lady, he knew that now. She worked so hard to convince everyone of that fact, but deep down she still hadn't convinced herself. And no wonder. Hadn't every person she'd come into contact with thrown her past back in her face—himself included? In fact, he'd been the worst of all. He thought of the way Jonas Sharpe had twisted her dreams into nothing more than a means to achieve his ruthless ends. He thought of the trial she'd endured, only to be convicted of murder and sentenced to life imprisonment. Then of her being delivered into the lewd, filthy hands of Sergeant Coombs, and finally passed on to him. No wonder she'd done everything in her power to escape.

But most amazing of all was that despite what she'd endured, Devon had never given up. Despite her father abandoning her, the cruelty of the asylum where she'd grown up, the loss of her brother, the meager existence she'd managed to eke out on the streets, she'd never given up. She hadn't walked into that icy river on a cold winter's day—a stark image that still filled him with horror. Instead she'd done what she'd had to do to survive, and done it with more grace and dignity than any woman he'd ever met in his life.

His resolve to catch Sharpe had increased tenfold after he heard Devon's tale. While it was too late for him to change any of the past, he could still make amends for his own part, for not having listened to her sooner. Capturing Sharpe seemed the most straightforward means to solve her problem.

That way, he reasoned, he would be able to clear Devon's name once and for all. He would do whatever it took to force Sharpe to confess that he and his man Ogglesby had been behind the murder of Lieutenant Prescott. That Devon had been nothing more than an innocent pawn in their scheme, in the wrong place at the wrong time. With the onus of murder removed from her shoulders, she would be able to do what she'd originally set out to do: to find a husband and leave the past behind.

Not that he was in the market for a wife himself.

Lord, no. He had enough on his hands right now. The timing was too impossible for him even to consider it.

Cole frowned as he deliberated on the narrow confines of society, unable to deny the injustice of what Devon faced. A woman with her past would receive nothing but scorn from ''proper'' society. But with his backing and connections, finding a husband for her shouldn't be too difficult. He thought of the men he knew in Washington, running over in his mind a list of likely candidates for her hand in marriage. After all, she had no one else to see to the task, and that made it his responsibility.

He searched his mind, listing the traits mandatory for a suitor for her hand. Definitely someone with money. Cole didn't like the idea of Devon ever wanting for anything again, no matter how slight. The man also had to be a Northerner, simply as a matter of principle. What else? Someone who would protect her, certainly, and accept her fully for what she was. Someone who would be damned proud to have her as his wife. Someone who would give her children. Devon had said she wanted a family.

Cole frowned again, thinking of how she'd felt in his arms. So soft, so sweet, so giving. As in everything else, she was a complete contradiction in that sense as well: a combination of breathtaking innocence and stunning sensuality. He remembered the feel of her hands as she traced them over his body, the honeyed taste of her lips, the enticing smell of her skin, and instantly vetoed the idea of another man ever getting anywhere near her. He knew he was being a bit dog-in-the-manger about the whole thing, but he couldn't help himself. Until he found a man worthy of her, Devon Blake was staying with him. And as far as he was concerned, that was the end of the subject.

''Why are you glaring at me?''

Cole started at Devon's question, abruptly realizing

that he'd moved from the general's study to the doorway of the parlor. She stood before him, her fists propped on her slim hips, her face flushed from the heat. It was hot and sticky in the little room, the air thick with the stale smell of sweat and illness. Even with the windows thrown wide open, it felt as though there wasn't enough air for so many bodies. "Glaring?" he answered, "I wasn't—"

"Yes, you were. As a matter of fact, you've been glaring at me for the past twenty minutes."

He lifted his shoulders in a casual shrug. "I was just thinking."

"Thinking?" Devon looked at him dubiously, then wiped the perspiration from her brow with the back of her hand. "Well, I don't believe it suits you. You looked awfully unhappy doing it."

Someone who finds her insults absolutely adorable, he mentally added to his list of traits for any suitor for her hand.

"McRae!" General Brader's voice boomed out from within the confines of his study. "Where the hell did you wander off to?"

"Right here, sir," Cole called over his shoulder.

The general lumbered out into the hall. His gaze moved to the wounded, then back to Devon. "You've been babying my men again, missy?" he demanded. "How the hell are they ever going to go back into battle with you giving them more attention than their mamas ever did?"

"You needn't worry, General, I'm quite finished," she replied.

"Hmph," Brader snorted, then asked in a softer tone, "They need anything?"

"Yes, as a matter of fact, they do. The man in the last cot on the left needs his bandages changed. They're all asking for more cool water, and a few are hungry again. There are some letters I left on the table that need posting.''

The general nodded, then turned to an aide standing idly nearby, pretending not to eavesdrop. ''Dammit, man, what are you standing there for? You heard the lady, now see to it!'' The aide jumped to obey. General Brader watched him for a moment, then, satisfied, turned back to Devon and Cole. ''Why don't you all come into my office for a spell? I need to talk to you, McRae.''

They followed him into his study. The general poured Cole a whiskey, then turned to Devon, the lip of the bottle hovering over a glass. ''What about you, little lady? I don't suppose you're partial to rotgut?''

''Tea will suffice.''

The general motioned to his adjutant, who left to relay the request to a servant. ''You all are leaving for Washington in the morning, is that right, McRae?'' he asked without preamble, barreling straight into the topic that was evidently on his mind.

From the corner of his eye, Cole saw Devon flinch at the question, and silently cursed the general for bringing the subject up now. He'd wanted to talk to Brader privately first and get his advice. As far as he could tell, he had only two options, neither of which was very palatable. If he didn't bring Devon straight to Old Capitol, he would be in direct violation of his orders and possibly face court-martial. On the other hand, knowing what he knew now, there was absolutely no chance that he would leave her in that rat-infested hellhole.

The only option seemed to be to leave her with his friends in Washington, where she would be safe until he captured Sharpe. But even as he considered that, Cole was left with the nagging fear that once his back was turned, Devon would slip away, out of his life forever. And that was a risk he was absolutely unwilling to take.

Aware that the general awaited his response, he nodded. "Yes. We leave for Washington in the morning."

He saw Devon stiffen as her expression slightly tensed, a reaction so subtle he would have missed it if he didn't know her so well. When the servant brought her tea, she went through all the motions of politeness, just as she'd been taught, no doubt. Stir the tea, place the spoon on the saucer, take a dainty sip. Everything tightly under control. Obviously she still thought he was taking her to Old Capitol. Dammit all, there was nothing he could do to rectify that now. He would speak to her privately, after he'd had a chance to confer with the general.

"Good," Brader said. "I need you to courier some reports up to General Halleck for me. It'll save me the trouble of sending my boys on the errand."

The sound of shouts coming from the front yard caught their attention. Glancing out the window, they saw a young recruit on horseback race to the front porch. He jerked back the reins and leaped from the saddle, leaving his mount behind sweaty and lathered. The soldier sprinted through the front entrance and down the hall toward them to appear in the doorway of the study, disheveled and distraught, breathing hard. He saluted, swayed to one side, then caught himself before he toppled over. "Corporal Sutter, sir. Request permission to report."

The general nodded. "At ease, boy. Tell me what happened."

Corporal Sutter licked his lips, his eyes wild, as if suddenly unsure where to begin. Behind him, two of the general's aides filed silently into the room. "We ran into some trouble, sir," he finally said. "Out near Taylor's Pond, down by the old mill."

"What happened?" the general pressed.

"Rebel scouts, sir. Six of 'em. Them boys was hiding inside the mill. We didn't even know they was there till they started firing at us. How are we supposed to fight properlike if we don't even know they're there? Somebody ought to tell them that that ain't the proper way to fight." His voice raised to high pitch. "It don't make sense. That ain't the way it's supposed to be. That ain't the way we're supposed to fight."

Cole recognized the signs of shock in a man who'd never been in battle before. There was no glory to it, no honor, none of the romantic notions that filled men's heads. A battle was a bloody encounter in which men fought and either lived or died. No more, no less.

"Easy, Corporal," the general soothed. "Was anyone hurt?"

"Yes, sir." The man swayed again, clearly exhausted.

"Do you need to sit down, Corporal?"

"No, sir."

"Then answer my question. Was anyone hurt?"

"Yes, sir. Three men, sir." The corporal's voice came out a rough whisper. He cleared his throat and began again. "Sergeant Samuel Wright had his horse shot out from under him. Busted his knee pretty bad when he fell. Private Jimmy Johnston, shot in the arm. Private Emmett Brader . . ." He paused, his features tight with strain, his Adam's apple bobbing furiously. "Private Emmett Brader was wounded . . . mortally, sir. Shot through the neck. I'm sorry, sir."

A collective gasp filled the room. The general sat motionless as the color drained from his face, leaving behind a white mask of pain. Devon stiffened in shock, then closed her eyes, her lips moving in what looked to be a silent prayer. Cole felt his gut twist painfully, as though someone had just split open an old wound with a dull knife. He slowly rose, crossed to the general, and placed his hand on the man's shoulder. "Beau,

I'm so sorry," he said, addressing the general by his first name, hating how pathetic the words sounded, how small and meaningless. "I'm so sorry."

General Brader nodded, staring straight ahead, then turned his gaze back to the corporal. "Give me the rest of your report, boy."

Corporal Sutter's eyes widened in shock. "My report? But, sir, didn't you hear me? Emmett Brader—"

"Yes, goddammit, I heard you! Now give me your report!"

The corporal stammered out what information he'd been able to obtain from one of the Rebel scouts they'd captured. Devon rose, her face etched with sorrow as she slipped quietly from the room.

Cole remained in the general's office, assisting as Brader and his staff fired off cables and sent out reports detailing Stonewall Jackson's probable troop strengths, weaponry, even the route he would most likely be taking. Through it all, General Brader operated with cool military efficiency that left his aides, and even Cole, stunned. It wasn't until two hours had passed and he'd done everything he could to get the word out that Brader finally dismissed them.

Cole left with the others, then realized that the general had forgotten to give him the reports he wanted taken to Washington. He went back to the general's study, tapped softly on the door, and edged it open. He took two steps inside, then froze. General Brader sat hunched over his desk, his head cradled in his arms, his massive shoulders racked with great, silent, shuddering sobs.

Cole backed out of the room and closed the door softly behind him.

Chapter 11

~~~⌒⌒~~~

Devon glanced at Cole, who rode on horseback next to her as they traveled north on their way to Washington. Though he was physically near, in every other sense he was miles away. He wore his hat pulled down low over his brow, shielding himself not only from the sun but, she suspected, from her gaze as well. His rugged features were completely shadowed, giving her absolutely no insight into what he was thinking or feeling.

She doubted if they'd said more than a dozen words to each other since leaving General Brader that morning. With each passing moment, she could feel Cole withdraw a little further away from her. Somehow the fact that they couldn't share their sadness over Emmett's death only made it worse.

They traveled as they had before, staying off the main trails, moving along back roads that carried them past small farms, weaving through dense thickets of woods and into broad open fields. They rode until dusk, stopping only when the horses were too weary to continue. Cole helped her down from her mount, releasing her as soon as her feet touched the ground. He wasn't cold, but there was no gentleness in his touch either. The absence of any emotion in his touch hurt almost as much as the silence.

She watched him without comment as he went about making camp. When he finished tending the horses and spreading out blankets for them to sleep on, he straightened and looked at her. "Are you hungry?" he asked.

Devon was about to shake her head no, then thought better of it. Eating would give them something to do, a routine that might make things more normal between them. "I suppose so," she answered, mustering up what little enthusiasm she could.

He nodded and removed their provisions from within his saddlebags and passed the food to her. Devon took a couple bites of the meal before her appetite deserted her completely. The meat—she guessed it was rabbit—tasted hot and greasy, the cornmeal biscuits coarse and dry. She set the food aside, noticing that after a couple of bites Cole did the same.

Devon studied him from beneath her lashes, watching the moonlight dance across his rugged features. Dark shadows hung beneath his tawny eyes; his shoulders were stiff with tension. She doubted if he'd slept at all last night. After leaving General Brader's office, she'd returned to see to the wounded, then, hours later, curled up in a deep chair in a back parlor. She'd awakened at some point in the night to find Cole standing in the doorway, watching her sleep. He'd said nothing, simply moved toward her, tucked a blanket around her, then left as wordlessly as he'd come. She would have dismissed the whole incident as a dream had she not awakened the next morning to find the blanket still wrapped around her and her tapestry bag at her feet. Given the late hour, apparently he'd gone back to the boardinghouse to collect their belongings by himself, rather than disturb her sleep.

"We'll be in Washington by tomorrow night," he said, breaking the thick silence that hung between them.

Devon nodded, ignoring the ache that exploded inside her as his words confirmed what she'd been fearing all along.

"I wanted to discuss this with you last night," he said, "but—"

"Yes, I know. Emmett," she said, cutting him off. She didn't need to hear any more. Perhaps he would say he believed her story, perhaps he wouldn't. The bottom line was that he was just obeying orders, the matter was out of his hands. She'd had a trial and been found guilty, and that was the end of it. He might regret what he had to do, but that wouldn't change anything. He couldn't or wouldn't help her. She might even be able to bear it, as long as she didn't have to hear him say the words.

"I have friends in Washington that you can stay with," he continued. "It may just be a matter of weeks, it may be longer—"

Devon stared at him blankly. "What are you talking about? I thought you were taking me to Old Capitol."

"No," he said firmly.

"But what about your orders?"

"The hell with my orders."

Devon studied him, suddenly apprehensive. He was acting like a man who'd made his mind up about something and then put the matter behind him. Unfortunately she couldn't help but feel that the matter he'd put aside was her. "If you're not taking me to Old Capitol," she said, striving to keep her tone level, "then what exactly do you have in mind?"

"Like I said, I have friends you can stay with. For as long as it takes me to capture Sharpe. It may be weeks, it may be months, but I will stop him. And you'll be safe there in the meantime. When I come back, we'll have the proof we need that you weren't involved in the murder."

"I see," she said slowly. "And after that, once we have the proof we need?"

Cole hesitated, then forged ahead with grim determination, "After that, you won't have this hanging over your head. You can start over, Devon, have the life you wanted. Washington is still a lively city, despite the war. There are dances and parties nearly every night. I can introduce you to the best of society, find you a place to stay, give you enough money so you don't lack for anything. You'll be free to do what you came here to do—find a husband and settle down,'' he finished flatly.

Devon took a deep breath, struggling to hide her despair. He was leaving her. Honorably, of course, but he was leaving her just the same. ''That's very generous of you,'' she managed.

Cole nodded curtly, looking as though he was deriving as little enjoyment from the conversation as she was. ''You'll be safe in Washington, but I can't be there. I have to stop Sharpe, and I may not come back. Do you understand that?''

Devon ignored the lump that gathered in her throat at the thought of anything happening to him and struggled instead to stay focused on his words. ''Because . . . because of what he did to your ship?''

''No.'' He tugged his hand through his hair, his expression strained. ''Not because of what he did to my crew, or even because of what he did to you. It's more than that, Devon. I can't afford the luxury of revenge any longer. Not when hundreds of boys like Emmett are dying every day. And as long as Sharpe keeps breaking through the blockade with ships loaded with guns and munitions, more will continue to die.''

She nodded, considering his words. ''Then take me with you. Let me help you find him. I have connections that you don't, ways of getting information—''

''No, it's too dangerous. You should never have been involved in this in the first place.''

Devon studied him, seeing the futility of trying to argue. Clearly Cole had already made up his mind.

Tomorrow it would all be over, but she still had tonight. "I suppose it's all settled then," she said.

"Good."

"There's just one last item to attend to." She reached into the pocket of her skirt and retrieved the gold watch she'd stolen from him on the first day they'd met. "I believe this belongs to you. I should have returned it days ago."

Cole didn't move. He stared at the watch, then, with a reluctance that confused her, stretched his arm forward and allowed her to drop it into his palm.

Devon frowned at his reaction, thinking of the inscription she'd seen on the inside. *To Cole, With Love, Sarah.* She'd wondered about it at first, then hadn't given it any further thought. Now she had to know. "Is Sarah your wife?" she said, ashamed of herself for asking, hoping he couldn't hear the trembling note in her voice as she did.

"I don't have a wife, Devon."

She nodded, then lowered her gaze in defeat. "I see."

"Sarah is my sister-in-law."

His answer caught her off-guard. There was something in his tone, but she couldn't quite grasp what it was. She felt as though she were skirting along a cliff in darkness, and one wrong step would plunge her into an abyss. But the other side held the promise of light and understanding, if she could just find her way. "It's a lovely gift," she said cautiously. "You must be very close to her."

Cole's hand tightened around the watch and it disappeared within his big palm. "We were. But that was before . . ." He hesitated, his expression grim. "Before the war." He tucked the watch, not within his shirt pocket, but deep in his saddlebags. As if he wanted it far away. "We'll need to get an early start in the morning if we want to make it to Washington by nightfall."

Devon had come too far to retreat now. "Tell me about the battle," she said quietly. "The one you had with Sharpe." When he didn't reply, she forced herself to continue. "In your dream, you call out Gideon's name, and you can't move. Why can't you move?"

A soft breeze stirred the air, sending flickering moonlight shadows across his face. Devon held her breath, sensing that Cole needed to talk about it as much as she needed to hear, but ultimately, the choice was his. After a long pause, he finally answered. "Gideon was my nephew. Sarah and Richard's only child."

"Richard is your brother?"

"Yes."

"And Gideon was killed in the battle with Sharpe," she said softly, knowing that it was true.

A look of harsh regret crossed Cole's features. "He wouldn't have been, if only I'd been tougher, stricter. If only I hadn't encouraged him."

"What did you encourage him to do?"

"Everything," he answered in disgust. "Richard and my father are so alike, so stiff and proper, but Gideon was always more like me. He followed me around, did everything I did. We even looked alike. He had that same restless, wild streak, and I did nothing but encourage it."

Cole's love for the boy was clear in his voice. Devon studied him, so tall and strong and certain, understanding what a dashing figure he would make for a young boy like Gideon to idolize.

"Whenever I returned from a voyage," he continued, "I filled his head with romantic tales of life at sea. So naturally, once Gideon turned eighteen, he wanted to sign up with my crew. Richard and Sarah insisted on sending him to the university, but I convinced them to give Gideon just one year of freedom first. I promised them I would look after him."

"So he joined your crew," Devon prompted into the long silence that followed.

Cole shook his head, a dark scowl on his face. "Jesus, that was so idiotic. The middle of a damned war, and I encourage the boy with tales of the sea." He lifted his gaze to hers, as though searching for absolution. "I wanted Gideon to know that there was more to life than the strict confines of society. And at that point, nothing had happened. I'd chased down a few runners, fired a few shots, but that was it. The whole thing seemed more a sport, I didn't think there was anything I couldn't handle."

A chill ran through Devon. "And then you went after Sharpe."

"Yes." His eyes were no longer on her, but far away. "I spotted a runner heading out to sea—it was Sharpe. His ship looked damaged, an easy catch. I ordered my men to their stations and went after him. We followed the runner out a bit, then drew close and fired a warning shot. Sharpe turned and fired back, joined by two other ships bearing down on us. I'd led my crew right into a trap. I should have seen it, I should have known it was too easy, but I didn't . . ."

"You couldn't know . . ." she offered, not knowing what else to say.

"The battle exploded. We were outgunned, outmanned, outmaneuvered. Shells started exploding all around us, tearing up the hull, setting the sails aflame. I had a good crew, Devon, good men. But there was so much chaos, so much smoke and fire and screaming. Sharpe gave us no time to surrender, no time to do anything. Within minutes, the decks were so slick I thought we were taking on water."

Devon summoned her voice to ask, "Were you?"

He shook his head. "The deck was running with the blood of the wounded. We couldn't stop to take them below . . ." His voice faded away. He stared at her for a moment, then forced himself to continue. "A cannon broke loose, and I heard it rumbling behind me, but by the time I turned it was too late. I was pinned between the gun and deck rail and I couldn't move. That was when I saw Gideon."

Cole paused, the pain in his eyes so intense, Devon could hardly bear it. "He hadn't listened to me," he continued. "He hadn't gone below, like I'd ordered him. Instead he'd stayed on deck and was working with the forward gun crew. I screamed at him to go below, to get down, out of the way, but he wouldn't listen. He wouldn't listen. After all those years that I'd encouraged him to be wild, reckless, to disobey, it had never occurred that he wouldn't listen to *me*."

"Cole . . ."

"I couldn't move, I couldn't get to him. God, if only I could have moved . . . I heard a shell shrieking toward them, but there was nothing I could do. The shot exploded, killing all of them instantly. Except Gideon. Gideon didn't die right away. The impact blew his arms off at the shoulders, knocked him flat."

Devon closed her eyes, feeling as though all the air had just been knocked from her chest. She couldn't breathe, couldn't speak. Cole continued as if he'd forgotten she was there, talking in a voice that had gone absolutely flat, toneless.

"Gideon tried to get up, but he couldn't. He kept slipping in all the blood. He kept slipping and falling. I don't know if he knew . . . if he knew . . ." Cole stopped, his fists clenched at his sides, and drew in a ragged breath. "When he saw me, he started screaming, crying for me to help him, but I couldn't. I was pinned behind that damned gun. Sharpe kept firing and firing, he wouldn't let up. Finally a shell hit hard enough to jar the hull and shake the cannon free. But by then it was too late. Gideon bled to death in front of me, begging for my help."

Devon was trembling, aching inside. She'd wanted to know, and now she did. Now she knew why Cole had treated her with such burning contempt back at Fort Monroe. Now she understood his harsh words, his painful silences, and why the nightmares never went away. After what he'd been through, how much he must have hated her, thinking she was Jonas Sharpe's agent. And yet he'd risked his life to save hers. He'd actually listened to her, when no one else would. Despite everything, he was still trying to do what was right, what was honorable.

She leaned forward, willing to trade her soul at that moment for the words that would take his pain away. She laid her hand gently on his leg and said, "Cole, it wasn't your fault. Just like Emmett dying wasn't General Brader's fault. It's the war . . ." Her words dropped like stones, with no impact whatsoever. She should have known as much, she thought, and immediately changed her tack. "Tell me something about Gideon."

He turned toward her, his face still haunted with pain. "What do you want to know?"

"Anything. As long as it has nothing to do with the war or the battle. Tell me something that only you would know."

Cole shook his head, unable to think. He felt as though his skin had been peeled back, leaving every nerve raw and exposed. The shock of Emmett's death had brought back all the feelings he'd been trying so hard to bury. All the shame, all the guilt, all the sorrow and impotent fury . . . there was no place to put it, no way to control it. He couldn't keep shoving it down inside him, but letting it out, talking about it, hadn't solved anything either.

"Please, Cole," Devon said. "Tell me something about Gideon."

He knew what she was trying to do, but it wouldn't work. He couldn't let go of the anger and regret long enough to remember anything else. But because she looked so upset, so desperate to help, he struggled to find something to tell her. "He cheated at cards," he said at last, the thought striking him like a bolt from the blue sky.

She looked startled, then visible relief washed through her expressive eyes. "He cheated at cards?" she repeated.

Cole nodded, grasping the memory tightly in his mind, as though it might slip away. "He didn't call it cheating, of course. He referred to it as card tricks." He paused, shaking his head. "He would have given you and Uncle Monty a run for your money."

She smiled. "Tell me something else about him."

Cole thought again. Bits and pieces of memories washed over him, fragments of the past that were still painful to look at, but for the first time, it was a pain he could manage. "Gideon loved the sea," he said at last. "He and I were alike in that regard as well. From the first time I took him with me on one of my voyages, when he was still a boy. He loved everything about it: the smell of salt air, the rolling pitch of the deck, the foreign ports ..."

With her encouragement, Cole began to talk. Hesitant initially, then with greater ease. He regaled her with stories of the sea, the details of the trips he and Gideon had taken. When he finished, he saw that the stars had shifted overhead. He looked at her in astonishment, amazed at how long he'd spoken.

"Those are the things you have to remember, Cole," she said softly. "When you think of Gideon, remember why you loved him, and he'll always be with you. If you don't, you'll never be able to let the pain go, and you'll lose him forever."

He stared at her in sudden understanding. "Is that what you do, Devon?"

She nodded. "I collect memories."

As Cole considered her turbulent past, a feeling of aching tenderness exploded in his chest. "Will you share a few with me?"

Devon drew her legs up and wrapped her arms around them, resting her chin atop her knees. "I remember the time my father came home from one of his trips," she began, "and he brought Billy a pair of long pants as a gift. Billy was so proud of his grown-up pants. It was literally weeks before my mother and I could convince him to take them off long enough for us to wash them." She paused, smiling softly. "Are all boys so wild about their first pair of grown-up pants?"

"Absolutely," Cole averred. "Though I must confess that I didn't get my first pair of grown-up pants until I was nearly thirteen."

"Thirteen?!" she gasped, choking back a giggle.

"Go ahead, laugh," he said. "I've already spent three of the most wretched years of my life defending my honor in the schoolyard because I didn't have those blasted pants. And now I can see that I've completely discredited whatever dashing image you might have had of me."

"Completely," she agreed at once. Her eyes danced with merry amusement, two captivating dimples framed her mouth.

"If you're through laughing at my expense," he teased, "I'd like to hear something else from your collection."

She tilted her head to one side, thinking. When she spoke, her voice was rich, warmed by her memories. "I remember the spring my mother and I were planting flowers and we found a bird's nest with baby robins in it. I remember Uncle Monty sitting by my bed and reading me fairy tales one time when I was ill, even though I was far too old for them. I remember how delicious it tastes to catch the very first snowflake on your tongue in winter, and how lovely the sun feels in the spring.''

He matched her sentimental smile. ''What else do you remember?''

Devon stared at him, then said with total solemnity, ''I'll remember you, Cole McRae.''

Cole's heart slammed against his chest. Their eyes locked as the quiet stillness that surrounded them seemed to pulse, as if the night itself had suddenly come to life. He moved toward her, closing what little space there was between them as he reached out and lightly brushed her cheek. Pain and regret knifed through him. ''It would be better if you didn't.''

Devon ignored that. ''Will you remember me?''

He stared at her for a never-ending second. ''Always,'' he whispered roughly.

She lifted her hand, catching his fingers in her own. ''Are we going to make love, Cole?''

He drew in a sharp breath, his entire frame suddenly racked with tension. She asked the question without any artifice or pretension, but merely the forthright candor and quiet courage that he'd come to expect from her. It was a simple acknowledgment of what they both knew: they'd been drifting toward this moment for days, carried toward each other as irreversibly as a river empties into the sea.

But it was wrong, and Cole knew it. Devon deserved a hell of a lot more than what he had to give her. She deserved a home, a family, security—he couldn't promise her any of that. Not now. All he would be doing was taking from her. Taking her warmth, her strength, her passion, and her virginity. Giving her nothing in return.

But even as he played out the argument in his mind, the delicate scent of her skin drifted toward him, like a gentle, moonlit caress. Her eyes glowed as though lit by an inner fire. Her lips were slightly parted, ready for his kiss. She waited in silence, watching him, her expression one of tender vulnerability.

Devon might be savvy with regard to cons and crimes, but she was absolutely sheltered when it came to experience with men. He'd felt that in her kiss, in her passionate, unrestrained embrace. She was too trusting, too giving. Naive and untutored in the ways of making love. As a rule, he preferred sophisticated women who understood the rules of the game, who expected no emotional attachment. Women who knew the difference between love and lust. Until now, that had always suited him. But never before had he experienced the driving, aching need that Devon Blake aroused in him.

In that instant, Cole knew exactly what he should do: ride until he found an icy creek and plunge himself in headfirst, staying there all night if need be, until he cooled his ardor and came to his senses. Explain to her—gently but firmly—all the reasons why they shouldn't become lovers. Take her to Washington and find her a husband who could give her everything she'd ever dreamed of. But he wasn't going to do that. Despite the fact that he knew better, that his conscience was screaming at him to stop, not to take advantage of her warmth and innocence, he wasn't going to do that.

Instead, bastard that he was, he was going to seduce her.

Cole moved ever so gently, easing her down on their blanket as he stretched out next to her. He propped himself up on one elbow, studying her face. Brushing a strand of dark hair from her eyes, he quietly asked, "What do you know of making love?"

Not knowing how to interpret his question, Devon could only respond with the truth. "Not much," she admitted. "But I do know how it's done."

Cole quirked a brow. "Do you?"

She nodded as a delicate pink tint infused her cheeks.

"Sort of a cross between kissing and dancing. Only messier, and much more embarrassing."

A lazy grin spread across Cole's face. "Much more enjoyable," he amended softly, leaning down to brush a light kiss at the base of her throat. "Much more satisfying." His kisses moved over her collarbone, sending a shiver racing down her spine. "Much more intense." He wrapped his arm beneath her waist and pulled her tightly to him, capturing her mouth with his.

Stormy desire shot through her as his kiss robbed her of all breath and thought. Devon responded purely on instinct, her body locked beneath his as they established a rhythm that mimicked the heat and passion of their kiss. Cole traced his hands over her body, exploring her every curve, as a hot, quivering yearning spread through her limbs. She arched her hips and pressed herself tightly against him, aching for more.

Cole pulled back, his eyes dark with passion. "Let me see you, Devon," he murmured huskily, his breath softly fanning her neck. She leveraged herself up to a sitting position and with trembling hands slowly released the buttons of her gown. He reached up to help her, rolling it off her shoulders and over her hips until it lay wadded beside them like a limp rag. Her boots came next, leaving her in her stockings and undergarments. She reached for the delicate blue ribbons that held her chemise in place.

His hands came up immediately, covering hers. As his eyes met hers, she saw a question in their depths, and knew he was asking her to let him do it. She brought down her hands in silent answer. But instead of reaching for her chemise, he first removed the pins that held up her hair, letting it cascade down her back and over her shoulders. He brushed the long, dark, silky strands away from her face, touching her with an almost reverent tenderness.

After a moment, his hands returned to her chemise.

Nervous tension flooded through her, making her body tremble once again in anticipation of his touch. With infinite care, he undid each ribbon, then parted the material and let it fall away. She heard his subtle intake of breath, then he reached for her, gently caressing her skin, brushing her body with soft kisses as he slowly worked her clothing free. Her undergarments and stockings soon joined her gown, tossed carelessly in a pile near their feet. Cole pulled back and knelt above her, absolutely still as his burning, tawny-gold gaze moved silently over her delicate form.

Insecurities Devon never knew she had suddenly rose to greet her. Her small size had always been an advantage before, for it made her look younger when she and Uncle Monty were working a con. But she wondered now if Cole like the way she looked. Or if he preferred women with lusher hips and fuller breasts. When he didn't say anything, only continued to stare at her, she reached for her dress, anxious to cover herself.

"Please, Devon," Cole whispered hoarsely, stopping her. "You're so beautiful, I just need to look at you for a moment. Is that all right?"

The tension slowly drained out of her. "I'm not too—"

"You're perfect," he answered firmly.

Thrilled and embarrassed by the compliment, she reached for him, running her hands beneath his shirt. "Now can I see you?" It took far less time to remove his clothing than hers. Within mere seconds, Cole had torn off his shirt and pants and flung away his boots. He knelt above her in naked, golden, all-male splendor, giving her a full and complete view of what she'd only seen hints of before. Every inch of his body was corded, sinewy muscle, raw masculine beauty. Her gaze traveled down to the most intimate part of him, then quickly moved away as courage deserted her.

Devon wasn't comfortable in unfamiliar situations,

and this was utterly foreign. Cole was so big, so strong, such a contrast to herself in so many ways. Years of instinct to protect herself, to shield herself from the unknown, suddenly took root. He must have seen it in her eyes, for he went completely still, something that looked akin to pain flashing across his face. "Devon, if you've changed your mind—"

"No," she said immediately, thinking how green she must look to him, how naive and unsophisticated. She reached out for him, then hesitated, suddenly lost. She lifted her gaze to his, searching his eyes. "Is it all right if I touch you?"

"Yes," he said, his breath coming out in a rush. Devon realized then how still he was holding himself, how badly he wanted her to do just that. She placed her hands on his shoulders and felt his muscles leap beneath her palms in response. His reaction not only amazed her but gave her a quiet sense of power, knowing that her touch could affect him the way his affected her. She moved slowly, taking her time in exploring his rugged male physique. Familiarizing herself with the hot, rough velvet feel of his skin and the clean, masculine scent of his body. She traced the broad expanse of his chest, weaving her fingers through the coarse, spongy blond hair she found there, then let her palms drift downward, over the flat, rippled muscles that lined his stomach. She drew her hands over his lean hips, the firm curve of his buttocks, and his rock-solid thighs, never losing contact with his skin, turning her aimless exploration of his body into one long, lingering caress.

Cole remained rigidly still, letting her explore his body, sensing instinctively that this was what she needed to do. Her confidence slowly returned. Touching him gave Devon the time she needed to accept and adjust to the fact that this was still Cole, the Cole she'd always felt so safe with, and the simple fact that they were naked wouldn't change that. As her fear lessened, her curiosity returned. She glanced down at him and asked, "Can I touch you . . . there?"

A muscle leaped in his jaw as he nodded tightly.

Her hand moved down, and her fingers lightly traced his erection. The skin felt softer than the rest of him, but every bit as hard and rigid. As she grasped him delicately in her hand, she saw a shudder run through him. "Devon, please—" he rasped out.

She looked up at him, then jerked her hand back, alarmed by the expression of pure agony on his face. "Did I break it?"

He made a sound that was part laughter, part groan. "No, you didn't . . . I love the way you touch me. But I need time, don't want to rush . . ." Realizing he was stammering, he wrapped his arm around her waist and lowered her to the blanket. "Let me love you, Devon."

His words found their way straight to her heart, breaking through all her defenses, crashing through the barriers she'd hidden behind for so long. Leaving her more open, more vulnerable than she'd ever been in her life.

Cole pulled her instantly back into his embrace. His hands moved wildly over her body, as if desperate to make up for the time when he hadn't allowed himself to touch her. He traced the rounded curve of her buttocks, the silky smoothness of her thighs, the gentle curve of her hips, and the tiny span of her waist. He cupped her breasts, brushing his palms over her nipples in a light, teasing touch until they grew hard and firm beneath his hand. Devon arched her back, her breasts straining against his palms as the motion grew rougher, faster. He gently squeezed her nipples between his fingers, then leaned forward, bringing a firm, rosy peak into his mouth.

Shock and delight screamed through her as Cole shifted from one breast to the other, giving each the same loving attention. Unlike the rough, gentle touch of his hands, his mouth felt slick and hot as he licked and teased and suckled. Then, when the pleasure became so great that Devon thought she couldn't stand it anymore, he moved lower, trailing hot, lavish kisses over her ribs, across her stomach and the tops of her thighs. He covered her body with his mouth, claiming her with a savage hunger that found every sensitive inch of her.

She echoed his movements, letting him lead, worshipping his body as he was hers, loving him with her mouth, her tongue, her hands, lost in the sensations she was giving and being given. It was all so new, so amazing, and yet so incredibly right. Skin on skin, male to female, touching, tasting, feeling. Primal passion and hot sensuality . . . Cole's hand drifted between her legs, his fingers gently probing the warm wetness he found there.

Devon tensed. Heat coiled tightly in her belly and then spread, making her limbs quiver, shaken by a desperate need she could feel but not identify. As Cole captured her mouth with his, she locked her arms around his neck, returning his kiss with a fervent, wanton longing. Her body molded itself to his, as if begging for more. Hunger she barely recognized rose within her once again, laced now with stunning urgency and sweet, possessive fire.

Cole drew back and raised himself on his forearms above her, the tip of his erection poised at her entrance. His eyes locked on hers, he slowly inched his way into the warm, wet place deep inside her. Devon's eyes grew wide with wonder as she felt her body stretch to accommodate him. Then, as quickly as she adjusted to the incredible sensation of having him inside her, he pulled back, leaving her achingly empty. "Devon, I'm sorry," he said hoarsely, his breath fanning her neck. Before she could figure out why he was apologizing, or why he'd stopped, he lifted his lean hips and pushed forward, filling her completely.

A sharp, stinging sensation tore through her. Devon froze, shocked by the intrusion of pain, realizing belatedly why Cole had stopped. Even now, he was poised above her, not moving, as if afraid he would hurt her again, the strain of holding back etched on his features. Tenderness poured through her, along with the driving desire to give him everything he was giving her. As the pain ebbed away, she reached up, running her hands over his shoulders and down his arms. "Cole," she whispered. "Love me."

An expression she'd never seen before crossed his face. Something darker than passion, deeper than lust. He stared down at her, his eyes burning with golden fire. He leaned down, his lips slanting over hers in a kiss of such heat and passion, such silent eloquence of need, it seemed to scorch her very soul.

Then he began to move. Slowly at first, moving almost teasingly within her, until they found the ancient rhythm that brought them together as one. Silent wonder exploded within Devon as she arched her hips to meet his. She felt her body straining, aching for something she couldn't define. Each long, loving stroke carried her closer, nearer to what she needed.

She dug her fingers into Cole's shoulders and he moved faster, deeper, responding to her silent plea. At last he sent her over the precipice she'd been struggling to reach. Every nerve in her body seemed to take flight, exploding in a wonderful, shattering bliss. Pleasure shot up her spine and raced down her legs. She called out Cole's name in a low, throaty groan she barely recognized as her own. The moment she did, he tightened his arms around her, then drove deep inside her, a shudder running through his large frame as he poured himself into her, at last finding his own release.

Cole abruptly collapsed on top of her, then rolled

over, taking Devon with him. She lay splayed across his chest, still intimately joined. His heart was pounding in rapid tempo beneath her ear, his breath coming in deep gulps. He ran his hands gently over her back, as if memorizing the feel of her soft curves. After a few minutes, he asked softly, "Did I hurt you, Devon?"

"No," she whispered, her throat aching at the concern she saw in his eyes. In fact, just the opposite was true, she thought, filled with bittersweet regret. He'd given her more than she ever could have imagined. While she lay in his arms like this, she felt so safe, so protected, so . . . loved. There was no other word for it. Loved. As if every silent wish she'd ever wished had momentarily come true. Devon was overwhelmed by the emotions bubbling to the surface, like a pot that had been left too long to boil. She felt tears sting her eyes and quickly lowered her head before he could see them.

She was too late. She felt Cole tense beneath her, then he gently tipped her chin up. His face went dark with regret at the sight of the wet tears streaming down her cheeks. "I did hurt you—"

"No." She shook her head, fighting to control her emotions, trying to find the words to express herself. "I wasn't prepared, I didn't know . . . I didn't think you would touch me like that."

Panic and self-loathing filled Cole's eyes. "Devon, I'm sorry, I thought you said you knew how it was done. I shouldn't have—"

"No, not the way you touched my body."

He studied her, clearly upset and thoroughly confused. "Then what—"

"The way you touched my heart."

Cole stared at her, completely stunned. Finally he seemed recovered enough to speak. "Devon," he began softly, reaching for her.

"Please, Cole," she said, smiling absurdly through

her tears. She knew she was making a mess of things, but she didn't care. "Can we make love again?"

Devon shifted onto her side, watching Cole as he slept. They'd made love a second time, with exquisite tenderness, slowly and gently, with less of the explosive passion of the first time. Much to her relief, she'd been able to keep her emotions under control. She wondered if it was simply the pure physical release that had shaken her so, but discarded the notion as quickly as it had occurred.

What had shattered her composure was an emotion that felt incredibly like love, bursting open within her. She hadn't wanted it, hadn't expected it, and certainly hadn't been prepared for it. She had no place for that emotion in her life. And neither did Cole—at least not as far as she was concerned.

Devon slipped out from beneath his arm, which was flung casually over her waist. She stood and padded softly around their camp, allowing the light of the moon to guide her as she collected bits and pieces of her scattered clothing. Her body, sore from making love, ached in unfamiliar places as she dressed. She ignored the discomfort and saw to her horse, using her already strained muscles to lift and secure the saddle.

That task quietly finished, she walked back to camp, staring at Cole where he lay sleeping. His breath came deep and regular, telling her he hadn't been disturbed by her motions. She knew he hadn't slept at all the night before, and suspected he'd slept very little at the boardinghouse. No wonder he was so exhausted. He'd probably passed those nights trying to decide what was the right and honorable thing to do about her.

The only trouble was, Devon couldn't abide by his decision. If Cole didn't deliver her to Old Capitol, he would likely face court-martial, and that was a risk she couldn't let him take. Nor would she let him become a laughingstock by trying to pass her off as a lady among his friends. No matter what Cole said, Devon knew better. For a few days, they might believe it, but with time her past would come back to haunt her. It always did.

She wouldn't burden Cole with that. She owed him at least that much. If she escaped, he might face a slight reprimand, but that would be it. Perhaps he'd be angry at first to discover that she'd left, but in time he would be thankful. It relieved him of any obligation he might feel toward her. He could dismiss her completely and get back to his own life, back to the world where he belonged. A world of which she would never have any part.

She glanced up at the night sky and saw that she had a few hours left until dawn. Devon stared at Cole for one last time, committing every line and detail of his rugged face and glorious body to her memory. She walked to where she'd left her horse and mounted quietly. Her final words were a whisper, barely audible above the wind. ''Good-bye, Cole McRae.''

Chapter 12

~~~CCCC~~~

The Pig's Head Inn was no different than any of the other dozen or so waterfront taverns Cole had visited since reaching St. George two days ago—dirty, crowded, teeming with people from all walks of life. Rebel sailors on shore leave mingled with blockade runners, businessmen, prostitutes, and Yankee spies. They all merged together in the giddy atmosphere created by tremendous risk and sudden riches. This small Bermuda tavern did have one particular distinction, however: it was Cole's last chance to find Devon.

He'd already scoured every other waterfront dive, hotel, and restaurant on the island, coming up without a trace of her, which only served to intensify his nagging fear that perhaps he'd been wrong in coming to Bermuda. Perhaps Devon had gone to Nassau in the Bahamas instead, another notorious port for blockade runners. There, as here, she'd have her choice of dozens of wide-bellied cargo ships to take her back to England, along with the cotton they'd smuggled out of the South.

She'd left no trail, disappearing from his life with the same explosive intensity with which she'd entered. Cole remembered with grim clarity the morning he'd awakened back in Virginia when the emptiness beside him told him she was gone. Christ, did she still believe that he was taking her to Old Capitol? After the night they'd spent together, how was it possible for her not to trust him?

The questions were eating him up inside. It was the middle of the damned war, for God's sake. He didn't have time to chase after her. But his only other alternative, to forget her and go about his business, was unthinkable. Not until he knew why she'd left him. Not until he knew she was safe.

Not until he got her back.

It had taken him a week to return to Fort Monroe. There he had spent an additional two weeks overseeing the completion of repairs to his ship. That totaled three weeks: more than enough time for Devon to have slipped past him, for her to be well on her way to England by now. He'd spent his nights prowling the docks, interrogating any sailor he could find for news of runners that had slipped through the blockade. Hoping for word from someone who might have seen Devon. In the end, he'd found nothing. Nothing but blank stares and negative responses.

When Cole left Fort Monroe, Admiral Billings had given him one month's leave to pursue Jonas Sharpe. After that, he was required to return to blockade duty. One month. That was all the time he had.

Cole pushed open the doors to the Pig's Head Inn and made his way through the tavern. He found a table near the back, kicked out a chair, and sat down. Despite the fact that it was midday, the bar was teeming with drunken revelers. Thick plantation shutters at the doors and windows filtered the light and air, allowing entrance to the salty sea breezes that blew from the harbor, but it wasn't enough. The air stank of the hot press of bodies and stale alcohol. A man who looked to be the owner approached his table. He wore a coarse apron blotched with stains, no shirt beneath, his skin glistening with sweat. He flicked a greasy rag across the table and asked Cole for his order.

"I'm looking for a woman."

The man glanced up, studied Cole for a minute, then

nodded. He motioned across the room to a dusky-skinned beauty whose dress was split open nearly to her waist. "Her name's Bettina," he said in a bored voice. "You can have her for an hour. Pay me when you're finished."

Cole shook his head. "Not her."

"You prefer yellow hair?"

"The woman I'm looking for is English, small, with dark hair and green eyes."

The man shook his head. "No," he said, flicking his rag once again over the table. "I have thirsty customers to attend. Do you drink or not?"

Something in his voice, or perhaps the furtive glance of his eyes, gave him away. Cole felt a tightening deep within him. "Where is she?"

The owner studied him once again, then finally asked, "What do you want with her?"

Cole didn't answer, but simply opened his billfold, removed a crisp hundred-dollar bill, and set it on the table before him. "Where?" he said, his tone cold and flat.

The man stared at the money, his eyes dark with greed, but shook his head. "She makes more for me than that. More than even Bettina makes."

Cold fury shot through Cole. "The woman I'm looking for isn't a whore."

"No," the owner quickly agreed. "No, not a whore. She ... brings in customers. Fancy customers." It took Cole a minute to follow the man's meaning, then understanding slowly dawned. Not bad. Devon lured the marks in, coaxed them into getting drunk and running up lavish tabs, then freed them of their watches, wallets, and any other sparkling fob they might possess. The owner not only got the additional business, but presumably a hefty share of Devon's take as well. He coolly eyed the owner, testing his theory aloud.

The man promptly began to look uncomfortable. "I run a proper establishment—"

"Yes, I'm sure," Cole said in disgust. He set another hundred-dollar bill on top of the first. "Consider that a reward for your honesty and integrity. Now tell me where I can find her."

"I don't want any trouble—"

"Where?"

The owner reached out, grabbed the money, and shoved it deep within his pocket. "Wait here. She'll be back in an hour, maybe two."

Cole settled in his chair, refusing to let himself build any false hopes. The man could be lying, or he could simply be wrong. Or perhaps there was another woman who fit Devon's description. He ordered a glass of whiskey and nursed it as he waited, watching the crowd. The war had temporarily lifted all societal boundaries, he noted. Every section of society, both men and women, seemed duly represented. Rich patrons from the pompous enclave of Rose Hill mingled with lowly wharf rats. All were anxious to partake in the excitement that surrounded them, reeling with the thrill of misbehaving, intoxicated by the jubilant pandemonium that had overtaken the tiny island.

He watched as another high-society group entered the door, then he turned away, only to snap his head back to the scene; his gaze focused on the woman in their party. His breath caught in his throat as he stared.

Devon.

He almost didn't recognize her.

She wore an emerald-green silk gown edged in black lace and carried a matching parasol. Her hair was coiffed in an elegant chignon. She looked poised, polished, and absolutely, stunningly beautiful. Another fact struck him at the same time: she was standing altogether too close to the two men who escorted her into the tavern.

He quickly sized them up. Judging by their meek builds and fancy frock coats, she'd found a couple of dandies out slumming. Cole nodded in approval; she chose her marks well. He felt his heart constrict as he watched her walk gracefully across the room. He didn't move or make a sound, but simply watched as they settled into a table. For the first time since she'd left him back in Virginia, he felt as though he could breathe again.

After a minute, he stood and made his way through the crowded bar toward them. He didn't take his gaze off her, half-afraid that if he blinked she would disappear again. She was smiling and laughing, but he knew it was all a performance. None of it reached her eyes. He stopped just short of their table, listening as one of the men recommended the house brandy. "Actually," Cole said, his eyes focused entirely on Devon, "brandy doesn't agree with the lady."

He watched her freeze, then she slowly lifted her gaze to his. A myriad of emotions flashed across her face, all passing too quickly for him to read. Her mouth dropped open, but it was a moment before any sound followed. When she finally spoke, it seemed one word was all she could manage. "Cole."

He politely inclined his head. "You remember my name. I'm flattered."

"You—you thought I would forget?"

"In light of the other things you forgot, such as the proper way to say good-bye, yes, it occurred to me that you might."

The two men with whom Devon had entered watched the exchange in stupefied silence. Finally one of them rose nervously to his feet and cleared his throat. "Pardon me, sir, but this is a private—"

"You'll excuse us, then," Cole said firmly, reaching for Devon. "The lady and I have unfinished business to attend to."

The dandy sputtered in outrage, but after sizing up Cole's powerful build and angry demeanor, he wisely made no move to stop him as Cole escorted Devon back to his table. They sat opposite each other in silence, as if taking each other's measure once again. Cole still hadn't adjusted himself to this new side of her. In the dim light of the tavern, her eyes were no longer a soft green, but a deep, glittering emerald. Her skin glowed—delicate ivory with hints of rose. Every strand of her dark, silky hair was neatly coiffed. She'd looked pretty in her sky-blue calico, but nothing had prepared him for this.

This was a Devon he'd never seen before—certainly not the Devon he thought he'd find. In his mind, he'd pictured her wild and reckless, tossing his threats and insults back in his face. He remembered the way she looked the morning when they broke camp, all soft-eyed and sleepy, her hair mussed and adorable. And most of all, he remembered the way she'd looked when they'd made love, her body bathed in moonlight, her skin soft as satin to his touch. Now she looked so prim and proper, so untouchable. He frowned. "You're wearing one of those corset things, aren't you?"

Her eyes went wide. "*That's* what you have to say to me?"

No. As a matter of fact, Cole didn't give a damn about what she was wearing. He had rehearsed dozens of stinging lectures and gentle discussions in his mind, but now that she was here, he couldn't remember a word of any of them. Instead all he could focus on was the one question that had been burning through his soul for the past three weeks. "Why did you leave me, Devon?"

She stared at him silently for a moment, then sighed. "You're angry, aren't you?"

"How the hell did you think I would feel? To wake

up and find you'd snuck off like a th—'' he stopped abruptly, cursing himself.

"Go ahead," she said quietly. "Say it. Like a thief in the night."

"Dammit, Devon, that's not what I meant."

She shrugged. "Why not? It's the truth, isn't it?"

"It doesn't have to be."

She gave a bitter laugh. "Is that why you're here? You want to reform me, to lead me down the path of righteousness? Well, forget it. I tried that and nearly spent the rest of my life locked away in prison." She rose to her feet. "I'm not your responsibility anymore, McRae. You can leave with a clear conscience."

"Devon, wait." He stood and grabbed her arm, easing her back into her chair as he frantically searched for the words he needed to say. "That's not why I'm here."

"You shouldn't have come. Can't you see that I was doing you a favor—"

"You call running out on me in the dead of the night a favor?"

Devon drew in her breath as pain flashed through her eyes. "It wouldn't work, Cole. I thought I could pretend to be something I'm not, but I can't. It would have only made matters worse for both of us if you'd brought me to Washington and tried to pass me off as a lady to your friends—"

Shock tore through him. "Did you think I actually intended to go through with that?" He realized she didn't know him at all if she still believed, after the night they'd spent together, that he could ever willingly give her to another man.

"That's what you said you were going to do."

"Obviously I changed my mind."

"I see." A dark shadow passed across her face. "So you were taking me to prison after all. That's why you're here now."

"Prison?!" he exploded. "Good God, is that what you think of me?"

"I don't know what to think. I don't know what you want or why you're here, I only know that I'm going back to England."

Despite her cool demeanor, Cole saw that she was gripping the edge of the table hard enough to turn her knuckles white. This definitely wasn't going the way he had planned. He had decided weeks ago exactly what would happen once he found her: first a stinging lecture for leaving him like that, followed by her profuse apologies and promises never to do it again. Then, once that had all been settled, he'd looked forward to sweeping her into his arms and carrying her off to make love all night.

Instead they were sitting across from each other like adversaries, separated by the same barriers that had always kept them apart. Worse, they'd become intimate strangers. Too much had passed between them to go back, too little to go forward. He'd idiotically assumed that Devon would be as thrilled to see him as he was to see her. Now he couldn't think of a reason in the world why she should be. Not after the way he'd treated her. If he could just buy a little more time somehow, he'd find a way to convince her to trust him. All he needed was a little more time.

"We need to talk," he said. "Privately. My ship's in the harbor, we can go there."

"We have nothing more to say to one another."

He let out a breath of disgust as his gaze shot around the squalid room. "That has to be the most asinine thing you've ever said. Unless, of course, spending the rest of your days rotting away in this seedy tavern is exactly what you always wanted for yourself."

Devon tilted her chin. "Not that it's any of your business, McRae," she bit out, "but I happen to *like* it here. Not once have I been shot at, awakened at dawn and tossed on the back of a horse, pushed out of a speeding train, or rolled in slimy goose droppings. Why, compared to a week spent with you, this wretched tavern is the pinnacle of luxury.''

Cole regarded her steadily as silence stretched between them. He reached across the table, gently capturing her hand in his. ''Was it all that bad between us, Devon?''

Panic flashed through her eyes. She tugged at her hand, and he reluctantly released it. ''I'm leaving,'' she announced, her voice high and tight. ''I'm going back to England. I sent word to my uncle a while ago asking him to wire money to me here, in care of the hotel. I expect the funds should arrive any day.''

''Five minutes, Devon. That's all I ask.'' He had no idea what he was going to say to her once he got her aboard his ship, but the idea of locking her in his cabin until he figured it out held a certain appeal.

Her gaze narrowed, then she finally nodded. ''All right, I'll go. But just to talk, is that understood?''

Cole slowly let out his breath, aware only then that he'd been holding it. He reached for his wallet to pay for his drink, then frowned and felt in his other pocket. He searched his vest, realizing that not only was his wallet missing, he'd lost his gold watch as well. ''If you don't mind, Devon, I need to pay for the whiskey.''

''Go ahead.''

Cole held out his hand. ''Well?''

She arched a dark brow. ''Surely you don't expect me to pay for it?''

''No. I'd simply like you to return my billfold and pocket watch.''

Shock and anger flashed across her face, then she rose to her feet once again, her expression glacial. ''You know as well as I do that those items were returned to you before I left. If you've come all this way just to accuse me of stealing—''

"You mean you don't have them?"

"Certainly not."

"Well, I'll be damned," Cole muttered to himself, glancing around the crowded barroom.

Devon frowned, watching him. "Are you sure you had them?"

"I had them five minutes ago when we sat down."

"You mean to tell me someone lifted them while I was here?" She shook her head. "Impossible. No one's that good. No one except me and perhaps..." Her voice trailed away as her eyes fastened on a large man who stood with his back to them. A startled smile flashed across her face, then fell away as she looked back at Cole. "Let's go back to your ship," she said, rising to her feet so abruptly, she nearly tipped her chair.

He followed her gaze, noting that the man had turned and was looking at them as well. Cole quickly sized the stranger up. He was tall and big; what had once probably been muscle was now settled thickly across his midsection. He wore the loudest plaid suit Cole had ever seen and carried a black derby in his hand. He was almost entirely bald, but what he lacked on the top of his head he more than made up for with the luxurious growth of dark muttonchop whiskers that covered the lower half of his face. He set down his drink and began walking toward them.

"Please, let's go," she urged.

Cole studied her curiously. Whoever the man was, Devon seemed desperately eager that they not meet. Which, of course, only made him all the more determined that they should. He leaned back in his chair and gestured casually to his drink. "There's still the bill to be settled."

She opened her reticule, snatched up a coin, and slapped it on the table. "Now!" she hissed.

He picked up the coin and frowned. "That's hardly enough for a proper tip."

"Dammit, McRae!"

"Devon, my girl! I thought that was you!" The stranger boomed out from behind her.

With a look of weary resignation on her face, Devon turned, only to be immediately engulfed in the big man's embrace. When she pulled back, however, her smile was genuine, as was the affection that shone from her eyes and the warmth that softened her voice. "Hello, Uncle."

Uncle Monty. Of course. When he received Devon's telegram, the man must have decided to come in person, rather than simply wire her the funds she requested. Cole would have done the same damned thing. "Aren't you going to introduce us?" he drawled, coming to his feet.

"Well, er—" Devon stammered, her worried gaze shifting from Cole to her uncle.

"My good friend," the man boomed, not in the least put off by Devon's awkwardness. "Montgomery Persons at your service." He pumped Cole's hand, his face wreathed in a jovial smile. "You must be Boris—"

"No, Uncle Monty," Devon quickly intervened. "There were some, ah, difficulties. This is Captain Cole McRae."

"I see," Monty's smile faded for an instant, then it was back, bright as ever. "In that case, Captain, perhaps you'd be interested in hearing about an investment syndicate I'm putting together. Absolutely no risk, and I guarantee you'll triple your money within a fortnight—"

"Uncle Monty," she broke in again, "this may not be the best time."

"Of course it is, my girl. It's always a good time to learn how to make a fortune overnight, isn't that right, Captain?"

"Actually," Devon said as she stared up at Cole, her expression one of silent pleading, "the captain and I were just saying good-bye. Weren't we?"

Cole met her gaze, then slowly grinned. "Not even close."

She shot daggers at him with her eyes, then turned back to her uncle. "Why don't I meet you later, back at your hotel—"

"Devon, my girl—"

"Please, Uncle."

Monty stopped, looking from Cole to Devon. After a long, weighty pause, he said to her, "Maybe you'd like to tell me about those 'difficulties' you ran into."

"I will, but later—"

Monty shook his head. "There's no wedding ring on your finger, my girl. You're not settled down in a fine house with your banker husband in Virginia. Instead, I find you in a waterfront tavern with a stranger, and you can't quite seem to look your Uncle Monty in the eye." He reached out, lightly cupping Devon's chin as he tilted her gaze up to his. "Now."

Devon licked her lips, looking worried. "I don't want you to get upset. Remember what the doctor said."

"I never get upset."

Cole watched Devon roll her eyes. She took a deep breath, as if fortifying herself. "You see," she began hesitantly, "there was a slight misunderstanding at the docks . . . minor, really . . . hardly a problem at all . . ."

"Jonas Sharpe and his man Ogglesby framed Devon for murder," Cole interrupted curtly. "She was tried and convicted, sentenced to life imprisonment in Old Capitol Prison. I was charged with the duty of escorting her there."

Devon balled her fists on her hips, glaring furiously at him. "Oh, fine, McRae. You just couldn't let me tell it, could you? That is *exactly* why I didn't want the two of you to talk."

Cole didn't bother to reply. His attention was focused solely on Montgomery Persons as the man went from pink to scarlet to the most magnificent shade of purple he had ever seen.

"What?!" Monty roared, his booming voice sounding like an explosion in the noisy room. All sounds abruptly ceased as every head in the place swung to study the cause of the roar. "What?! He did what?!" he bellowed, bringing a beefy fist crashing down on top of the table, which nearly collapsed beneath the blow. "That low-life—son-of-a—bloody hell—" he choked out, too enraged to form a complete sentence.

Cole stepped protectively in front of Devon at the start of the outburst. But rather than being alarmed or frightened by her uncle's temper, she simply sighed and sat down, completely immune. She glanced up at Cole and shrugged. "Nice work, McRae," she said. "It'll be a while now."

"A while" turned out to be thirty minutes of cursing and fuming, until Monty recovered enough to bring his anger back under control and sit down. Cole listened as Devon related what had happened, carefully minimizing the details so as not to set her uncle off again. As far as explaining Cole's own part in her misadventure, she said nothing more than that she'd been transferred into his care in Fort Monroe, only to escape later outside Washington.

When she finished, Monty leaned forward and patted her softly on the knee. "I'm sorry, my girl," he said. "Your Uncle Monty delivered you out of the water and straight into the shark's jaws, didn't he?"

"No, everything's fine now—"

"Hmph," Monty snorted. "It won't be fine until Mr. Jonas Sharpe gets back a piece of what he gave to you." He swiveled around and looked at Cole, truly focusing on him for the first time. "You've finished your business here, Captain. You can go."

"Not without her," Cole answered.

Monty stared at him, his eyes hard, then he slowly rose to his feet. "I don't care what your orders are, Captain," he said, his voice dangerously low, "or what happened at that trial. I know my niece, and she would never stab a man in the back." With a quicksilver motion, he produced a knife from the back of his coat and set it calmly on the table. "I, however, wouldn't hesitate to do so. I can prove that to you within the next two seconds, or you can get up and leave now. The choice is yours."

"Uncle Monty!" Devon gasped.

Cole stared up at him, remaining right where he sat. He glanced at the knife, then back at Monty, seeing that the man meant every word he'd said. Instead of being furious at the bald threat that had just been thrown in his face, he felt nothing but overwhelming relief. It was exactly the sort of fierce, protective gesture Cole would have made had their roles been reversed. "You've taken care of her, haven't you?" he said.

"You're damned right I have," Monty growled. "And if you think—"

"Thank you."

Monty blinked. He looked from Cole to Devon, then sank slowly back into his seat. "What exactly is going on here?"

"Nothing," Devon answered quickly.

"Is that a fact," Monty muttered, looking thoroughly unconvinced. He ran his fingers over his beard, his gaze speculative as he focused on Cole. "Have you come to drag my niece off to prison?" he demanded.

"No."

"Then what the hell do you want with her?"

Cole cursed inwardly at the question. He hadn't been able to sort out for himself what he felt for Devon.

Defining it now for her uncle was impossible. Still, the man expected some sort of answer. "Devon and I—"

"What are you doing here, Uncle Monty?" Devon blurted, drowning out his words. She gave Cole a sharp kick under the table, as though she'd expected him to finish his statement with "Devon and I became lovers . . ."

Monty patted her hand, his tone distracted as he pulled his gaze away from Cole long enough to answer. "Did you think I wouldn't come after receiving your wire? Besides, I missed you, my girl. Business hasn't been the same without you."

She looked both surprised and pleased. "You came all this way just to see me?"

"Damned good thing I did too," Monty grumbled. He turned back to Cole, an intense frown on his face. "How long were the two of you in Virginia together? And no more interrupting me or kicking the captain beneath the table, my girl," he added sternly, glancing at Devon. "I know all your tricks, and they won't work with me."

The man was sharp, Cole had to give him that.

"How long, Captain?" he repeated.

Cole leaned back and folded his arms over his chest, mildly curious to see where Monty was going with this line of questioning. "Long enough," he answered coolly.

"All by yourselves?"

"Uncle Monty," Devon broke in, "this has nothing to do with—"

Monty held up his hand to silence her, his eyes locked on Cole as he waited for him to speak.

"From time to time."

"I presume you made arrangements for separate quarters."

"I'm afraid not."

Monty sank back into his chair, his dark eyes moving

slowly over Cole. He shifted his gaze to Devon, whose face was scrupulously averted as she busily arranged the folds of her skirt. "I see," he said.

Devon finally lifted her head, revealing the soft rosy stains that flushed her cheeks. "Uncle Monty, I really think we should—"

"Now, now, don't rush me, my girl. You know I don't like to be rushed." He let out a contented sigh and smiled at Cole. "How fortuitous it is for us all to have come together here, is it not? Amazing where fate will steer us . . ."

Cole wasn't impressed by the man's sudden burst of goodwill. Devon's uncle was up to something. He studied Monty's predatory smile and knew it instinctively. But whatever the scheme he was brewing, Cole wasn't having any part of it.

"We all have our own motivations for stopping Jonas Sharpe, do we not?" Monty continued, as if musing aloud. "Devon needs to clear her name so she won't have the accusation of murder hanging over her head for the rest of her life. You, Captain, need to stop Sharpe because of the threat the man poses to the Union blockade. And I, of course, must undo the damage that's been done to my reputation."

"Really?" Cole drawled. "And what reputation might that be?"

"I happen to be a professional," Monty replied. "If word got out that someone of my caliber and expertise was taken in by the likes of Jonas Sharpe, my career would be ruined."

"Of course," Cole said, amazed at the absurd turn the conversation had taken. "Your career as a thief, con artist, embezzler—"

"I do no such things," Monty retorted sharply. "It's people like that who give stealing a bad name. I simply liberate funds that have been neglected due to carelessness. From time to time, I've also gratuitously acquired a few select pieces of art and jewelry. But no one has ever been hurt in the process.''

Cole arched a tawny brow and looked at Devon, but she merely shrugged as if she'd heard the outrageous rationalization many times before.

''In any case,'' Monty continued, ''this is steering us away from the matter at hand.''

''Really? And what matter is that?''

''Jonas Sharpe, of course. I presume you have a ship in harbor, Captain.''

''I do,'' Cole answered. The *Islander* had been completely refitted and repaired and was stronger than ever. Where she'd been primarily a sailing vessel before, she now boasted an engine and sturdy screw propellers aft, giving her more power and maneuverability. Taking the lead from the runners he'd pursued, Cole had ordered the ship painted a dull gunmetal-gray, thus giving her the same cloak of invisibility as the runners. There had been one final change: for all intents and purposes, the *Islander* had been destroyed that fateful day at sea. Cole christened his newly fitted ship the *Ghost*.

''Hmmm . . .'' Monty nodded, as if deep in thought. ''Capable of running the blockade, do you suppose?''

Cole frowned. ''My duty is to man the blockade, not run it.''

''Yes, yes, of course.'' Monty sighed heavily. ''I suppose that won't work, then.''

''Good, it's all settled,'' Devon, who'd remained silent until that point, hastily broke in. ''Uncle Monty, we really should be going—''

Cole knew he'd probably regret his next question for the rest of his life, but that didn't prevent him from asking it. ''What won't work?''

Monty smiled broadly, his dark eyes gleaming with satisfaction. ''You see, Captain, a man in my position is privy to certain bits of information that may not be available to others. Take for example the rumor I heard when I first reached this lovely island. Jonas Sharpe has run into a bit of bad luck. You know, of course, that one of the warships Sharpe had constructed left Liverpool approximately a month ago. But it seems that you Yanks recently captured Captain Nathan Daniels, the man slated to take over the helm.''

Cole recognized the name, for he had heard as much while he was in Fort Monroe. The capture of Captain Daniels had been quite a coup for the Union Navy. What neither Cole nor anyone else had known, however, was that Daniels was the man Sharpe had chosen to take on the first in his fleet of iron rams.

"The word is out that Sharpe is looking for a new captain for his ship,'' Monty finished.

Cole drew his brows together, studying Monty. "The Confederate Navy is full of commissioned men waiting for a ship. It should be no trouble at all for Sharpe to find a replacement for Daniels.''

"A commission in the Confederate Navy is a mark of neither ability nor experience, but simply the right political connections. Jonas Sharpe knows this as well as you or I. The best men are the ones running the blockade, and those are the men Sharpe is attempting to lure to his side.''

Cole leaned back in his seat, reassessing Montgomery Persons. He might be a thief, but he was also thoroughly knowledgeable about naval matters, incredibly resourceful, and apparently well-connected. And strangely enough, despite his glib talk and quick fingers, the man wasn't completely unlikable.

"Of course, Sharpe won't hand over his ship to just anyone,'' Monty continued. "The man must be willing to prove his worthiness as a seaman. Whoever wants a go at captaining the frigate must first demonstrate his skill and daring by running the blockade into Wilmington.''

Cole considered Monty's words, recognizing at once

the incredible opportunity laid out before him. If he succeeded, not only would he be handed the battleship straight from Liverpool, but he would be able to use Sharpe's own ship against him. All in all, the reward far outweighed any risk he might have to take.

Monty regarded him steadily. "Within an hour's time, Captain, I can not only build you a reputation as one of the South's most notorious blockade runners, but find you a profitable cargo to take into Wilmington." He let that sink in, then lifted his shoulders in a broad shrug. "Of course, if you won't consider it . . ."

The challenge was neatly and effectively thrown down. Cole had no choice, and they both knew it. There was simply too much at stake for him not to try. The run into Wilmington was one of the trickiest sea lanes open, but after two years of manning the coast, he knew it as well as any runner. He paused, considering the time and tides.

"You understand, of course," Monty said, "that my niece and I fully intend to accompany you on the voyage."

Cole snapped his attention back to Monty. "Running the blockade isn't a sport. You'll stay here until I return." He turned to Devon, fixing her with the full weight of his stare. "Both of you."

Devon coolly returned his gaze. "I have no intention of either running the blockade or remaining here," she stated firmly. "I intend to return to England at first opportunity."

"Now, now, my girl," Monty crooned, softly patting her hand. "You're upset, and I don't blame you, but you're not going anywhere with this murder hanging over your head." He turned back to Cole, smiling broadly. "Surely you realize that Devon and I have as much at stake in this matter as you do. I think it best for all involved that we work together, don't you?"

"Absolutely not."

Monty lifted his thick shoulders, still smiling. "In that unfortunate event, I'm afraid it's incumbent upon me to find another man capable of running the blockade. The island is no doubt brimming with men willing to try their luck."

The full import of his words was abundantly clear: you'll do it my way or not at all. The damned problem was, Cole couldn't do anything without Monty's connections. The man had him completely over a barrel, and he knew it.

Seeing his hesitation, Monty pressed his advantage. "Good, that's all settled then. I presume we'll want to leave at first light, Captain." He raised his hand and signaled to the owner. The same greasy little man that Cole had spoken to earlier appeared instantly, brandishing a bottle of the house's best champagne and three glasses.

The owner filled their glasses, then stood hovering at the table, waiting for payment. Monty looked at Cole. "Please, Captain, I wouldn't dream of depriving you of the honor of paying for our refreshments."

"How very considerate of you. Unfortunately I seem to have misplaced my wallet."

Monty clucked his tongue. "My good friend, what a dreadful shame. Perhaps you should check again."

Cole studied him for a moment, then reached into his vest, not at all surprised to find that the man had managed to work both his watch and wallet back onto him as nimbly as he'd taken them off.

"So easy to misplace the little things, isn't it?" Monty said, beaming. He raised his glass in a toast as Cole paid the bill. "To our illustrious partnership. May it be as profitable as the night is long."

"Uncle Monty," Devon immediately protested, "nothing is settled yet."

"I suppose you're right, my girl. We do have just one small bit of business left to attend, don't we?"

"Your fee, no doubt," Cole surmised dryly.

Monty frowned and waved that away. "Of course not. I'm acting strictly for the sake of my lovely niece." He paused and interjected smoothly, "Naturally, however, I will be due a percentage of the profit we make on whatever cargo we carry."

"Naturally."

"But all that can be discussed later, Captain," Monty continued brightly. "What is at issue here is undoing the damage that has been done to my niece's reputation. Though I'm certain it was unintentional on your part, surely a man of your standing and position understands how deeply sullied Devon's name will be if word gets out that she spent a considerable amount of time traveling unchaperoned with a man who was not her husband."

"It doesn't matter, Uncle Monty," Devon said softly, a pale rose tint lighting her cheeks. Cole saw the embarrassment streaked across her features and ached for her.

Monty placed his hand lightly on her knee. "Ah, but it does to me, my girl. It does to me." He transferred his gaze back to Cole. "Devon had her heart set on being a bride, and I aim to see to it that she becomes one."

"Uncle Monty, I told you, I've changed my mind. I don't want—"

"Now, my girl, don't interrupt your uncle. This is between the captain and me." His eyes locked on Cole's. "Devon will go as your wife, or not at all."

"Uncle Monty!" Devon gasped in horror. "No!"

Cole stared at the man, then looked at Devon. Decked out in her emerald silk finery, she was the picture of classic feminine elegance. Grace and beauty. But beneath that delicate exterior lurked one of the most willful, unpredictable, troublemaking females he'd ever met. If he had any brains left at all, he'd get up and run. Instead he smiled. "Agreed."

"What?!" Devon shouted, looking at him as though he'd just lost his mind. "You're crazy, both of you! I won't do it, do you hear me? Absolutely not!"

Monty looked from her to Cole, then took a deep sip of his champagne. He settled back into his chair, his lips split into a broad grin that engulfed his whole face. "Welcome to the family, my boy."

Chapter 13

Devon sat alone on a small bench outside the chapel where she was to be married. Married. It still didn't seem real to her. She didn't know how Cole had pulled it off, but somehow he'd managed to prepare everything within a mere twenty-four hours: the minister, the license, the chapel. She supposed it shouldn't surprise her any longer. The man seemed to be able to accomplish whatever he set out to do.

She wondered if it was a bad omen that she was the first one to arrive, then immediately chastised herself for the thought. Thinking of omens and superstitions was silly. Cole wanted her only because she and Uncle Monty could help him capture Sharpe. If he hadn't been so quick to agree to her uncle's outrageous demand, she would have been able to talk Uncle Monty out of it. Now it was too late. Obviously the thought of capturing Sharpe was worth anything to him, even being saddled with her as a bride.

Devon refused to lie to herself. It was a simple business arrangement, and she had to remember that. They were working together for a short time for the mutual good of all involved. Once Sharpe had been captured, she was sure Cole would want to be free from her and seek an annulment. They would dissolve their marriage as neatly and as unemotionally as they had entered into it.

But her rational side was overpowered by the emotions playing havoc with her nerves. Being this close to Cole was going to be sheer torture. She'd tried to force him out of her mind since the day she'd fled Virginia, but that had proved impossible. Cole McRae was with her every second of the day. He was her last thought every night and her first thought every morning. He haunted her dreams in between.

When he'd walked into that crowded tavern yesterday afternoon, she was sure she was only imagining him. Just another dream—a fantasy more vivid than any which had preceded it, but a fantasy nevertheless. Then Cole had spoken. Her had heart slammed against her ribs in response, expanding against her chest as if it would explode. Her lungs had swelled with joy, stealing away her breath and her words, leaving her speechless.

And now they were to be married.

A business arrangement, she amended silently, but still . . .

As always when she was nervous, she reached for her mother's wedding ring, which she wore around her neck. She felt a momentary shock of alarm to find it missing, then remembered that as of that afternoon she no longer wore it. She'd taken it off for the last time.

She sighed and stood, wishing the peaceful setting would calm her nerves. The chapel was a lovely, quaint building made of pink stone, situated on a hill overlooking the harbor. Rich vines of purple and scarlet bougainvillea cascaded down the outer walls. It was now early twilight, the sky filled with dusty shades of rose and lavender. A gentle breeze caressed her skin, carrying the thick scent of jasmine and gardenia. In the harbor far below, ships bobbed like tiny toys, in a sea that slowly changed from teal to sapphire.

Devon didn't feel that she belonged at the chapel, but rather that she blended into it. She'd changed out of her emerald-green traveling suit and into a frothy gown of the palest shell-pink. She'd purchased both upon her arrival in Bermuda two weeks ago. She'd hated to squander her money on the gowns, but at the time she had possessed nothing but the clothes on her back, she hadn't had a choice. In order to make money, she'd had to look as though she didn't need it.

Now, however, she was glad of the extravagant purchase. Glancing into the mirror as she dressed, she'd noted that the soft hue brought a delicate rose tint to her skin and made her eyes glow like those of a real bride. The gown was simple and unadorned, with a snugly fitted bodice and cap sleeves. The full skirt swished around her legs in hushed whispers of silk. She wore her hair up in a loose chignon, a spray of tiny white orchids tucked behind her ear in lieu of a bonnet.

She clutched the pale pink silk reticule that had been made to match her gown tightly in her hands, kneading it between her fingers as she fought back her worries. Cole needed her help, it was as simple as that. No matter what it cost her, she would give it to him. Nothing else mattered.

She heard the sound of hoofbeats, a horse racing up a steep path that led to the chapel. She froze, knowing it was Cole. Within seconds, he appeared in view, looking strong and in command—and unbearably handsome in his summer uniform. The deep gold braid of his trim navy jacket accentuated his broad shoulders and the narrowness of his waist and hips. Crisp, white linen trousers encased his long, powerful legs; his black boots were polished to a high sheen. He wore his thick golden hair brushed back, away from his face.

He leaped from his horse and secured the reins to a low branch. He turned toward the chapel, then stopped, scanning the grounds. An expression of regret, anger, and anxiety marred his strong features. It was then that Devon realized she truly did blend into the chapel, due to the color of her gown and the fact that she was standing motionless in the fading twilight shadows. Understanding immediately that he thought she hadn't come, she stepped forward.

Alerted by her movement, Cole jerked his head around, relief coursing across his face as he found her. His expression deepened as his eyes traveled slowly over her. She was held captive by his gaze, reading in his eyes everything she'd ever longed for him to say. She saw approval, possessiveness, and a burning hunger that she understood all too well. For one incredible moment, time seemed to stand still. The world stopped spinning and the sea no longer crashed against the shore. Nothing existed except her and Cole.

A kaleidoscope of images tumbled through her mind, searing her very soul. She remembered the first time she'd set eyes on Cole, so wounded and raw and angry, yet there'd been something about him that had drawn her to him even then. She remembered his gentle touch as he removed the iron shackles that had bitten into her wrists. She remembered him leaping onto the train to save her life, laughing with her as they talked, and the anguish on his face when he'd told her about Gideon. And finally she remembered making love to him in a wooded glen, beneath a midnight sky that shimmered with stars.

Looking back, she saw that each step had been part of a dance led by fate, bringing her to this very spot. To this man. To a pink chapel nestled between a lavender sky and a sapphire sea. This was where she was meant to be.

Cole moved forward, his long strides bringing him quickly to her side. He took her hands in his and said simply, "You came."

"Yes."

"I'm sorry I'm late. It took me longer to set the crew to storing the cargo than I'd expected."

"It doesn't matter."

"Your uncle sent a note, he won't be here for the ceremony. Apparently he was able to arrange a meeting with one of Sharpe's agents."

Devon nodded, ignoring the disappointment that shot through her at the news. She let out a shaky breath and attempted a smile. "I guess that just leaves the two of us then, doesn't it?"

He frowned as he studied her, then reached out and softly brushed her cheek. "Nervous?"

"You don't have to do this, Cole. I'll talk to Uncle Monty, just give me a little time. I can convince him to help you, to give you everything you need."

Silence hung between them as he seemed to consider her words. Finally he said, "Everything except the one thing I need most of all."

Devon searched her mind. The cargo, the connections, the ship, Sharpe's agent ... She shook her head in bewilderment, wondering what she'd missed.

"You."

Devon sucked in her breath. She searched his eyes, finding nothing but tender solemnity in their tawny-brown depths. He looked absolutely serious, but did she dare believe it was true? Incredible as the thought might be, she didn't know if it was worth the risk to actually find out.

"What is it?" he asked gently. "What's wrong?"

"It's just that ..." Her voice trailed off as she searched for the proper words to convey her feelings. She'd left England for exactly this sort of arrangement. Only then she'd been promised to a man she'd never even set sight on, a man for whom she cared nothing. Now she was actually going to marry Cole. *Cole*. The one man in the world capable of twisting her heart into knots and turning her brain into jelly. "It's just that ... You're not Boris Ogglesby."

He slowly grinned. "You'll have plenty of time to

thank me for that later. Now come on, the minister's waiting.''

Cole took her hand and led her into the chapel. Devon glanced around, studying the decorations. Obviously they were left over from a previous ceremony. The flowers were wilted and the candles were partially melted down, giving the room the air of a party that had been abandoned. Her mind strayed once again to thoughts of omens and bad luck, but she resolutely pushed them aside.

Cole frowned. "Devon, I'm sorry. I didn't realize—"

"No, it's all right," she said, forcing a cheerful note to her voice. "It doesn't matter, truly it doesn't.''

She found herself repeating the same thing near the end of the ceremony when the minister asked him for the ring and Cole's expression changed to one of shocked horror. He'd forgotten to buy one. The minister shrugged and continued, speaking in a monotone voice of Scripture, vows, and promises. Finally he pronounced them husband and wife. Devon doubted if the entire ceremony had taken more than ten minutes.

She left the chapel feeling dazed, not quite believing that it was all real. Cole sent Devon's driver back with his horse, then assisted her into the carriage she'd rented earlier. Night had fallen quickly, murky darkness replacing the hazy twilight. They moved back onto the narrow, winding path that led back to the docks. The path had been cut into the mountain, where one side hugged the wet, green, tangled face of the cliff, while the other side—the side where she sat—was nothing but a sheer precipice that dropped off to the sharp rocks and crashing waves below.

Devon clasped her hands tightly in her lap and tried to ignore the nervous flutter in her stomach. Just as she was about to congratulate herself on her bravery, the rear wheel rolled over a rock, jarring the carriage as it swayed around a curve. She gave a tiny yelp, then bit down hard on her lip.

Cole swung his head around to look at her. "What's wrong?"

"Nothing," she lied.

"Devon . . ."

He reached for her just as the carriage hit another bump in the road. "No! Cole, don't touch me! Keep your hands on the reins, please!"

He obeyed, but his focus was almost entirely on her now instead of the road. "Devon? What is it?"

She shook her head tightly, then admitted in a small, unsteady voice, "I'm afraid I've never been overly fond of heights."

"Don't look down."

"Now there's a forty-carat jewel of wisdom. Original, too. Where else am I supposed to look? We're careening down the side of a mountain in a rickety trap of a carriage and you tell me—"

"Devon?"

"What!"

"Come here." Cole kept his hands on the reins, just as she'd asked. He lifted his arm, allowing her room to slip beneath his elbow. Devon hesitated for less than a second before she slid across the seat and snuggled up against him. He lowered his arm and brought her tightly into his embrace. "Now close your eyes," he instructed.

Devon obeyed. She breathed in his familiar scent and soaked up the heat of his body. Within minutes, she felt safe and protected, just as she always did whenever Cole was near. The terror of the jagged cliffs slowly faded from her mind. "How's that?" he asked.

"Better."

"Why didn't you tell me you were so afraid of heights? I would have met you at the ship and brought you to the chapel myself, rather than sending you with a driver you didn't know.''

"It wasn't so bad on the way up."

"Why not?"

"I didn't have to look down, for one thing. Besides, at the time there was something which terrified me even more."

She felt his chest move as he shifted to look down at her. "What?"

"Marrying you."

Cole was silent for a long moment, then his hand drifted over her back in a light caress. "That bad, was it?" Though she couldn't see his face, his smile was clear in his voice.

She snuggled against him and let out a deep, heartfelt sigh. "Awful." She thought for a moment, then shook her head. "I don't know you, Cole. In some ways I do, but in other ways we're still strangers. I don't know your birthday, your favorite time of the year, or your favorite food. All the details, all the things that might one day bring us closer together, are missing." Even as she spoke, Devon wondered if any of that really mattered. Perhaps all that mattered was the way she felt right now, with Cole's arms locked tight around her. Perhaps all she needed was more time, more closeness, more . . .

"May eighth, the fall, and roasted chicken."

Devon choked back a laugh. "Cole, I didn't mean literally—"

"Your turn."

She smiled. Of course. In Cole's logical, male mind, all they had to do was fill in the blanks and everything would be fine. Not knowing what else to say, she replied, "November twenty-first, springtime, and cherry cobbler."

She glanced up at him. "By the way, what's your

middle name? I couldn't quite make it out on the license we signed."

Cole shifted uncomfortably. "You already know it."

Devon frowned. "I don't remember you ever telling me."

"Cole is my middle name. It was my mother's maiden name."

"Then what—"

He let out a sigh of weary resignation. "Sherman. My first name is Sherman."

Devon bit down hard on her inner lip to keep from laughing. She took a deep, steadying breath, and said, "Sherman. Well. Isn't that . . . something? Actually, I believe it quite suits you—"

"Devon," Cole began warningly.

"Honesty like that deserves a reward," she rushed on. "I'll tell you something I'll bet you didn't know about me: I can't dance."

"You mean you don't like to?"

"I mean I can't; I never learned how. I was too young when my mother died to remember anything she showed me. Mrs. Honeychurch certainly didn't give lessons, and Uncle Monty . . . Well, he and I stayed away from the fancy balls and such. He thought there was too great a risk that we might run into someone we'd, er, done business with in the past. Our forays into high society were limited to small dinner parties and the like."

"I'll teach you," he answered, then transferred the reins to one hand, leaving his other free to lightly stroke her back. They drove on for a few minutes in silence. "Do you feel better now?" he asked.

"Hmmm," she answered, in a voice so relaxed it was almost drowsy. "I'm not frightened anymore, Cole."

"That's what husbands are for."

Devon smiled. "What are wives for?"

Cole bit back a groan, squelching the answer that sprang automatically to his lips. Devon had shifted herself entirely onto his lap, nearly purring in response to his touch. Her thighs stretched across his, her breasts rubbed softly against his chest. Her every movement tortured him. The soft silk rustle of her gown, the delicate scent of her body as she rubbed up against him, the feel of her warm breath lightly fanning his neck . . . Each innocent brush of her skin against his, each rocking, rolling motion of the carriage that sent her swaying into him, had become almost painful.

He dropped the reins, set the brake, then took a deep breath in an attempt to gain control. "We're here," he announced, thankful he'd kept his jacket on. He didn't relish the prospect of walking aboard and introducing his wife to his crew while in the throes of the biggest erection he could ever remember. At least his jacket would cover it—or so he hoped.

Devon opened her eyes, glanced around the dock, and scooted off his lap as he bit back another groan. "We're here? Already?" she said, clearly delighted.

Cole climbed stiffly from the carriage and helped her down. As they moved toward the *Ghost,* Devon tugged his hand and stopped. When he turned to look at her, she was frowning. "What's wrong? Why are you walking like that?"

He swore silently as he considered his options. He could take her directly into his cabin and spend their wedding night ravishing her, which was exactly what he wanted to do. Or he could take it slow and easy, wait in torment for his aching state of arousal to subside, and give her the proper welcome she deserved as his new bride. Devon stood silently looking at him, all soft pink innocence. His answer was gruffer than he intended. "We've been sitting too long. My damned leg fell asleep. It'll be all right in a few minutes."

Her brow knit with concern. "Why don't you show

me where it hurts and I'll rub it for you. Sometimes a good massage is all—"

"No!" Cole took a deep breath, forcing that image away. Seeing her startled expression, he continued gently, "Thank you, Devon. That's very considerate of you, but I'm sure it'll be fine in a few minutes."

She shrugged and turned to look at his ship, studying it in silence. Taking advantage of her distraction, he led her aboard and gave her a cursory tour. Twenty minutes later, his self-control markedly improved, he brought her back to his cabin.

He watched her face as she moved into the room. The small, tight quarters had never bothered him, for he didn't spend a great deal of time there. But now, seen through her eyes, he imagined it must look rather stark and dreary. The cabin held only the bare essentials. A bed lined with crisp white sheets and a dark navy blanket took up most of the space. His desk was cluttered with nautical equipment. Beside it was a chest that held his clothing and personal items; a washstand with basin and pitcher stood next to that. A table with two chairs sat cramped against the corner wall. He wished now he'd thought to pick up some flowers to soften the space a little for her. Women liked that sort of thing.

Devon wandered into the tight room, exploring with open curiosity as Cole watched her. She looked small, feminine, and dainty against bulky, masculine furnishings. But oddly enough, she didn't look out of place. She looked as if she belonged there. In the same way, she'd walked into his life and exploded into his heart and what should have been completely wrong, turned out instead to be completely right. She belonged in his heart as well.

She turned to him and nodded, smiling softly. The twin dimples that had so captivated him before made an appearance. "It suits you," she said.

Cole stared at her for a long moment. "Perhaps," he said. "Five minutes ago it was just a stark, barren room. Then you stepped into it, and everything changed."

She looked as stunned at hearing his words as he was at having said them. "Cole, you don't have to say things like that. I don't expect—"

"I know you don't. But I meant it, Devon."

Her eyes glowed as a steady current pulsed between them. "Now what do we do?" she asked.

He studied her, suddenly at a loss for words. He knew what he wanted to do. But whether Devon was ready to make love was an entirely different matter. In all his life, Cole had never felt such an overwhelming need to get a woman into his bed. Nor had he ever felt such stumbling, groping awkwardness about how to accomplish it. He searched his mind for the words to gently introduce the topic. "Well, I believe it's customary after the wedding day to have a wedding night."

A soft pink blush rose to her cheeks. "Yes, that is the custom, isn't it?"

Her words told him nothing. *Do you want me, Devon?* He wanted to scream. *Do you want me as badly as I want you?* She turned to look at the bed, a worried frown on her face. "What is it?" he asked. "What's wrong?"

"It's just that . . ." She paused, a wobbly smile on her face. "I'm afraid I'll disgrace myself again. When you touch me like that, Cole, it stirs something up inside me. I just know I'll start crying when we're done and look like a complete fool."

Her words shot straight to his heart. Cole moved forward and pulled her tightly into his arms, aching with a desire that went far beyond the mere physical needs of his body. When he finally spoke, his voice was strangely hoarse. "I'll thank you to watch what you say," he reprimanded softly. "The woman you're speaking of happens to be my wife."

She pulled back and looked up at him, her beautiful eyes sparkling with joy. "Cole—" she began, but whatever response she would have made was prevented by a knock at the cabin door. Cole reluctantly released her and reached to open it. A young steward entered carrying an exquisite crystal vase brimming with an enormous bouquet of orchids, lilies, jasmine, and gardenias. "Flowers for the lady," the boy said. He set the heavy arrangement down on the chest near the bed, then quickly exited.

"Oh, Cole," Devon exclaimed as she bent to examine the flowers, "they're beautiful, absolutely beautiful. Thank you."

Cole dug his hands deep into his pockets. "Unfortunately they're not from me."

She lifted her head, her expression quizzical. "They're not?"

"I was just wishing five minutes ago that I'd thought to do that."

"Oh." Devon reached into the arrangement and withdrew a slim white card. As she read it, a slight frown creased her brow, then she tucked it swiftly into her pocket. "They're from Uncle Monty."

She looked worried, and Cole wondered what had been on the card that upset her, but manners precluded him from asking. "That was quite thoughtful of him," he said in an attempt to draw her out.

"What? Oh, the flowers. Yes, it was." With visible effort, she seemed to shake off whatever was bothering her. She hesitated for a moment, then reached into her reticule and withdrew a slim box wrapped in gold paper and tied with a black satin ribbon. She looked up at him, her expression suddenly shy. "While we're on the subject of gifts . . ."

Cole froze, his stomach plummeting with dread.

Dammit to hell, how could he be so stupid? He'd been so worried about getting his ship and crew prepared for the run into Wilmington, worried about making the wedding arrangements and getting to the chapel, worried about being separated from Devon for even an hour, afraid that she might slip away from him once again, that he'd forgotten the ring, the flowers; he'd forgotten to buy her a gift.

She smiled at him, holding out the box. "I believe it's traditional for the bride to give the groom a gift."

Actually tradition called for the groom to give the bride a gift, not the other way around, but he didn't correct her. He stared at the shiny gold box she held, feeling lower at that moment than he ever had in his life. If there was a snake in the room, he could have walked beneath its belly without so much as ducking down. "Devon," he began haltingly, "I didn't—"

"It doesn't matter," she rushed to assure him. "This was purely a whim on my part, that's all. It's nothing, really, but . . . I'd like for you to have it."

He reluctantly took the gift from her hand. "I don't deserve it."

"You're right, Sherman, you don't," she answered cheekily.

Cole groaned. "Remind me never to share any secrets with you again."

"I can't take it back, so why don't you just go ahead and open it?"

He peeled off the wrappings and lifted the lid to reveal an elegant gold stickpin, mounted at its crest with a stone of glowing tiger's eye. It was simple and yet exquisitely crafted. Devon moved to stand beside him. "The stone reminded me of your eyes," she said softly.

Cole stared down at her, more moved by her thoughtfulness than he cared to admit. "It's beautiful, thank you. I only wish I had something to give you."

"I'm afraid Uncle Monty has decided that you are my wedding gift," she answered with a laugh. She glanced at the stickpin then back at him, searching his face for approval. "But you like it? Truly? I wasn't sure . . ."

"It's perfect. My only fear is that it was too expensive. You should have spent your money on you, not me."

Devon waved that away. "You needn't worry about that. I'm afraid what little money I made on the island I spent entirely on the two gowns I bought."

Cole frowned as an uncomfortable suspicion suddenly rose to life in the back of his mind. "Then how did you—"

"It's very ungracious of you to ask," Devon replied lightly. "But you needn't worry. After all, there's more than one way to acquire jewelry."

"You didn't actually buy this, did you?"

She turned away from him, looking embarrassed. "Well, no, not exactly, but—"

"I see." Cole closed the lid on the box and set it down. He sat down on the edge of the desk and pulled her to him, bringing her to stand between his knees so they were eye to eye. He hated what he was about to say, but had no choice. Issues like this were best tackled head-on, and the sooner the better. "I think we need to have a little talk," he said, striving to keep his tone nonjudgmental.

"What about?"

"This gift."

"You don't like it, do you?"

"It's not that, the pin is lovely. But if I were to bring it back to the shop tomorrow, what would the owner say?"

Devon bit her lip, blushing furiously. "Actually, Cole, I'd rather you didn't go there," she said quickly.

"Why not?"

"Just tell me what you want and I'll get that for you instead."

Cole took a deep breath. "Devon, in the future, if you want money for anything you need only ask me. In fact, you won't even have to ask. I'll see to it that you have ample funds at your disposal—"

"That sounds very generous, but I could hardly ask you for money to buy your own gift, could I?" she countered with a small laugh.

"You don't have to steal anymore, Devon."

The amusement he'd seen on her face drained away. Pain streaked through her eyes as she stiffened and pulled back.

Cole caught her hands in his and held her near. "Sweetheart, I don't mean to embarrass you. It's not your fault, I don't blame you. You've done whatever you had to do in order to survive, but it's no longer necessary." He gave her hands a gentle squeeze and smiled encouragingly. "Consider it a bad habit that you have to break. You may still get the impulse now and again, but I'll help you through it. I think, once you feel fully secure . . ."

His voice trailed away as he studied Devon. She was no longer looking at him, but through him. He brought his hands up and rubbed them softly from her shoulders to her elbows, hoping for a response. She remained absolutely still, as if stoically enduring his touch. Cole shook his head. "Please, sweetheart, I'm asking you to trust me, that's all. Part of that trust is knowing that I'll take care of you." He tried to inject a note of humor. "I don't want to spend my time bailing my wife out of jail."

Her expression didn't change. "I'll return the pin in the morning."

"Never mind," he said wanting to spare her any further embarrassment. "We're leaving with the tide at dawn. Just give me the name of the shop and I'll send a boy over with sufficient funds to cover the purchase."

She pulled out of his grasp and turned away. "I don't remember."

"Devon—"

"I'll take care of it myself. It was my mistake."

He studied her ramrod-stiff back, wishing she would turn around so he could see her face. "Devon, the thought behind the gift was lovely, more than I'd—"

"Would you mind leaving me alone now?" she asked softly, her voice perfectly polite. "I seem to have developed a touch of the headache. I think I'd like to lie down for a few minutes."

"Certainly," he answered automatically, but he didn't move. He remained right where he was, loath to leave when she was so clearly distraught. "Devon, this doesn't change anything between us—"

"Please, Cole." Her voice was strained and tight.

Five minutes ago they'd been laughing and ready to make love. Now the moment was over, stamped out like a tender flame. He hesitated, then reached for the door. "I'll let you rest," he said and backed quietly out of the room.

He stood on the other side of the door, listening, though he didn't know what he expected to hear. There was no sound, no movement of any kind. He imagined her standing exactly as he'd left her, rigidly still in the middle of his small cabin. "Damn," he muttered to himself, letting out a dark sigh as he closed his eyes and leaned against the passageway wall.

Obviously he'd handled the matter clumsily, but he'd had no choice. For the sake of their marriage, she had to learn to trust him, to believe that he would take care of her. She had to leave her old habits behind. It would take time, that was all. Just a little more time. That decided, he moved reluctantly away, giving her the space he knew she needed.

He checked on the loading of the cargo and found that the work was proceeding smoothly. His crew didn't need him. There was still no word from Monty about the outcome of his meeting with Sharpe's agent. He thought about returning to his cabin but abruptly dismissed the idea, knowing that it was still too soon.   He wandered around his ship, finding himself entirely at loose ends. Restlessness crept over him like an itch that festered beneath his skin.

Cole left the ship and meandered along the docks, looking for something to distract him from his bleak thoughts. The lights and laughter spilling out from a busy tavern drew him. He went in and ordered a whiskey, then sat in the back and nursed it, watching the crowd with complete detachment. One or two women approached, but his look was enough to send them away, for they retreated without a word.

God, he'd acted like an idiot today. Today? Hell, he hadn't been thinking straight since the first time he'd set eyes on Devon. Once he'd convinced her to marry him, he hadn't wanted to let her out of his sight. So he rushed her. No ring, no flowers, no wedding gift. No time to change her mind. He wondered if she'd noticed that the minister who performed the ceremony had been drunk. He sighed, disgusted with himself. She deserved better than that. Perhaps it was having lost Gideon that created this overwhelming fear of losing someone else he loved.

Cole blinked, shocked by his rambling thoughts. *Someone else he loved.* His hand tightened around his glass. He loved her. When he'd tried to rationalize what he was doing and why, he'd come up blank. Now the answer came through with stunning, crystal clarity. He loved her. He wanted to shout it out to the world. More importantly, he wanted to tell Devon.

He shoved back from the table and made his way through the door. As he strode back to the *Ghost,* he passed a lane known as Robber's Row, an extravagantly priced shopping district for the island's elite. He wasn't surprised to find that the shops still blazed with light, despite the lateness of the hour. The merchants purposely timed their business hours to coincide with those of the local taverns. Drunken sailors and profiteers were known to blow entire fortunes they'd made in as little as one night.

As Cole moved past the displays of rich merchandise, he determined to make up for at least one mistake by purchasing a wedding ring for Devon. He slowed his pace and searched the selection of ladies' jewelry, hoping to find something suitable. He turned, ready to move on, when a ring tucked near the back of the case caught his eye. He stared at it for a long moment, then walked into the shop.

The owner, a tall Frenchman, immaculately dressed, his hair and pencil-thin mustache neatly oiled, sized him up and issued an effusive greeting. Cole pointed to the ring, and the man frowned. "Surely monsieur would like to see something of better quality . . ."

"Show me the ring."

The Frenchman frowned again. "Certainly, monsieur." He reached into his display case and removed it, sniffing disdainfully as he passed it to Cole. "This is not the sort of merchandise I would normally carry, you understand . . ."

The man's voice faded away as Cole stared at the ring in his hand. He recognized the gold band immediately: thin, badly scratched, set with a row of tiny diamond chips. He hesitated, icy dread coursing over him as he peered at the tiny initials engraved inside. *ELB.* Elizabeth Layton Blake. Devon's mother's ring.

"Monsieur, is there something—"

"Where did you get this?"

The shop owner regarded him strangely, then shrugged. "A young woman came in this afternoon

wanting to barter it for another piece of merchandise,"
he answered. "Ordinarily I wouldn't have bothered, but
I am a sentimental man, and she was a bride in need
of a gift for her groom."

Cole sucked in his breath and squeezed the ring
tightly in his palm. Regret exploded inside him and
shot through his veins like acid. She hadn't wanted him
to come to the shop because she hadn't wanted him to
see what she'd sacrificed for him, what she'd had to
give up to buy him that pin. That's why she hadn't told
him. And he, of course, had assumed the worst. *You
don't have to steal anymore, Devon. It's not your fault.
I don't want to spend my time bailing my wife out of
jail.* His voice echoed through his mind, sickening him.
Then, after everything he'd said, he'd dared to lecture
her about trust.

"Monsieur, perhaps—"

"I'll take it."

"Pardon?"

"The ring. I'll buy it. And I need another."

The owner blinked. "You need *two* wedding rings?"

Cole glanced at the display case. "Have you anything better?"

"Monsieur, that is the finest selection of—"

"Never mind, then. Just—"

"*Attendez, attendez!*" the owner cried, holding up
his hands. "Allow me a moment, if you please. Obviously you are a man of discriminating taste. As it happens, I do have a small collection of pieces I reserve
for my better clientele." He disappeared into a back
room, returning a moment later with a small velvet tray
and metal box. He unlocked the box and spread three
glittering rings on the tray. "Perhaps these are more to
your liking, monsieur."

Cole knew instantly which one he wanted. He selected a glittering gold band with a huge diamond,

framed on either side by a matching emerald. "Yes," he said slowly. "That will do."

He settled the bill, leaving the ecstatic owner bowing over his feet as he left the shop. The rings burned in his pocket as he made his way back to his ship. If they didn't help to make it up to Devon, he'd try something else. And keep trying, until he found a way back into her heart, until she'd forgiven him for his stupid, senseless blunder.

He went straight to his cabin but found it empty, no sign of Devon anywhere. He stepped out in the passageway, grabbed the first crewman he saw, and hauled him up by the shirt collar. "Where's my wife?"

The sailor's eyes went wide. "Who?"

"My wife! The only woman on the whole blasted ship! Where is she?"

"I didn't take her, sir! I swear it!"

The man's words stunned some sense back into him. Abruptly recalling himself, Cole let the innocent crewman go. "I'm sorry, Ensign. Carry on." Not ready to sound an alarm, he proceeded to search the ship himself, beginning with the upper decks. He found her almost immediately, standing alone at the starboard bow. She stood bathed in moonlight, staring out at the peaceful sea. A gentle trade wind tossed her hair around her shoulders and rustled her skirts.

Though she must have heard him approach, she did not acknowledge his presence. He waited quietly, then spoke. "Devon."

She slowly turned toward him, her face carefully expressionless. As though he were a stranger who had disturbed her solitude and she was patiently waiting for him to speak, then go away. "I'm sorry," he said.

She looked at him blankly. "For what?"

"For this." He produced her mother's ring from his pocket and held it out to her.

Devon stared at the ring for a long moment, then

reached out, allowing him to drop it into her palm.
"How did you find it?"

"Purely by chance. I was walking by the shop."

"I see." She looked at the ring, then slipped it into
her skirt pocket. "I suppose it was silly of me to have
kept it for so long. It never brought my mother much
luck either." She turned back toward the sea, pointedly
dismissing him.

Cole took a step closer. He ached to reach for her,
but knew instinctively that his touch wouldn't be welcome. "Devon, tell me what I can do to make it up
to you."

She shook her head. "You don't have to do anything.
I told you before, once people know you're a thief,
they never let you forget it. It always comes back—no
matter what you do, no matter how hard you try. It
always comes back." She turned and looked him
straight in the eye. "You're no different than anyone
else. I don't know why I thought you would be."

Cole knew why. Because he was her husband. Because he knew better. Because he loved her, for God's
sake, and instead of showing it, all he did was continu-
ally hurt her and ruin any chance they might have.
"Devon, if there was any way I could take every word
back—"

"Then we'd have the thoughts between us, the silent
accusations. No, it's better this way. It's better that we
both know where we stand." She looked up at him,
her gaze filled with cool determination. "I'll stay with
you until you capture Sharpe. I'll help you in whatever
way I can, just like I promised." She paused and took
a deep breath. "I want you to promise me something
in return, Cole."

"Anything," he swore.

"When we're done, I'm leaving. I'm going back to
England. Promise me you won't come after me when
I go."

Her words slammed into him with the intensity of a blow to the gut. ''Devon, please—''

''Swear it or I'll leave right now.''

Cole took a long, deep breath, then slowly nodded. ''I won't go after you.''

''Thank you.''

He watched her lift her skirts and move gracefully away from him. If she left, he wouldn't go after her. He'd given his word. Despite what it cost him, he would let her go. Which meant he had only one course of action left: move heaven and hell, if that's what it took, to convince her to stay.

Chapter 14

⟨ ∞ ⟩

Cole frowned into the mid-morning sun as he stood at the helm of the *Ghost*. They'd left harbor at dawn, just as planned. Normally he enjoyed the start of a voyage, but this trip was definitely an exception. His body ached with exhaustion, and the hot glare of the sun only worsened the fierce pounding in his head. He'd been up all night supervising his crew as they loaded the last of the shipment they were carrying into Wilmington. Not because they needed his help, but because even the heavy work of loading cargo was preferable to going back to his cabin and facing Devon.

Cowardly, perhaps, but there it was. He'd slunk around and hauled cargo all night, simply because there was no place else on his damned ship for him to go. Cole let out a sigh of disgust and rubbed his hand across the stiff muscles at the back of his neck. His mood didn't improve as he watched Montgomery Persons stride toward him from across the deck.

Reginald Teller, he reminded himself, for that was the name Devon's uncle was temporarily using. Judging by the ease with which the name slipped off Monty's tongue, Cole presumed it was an alias he used quite often. Monty had bestowed upon him the unimaginative title of Captain Cole Smith. The necessity for the assumed names was clear: it wouldn't do at this point in the game for Sharpe to know who was behind arranging the run.

Monty wore a dapper three-piece suit of burgundy plaid that made him look even rounder. A trim bowler hat sat at a jaunty angle on his head. "Lovely morning to run a blockade, is it not?" he said, his voice gratingly cheerful.

"We won't be running the blockade for another three days," Cole answered tersely. It would take them at least that long to reach the inlet of Cape Fear River.

Monty shrugged, seemingly oblivious of his tone. "Well then, it's a lovely day to be at sea."

Since the man obviously had no intention of leaving, Cole decided that now was as good a time as any to press him for the information he needed about Sharpe. "Where's Finch?" he began, referring to Sharpe's agent. The man, sent to accompany them on the run, had boarded last night.

"Ingratiating himself with your crew, I imagine. Probably at this very moment trying to discover if we are who we say we are."

Cole had spoken with his men at length about his plan, and he trusted them completely. He had a good, solid crew. Still, he didn't like the idea of Finch poking around his ship, looking for trouble. He leveled Monty with a cool stare. "You sound awfully blasé about it."

"My good friend, I'm thrilled. We've baited the trap, now it's up to the rat to bite the cheese. I've done what I needed to do to get Sharpe's man aboard. If everything goes as planned, Finch will lead us straight to Sharpe himself."

"Any idea where that frigate's being routed?"

"All in good time, Captain, all in good time."

Cole managed to temper his anger. That was exactly the sort of answer he'd come to expect from Montgomery Persons. Neither a yes nor a no, but rather a reply that cheerfully slithered around his words until the original intent became either convoluted or forgotten entirely. That trait, combined with the fact that they had nothing but the most tenuous strands of a plan at this point, fortified the ever-increasing doubts he harbored about Monty. Despite his glib assurances that all would be well, there was too much about the man that he didn't trust. "You sound as if you're enjoying this."

"Of course I am. Why do you think I made it my life's calling? There's nothing like the thrill of watching a cleverly executed con unfold."

"And you have no conscience as to anyone else who might get hurt along the way."

Monty looked surprised. "Hurt? Who am I hurting?"

"Let me guess. This is where you give me the bit about not being able to swindle an honest man."

"Nonsense. Anyone can be swindled," Monty asserted gruffly. "An honest man simply requires more work." He shrugged. "That's a moot point in any case, Captain. When the Lord has chosen to make the greedy and stupid so plentiful, who am I not to share in His bounty? The way I see it, the fools in this world are like certain species of fish. They fill their place in nature as sustenance for the sharks."

Cole shook his head in disgust. "Remarkable. You have an answer for everything, don't you?"

"My good friend, I'm a professional. Part of an elite group of the most talented scoundrels alive today. But there are three rules to this trade by which even I must abide. One, never take a man's last dollar. Two, never betray a friend."

"And the third?"

Monty beamed. "The most important rule of all: never get caught."

The conversation was doing little to improve either Cole's disposition or his headache. Instead it served only to amplify the foolhardiness of the scheme upon which they'd embarked as well as his own dismal judgment at having allowed Devon's uncle to lead them this far. But at this point, it was too late to go back. There was nothing for him to do but make his own position clear.

"Allow me to demonstrate the secret of my success," Monty said as he pulled a playing deck from his coat and spread three cards on a nearby crate. He flipped them over to show three queens, then turned them facedown again. "Surprise, Captain, that's what I always say. Surprise a man and he won't know what hit him." With that, he flipped the cards once more and the queens were gone. Sitting faceup on the crate were a three, four, and five of clubs.

"Impressive," Cole acknowledged. "Maybe now you'd like to hear a little saying of my own."

"I'd be delighted."

With a flash of movement, Cole reached across and grabbed Monty's wrist. He pulled three queens from the man's sleeve and tossed them on the crate. His gaze locked on Monty's as he said in a low growl, "Don't piss down my back and tell me it's raining." He tightened his grip on Monty's wrist, then slowly let go. "I hope we understand each other."

Monty pulled back and adjusted his sleeve. "Crude, but effective. I believe your point has been made."

"Happy to hear it."

"By the way, Captain, I'm on your side."

"Now why don't I believe that?"

Monty smiled broadly. "No one ever does."

Cole watched him walk away. He remained at the bridge for an hour after Monty left, unable to pinpoint the exact cause of his unease. Despite Devon's blind devotion to her uncle, a twisting sensation in Cole's gut told him something was wrong. Ordinarily he wasn't a man to believe in premonitions, but he'd spent too many years at sea to discount them completely. The sky might read bright and clear, but if he felt the coming of a storm in his bones, he made damned sure both his ship and his crew were prepared.

Given his current state of mind, it was probably not the most auspicious time to face his reluctant bride, but Cole decided there was no sense putting off the confrontation any longer. He strode to his cabin, tapped lightly on the door, and edged it open. He was just in time to see Devon, standing with her back to him, drop to the floor in a dead faint.

Cole shot forward, falling to his knees beside her in an instant. But just as he reached for her, Devon straightened and sat up. She looked up at him and blinked in surprise. "Oh, hello."

He hesitated, his hands stopped in midair as he searched her face for signs of illness or injury. "Devon?"

"How was I?"

"Excuse me?"

"My swoon," she clarified. "I've been practicing all morning. Uncle Monty says I'm dreadful at it, but I don't think that last one was so bad." She frowned and tilted her head to one side, thinking. "Do you suppose it would be better if I swayed a bit more before I fell?"

"You've been practicing . . ." he repeated blankly.

"Of course. It has to look real, even if it's not."

Cole jerked to his feet. He turned his back to her and tugged his hand through his hair, taking a deep breath in an attempt to slow the furious pounding of his heart. When he spoke, his voice sounded more than a little strained. "Devon, in the future I'd appreciate it if you'd warn me—"

"Well how was I to know you'd come barging in here?"

He turned slowly around, making every effort to summon his patience. "In the first place, I didn't barge, I knocked. In the second place, this is my cabin."

Devon considered that, then frowned. She rose to her feet and dusted off her dress. He noted that she wore the blue and lavender calico he'd bought for her in

Virginia, and wondered if he could take that as an indication that her feelings toward him had softened a bit. "You could do with a rug in here," she said. "This wood floor makes swooning awfully hard on a body."

Cole propped one slim hip up against the washstand and crossed his arms over his chest. "Guess I don't swoon enough to notice it."

Her eyes wandered briefly over his body. "No, I suppose not."

"Would you mind explaining what you were doing?"

"I told you, I was practicing."

"Why?"

She shrugged. "Once you've captured Sharpe, Uncle Monty and I can return to Liverpool and go back into business. Then everything will be just like it was before I ever—" She stopped abruptly and looked away.

Before I ever met you, Cole finished for her, knowing that was what she'd been about to say.

"Before I ever left," she finished awkwardly.

"I see."

"Fainting dead away can come in very handy, you know. A limp is useful as well. I do that much better, if you'd care to see."

"Thank you, no."

She looked at him expectantly, as if waiting for him to speak. When he didn't, she glanced around the small room. "I've been monopolizing your cabin, haven't I? I'm sorry, I'll get out of your way."

"You've never been in my way, Devon."

A melancholy smile touched her lips, then flitted away. "We both know that's not true, now don't we? Excuse me—"

"Devon, wait." His words stopped her as she turned toward the door. He saw her stiffen, then turn reluctantly back.

"Was there something you wanted?"

He studied her in silence for a moment, then nodded. "Several things actually, but we can begin with this." Cole moved back to the doorway then reached for the tapestry bag he'd dropped when he saw her swoon. He crossed the tiny cabin in two long strides and set it on the bed. "You left a few things behind in Virginia. I thought you might want one of them."

Devon had left exactly two things behind in Virginia, and they both knew it. One item was the bag full of stolen contraband that he'd just set on the bed; the other was Cole himself. Devon focused on the bag. "Thank you," she murmured. "That was very considerate."

Not knowing what else to do, he leaned against the washstand and watched her unpack. If he moved a mere inch in her direction, they would be touching, but Devon seemed blithely unaware of that fact. She went about the task with cool efficiency, ignoring him completely. "I'll have the cook send up a tray," he said after a few minutes. "We can eat here in the cabin—"

"Actually I thought I might dine with Uncle Monty today. I had so little time to visit with him yesterday."

"Of course," Cole said. "Perhaps supper then."

"Supper? Well, you see, I generally like to eat rather late, and I wouldn't want to hold you up . . ."

"A late supper is fine. That's usually how I like to dine."

Devon paused in the midst of cluttering his washstand with her various creams and ointments. She glanced at him, then quickly averted her gaze. "Did I say late? I meant early. I like to dine early. Sometimes I'll eat my supper immediately after lunch. It's a rather bizarre habit, I know. I wouldn't want you to change your schedule just to accommodate me."

Cole stared at her for a long moment, his face carefully blank. "I see." So that was the plan. She was going to avoid him at all costs until she could finally slip away. Damned if he was going to let her. "Devon," he said firmly.

She let out a weary sigh. "Is there something else you want?"

"As a matter of fact, there is. I should have taken care of this yesterday." Cole straightened and moved toward her. He reached into his pocket and withdrew the glittering wedding band he'd purchased last night. With tender solemnity, he asked, "Would you do me the great honor of accepting this?"

Her startled gaze flew from the ring to him, as shock and pain flashed through her expressive eyes. She shook her head, her voice slightly unsteady as she said, "You didn't have to do that."

"Yes, I did."

Devon hesitated, then looked away. "I suppose it would look odd if I didn't have a ring."

"Will you wear it?"

He watched her run her hands over her skirts, the gesture that always evidenced her nervousness. She drew her brows together in a worried frown, then reluctantly accepted. "Fine."

She reached for the ring, but Cole caught her hand instead. He traced the rough pads of his fingers over the flesh of her palm in a gentle caress. He turned her hand over and lifted it to his lips, his eyes locked on hers as he brushed her skin with a gentle, lingering kiss. Then, moving with infinite slowness, he slipped the ring onto her finger.

The second he released her, she pulled her hand away, holding it as though it had just been burned. "Don't worry," she said with a shaky laugh. "I won't forget to give the ring back to you when this is over."

"I didn't ask you to do that, Devon."

"Yes, well . . ."

"Will it be so awful for you then, being married to me?"

"Cole . . ." Her voice was little more than a whisper. "Will it?"

She spun away from him and resumed unpacking, removing the items from the tapestry bag with slow, careful precision. "You know," she finally remarked, "once when we were in London, Uncle Monty took me to see a traveling show. There was a man there who had an ax stuck in the middle of his forehead. The doctors wouldn't remove it for fear that he might bleed to death." She glanced at him and lifted her shoulders in a light shrug. "If that man could learn to live with an ax in the middle of his forehead, I suppose I can learn to live with you. After all, it's only for a short time, isn't it?"

Wonderful. Of all the things she could learn to tolerate in her life, being married to him ranked just above being struck in the forehead with an ax.

"Devon, if there was any way I could take back every blasted word I said last night, anything I could do—" Cole shook his head, searching for the words he needed to get through to her. What he found instead were barely coherent thoughts that seemed to tumble straight from his soul. "I keep making mistakes, don't I? Stupid, unforgivable mistakes. I used to feel that I was in complete control of my life, but now I see that was nothing but arrogance. I would give anything for just one day, one hour, to go back and do it all over." He stopped and drew a ragged breath. "But I can't go back, Devon. I'm asking for another chance. Please, let me make it up to you. Give me another chance."

"Actually, there is something you can do."

Relief coursed through him. "What?"

Devon pointed to her gowns, which lay spread over his trunk. "I'll need a peg to hang those on or they'll be nothing but wrinkles by tomorrow."

Cole froze, feeling as though he'd just been struck by a pail of ice water. He nodded tightly and moved toward the door. "I'll send a steward to see to it right away." He gave her a brief, polite bow. "If you'll excuse me, I can see that you're busy—"

"Cole, wait," Devon cried. She stood in the center of the room, clutching her skirts. She bit down hard on her lip, then blurted out, "Where did you sleep last night?"

"I didn't." He stared at her for a long second, then sighed. "I'll need to tonight, however. I'll try not to disturb you when I come in."

Devon watched him leave, then sank onto the bed, swallowing past the fist-sized lump in her throat. *Don't do this to me, Cole. Don't make this any harder.* She wasn't going to start crying. She'd already spent the better part of last night bawling, and she refused to give in to that wretched impulse again.

She clutched her hands tightly in her lap and drew in a shuddering breath. Last night she'd cried because he'd rejected her. Today she wanted to cry because she'd rejected him. The whole situation was hopeless. She felt in her pocket for a handkerchief and came up instead with the note Uncle Monty had enclosed with the flowers he'd sent.

She read it again, frowning as she did so. *Trust me. I have a plan.* He hadn't even signed it, but the note had to be from him. No one but her uncle would be audacious enough to send that message, or to use her marriage as a means to an end for one of his schemes. She rose wearily from Cole's bed, thankful to have something to distract her. Whatever Uncle Monty's plan was, she was about to put a stop to it.

She found him on deck, deep in conversation with a man she'd never seen before. Judging by the fancy suit the man wore, he wasn't a member of the crew. He was of medium height and build, with thinning brown hair and cool gray eyes. She guessed him to be somewhere in his early forties. He looked entirely out of place aboard ship. Devon pictured him seated at a desk with a book of ledgers spread open before him. Seeing her approach, the two men stepped apart, their conversation abruptly ended.

Monty smiled broadly. "Ah, there she is now, Mr. Finch, my lovely niece, Mrs. Smith."

"Hello, Uncle," Devon said cautiously, giving Monty a light kiss on the cheek. She turned to the stranger next. "How do you do, Mr. Finch."

Finch nodded, clearly sizing her up. His gray eyes swept over her, cool and analytical. She saw him even glance at her finger to check for a ring, as if suspecting she was no more than the captain's mistress. He bypassed all the usual social pleasantries and said, "It's rather odd for a woman to want to run the blockade, isn't it? If a battle erupts, we won't have time to cater to your frail sensibilities. I hope your husband made that clear."

Devon had perfected the art of the icy stare, and she used it now. "I believe I'll manage, sir."

"Newlyweds," Monty broke in smoothly. "They couldn't bear to be parted. Lovely, isn't it?"

Finch sniffed disdainfully. "Quite."

Devon ignored him. "If you don't mind, Uncle, I should like to speak to you." She paused and glanced at Finch, adding with deliberate rudeness, "Privately."

Finch bowed stiffly. "You'll pardon me then." With that he took his leave, wandering off below decks.

"What a wretched little man," Devon murmured absently, watching him go. "Who is he?"

Monty patted her hand approvingly. "You always were a fine judge of character, my girl. He's our link in the chain that will lead us to Jonas Sharpe. Finch will either approve or disapprove of us. He knows where the ship is being routed, but wants to see us run the blockade before he'll share that bit of news."

Devon nodded, silently absorbing the information. "Who are you, by the way?"

"Reginald Teller."

She smiled. "Uncle Reggie, is it? We haven't seen him in ages." She tilted her head to one side, considering. "Do I need to change my name?"

"That's already been taken care of, my girl. There's no reason for Sharpe or anybody else to connect Devon Blake to the wife of Captain Cole Smith."

Devon was not yet accustomed to hearing herself referred to as Cole's wife—regardless of the name he was using. She looked away and said hollowly, "I suppose so."

Monty frowned. "That's hardly the response I'd expect from a blushing bride."

The image of herself as a happy, blushing bride was so opposite the reality of her situation that Devon found tears once again rushing to her eyes. She blinked them back, swallowing past the sudden ache in her throat as she shook her head. "Oh, Uncle Monty," she choked out, "I think we made a dreadful mistake."

Monty wrapped his arm around her, instantly concerned. "What is it, my girl?"

"Cole and I never should have married. Even if it's only for a little while, it's all wrong—"

"Who said it's only for a little while?"

"I do. We forced him into it, and I have no intention of holding him to a promise he never wanted to make. It was nothing but blackmail. If he weren't so desperate to capture Sharpe, he would have turned you down flat."

"Is that a fact?" Monty countered. "Seems to me the man was here on the island to track you down, and capturing Sharpe was nothing but an afterthought."

Devon accepted the handkerchief he offered her. With an embarrassed smile, she wiped away her tears and blew her nose. "That doesn't mean anything. Cole has this absurd sense of honor. It was his duty to bring me to Washington; he came after me only because I escaped. Trust me, all he cares about is capturing Sharpe.''

"Suppose you tell your uncle why you feel that way.''

She nodded miserably. "Last night—what was supposed to have been our wedding night—well, it was awful, truly awful.''

"Ah, so that's it.'' Monty shifted, looking distinctly uncomfortable. "Devon, I should have spoken to you about this sooner. Obviously I've neglected my duties in educating you about the ways of life.'' He shook his head, his expression mournful. "Quite frankly, I thought you would just pick it up in the streets, but I suppose that was too much to hope for.''

Devon stared at him, drawn out of her own misery for a moment. "Uncle Monty, you've done everything for me.''

"If that were true, my girl, you'd know that there are certain ways that a man will want to touch his wife. Now it might seem shocking to you at first, perhaps even vulgar, but—''

"Oh, Uncle Monty, that's not it. Cole taught me all about that back in Virginia when—'' She stopped abruptly, appalled at what she'd let slip out.

Monty's eyes went dark. "Oh, he did, did he?''

"It was all my idea,'' she rushed on, "but I convinced him to go along.''

"How generous of the man to oblige.''

Devon let out a deep sigh. "He thinks I'm a thief, Uncle. Last night, I gave him a wedding gift and he accused me of stealing it.''

"That doesn't sound like the man,'' Monty replied, studying her intently. "What exactly did he say to you?''

She took a shuddering breath as she remembered

Cole's words. "He told me that I never had to steal again, that he was going to take care of me, and that all I had to do was trust him."

Monty smiled. "The bloody brute. No wonder you're upset."

"This isn't funny," she cried. "He had no reason to believe that of me, no reason at all."

"No reason at all? I suppose you never dipped your fingers into his pockets while you were together?"

Devon frowned. "Well, yes, but—"

"And he didn't find you merrily back in business in that tavern in St. George?"

"Well, yes, but . . . Uncle Monty, you're taking his side!"

Monty clucked his tongue. "Now, now, my girl, I'm just pointing out that your captain has some justification. A fact you seem to have overlooked." Her uncle lifted her hand and continued, "Besides, if he thought you were a thief, would he have given you a ring with stones the size of which would rival the royal jewels?"

"The ring doesn't mean anything. It's just so the marriage looks real. I'm going to give it back as soon as we've captured Sharpe."

"In that case, my girl, might I suggest we return it with creative glass substitutes for the stones? Hardly detectable, except to the discerning eye . . ."

Devon gasped and pulled back her hand. "Uncle Monty, not my wedding ring!"

"I thought you said it didn't mean anything."

"It doesn't," she replied.

"Ah, I see. So that's the way it is." He nodded sagely, his gaze focused entirely on her. When he continued, his tone was completely blasé. "You know, your captain and I had a little talk this morning, and I believe we were able to come to an understanding."

Devon regarded him warily. "About what?"

"Oh, this and that. He's not a bad man, my girl. A

little too straight and narrow for my taste, of course. He also has a rather primitive way of phrasing things, very little sense of adventure, and I imagine he's rather stubborn. Why, now that I think on it, he's a most unpleasant chap. I can certainly see why you wouldn't want to be married to someone like that."

"No, Uncle Monty, Cole's not like that at all. He's . . . he's perfect. That's the problem," she choked out.

Monty shuddered. "A perfect human being. What a ghastly thought. No wonder you can't stand the man."

Devon gave him a trembling smile. "It's even worse than that. I love him, Uncle Monty," she admitted miserably. "That's why everything is such a wretched mess. I've been trying not to, but I can't seem to help myself. I love him."

"How does he feel about you?"

"He doesn't love me."

"Are you sure?"

Devon nodded as tears flooded her eyes once again. "Positive."

"Hmmm." Monty rubbed his fingers over his beard as he considered. "Perhaps he does, perhaps he doesn't. But I saw him just a few minutes ago as he was leaving your cabin, and I've never seen a more miserable fellow in all my life."

She let out a shaky breath. "You see? It's impossible."

Monty shook his head. "On the contrary," he said, smiling brightly. "You should be damned proud of yourself. It takes a special woman to make a man that unhappy."

Devon felt a surge of hope. "Really?"

"Absolutely. Now stay out of my way. Your Uncle Monty has some thinking to do."

She blinked. "But what am I supposed to do now?"

"Have you ever seen a tree growing on the edge of a cliff, with what looks to be nothing but bare rock to support it? There it will stand, through fire and the fiercest storm, the roots digging in hard and deep to hold on. Yet another tree, one which is anchored in the finest, loose soil, will topple over if a breeze so much as blows the wrong way.''

"What does that have to do with anything?''

"The sturdiest of trees grows in rocky soil, my girl.''

Devon sighed. "Uncle Monty, we're talking about my marriage here, not planting trees.''

"The same principle applies. Go water the roots, my girl. Go water the roots.''

Chapter 15

~~~~~oGo~~~~~

Devon wasn't exactly sure how she was going to go about watering Cole's roots, but wearing a cotton nightgown so sheer it was nearly diaphanous seemed a good place to start. She'd purchased it along with her gowns, undergarments, and other necessities when she'd arrived in Bermuda. At the time, she hadn't thought about how sheer the shift was, her primary concern then being to find something cool in which to sleep. She glanced down at herself in nervous hesitation, then shrugged. If nothing else, she was fairly certain she would get his attention.

She wore nothing beneath the gown, allowing the smooth, cool cotton to flow softly over her body as she moved. She'd deliberately chosen to leave the satin ribbon that gathered around the yoke undone, as though she was ready to slip the garment off entirely. Not wearing any underthings beneath the shift seemed a shocking indecency, but the pure naughtiness of the act helped to bolster her courage.

Devon had spent most of the afternoon primping and pampering, beginning with a steaming hot bath. Once her hair was squeaky clean, she brushed it until it shined with a rich sable gloss, then let it cascade over her shoulders and down her back. She rubbed lotion over her entire body, then dabbed her wrists and throat with the barest touch of scent.

It was a strange, almost sensual experience to know

she was preparing herself for Cole. Touching herself in places he would soon—she hoped—be touching. Memories of the last time they'd made love caused a burning sensation to gather in her belly and spread through her like a slow heat. Knowing what she was going to do, she hadn't been able to eat a bite of dinner. Her nerves were simply too heightened, her body too restless, to focus on anything as mundane as food.

Once she finished preparing herself, she turned her attention to the room. She lit the lamps and turned them down low, until the burning wicks gave off nothing but a soft golden glow. The bedding was pulled back and rumpled, the pillows tossed about in wanton disarray. She pushed the portholes open and let the ocean breeze slide through the room, filling the cabin with the fresh, salty scent of the sea. Finished, she selected a book from Cole's desk and seated herself at the table. There was nothing more for her to do but wait.

It was nearly midnight when she heard a soft tap, followed by the sound of the door handle jangling. The door opened and Cole stood there, the light from the passageway framing his rugged form in dark silhouette. Her senses were so finely tuned to his that Devon felt connected in an almost animal sort of way. Cole's presence changed the very air around her, filling it with currents and strange pulses.

There was a moment of silence between them, then Cole stepped into the room. His gaze moved directly to the chair where she sat. "You're awake," he said. He didn't sound disappointed exactly, simply hesitant, as though unsure of his welcome.

"Yes." Devon set down the book she'd been holding and rose to her feet. She watched his eyes widen with shock as his gaze traveled slowly over her. She summoned her courage and said, "I was hoping, if you're not too tired, that we could talk for a few minutes."

She wasn't naked, but she may as well have been.

The pale light of the lamps turned her chemise to nothing but the barest of coverings. A gentle breeze blew into the room, tossing her hair and molding the gossamer fabric to her breasts, thighs, and belly. Desire darkened Cole's face, golden fire shone from his tawny-brown eyes. Devon watched him, her body reacting instinctively to the naked hunger she read on his face. The swelling heat that had been building within her all afternoon seemed to rise to a crescendo, sending a delicious warmth flooding through her limbs. Her resolve weakening, she considered abandoning her plan and walking straight into his arms right then and there, but stubborn pride made her reject that notion. Not until she'd said what she had to say.

"Cole?" she prompted.

He dragged his gaze away from her body. "Yes?"

"Is that all right?"

"What?"

"If we talk."

He stared at her blankly for a second, then seemed to shake himself out of his stupor. "Fine," he said curtly. Apparently realizing that he hadn't moved an inch since she'd stood, he turned and closed the door behind him, taking what seemed to Devon an inordinate amount of time to see that the latch was properly fastened. Finally, when he could delay no longer, he turned back around.

He looked beautiful. Tired, perhaps, but ruggedly handsome. She noted faint shadows beneath his eyes, and the dark stubble on his cheeks told her he hadn't shaved that morning. But as far as she could tell, those were his only flaws. The sun had turned his skin a glowing bronze and woven thick, brilliant streaks through his golden hair. His long legs were encased in neat black trousers that hugged the powerful muscles of his thighs; his black boots were polished to a high sheen. He wore a white, billowy shirt that was loose at the collar and sleeves, allowing her a glimpse of his broad, deeply tanned chest.

"Won't you sit down?" she said, gesturing to a chair. Her tone was perhaps a bit formal considering their circumstances, but Cole didn't seem to notice. He slipped into the chair, his focus remaining entirely on her. Devon felt a flutter of nervousness, as though she were a new hostess entertaining guests for the first time. She lifted a bottle of brandy she'd found while unpacking. "Would you like a drink?" she offered politely.

Cole shrugged, a movement she chose to interpret as assent. She uncorked the bottle, then realized she had no glass. Cole tilted his head toward his desk. "Bottom drawer on the left."

Devon crossed the room to his desk, feeling his eyes on her as she moved. She bent and rummaged through the drawer, shuffling aside papers and bills of lading. Well-aware of the view she presented, she tried desperately not to be embarrassed. It belatedly crossed her mind that it might have been smarter to leave her dressing robe on until they'd finished talking, but it was too late for that now. She found the glass, straightened, and turned around. Cole's eyes lingered exactly where she'd thought they'd be, then moved slowly up her body. "That's quite a gown," he said.

Devon nodded and brushed her hands lightly over the fabric. "Yes, well, since you didn't get any sleep last night, I assumed you'd be rather tired. I thought this might help to wake you up."

"That gown would wake me up if I'd been dead for three years."

A fleeting smile crossed her face. She assumed that was a compliment, but judging from Cole's grim tone as he said it, she couldn't be certain.

She poured his drink, hoping he wouldn't notice the

slight trembling of her hand. But that was exactly where his eyes were now focused: on her hand.

"You're not wearing your ring," he said, ignoring the glass she set before him.

Devon sat down and folded her hands primly in her lap. On the table sat both her wedding ring and the stickpin she'd given him. "No, I'm not. That's what I wanted to talk to you about."

She saw his expression harden as his lips formed a thin, somber line. "I see."

Devon took a deep breath, praying that Uncle Monty had been right, that there still was some tiny spark that existed between them. "Cole," she began, "neither of us wanted this marriage. It was merely the result of unfortunate circumstances. Uncle Monty blackmailed you into taking me as a wife, even if it's only for a little while—"

"Devon, I—"

"No, please, let me finish. This isn't easy for me to say." She bit her lower lip, suddenly nervous. "Despite all of that, it seemed for a little while yesterday that our marriage might not be so bad after all. That perhaps we could be happy together, even if it was for just a short time."

"Until I acted like an ass and accused you of stealing that pin."

"You weren't an ass. You were just being . . . logical."

Cole grimaced. "An ass."

"You couldn't possibly feel any worse about that than I do for turning you away when you came to talk to me today," she said softly. "I'm sorry, Cole."

He looked stunned by her apology. "Devon, you don't—"

"Yes, I do. I owe you at least that much." She clenched her hands in her lap as a silence fell between them. "Hardly a stellar beginning to our marriage, is it? All of these apologies and regrets."

Cole clenched his hand around his glass as a muscle leaped furiously in his jaw. "What are you trying to say, Devon?"

"Well ..." She hesitated, gathering the last of her courage. "I was thinking about what you said this afternoon, about wanting to go back and do everything over ... I want to go back, Cole. Just twenty-four hours. One day. One more chance to do it right, at least for a little while." She stood and lifted the stickpin she'd given him last night. "I thought, if it's all right with you, that we could begin again from this point."

He stared at her in silence, stunned disbelief etched on his rugged features. Deciding to take that for encouragement, Devon pushed forward.

"I'd like for you to have this, Cole. I wanted it for you because the stone reminded me of your eyes. It's a wedding gift, with no strings attached. I don't expect anything in return." She gave him a knowing look and arched a dark brow. "And you needn't worry—I didn't steal it."

His expression carefully blank, he accepted the pin. "It's a lovely gift, Devon. Thank you." He took her hands in his and pulled her forward, brushing his lips lightly over hers. The kiss was altogether too brief. Before she knew it, he released her.

She hid her disappointment with a jaunty smile. "Now it's your turn," she informed him, glancing pointedly at the ring that sat on the table.

"So it is." He lifted the ring, studying it as though it were the first time he'd seen it. "I'd like to tell you that this reminds me of your eyes," he said, echoing her sentiment, "but unfortunately, I can't. The emeralds don't compare. They're nothing but lifeless stones next to the fire and beauty dancing in your eyes."

Devon took a deep, shaky breath. "The ring is lovely, Cole."

"Will you wear it?"

"Yes, I'll wear your ring." The words seemed to stretch between them, as though she'd just promised so much more than that.

Cole must have felt it as well. She studied his eyes as he slipped his ring back onto her finger, seeing triumph in his tawny gaze, as well as what looked to be profound relief. He gave her hand a gentle squeeze. "There's just one other thing you should know about that ring."

"Oh? What's that?"

He gave her a slow, teasing grin. "I didn't steal it."

Her heart melted. "It's reassuring to know that I haven't corrupted you with my wicked ways."

He looked at her for a long moment, then slowly reached out and brushed her hair back over her shoulder. "Ah, but you have. You've corrupted me completely."

His deep voice was low and husky; his words drifted over her skin like a velvety caress. Devon swallowed hard and said, "I believe we still have one more debt to settle."

"What would that be?"

She stepped away from him and moved toward the bed. Moonlight streamed through her gossamer shift as she softly said, "You owe me a wedding night, Mr. McRae."

Cole didn't move. He stared at her intently, as though committing every detail and line of her body to memory. Under his intense gaze, her courage fled. Devon spun about, staring blindly out the porthole at the midnight sea. She brushed her hands nervously over her gown, which suddenly seemed a huge gaffe. Doubtless she looked too needy to him, too eager. "Of course," she managed in a small voice, "if you're tired, we can wait for another night."

Cole was suddenly behind her. "Devon," he said. She started to turn around, but he caught her shoulders and held her still. He slid his hands down her arms in a light caress, then started back up again. She leaned back against his chest, surrendering completely. His voice husky, soft, just a gentle murmur in her ear. "You have no idea what you do to me, do you? No idea how much I want you."

His words shot tremors down her spine. He brought his hands up beneath her gown, pressing her against him as his fingers brushed over her body in playful, loving strokes. Devon was lost in the feel of his touch, helpless, aching for more. A gentle breeze blew in through the porthole and rippled the fabric of her gown, caressing her skin as Cole's words caressed her soul. "You're so beautiful, Devon, so damned beautiful . . ." Meaningless, meandering thoughts and jumbled words, revealing that he was perhaps as lost as she was.

He nibbled her ear, then brushed hot, lingering kisses along her neck and collarbone. A curious, pulsing sensation centered at the junction of her thighs as his hands skimmed over her hips and belly. She caught her breath as he moved lower, winding his fingers through her tight tangle of curls, cupping the warm center between her legs, leaving her hot and moist and aching for more. "Do you like that, Devon? Do you like the way I touch you?"

A soft moan escaped her lips. It was all she could manage in response. She felt drunk, light-headed, and yet acutely aware. Her head lolled against his shoulder, and she closed her eyes. His strong arms wrapped around the front of her as he captured her breasts in his hands. Her nipples were tight and hard, straining against the rough calluses on his palms as he gently caressed her.

Cole was losing control. She could feel his arousal against her back, sharp and jutting, straining against the trousers he wore. That excited her even more. Primitive longings stirred deep within her and a slow heat pounded through her veins. His voice became hoarse, his breath heavier, hot against her ear. There were no more words. Just her name, over and over.

With a low groan, he dropped his hands from her breasts and locked them about her waist, holding her steady. Then with one swift motion, he lifted her into his arms. It took only two strides to reach his bed. Cole sat and laid her down beside him. Devon reached for her gown, which was rumpled and pooled about her hips, but Cole was there first. He gathered it in his hands, eased her arms free, then slipped it gently over her head. His gaze, burning with naked hunger roved over her body.

Devon reached out and touched his chest, her fingers moving clumsily over the buttons. Cole tore off his shirt and sent it sailing across the cabin. His pants and boots quickly followed. His desire was evident, rising proudly erect and just as strong and large as she'd felt it. She ran her hands over his body, familiarizing herself once again with the feel of him: the power of his muscles, the texture of his skin. So hot and smooth and rough, so purely male.

Cole drew her to him, wrapping her in a fierce embrace. His lips slanted over hers in a kiss of savage, aching need. Their tongues met and their bodies molded together, moving as one. He pulled slightly away, his lips tickling the sensitive skin below her ear and trailing hot kisses down her throat. He moved lower and drew her nipple into his mouth, gently sucking and teasing.

Devon arched toward him, her fingers digging into his shoulders. When he pulled back, she nuzzled his neck, licking the hot, salty sweat from his skin. Their lips met again, then Cole eased her back, trailing kisses along her ribs, across her belly, and over the tops of her thighs. She felt him touch his lips to her innermost part and went stiff as alarm shot through her. "Cole! No . . ."

He lifted his head and brushed his hands soothingly over her thighs. "Just one kiss, Devon. Please. Let me taste you . . ." The rough stubble of his cheek rubbed against the soft flesh of her inner thigh, sending hot jolts of desire surging through her body. He pressed his lips against her again, parting the crimson petals of her sex with his tongue, nibbling and teasing until all thoughts of restraint were driven from her mind. She bunched the linen sheets tightly in her fists as she strained toward him, driven by reckless abandon.

The burning heat that had been building within her suddenly turned to aching, throbbing emptiness. "Cole, please . . . I need you. I need you." She didn't know where the words came from, but he seemed to understand. Cole stopped and rose above her. He captured her mouth in a long, deep kiss, then pulled back and drove into her. Not slowly and gently, but fast and hard, which was exactly what she needed, what she had to have. Fast and hard, pounding into her, noisy and deep. Devon drove her nails into his shoulders, clutching herself against him, her fingers slipping over his slick, hot skin. Her release came like an explosion. Every nerve in her body burst open, splintering into fragments of shattering joy.

From somewhere deep within her, she felt Cole freeze, then thrust one final time before he poured himself into her, his body jerking in release. He sagged onto his side, pulling her tightly against him. They lay gasping for breath, exhausted, tangled in their embrace. In some dim corner of her mind, Devon noted that she didn't feel like crying this time. Instead she felt absolutely complete and totally whole.

She listened to the furious pounding of Cole's heart,

felt his chest move as he struggled to gather his breath.
After a few minutes, she heard his deep sigh.
"Devon?"

She tilted her head back and looked into this eyes.
"What?"

"I hope you know how to run a ship."

"Why?"

"Because I doubt I'll ever be able to move again."

Two nights later, Devon paced the deck, her thoughts
wandering aimlessly. She and Cole had finally come
together, and in more than just a physical sense. Ever
since their wedding night, things had changed between them.

Before, her feelings toward Cole had been elusive
bits of hope and fear, torn apart by the slightest ill
wind. But the past two days had changed all that. Her
emotions were now solid, grounded, and not easily
chased away. As Uncle Monty would have said, they'd
grown roots.

They spent hours in Cole's bed talking of important
issues, holding fiery debates, and telling bawdy jokes.
Devon didn't know where the talking ended and the
lovemaking began; there was so much they wanted to
do of both. She'd discovered that Cole was adventurous
and curious, and he whetted the same appetites within
her. Their unions were a blend of fiery passion and
playful teasing, ludicrous positions that had them both
tumbling out of bed laughing until they cried. They
made love on the floor, across Cole's desk (not very
comfortable), tried it while sitting in a stiff-backed
wooden chair (better, because she was astride his lap),
and standing up against the wall. What little sleep
they'd had was enjoyed curled up in each other's arms.

There'd been not only physical discoveries, but emotional ones as well. Devon had gone looking for Cole
yesterday and found him sitting on the starboard rail.

His posture was that which she'd always identified as uniquely his own: one knee drawn up against his chest, his arm thrown casually over it. The wind whipped back his shirt and tossed his hair. Beyond him, the sun streaked the sky with gold and crimson, a fiery ball that sank into the deep teal sea. Gentle, rolling swells rocked the ship and filled the sea with small, white-crested waves.

She'd stopped and stared, her breath caught in her throat. He was a picture of rugged male perfection, yet he seemed to pulse with life. He wasn't just riding out the sea, but was leaning forward, as if a part of it. The ship and the sky, the sea and the man; all molded into one. It revealed a different side of him, a part of Cole she had glimpsed but never fully understood.

There was a sense of healing about him as well. A slow, steady reconciliation, taking place deep within himself. The rough, sharp edges, so spiked and painful when they'd met in Fort Monroe, were finally beginning to be smoothed away. The nightmares had begun to fade as well.

Devon had backed away, not wanting to intrude on his solitude, when Cole turned, as if suddenly sensing her presence. He'd smiled at her and held out his hand. She had hesitated, then moved forward, feeling as though she were walking into a dream. She remembered little of what they spoke of, only that the sun had sunk and disappeared. The stars had risen one by one, and faint glimmers of light slowly imbued the indigo sky with sparkling, shimmering brilliance.

All the while, Cole had held her hand. Touched her in a way that wasn't sexual, but simply brought them together as they talked. Establishing a trust and friendship that added a different dimension to their relationship; one that was pure and bright. Distinctly unlike the smoky haze and passionate fire of their lovemaking, but equally powerful.

As she remembered that moment, a soft smile lit her features as she paused in her evening stroll and leaned against the deck rail. Devon stared absently at the sea, unable to contain her joy. When the worry that their marriage was nothing but a temporary arrangement threatened to intrude, she abruptly banished it. If she was to be crushed later, so be it. She'd accumulated more than enough memories to last her the rest of her life. For now she was content to live only for the moment, to let the winds of fate carry her wherever she was destined to go. Right now, if she was meant to be with Cole, she would be. Totally and completely.

Just as she'd resolved that in her mind, an order was passed among the crewmen to extinguish the lights; the ship was plunged into darkness. Though she'd been expecting it, the eerie quiet and total blackness sent her heart racing, for it could mean only one thing. It was time to run the blockade.

Devon lifted her skirts and moved gropingly along through the darkness, making her way up to the bridge. There she found not only Cole and the ship's pilot, but her Uncle Monty and Mr. Finch. She slipped quietly into their midst. The only other place for her to go was back to her cabin, but the thought of sitting alone all night, not knowing anything, was intolerable. At least here she'd have Cole's presence to comfort her. Even now, as she studied his rugged profile, she felt some of her fear and nervousness begin to slip away.

Last night, he'd explained to her in nautical terms what they faced in running the blockade, and she focused on that now. They'd made good time out of St. George. Too good, as a matter of fact. At noon, Cole ordered the sails lowered and the engines cut, allowing them to drift around Cape Fear and approach the river to Wilmington from the northern end of the blockade, which was their present position. Devon glanced at the sky. It was a moonless night and a slight fog enveloped them—a runner's dream—better conditions than they ever could have hoped for.

As they crept cautiously forward, a thick tension spread over the ship. Orders were passed back and forth in whispers. The ship's compass was draped with a dark cloth, shielding the tiny light from view. There was no noise but the dull rumble of the engines and the gentle, splashing wake created by the *Ghost*'s screw propellers.

Dead ahead, she saw a looming mound of earth, which she recognized from Cole's description as Smith Island. It divided Cape Fear River at its mouth into two channels: New Inlet to the north, guarded by the guns of Fort Fisher, and the main channel to the South, guarded by Fort Caswell. She strained her eyes, looking for the signal that would guide them into the channel.

"There!" Devon cried softly, seeing a soft glow through the thick fog. Soon she was able to make out the second lantern as well.

"All right, let her drift," Cole said.

He gave the command without any hesitation, though Devon was well-aware of the risk. The *Ghost* was to drift north, keeping the lights in view, until the two lights merged into one. Only then would the ship be in position to make it over the sandbar without trapping the hull. In theory, it was a sound plan. But too much could go wrong. The Federals could have learned of the run and moved the lights, sending them crashing ashore. Their position could have been miscalculated by the Rebels who set them out. A strong gust of wind could have blown one lantern over, setting it off just enough to ground them.

Cole's voice was cool and in control. "Steady . . . Steady . . . There. Send her in."

Devon held her breath, waiting for the grinding roar that meant they were trapped.

They sailed cleanly through the narrow passageway.

She heard a low rush of air as every man aboard let out his breath. Beside her, Finch reached into his pocket and pulled out a cigar. With a trembling hand, he struck a match and raised it to the end.

Cole spun around furiously, grabbed the cigar in his fist, and jerked it out of Finch's mouth. He knocked the match from his hand and ground it out with his boot. "What the hell are you doing?" he hissed.

Finch stared at him in stupefied amazement. "Why, I just ... I didn't think—"

"Captain! Off the starboard bow," whispered the pilot urgently.

Cole turned his back on Finch and focused his attention on the river. Devon peered into the fog but saw nothing. Cole's voice was little more than a cool, steady whisper. "Yes, I see her. Starboard a little. Keep her steady." They inched through the water, and still Devon saw nothing. She felt a subtle shift beneath her feet as the *Ghost* strained against tide. The black, motionless hulk of a Yankee gunboat materialized to her right as they slid past. She caught her breath, expecting at any moment to see the angry flash of guns as Yankee cannon exploded at them. Miraculously, they sailed by undetected, cloaked by the fog and inky blackness of the night.

They moved perhaps another hundred yards when she felt Uncle Monty's fingers digging into her arm. "There!" he cried softly, "I see one!"

"Hard aport," Cole ordered in a rough whisper. "Cut the engine. Just the starboard, dammit! Now!"

The pilot obeyed and the *Ghost* swung in a hard ninety-degree angle to the left. The Yankee gunboat slid past on their right. The ship was so close that Devon could hear the conversations of the crewmen aboard the other vessel. Her knees buckled, and she gripped the rail in an effort to remain standing.

A phantom ship rose from the fog dead ahead of them, crossing the bow.

"Stop her," Cole said.

The pilot obeyed once again, cutting the port engine. The *Ghost* sat silent in the water. But their momentum and the current continued to push her forward, directly in the path of the steamer. Devon closed her eyes, bracing herself for the impact of the collision. Instead they passed so close to the steamer's stern that the spray of the paddle wheel soaked the deck.

Relief surged through Devon. She longed to collapse in an undignified heap in the middle of the bridge, laughing and crying at the same time. She felt Monty sag against her. The pilot slumped against the helm, and Finch leaned against the rail as though he were about to be sick. Only Cole remained unaffected by their near-disaster. "I need a reading," he said.

The order was relayed forward, where a man handling the forechains lowered the lead and checked the depth and condition of the bottom. The information obtained was sent back to the bridge in whispers.

Devon saw quickly why Cole hadn't been relieved at their near-miss. What he'd been unwilling to explain to his shaky passengers, he and his crew knew only too well: they'd barely begun their run. The *Ghost*'s engines were stoked once again and they inched on through the night, dodging enemy warships as they went. To Devon's increasingly strained nerves, each near miss and close encounter was more terrifying than the next.

Periodically Cole weighed anchor and requested a reading. He listened to the report on the river conditions, using that to adjust their heading. In short order, the helplessness of their position was made frighteningly clear. Cole was sailing the river blind, with nothing to guide him but memory, instinct, and what little information he was able to obtain from the readings.

He had told her that it normally took two hours to sail from Cape Fear to Fort Fisher. He'd anticipated they would make it in four. It had been six hours now since they'd entered the river. With all of their stops, starts, and wild maneuvering, it was even possible they'd turned completely around and were headed back out to sea, a position that would leave them wide open to attack, completely surrounded by enemy vessels.

Devon glanced anxiously at Cole. His mouth was grim; tense lines of strain showed around his eyes as the ship crept warily forward. In the past hour, he'd been stopping for more and more readings. To the east, the sky was tinted with a rosy glow as the sun began its ascent. They were about to lose their cover entirely.

"You don't know where we are, do you, McRae?" Finch hissed, his face white with fear. "You've got us trapped—"

Cole ignored him and turned to the pilot. "I need a reading."

"Another?!" shrieked Finch, his voice laced with panic. "Can't you see the sun is coming up? There's no time!"

Unfortunately he was right. A flash of red streaked through the rosy sky. A whirring shriek filled the air above their heads, followed by the roar of an explosion as a shell landed in the water behind them.

Devon spun around, her heart slamming against her chest. Six enemy warships bore down hard and fast, their guns blazing.

Chapter 16

❦

"Fire the engines!" Cole shouted below. "Give me all the steam she's got!" He felt the thrust of the engines beneath his feet as the *Ghost* roared to life, churning up water in their wake. No more inching, creeping along the river. Speed was their only chance of survival now.

Shots rained furiously around them. The warships were still too far behind to have any sort of accuracy, but they were closing in fast. His crew, ready at their stations, manned their weapons. "Fire, sir?" a young recruit yelled from his position behind a fifty-pound pivot gun.

"No," Cole called back. "Hold steady, men! Wait for my order!"

"No?!" echoed Finch in furious disbelief. He turned to the crewmen and waved his fist. "Fire, dammit! Shoot the bastards! Fire!"

The crewmen ignored Finch and stared at their captain instead as shots rained in all around them. Cole turned and yelled down to the engineer, "We need more speed!" But smoke poured through the stacks even as he shouted the command. He knew the men in the engine room were shoveling coal into the furnace as fast as they could. He couldn't expect the ship to go from a near-crawl to full speed in a matter of seconds.

Cole raked his fingers through his hair, his gut clenched with sick dread. He'd failed. Dammit to hell, he hadn't gotten them through. The Federals were closing in. He glanced at the warships, able to identify them all. He knew most of the men commanding them by name, a few he even counted as friends. Now he had to do his best to blow them out of the water. The shots exploded closer, and he knew he had no choice. The fight was on. "Arms!" he called. "Ready to fire!"

A flash of pale blue calico caught his eye. *Devon*. He grabbed her by the arm and turned her toward the ladder that led from the bridge to the main deck. "Get below and wait for me in my cabin," he ordered curtly.

She shook her head. "But what about—"

"Dammit, Devon, now! Get below!"

"Captain!" the pilot shouted. "Dead ahead! Big Hill!"

Cole whirled around, peering along the flat coastline until he saw the bump in the sand to which his crewman was referring. He relaxed his grip on Devon's arm as icy relief poured through him. They'd made it.

Just beyond Big Hill lay the Confederate batteries of Fort Fisher. Within seconds, the roar of cannon fire exploded in the air. Hot lead shots sailed over the *Ghost*, striking within threatening range of the Federal ships. The warships pulled up short, clearly outmanned by the Rebel guns of the fort. They fired off a couple of angry, useless blasts, huddling in the distance like a pack of snarling dogs, then sensibly retreated. The jubilant cries of his crew mingled with the triumphant shouts of the men at the fort as the *Ghost* crossed the bar, her path to Wilmington now free and clear.

Monty's hand came down hard on his shoulder. "My good friend." He beamed. "Nice bit of work. Very nice, indeed."

Finch pulled out his handkerchief and mopped his brow. "For a moment there I didn't think we were going to make it." He glared up at Cole, his tone suspicious. "You cut it awfully close, Captain. Why didn't you fire on those ships?"

"I'm not in the habit of wasting ammunition. The South needs all she can get," he answered with a reasonable lie.

Finch frowned and shoved his handkerchief back into his pocket. "I would have fired anyway."

"Maybe that explains why I'm captain of this ship and you're not." Cole turned and reached for Devon's hand. "If you gentlemen will excuse us, I have duties to attend to before we dock, and I believe my wife is in need of some rest."

He ushered Devon across the deck and through the narrow passageways that led to his cabin. Neither one spoke a word as they moved. Once there, he brought her inside and kicked the door shut behind them. Cole wrapped his arm around her in a fierce embrace and pulled her tightly to him. His lips slanted over hers in a kiss of savage hunger, in a need to release his pent-up fear and frustration.

Finally he was able to pull back. He ran his hands over her back and breathed deeply. "I should have never brought you. That was too close, Devon. Too damned close."

She pulled back and stared up into his face. "That doesn't matter. You made it. You got us through."

"Barely. I didn't know what the hell I was doing."

"I never doubted you for a moment."

He stared down at her, amazed by the absolute conviction in her tone, the complete trust and approval glowing in her eyes. He felt overwhelmed—and totally undeserving. "What am I going to do with you?" he asked huskily.

"I don't know, but I suspect you'll think of something."

The invitation was clear in her words. But as tempting as the offer was, she looked exhausted. He probably looked like something that had been wrung through a meat grinder. He sure as hell felt that way. Given that, it wasn't too difficult for him to be noble. "Later," he said gently. He brushed his fingers over her cheek, still entranced by the velvety softness of her skin. "Why don't you lie down for a little while," he suggested. "I'll join you shortly."

"Where are you going?"

"To check the cargo before it's unloaded." He let out a breath and ran a hand over the back of his neck. Every muscle in his body ached. Exhaustion made him thoughtless, or he never would have let his next words slip. "Thank God none of those shots came any closer. With what we're carrying, the ship would have gone up in—" He stopped abruptly, swearing silently.

Devon stared at him calmly. "Cole, I know."

He looked at her in disbelief. She couldn't possibly . . .

"Those crates marked hardware are full of weapons, aren't they?" she said. "The barrels marked wheat are full of gunpowder. You've other kinds of ammunition in the hold too, don't you?"

He let out a hollow laugh. "I can't imagine why I thought I could pull anything over on you."

She arched a dark brow. "Neither can I."

Half the crates stored below were filled with frivolous luxuries, the other half with rifles and munitions. Cole knew that the type of cargo he carried was equally as important as his ability to make it through the blockade. Bringing in the weapons should be interpreted as a sign of loyal dedication to the Southern cause, a trait that likely would appeal to Sharpe.

"I presume you took care of it," Devon said.

Cole nodded. "The firing pins on the rifles are bent beyond repair, the gunpowder has been soaked in saltwater, and holes were drilled into the shells to make them fire astray." He'd had to leave a few crates undamaged for checking and testing purposes, but the vast majority of the munitions were worthless.

"Good," she said, stifling a yawn.

"Get some sleep. I'll be back as soon as I can."

Cole found himself occupied all day, rather than just for a few hours. By the time he was finally able to return to his cabin, night had long since fallen. Normally Devon left a light for him, but tonight the room was pitch-black. He lit a lamp and turned it up low. She was lying in bed, curled on her side with her back to him, still fully dressed. The supper tray he'd ordered sent to her was sitting on the table, untouched. "Aren't you hungry?" he asked.

Devon didn't move or make a sound, though he knew she was awake.

Cole frowned as he walked to the bed and sat down. The mattress sank beneath his weight. Her body rolled back against his, her spine pressed against his thigh. She didn't move away, nor did she lean into him. Nothing. Cole fought back a rising sense of panic as he reached for her. Despite the warmth of the night, her skin felt cold and clammy. "Devon, what is it? Are you ill?"

She stared blankly at the wall, then softly said, "Let's leave Wilmington tomorrow, Cole. Run the blockade and get out. Forget about Sharpe, the war, everything. Just run."

He reached for her and gathered her into his arms, cradling her in his lap. He ran his hands over her, trying to transfer the heat from his body to hers. "Devon," he said, "I shouldn't have left you alone today. You're experiencing delayed shock from running the blockade. It's a terrifying experience for even the most seasoned—"

"No. No, that's not it." She tilted her face up toward his. Though she wasn't crying now, her eyes were red and swollen; the tracks of her tears still glistened on her cheeks. "We can't go after Sharpe, Cole. If we do, it's going to be bad. It's going to be very, very bad."

Cole looked down at her, his entire body aching with regret. Obviously she was more shaken up by the run than he'd suspected. "Where did this all come from?"

"I was sleeping and I saw it all," she said with a shuddering breath. "I saw exactly what's going to happen."

"You had a bad dream."

"No, not a dream. A vision. I get them sometimes when something bad is about to happen. It's as if God is trying to warn me. I had one before my father put me on that train, then again before Billy died, and once about a hotel at which Uncle Monty and I were staying. I saw that there was going to be an awful fire and there was, the very next night."

"And now you dreamed about Sharpe."

"You're not listening to me!" Devon shook her head against his chest, his shirt clenched in her fist. "It wasn't a dream. It's real, Cole. It's exactly what will happen if we go after Sharpe."

"Shhh," he soothed, rocking her back and forth. "I'm right here, Devon. I'm listening. Tell me about it."

She closed her eyes, her voice trembling as she said, "I don't know where we were, it's all so hazy. Everything had gone wrong. I was there, Uncle Monty was there, and you were there . . . but you weren't there. I don't understand it." She paused and took a deep breath. "Sharpe had a gun. There was blood all over my dress, all over my hands, and I couldn't stop screaming."

Cole's stomach clenched as he fought back the image her words created. He tightened his arms around her, thinking of his own dark premonitions the day they'd set sail for Wilmington. "That's not going to happen, Devon," he swore. "None of it, do you hear me?"

She pulled out of his embrace to study his face. "Does that mean you're not going after Sharpe?"

"Devon, I can't—"

"Cole, please . . ."

He stared into her eyes, hating the fear and desperation he saw there. "I have to do this," he said, refusing to lie to her. "We've come too far for me turn back now."

She regarded him in silence, then let out a shaky breath. "I know."

"I promise you, everything's going to be all right."

Her eyes welled with tears as she let out a choked sob. "There was so much blood . . ."

The sight of her tears slashed through his body like the sting of a whip. He pulled her tightly against him, brushing his hand gently over her hair. "It's going to be all right," he swore. "I promise, Devon."

Her nightmare wouldn't come true, and for one simple reason. When it came time for a showdown with Sharpe, Cole would make damned sure Devon was nowhere near.

Cole moved swiftly through the streets of Wilmington, stunned at the changes that had befallen the city in the year and a half since the war had begun. The streets were muddy and unkempt, the shops empty and barren. An air of poverty and distress hung over the town like a dark cloud.

He felt the furtive glances of people he passed, and wondered if there was something that gave him away. He wore pants and a shirt of decent quality, not too rich, but not shabby either. No Rebel uniform. He'd never claimed to be in the Confederate Navy, for that could be too easily checked by Sharpe. Instead he called himself a profiteer. Someone who ran the blockade for money, but who had strong Southern leanings. It was a bit ambiguous of a background, but he preferred it that way. No, there was nothing about him that gave him away. It was just that his nerves were still a bit on edge.

Devon had thoroughly shaken him three nights ago with her talk of visions and disaster. That, combined with his own dark premonitions, filled him with a deep sense of foreboding, despite the fact they'd gamely tried to brush it off the next morning as nothing but the result of strain and exhaustion. Monty seemed to be the only one who was handling the situation well. As a matter of fact, he appeared to be thriving.

Monty owned a different suit for every day of the week, and as near as Cole could tell, they were all plaid. That made the large man easy to identify. Especially now, as he stood on a crate before a swelling crowd. He was smiling, shouting, and carrying on, his grand gestures visible even from across the street. Cole shook his head and stifled a groan. A low profile, that's what Monty had promised him. But with Montgomery Persons, that obviously wasn't possible.

Cole glanced at the banner that hung over Monty's head: *Mrs. Winslow's Soothing Syrup. Miracle Cure-All.* Bottles of the syrup were stacked up neatly in the booth behind him, blazing with impressive red and gold labels that matched the banner. Cole had no idea where the syrup had come from, nor did he truly want to know. He spotted Devon standing next to the booth and went over to join her. She gave him a brief smile, then turned her attention back to her uncle.

"Of all the blessings this life has to offer," Monty boomed out to the crowd, "none can exceed the value of good health. Who among us has not fallen to grievous illness, only to recover and experience the bliss, the joy, the bounty of good health? And what a wonderful feeling that is, my friends, what a wonderful feeling that is!"

Cole was grudgingly impressed. Monty worked the

crowd like an evangelical preacher, offering praise and salvation one moment, heartache the next. "But what about those of you who suffer pain in silence, those who have loved ones who suffer? Do you think the world has forgotten you? Indeed, the world has not! Mrs. Winslow has not!"

"Why ain't you off fightin' the war?" a heckler called from the audience.

Monty handled the man with cool aplomb. "My good friend," he beamed, "I'm delighted you asked. For you see, I have as brave a heart in my body as any man, but the most cowardly legs you ever saw."

A chuckle ran through the crowd, and the heckler was pushed back. Monty grabbed a bottle and waved it around. "Speaking of the war, don't forget your loved ones in prison or in the camps," he called out. "One bottle will relieve the worst cases of sores, ulcers, scurvy, fevers, and bowel complaints. You there!" He pointed to two young men who stood nearby. "A side benefit of the syrup: when applied to the face it promotes a luxurious growth of whiskers—without staining the skin! Remarkable, you say? Yes, but true! All true!"

The townspeople surged forward, offering up their hard-earned bills. While Cole strongly doubted the cure-all would help any of them, neither did he figure it would hurt—except perhaps in the pocketbook. Most likely it contained a mixture of alcohol, water, peppermint, and whatever herbs were at hand when it was bottled.

After an hour had passed and Monty's stock was nearly depleted, a young girl fought her way to the front of the crowd. Cole's indifference immediately fled. She was barefoot, her dress made of coarse brown wool. In her arms she carried a squalling baby. The girl unclenched her fist, holding up a few coins. "Please! Please, sir, I have to have that syrup!"

Monty frowned. "Are you ill?"

"No, it's not for me, it's for the baby. She's been sickly ever since she was born."

Monty bent down and pulled back the thin cotton blanket that covered the child's face. "Your sister?" he asked gently.

The girl shook her head, a shy smile flashing across her face. "No, I'm her mama. Her daddy's off fightin' the war."

"I see," Monty said as he straightened. He looked at the girl for a second longer, then shook his head. "I'm sorry. The syrup is too strong to give to a baby."

The girl's smile faded as panic transformed her features. "It's the money, ain't it? I know it's not enough but it's all I've got. I don't have any more."

"I'm sor—"

"Wait!" she cried desperately. "I can dig up my garden! It's got carrots and potatoes. I'll give them all to you. Please, I don't need the food. I just need something for my baby."

Monty let out a deep breath, no doubt seeing what Cole was seeing. The girl was nothing but skin and bones. She needed every ounce of food she had and then some. "I don't want your food—"

"Oh, please," she choked out. "I'll give you anything. Anything. But I have to have a bottle of that potion."

"My dear girl—"

"Please, you don't understand," she said as she clutched Monty's leg. "Last night I prayed for a miracle for my baby, and now you're here. The bottle even says *Miracle* on it. That's why I have to have it. I know it's going to cure her, I know it will."

Monty studied her for a long, silent moment. Finally he let out a deep sigh and held out his hand. "Very well."

The girl dropped her coins into his palm, her face

wreathed with a glowing smile. "Oh, thank you, sir. Thank you." She reached for the bottle but Monty pulled it out of her grasp.

"Now, now, my dear. As I said, this is too strong to give a baby. Let me get you the other formula."

Cole watched in disgust as Monty pocketed the girl's coins. He moved forward, determined to stop the sale.

Devon caught his arm. "Let him be, Cole."

He stared at her in amazement. "What? We can't let him—"

"Let him be."

There was a quiet firmness to her tone. He shook his head, wondering why she wasn't as sickened as he was. Still, he did as she bid, watching as Monty ducked behind the booth, then handed the girl a box containing the syrup. He admonished her not to open it until she got home, lest she spill a drop. The girl thanked him profusely, then skipped away.

Cole frowned and said to Devon, "You can't believe that what he gave her will actually cure the babe."

Devon shrugged. "No," she said softly, "it won't cure the babe. But it will help, and that's all we can do."

Cole watched her move to join her uncle, taken aback by her faith in the cure-all. She gave her uncle a quick hug, murmuring words that sounded like praise. Cole's unease rose. Perhaps Devon had learned to tolerate her uncle's schemes and wiles, but he definitely had not. Her and Monty's absolute lack of remorse at taking the girl's only coin bothered him more than he cared to admit.

Realizing that they'd lost the momentum of the show, Monty and Devon dispensed the few remaining bottles free of charge to the wounded Rebel soldiers who lined the area in front of the booth. The men eagerly accepted the tonic, then hobbled off. Cole assisted Monty in dismantling the booth as Devon folded the banner.

When they finished, Devon excused herself and walked to the small shop across street, wanting to pick up a few items before they returned to the ship. Though Cole doubted she'd find much among the barren shelves, he welcomed the opportunity to talk to Monty alone. Cole had rented a wagon and a swaybacked old nag, the only horseflesh in town that hadn't been impressed by the army. As they loaded everything up, he said, "That was very well-done, Monty. I do believe you could charm the skin off a snake."

Monty shrugged. "So I've been told." He nodded to a passing coach, tipped his hat to the ladies inside, then turned back to Cole. "Speaking of snakes, I received a message from our good friend Mr. Finch today."

Cole tensed. "Where has he been?" The man had left the ship the day they docked and hadn't been seen since.

"Taking care of business, apparently. Evidently you passed on both counts, Captain. The cargo was in good order and no one has ever heard of you—either as a blockader or as a runner. Exactly what we wanted."

"So now what?" he pressed.

"Now we proceed as planned, of course. Your ship is loaded, ready to go. Finch will meet us aboard at five o'clock for departure, just as you requested."

Cole nodded. "Finch will be aboard for the return run?" he asked.

"Wouldn't miss it for the world."

That considerably offset the possibility that they were being led into a trap—at least while Finch was aboard. The man was rabid about saving his own skin. Still, Cole felt uneasy. He wondered why Finch had sent a message about departure to Monty rather than to him, as the ship's captain. There were hundreds of possibilities, none of which was very reassuring. His eyes locked on Monty's as he said, "You know, it could be that Finch has no idea where Sharpe is routing that ship. In fact, he may never have even heard of Jonas Sharpe. He could be nothing but a stooge you paid to lure me into making this run and providing you with a handsome profit.''

Monty brought his hand down on Cole's shoulder in a gesture of solid approval. ''Brilliant, my boy! Absolutely brilliant. I'm only ashamed I didn't think of it myself.''

''What I'm interested in is whether it's true.''

Monty smiled. ''Do you know what your problem is? You trusted me, and now you regret it.'' He sighed and shook his head. ''My good friend, it's a classic symptom—I run into it all the time in my line of work. You're angry at yourself and you're suspicious of me, but there's no going back. I offered you Jonas Sharpe and my darling niece in one neat package, and you leaped at the chance to have them both. You should have examined this thoroughly before you agreed, but now it's too late.''

''Listen, dammit, if you think this is some kind of a game—''

''A game? No, Captain, it most assuredly is not,'' Monty replied. For once, his tone was serious.

Devon approached the wagon, and Cole let the conversation drop. He helped her aboard, seating her between him and Monty as they made their way back to the *Ghost*. ''By the way, Captain,'' Monty said. ''Finch will be expecting a little payment from you. Five hundred dollars, to be exact.''

Cole pulled up the reins and brought their tired nag to a dead stop. ''For what?''

''Dock fees have to be paid, of course. Then there are the export taxes on the cotton and compensation for the extra hours the stevedores worked to assist your crew loading and unloading the cargo.''

''I've never heard of any of those charges. Sounds like Finch is getting greedy.''

"Either that or it's nothing but local graft." Monty thought it over, then shrugged. "A bit of both, I suspect."

"Finch expects me to hand over five hundred dollars in less than thirty minutes?"

"If we intend to leave Wilmington today, yes. The fees have to be paid first."

"That's impossible."

Monty frowned. "The money is of little consequence, Captain. We'll make it up at least a hundred times over once we sell the cotton we're bringing out."

"That's exactly the point. I have about ten dollars in Rebel notes left to my name. The cargo I carried in was swapped directly for cotton—there was never an exchange of currency." Cole had enough Federal currency in his cabin to cover the fees, but a Rebel blockade runner certainly couldn't flash Yankee bills around a Southern port. He'd managed to get his hands on some Rebel notes before he'd left St. George, but obviously not enough.

"I see. My, this is a tight fix, isn't it?" Monty said, not sounding the least bit concerned.

Cole let out a sigh of disgust, then brightened as he remembered the money the crowd had tossed at Monty for Mrs. Winslow's Soothing Syrup. While he hadn't approved, at five dollars a bottle Monty had earned at least what they needed to cover the fees. Probably twice that. "Pay Finch the money," he said shortly. "I'll reimburse you with Federal currency."

"Actually, Captain, I would prefer not to do that."

Cole stiffened. "And I would prefer not to pay the damned money in the first place. But it doesn't appear either of us has a choice, now does it?"

"Unfortunately I regret that I will not be able to oblige—"

"Now listen, Monty—"

"He doesn't have the money, Cole," Devon interrupted.

"Now, now, my girl, there's no need—" Monty protested as he shifted uncomfortably in his seat.

"What do you mean, he doesn't have the money?" Cole said. "I saw him take at least . . ." His voice trailed off as he remembered the elixir Monty had sold the young girl. Unlike the others he'd passed out to the crowd, hers hadn't been in a clear bottle. Instead he'd handed her a tightly sealed box and admonished her not to open it until she returned home. He recalled Devon's soft smile as she said, *It won't cure the babe. But it will help.* He turned and stared at Monty in stunned disbelief. "You gave it to that girl, didn't you?"

"Every penny," Devon answered for her uncle, "and probably every cent he had in his own pockets, as well."

Monty looked away, his expression thoroughly displeased. "Even I have my standards," he grumbled.

Cole shook his head in amazement. "I never would have believed it."

"I'll thank you to keep your mouth shut about it too," Monty snapped. "After all, I do have my reputation to consider."

Cole glanced at Devon, who wrapped her arm through her uncle's, looking both pleased and proud. With a flick of the reins, he set the nag in motion and brought his thoughts back to the matter at hand. "That leaves us with less than thirty minutes to come up with five hundred dollars in Rebel currency."

Monty brightened, happy with the shift in conversation, particularly since they were back in his area of expertise. He rubbed his hands together, his broad smile firmly in place. "Thirty minutes? Plenty of time, my good friend, plenty of time." He pointed to a waterfront tavern they were about to pass. "I think this should do nicely, Captain."

Cole drew to a stop and hitched the wagon. He secured the reins, knowing they had little choice. Obviously Monty was about to pick every pocket in the place. They moved into the dark, crowded tavern and took a seat at a table along a side wall. Monty studied a group of three men, listening intently to their conversation. Cole glanced at them as well.

The three looked wealthy and prosperous. Their conversation was easily overheard, as they were boasting loudly of the money they'd been making since the start of the war. A woman timidly approached, tapped one of them on the sleeve, and whispered a few words. The man scowled at the interruption. He made a remark to his friends about nagging wives, then turned back to the woman. "You just sit yourself down for a spell, Ma. Can't you see I've got business to take care of?" The woman turned and left the tavern, her mouth pinched and unhappy as the men resumed their drinking.

Monty smiled. "By jove, I think we've found our man."

"We couldn't have wished for better," Devon replied.

Cole sent him a stern frown. "Just make sure he doesn't catch you lifting his wallet."

Monty raised his brows and looked at Devon. "Crass, isn't he?" he asked.

"A complete cynic as well," she agreed. "No faith whatsoever."

Cole listened impatiently as they discussed his faults. Finally Monty turned to him and said, "Captain, I have no intention of stealing anything. Within ten minutes, that man will *offer* me five hundred dollars. In fact, he'll be angry if I don't accept it."

"Just how do you intend to accomplish that?"

Monty handed him a card. Cole took it and read aloud: "Calvin. Renowned astrologer and diviner of future events. Seventh son of a seventh son—"

"Ah. Pardon me," Monty plucked the card from his grasp and replaced it with another. It read simply:

HORACE GREELEY, ESQ.
LOTTERY AGENT

"I still don't understand—"

"You will, my good friend, you will. How much money do you have on you?"

Cole frowned and reached into his pocket. "Only—"

"Perfect." Monty removed the ten-dollar note from his hand and motioned to one of the serving women. "My dear," he said to her, "do you see that gentleman standing by the bar? Yes, the one in the blue suit. He's an old chum of mine from school, and I've quite forgotten his name."

The woman squinted at the bar. "You mean Edward Oakes? You went to school with him?"

Monty beamed. "Of course, dear old Eddy. The other fellows and I used to call him Spider Legs, but I won't bore you with that." He placed the ten-dollar note on her tray. "Be a love and don't tell him I couldn't remember his name. Most embarrassing, you know."

The waitress quickly pocketed the money, nodded, and left. Monty stood up, taking his card and hat with him. "You can time me if you like, Captain. Ten minutes, no more." With that he was gone, meandering back through the crowd and toward the front entrance.

Cole looked at Devon. "He can't possibly be serious," he said flatly. "No one can swindle five hundred dollars in ten minutes."

Devon watched her uncle walk away, then looked at the man about to be swindled. "You're right, not in ten minutes," she agreed as she stifled a yawn. "It can't possibly take him longer than five."

Despite her cavalier attitude, Cole was intrigued. He watched as Monty made his way from the front of the tavern toward the three men. Fortunately they were standing close enough for him to overhear their words. "Pardon me, gentlemen," Monty said as he broached their circle. "I was told I might find a Mr. Oakes here."

"I'm Oakes," said their prey.

"Ah, my good friend, how nice it is to meet you at last. It is indeed an honor, sir." Monty reached for Oakes's hand and shook it vigorously. "I was beginning to fear I would never find you."

Oakes frowned. "Who are you?"

"Forgive me, I've quite lost my head, haven't I?" Monty gave a small bow and handed over his card. "Horace Greeley at your service, sir. Representative of the Confederate States Lottery Commission. I have the privilege to inform you that your generosity to our dear cause has indeed paid off."

Oakes frowned. "I don't know what—"

"Most men only purchased five, maybe ten dollars' worth of tickets," Monty said to Oakes's friends, "but do you know what Mr. Oakes did? Why, he purchased one thousand dollars' worth of tickets! Granted, all of the funds are going directly to help our boys in battle, but we never expected such selfless giving, such glorious commitment to our cause." He paused, beaming up at Oakes as his friends stared at him in slack-jawed astonishment. Oakes looked as stunned as his companions.

"Imagine our delight at the lottery office," Monty continued smoothly, "to discover that Mr. Oakes actually won the raffle!"

"I won?" echoed Oakes.

"You did indeed. A fine, Arabian thoroughbred, the most magnificent piece of horseflesh I've ever seen.

Sired by the same stallion which was recently delivered to President Jefferson Davis himself. The saddle was made by the same craftsman who designed Jeff Davis's saddle as well. Doubtless you've seen the sketches in all the papers of the president sitting atop his magnificent steed. Now you, Mr. Oakes, will travel in the same glorious style. A style which befits a man of your station and generosity.''

''I will?'' said Oakes.

Monty nodded. ''We would like to submit sketches of you sitting astride Apollo to all the papers as well. I imagine the caption should read: Edward Oakes, Noble Confederate Patriot. That is, if we have your permission, sir.''

Cole watched as Oakes puffed up his chest, looking supremely satisfied. ''Of course.''

''My associates can deliver Apollo directly to your home tomorrow morning, if that's satisfactory.''

''That will do,'' he conceded grandly.

''Very good,'' said Monty. ''What a thrill this is. There are just a few more details, sir, and then I'll be on my way.''

''Yes?''

''You are Edward Oakes?''

''Of course.''

''The same Edward Oakes who purchased one thousand dollars' worth of lottery tickets from the Confederate States Lottery Commission?''

''I certainly did.''

Given that the Confederate States Lottery Commission didn't exist until five minutes ago when Monty made it up, Cole decided that was quite a feat.

''Very good, sir,'' Monty answered. ''I'll just need to see your ticket, then I'll be on my way.''

''My ticket?''

''Yes. There's also the matter of the delivery fee. As you recall, that's strictly the responsibility of the winner. Five hundred dollars to transport Apollo on the blockade runner that just came into port.''

"Five hundred dollars?!'' sputtered Oakes.

"Yes, sir. A negligible sum when compared to the value of the horse. Why, the saddle alone is worth more than that. Now, sir, may I see your ticket?''

"Well, I don't . . . That is . . .''

"Your ticket, Mr. Oakes?''

"I don't carry the damned thing on me, you know!''

"Of course, sir. But you understand I will need to see your ticket before I can deliver Apollo.''

Oakes reached for his wallet, removed five crisp hundred-dollar notes, and thrust them at Monty. "This is all you need to see.''

Monty glanced at the bills, his expression pained. "This is most irregular. I'm afraid I'm not authorized to deliver the horse until after I see proof that—''

"Are you calling me a liar?'' Oakes demanded hotly.

"Of course not!'' Monty stammered, clearly appalled. "Sir, I never intended—''

"Then take the damned money and bring me my horse. I bought the tickets and he's rightfully mine. I expect to see you first thing tomorrow morning.''

"Yes, sir.'' Monty accepted the bills and scribbled down his address. He shook the man's hand one last time. "You have no idea what a delight this has been for me, Mr. Oakes. Until tomorrow, then.'' He tipped his hat and made his way back through the crowd.

"He's quite something, isn't he?'' Devon said to Cole.

"Unbelievable,'' Cole answered, grudgingly impressed. He watched as Oakes's friends congratulated him on his good fortune, and felt not the slightest twinge of guilt at having taken the man's money. After all, Oakes had been eager to deprive a rightful owner of a thoroughbred Arabian. Had he at any point admitted that he hadn't bought the lottery tickets, he never would have been taken.

Cole escorted Devon from the tavern. They climbed into the wagon and rode the short distance back to the *Ghost*. Monty was waiting for them at the gangplank, his jovial smile firmly in place. "Cooperative chap, wasn't he?" he said, referring to Oakes. "Not overly burdened with brains, of course, but a pleasure to do business with just the same."

"How'd you know he wouldn't see right through your story?" Cole asked as he assisted Devon from the wagon.

Monty snorted. "I've yet to meet a smart man who called his wife 'Ma.' "

Cole looked from Devon to her uncle, taking stock of their situation. They were behind enemy lines, about to risk their lives once again to make it through the blockade. The closest thing he had to a father-in-law was the most outrageous con man he'd ever met in his life. His new bride was a convicted murderess he'd been blackmailed into marrying.

He'd never been happier in his life.

"I'm proud of you, Uncle," Devon said, standing on tiptoe to give him a quick kiss on the cheek. "There's just one more thing I'd like you to do for me."

"Anything, my girl."

"Give Cole his watch back."

Cole's eyes widened as he automatically reached into his shirt pocket and came up empty. Devon turned and moved toward the gangplank. Monty frowned and let out a deep sigh. He shook his head as he passed Cole his watch, a sorrowful expression on his face.

"I've done all I can, Captain," he said. "But I'm afraid it's hopeless. That girl's never going to make a proper thief. She's just too bloody soft, that's all there is to it, just too bloody soft.''

Cole watched the gentle sway of Devon's hips as she made her way up the gangplank. He couldn't agree more. Monty was right, she wasn't meant to be a thief. She was meant to be a lady. His lady.

Chapter 17

Devon felt the ship's engines rumble to life beneath her feet and steeled herself for the run. They'd made it into Wilmington, there was no reason they wouldn't make it out. Expect, of course, that on the way in they'd had the element of surprise on their side. This time, the blockaders would be waiting for them. Devon suppressed a shiver, fighting to keep her courage up. Cole would make everything all right. He always did.

She looked for him now, wanting to be near him as the ship pulled away from Wilmington. But the decks were piled so high with cotton, she couldn't see anything. In fact, every square inch of the ship was tightly packed with thick bales of their new cargo. Just crossing the deck felt like wandering through a maze. She lost her footing and stumbled a few times, for the ship seemed to be lurching from side to side. She frowned, wondering if they were having engine trouble.

Finally she made it to the bridge. Cole acknowledged her, then went back to his testing maneuvers. She understood now why the ship felt as if it had been jarring back and forth. He was putting his pilot through his paces, forcing him to make abrupt stops and hard turns. Testing the *Ghost* to see how she would react. Even Devon could feel that the ship was a bit sluggish, slower to respond to the commands. The hull sank lower in the water than ever before, and the ship groaned under the excess weight. She studied Cole's face to see if he was worried, that they might have trouble later. He didn't look upset, just serious, as though he were memorizing each slight pull and gentle sway the *Ghost* made.

They continued that way to Fort Fisher, executing the same jarring stops and starts. Uncle Monty and Earl Finch soon joined them on the bridge, assuming their same places. Conversation was kept at a minimum. "Captain," the pilot said as they neared the fort, "there's a barge heading our way."

"Go around her," Cole answered.

The pilot steered to port, attempting to maneuver around the small ship. The barge answered with a shotgun blast and made to cut across the *Ghost*'s bow. "Looks like she wants us to stop," said the pilot.

Cole frowned as he stared at the barge, then nodded. "Cut the engines."

The barge sailed toward them, lapping up beside them until they tapped against the ship's hull. "Permission to board, Captain," they called up.

"What the devil do they want?" Monty muttered under his breath.

"I'm not sure," Cole replied.

Finch turned at that and stared hard at Cole. "I thought you made this run all the time."

Devon stood still, wondering if they'd just given themselves away, but Cole merely shrugged. "I made it not more than three months ago," he coolly lied. "My ship was allowed to leave harbor quite unmolested."

Finch let the matter drop as Cole turned to his pilot and said the only thing he could under the circumstances. "Let them board."

His crewmen threw down a line. The men in the barge secured their boat, then climbed aboard. The group consisted of about ten men, each carrying a stick wrapped tightly at the ends in a dark gauzy fabric, as well as a thin iron pole. The last man to board carried a flaming torch. Devon caught her breath, imagining for a moment that they meant to put the bales of cotton to the torch. Instead they made no move, but waited quietly while their leader approached the bridge.

"Cap'n," the man said once he reached them. He wore linen pants and a shirt that might have been white at one time, but were now streaked with sweat and smoke. His skin was dark and coarse, a thick stubble of beard shadowed his cheeks. His hair might have been blond or brown, it was simply too dirty for Devon to tell. "Mighty fine ship ye got here," he said. "Mighty fine."

"Who are you?"

"Name's Lerner. Former overseer of the Clarke Plantation. Now I work for the county trackin' down runaways." He glanced around the bridge, his eyes widening as he noticed Devon. His lips curved into a lewd smile—a smile that made Devon feel as filthy as the man who bestowed it upon her. "Mighty fine cargo ye got aboard too."

"What do you want?" Cole snapped.

Lerner reluctantly dragged his eyes away from Devon and looked at Cole. "New rules, Cap'n. Any ship that leaves Wilmington has to be smoked and searched."

"I don't have time for this."

"Sorry about that, Cap'n, but it's the rules. Fort Fisher won't let nobody through unless we give the signal that you're clean. Won't take more than thirty minutes." He raised his hand and gestured to his men. "Get to work, boys!"

The men below touched their gauze-wrapped sticks to the torch. But rather than flare up, the sticks emitted an acrid, hazy smoke. Even from up above and removed as she was, Devon could feel her eyes and lungs begin to burn. She instinctively moved closer to Cole and felt the comforting pressure of his arm as he slipped it around her waist. They watched in silence as the men moved through the thick maze of cotton bales, applying their torches to the narrow spaces between. The minutes passed in torturous slowness.

"Hey! I got me one!" one of the men shouted, his voice thick with excitement.

She felt Cole grow rigid beside her as the men converged en masse. Two men stood at either end of the narrow aisle where the cry had come from and shoved their smoking torches down the tight space. The rest of the men scrambled up the cotton bales and positioned themselves above, jeering and shouting they swung into the aisle below with their long iron rods. Devon's stomach plummeted as she watched. She clenched her fists against the folds of her skirt, fighting to keep from crying out.

Finally the men ceased. One of them moved into the narrow aisle and dragged the captured slave out by his heels. The runaway was perhaps eighteen years old, no more. The boy doubled over, tears streaming down his face as he choked and gasped for air. His skin was torn, cut and bleeding from the vicious jabs.

Cole lurched forward, but Monty caught his arm and held him back. "Steady, my boy," he whispered. "Steady. There's nothing we can do."

Devon shot a glance at Finch, but he was too busy watching the furor below to notice the exchange. She realized with acute despair that Monty was right. They were in no position to help the slave. Had Cole known earlier that the runaway was aboard, he might have been able to do something. But not now. They wouldn't make it past Fort Fisher without Lerner's signal that the ship was clean and cooperative. Or without raising Earl Finch's suspicions that Cole was anything but a loyal Southerner.

Cole must have come to the same conclusion, for he

didn't move again when Monty released his arm. But knowing him as well as she did, Devon didn't miss the cold fury in his eyes as he watched the men shackle the slave's wrists and ankles, then toss him into the barge below.

Lerner turned to Cole, a gleeful smile on his face. "Hiding any more niggers, Cap'n?"

Cole swung around, glaring at the man with the full weight of his fury. Lerner's smile abruptly froze as he took a startled step backward.

"You got what you wanted," Cole said with a growl. "Now get the hell off my ship."

Lerner flushed with anger. "Fine," he spat. "You just watch your step goin' through that blockade, Cap'n. I wouldn't want my men to have to waste their time cleaning up pieces of your ship once it gets blown to bits and washed back down the river." With that he turned and shouted for his men to return to the barge.

Cole stared at him, then calmly asked, "You all done here, Mr. Lerner?"

"We're done," Lerner sneered.

"Good. Then allow me to assist you off my ship." Cole hauled him up by the collar.

"What the hell—" Lerner twisted and took an ineffectual swing, but he was too late. Cole dragged him to the rail and tossed him overboard like so much unwanted garbage. They heard a loud splash as Lerner hit the water, followed by the sound of furious and rabid curses.

"Well done, Captain," Monty said. "The man was desperately in need of a bath, wasn't he?"

Finch frowned and shook his head. "I hope you know what you're doing, Smith."

"This is my ship, Mr. Finch. I run it my way, and I don't have room aboard for scum like Lerner and his men."

"How do we know he'll signal the fort that we're clear to proceed?" Finch pressed.

Monty smiled. "Unless he's a complete fool—which, mind you, is not impossible—he'll stay out of our way. If we don't get past the fort, who do you think is the first one we'll go after, with all guns blazing?" He pointed to the barge as a small green flag was raised from the main mast. "There! What do you know, looks like our good friend Mr. Lerner figured that out all by himself."

Cole nodded to the engineer, and the engines rumbled to life once again. They sailed in under the protection of Fort Fisher and settled offshore to wait until dark. Devon stayed on the bridge as Cole made the rounds among his men, checking the guns and ammunition, offering words of encouragement. Finally they were ready to begin. Cole signaled to the man posted at the aft chains. Instead of raising anchor, the crewman merely pulled a pin out of the link, letting the chain slip quietly back into the water.

The night was clear, the sea calm, a crescent moon shining bright in the midnight sky—dangerous conditions for making a run. Nonetheless, the *Ghost* crept stealthily forward, moving like a phantom warship into an enemy sea. Their run had begun.

Devon's hope that she would be better able to stand the stress of their passage, since she'd been through it once before, was dashed within minutes of leaving the fort. Each stop and start, each near-miss, sent chills down her spine and turned her knees to jelly.

Judging from the strained expressions of her uncle and Mr. Finch, she wasn't alone in that feeling. Even the pilot looked done in; his face was pale, his shirt soaked with sweat. Only Cole looked relatively calm, his expression betraying nothing but fierce concentration. "Easy now," he said in a low whisper, speaking to no one in particular. ''We're almost there, just another mile or so.''

No sooner had he spoken the words than Devon heard him whisper harshly, ''Pilot, hard aport! Cutter on the starboard bow!''

Devon glanced ahead to see a small rowing boat with perhaps a dozen men patrolling the water. The ship jerked to the left, missing the cutter by a hair's breadth. Apparently the men inside the small boat were taken as much by surprise as the crew of the *Ghost*. Devon heard their shocked cries as their oars split against the hull.

They quickly recovered, however. Within seconds, the night sky was streaked with flares, signaling the *Ghost*'s presence to the other patrol boats. Monty clucked his tongue. ''Damned ungrateful of them, I'd say. Downright unsporting, as well.''

The brilliant sparks illuminated their position. Smith Island loomed dead ahead, marking the point where the mouth of the Cape Fear River opened into the sea. Devon glanced behind, and her mouth went dry. Coming up strong in their wake were three warships: a fifty-gun sailing frigate, a forty-gun steam frigate, and a twenty-four-gun sailing sloop. There was no chance of the *Ghost* being able to stay and fight it out. Nor could they run for the protection of Fort Fisher. Nothing lay ahead but the wide open sea.

''Open her up!'' Cole shouted to the engineer. ''Give me full speed! Men, hoist the sails—let's move!''

''Hoist the sails?'' Finch protested. ''They'll be shot to shreds!''

''Not at this range,'' Cole answered curtly. ''Why do you think they're not firing? As long as we can keep this distance, we'll be all right.''

''What are you going to do?'' Finch demanded.

''We're going to make a run for it—unless you have a better suggestion.''

"You should have run that damned boat over, that's what you should have done!"

Cole ignored him and shouted to his men below, "Move all that cotton off the bow," he instructed. "I want it piled aft, as thick and deep as you can get it."

Devon puzzled over the order until the men leaped to obey and she felt the subtle shifting of the deck beneath her feet. The cotton had been distributed evenly across the ship for balance, but now Cole wanted speed. Moving the heavy bales aft lifted the bow out of the water and submerged the screw propellers even deeper, giving them greater momentum. She only hoped that it would be enough.

The chase went on through dawn and well into the day. Maneuverability was the *Ghost*'s single advantage over the larger ships that trailed her, and Cole made the most of it. When the frigates closed in, he skirted the ship hard aport or hard starboard, leaving their adversaries twisting clumsily behind to adjust to their new path. Every now and then the frigates would fire their guns, testing the distance, but they had yet to close in enough for their weapons to reach.

The chase was exhausting body and soul. The crew worked in hour shifts, shoveling coal into the furnace as fast as possible, the men emerging covered in sweat and coal dust. Cole too, took his turn below in the scorching steam of the engine room.

Finally the bright light of day began to fade as hints of twilight showed in the sky. Devon approached Cole for the first time since they'd begun their run. "We're going to make it, aren't we," she said softly. It was more a statement than a question.

Cole reached for her hand and gave it a gentle squeeze. "We are. Once night falls, I can lose them in the dark. We've only an hour or so more to go—"

"Captain," a crewman interrupted as he rushed to the bridge. "Captain, I'm sorry, I didn't see it. We've been shoveling the coal so hard and fast, I thought we had enough to last—'' He stopped, dragging deep gulps of air into his lungs.

Cole abruptly released Devon's hand. "Are you telling me we're out of coal?"

"Yes, sir. I'm sorry, sir."

A heavy silence fell over the bridge. Devon glanced at the ships in rapid pursuit, knowing there was no way they could outrun them using sail power alone. Without the force of their engines, the *Ghost* would be brought to her knees in minutes.

"What about Wilmington? I thought we restocked there."

"We did, but all we could get was soft Southern coal, dug straight out of the mines. We can't use that."

Cole gazed up at the sky, studying the soft lavender twilight. "Stoke the engines," he commanded. "I want you and the men to pour it in as fast as you can. Shovel the coal dust in as well."

"But sir, the smoke . . ." The crewman halted his words as a slow grin spread across his face. "Aye, sir. Right away, sir." He leaped from the bridge and took off running toward the engine room.

Cole handed Devon a handkerchief and instructed her to tie it over her nose and mouth. As the *Ghost*'s engines faltered, the enemy warships drew in and began firing off shots, exploding in the water only meters away.

"What are you doing, Captain?" Finch demanded. "Aren't you even going to try to fight it out?"

"I'd put that on if I were you," Cole answered, gesturing to Finch's handkerchief. "You're going to need it."

Finch reluctantly obeyed. The rest of the men cloaked their faces as well, masking their mouths and noses. Within seconds, Devon understood the necessity. The acrid smoke they'd endured during the search for runaways had been nothing compared to what poured from the ship's flues now. The stacks made a loud belching noise, then thick, choking smoke gushed out, black as midnight, enveloping them all. It settled over the ship like a dark, heavy cloud. Soon it spread beyond them and over the sea itself.

Devon understood. Since Cole couldn't wait for the night, he was bringing the night to him. The thick smoke, combined with the twilight mist, rendered the *Ghost* nearly invisible. Gazing behind her, Devon could see nothing but black haze where just moments before the warships had ominously lurked. Only the thunderous explosions of their guns told her that they still followed.

Cole pulled down his handkerchief to shout to the men below, "Now lower the sails! Bring them in!" The men let loose the ropes, and the sails went slack. Cole turned to the pilot. "Hard starboard, then cut the engine."

The pilot obeyed, jerked the ship hard right, then let her drift into the murky black smoke. After their frantic sixteen-hour pursuit, the gentle drifting motion felt almost eerie. The *Ghost* sat absolutely still, cloaked by smoke and silence. The ploy worked. Devon held her breath as the warships continued to steam straight ahead, their guns blazing, blindly firing away at a prey that was no longer there.

The crew let loose a low roar of exuberant relief. Cole reached for Devon and spun her around in his arms. Before she could catch her breath, he yanked down the handkerchief that cloaked her face and kissed her hard on the mouth. Devon kissed him back, mindless of the others around them. He tasted like coal and sweat and smoke, his lips raw and gritty against her own.

"Well done, Captain, very well done indeed," Monty said as she and Cole pulled apart.

"The kiss or the escape?" Devon asked cheekily, too happy to care about propriety.

"Both," returned her uncle. He dug into his pocket and came up with a fistful of cigars. "I do believe the occasion calls for a celebration. Smoke, anyone?"

"Where to, Captain?" the pilot asked after the men had lit up and were puffing away contentedly.

Cole looked at Earl Finch. "I believe that's your call, Mr. Finch. Did I pass the test?"

Finch pulled the handkerchief off his neck and took his time wiping the grimy smoke off his face and hands. He dragged in deep on his cigar, then slowly let out his breath. "Captain, there were at least a hundred times I thought we were all dead for sure. You took risks no sane man would take. And not once did you fire a shot at the enemy." He paused, a fierce frown of disapproval on his face. "But you got us in and you got us out, and that's all Mr. Sharpe asked me to bear witness to."

"Captain?" the pilot repeated, his hand on the helm.

Cole looked at Finch.

"Mr. Sharpe will be waiting for you in Nassau," Finch said. "I'll set up a meeting once we arrive."

Cole didn't move, nor did his expression change. But for just a second, Devon could swear she saw the ghost of a smile flash across his face. He nodded to his pilot. "You heard the man. Chart a course."

Devon stood alone at the ship's rail, gazing up at the stars as a midnight breeze blew over her skin. The sea was smooth and calm, a sheet of dark glass that mirrored the sky above. They skimmed lightly across the surface, propelled by just the wind. She tipped back her chin, letting the breeze fan her neck and shoulders. She'd been too restless to stay inside, so she'd wandered out on deck to do her thinking. The sound of Cole's voice broke into her rambling thoughts.

"I looked for you in the cabin."

Devon turned to him and softly smiled. "I bet I wasn't there."

"You weren't."

"Imagine that."

Cole smiled and reached out, running his fingers gently along the nape of her neck. He settled in beside her, bracing his elbows against the rail. They stood in silence, absorbing the peace of the night and the silence of the ship.

Devon studied him from beneath a sweep of lashes. Like her, he must have bathed earlier, for all traces of soot and grime were removed from his skin. He looked virile and bronze; his rugged profile was chiseled perfection in the moonlight. Her eyes went to the jagged scar that marred his cheek. Every day the healing progressed a little bit more.

He turned toward her, eyeing her with tender concern as he asked, "How are you?"

"I'm fine."

"No aftermath shakes?"

She held out her hand; it was smooth and steady.

Cole shook his head. "Incredible. Most women would have collapsed at the first sign of trouble. Hell, most men. Half my crew is snuggled up in bed with a brandy bottle as we speak."

She shrugged. "I'm a professional, remember? I've been trained since an early age not to show fear." She gave him a rueful smile and amended her lofty statement with, "Except, of course, if you have me dangling over the side of a cliff in a rickety old carriage."

"A situation I will endeavor at all costs to avoid in the future, Mrs. McRae."

"Thank you, Mr. McRae."

A silence fell between them as his gaze ran slowly over her. "What are you doing out here?"

She shrugged again. "Nothing really."

"Wishing on stars?" he guessed, glancing at the brilliant midnight sky.

She laughed and shook her head. "Never."

Cole smiled and lifted a brow at that. "What kind of a woman did I marry?" he asked. "You're able to run the blockade without a single tremor, you can leap from a galloping horse onto a speeding train, start barroom brawls by just fluttering your eyelashes, but you don't know how to dance, and you never wish on stars."

He was using the voice she loved best: low and husky, gentle and teasing. The voice she heard only when they were alone, usually whenever they made love. And sometimes the morning after as well, when they lay with their limbs entangled and their eyes closed against the soft dawn light, neither one willing to come fully awake. Or to move at all. The voice that washed over her soul like a tender caress. A voice of murmured promises and tender passion.

"So tell me," Cole continued, "why don't you wish on stars?"

"I don't do it right."

He grinned. "There's a proper way to make a wish?"

"Of course," she answered, struggling to remain focused on their conversation. "One should wish for simple things. Like a few extra shillings, a bit of cake, or a new gown."

"But you don't do that."

Devon gazed up into his eyes. "No."

"What do you wish for, Devon?"

I wish you would love me. The thought sprang unbidden to her mind, fully formed and achingly real. She shook her head and looked away, swallowing hard past the lump in her throat. "Impossible things."

He moved a step closer. "Tell me."

She searched for a suitable reply, then finally answered, "I wish we could just sail away into the night. I wish we didn't have to go after Jonas Sharpe."

Cole sobered immediately. "Did you have that dream again?"

An icy chill raced down her spine. Devon bit down hard on her lip and shook her head, pushing that memory away. "No."

He slipped his arm around her and pulled her to stand in front of him. His arms wrapped securely around her waist, Devon idly traced her hands over his forearms, content to stand with him like that forever. "We've been through the worst of it," he said. "Finch doesn't suspect anything, and there's no way for Sharpe to find out about us until it's too late."

She rested the back of her head against his chest and closed her eyes. "You sound so sure," she said. "So positive that everything's going to work out."

"And you sound worried."

"I'm trying not to."

He tightened his arms around her and gently teased, "Trying not to sound worried, or trying not to be worried?"

"Both."

"Devon, it's only a matter of days now, and it will all be over. Try just to think of that."

That was the last thing in the world she wanted to think about. In two short days, they would reach the Bahamas. Once they'd captured Sharpe, she was honor-bound to keep her end of their bargain. Uncle Monty had blackmailed Cole into marrying her. She had no intention of holding him to a promise he hadn't given of his own free will. Logically she knew it was the right thing to do. There was no place for her in his world. But the thought of not being with Cole, of never feeling his arms around her again, cut through her heart like jagged pieces of glass.

"I don't want to think about that," she said.

"Very well." Cole rocked her softly back and forth. "I'll teach you to dance."

She smiled. "Right here?"

"Absolutely."

"Are you going to sing for me as well?"

He sighed. "Have you ever heard a dog howl at the moon?"

"That bad, is it?"

"I'm probably insulting the dog."

Devon twisted around in his arms. She raised herself on tiptoe and tilted her head back to touch her lips to his, kissing him with all the fervor and passion and ache within her soul. Kissing him to memorize the taste of his lips, the feel of his hands on her body. Kissing him so she could conjure up the feeling on all the long, lonely nights that lay ahead of her. So she could capture the radiant joy that spread through her whenever he was near and hold it in her heart forever.

She pulled away, almost out of breath, and gazed up into his eyes. They were dark with passion and fire, lit within by a golden glow that sent her pulses racing. "What was that for?" he asked huskily.

"Do I need a reason?"

"Never." He took her hand. "Let's go back inside."

Devon shook her head. "I'm not sleepy."

Cole reached down and lifted her into his arms. His long strides carried her swiftly through the maze of cotton and toward his cabin. "Good."

Chapter 18

The streets of Nassau pulsed with energy. The city was awash with color, framed by a sapphire sea and dazzling white beaches. Natives attired in vivid garb strolled casually by, calling out in the soft dialect of the island. Tall palms swayed in the gentle trade winds. Perhaps it was just the contrast with the dreary poverty and distress she'd seen in Wilmington that made the city seem so prosperous and happy. Whatever the reason, Devon was determined to enjoy it.

She drank it all in as she rode in an open buggy seated between Cole and her uncle. As was his habit, Earl Finch had disappeared as soon as the ship had docked. She, for one, would not miss his presence. She pushed thoughts of Finch from her mind and focused instead on the sights around her.

Although she knew Nassau was a Rebel gun-running port, just as St. George had been, the difference was amazing. St. George had been quaint and charming, but filled with a sense of giddy desperation and greed. She felt none of that here. The island was more formal than she'd expected, graced with stately mansions and classical government buildings, carefully tended parks and gardens. The narrow streets and dimly lit pubs had a decidedly British feel to them and made her feel right at home.

They passed Straw Market, a rowdy square that was alive with noise and color. Vendors with bulging booths and trestle tables sold every conceivable item from fish and fruit to lace and tobacco. The Grand Hotel, where the hitching posts were thick with horses and carriages, appeared to be one of the island's busiest establishments. Glancing through the windows, Devon saw that the tables in the glittering dining room and salon were tightly packed. The dull roar of voices spilled out onto the street. She recognized the same breed of men as she'd seen in St. George: Americans fleeing the war, blockade runners, officers of the Confederacy, and Yankee spies.

Cole directed the carriage east of town, along a pretty, winding street that moved gradually uphill. It was quiet and peaceful, unlike the bustling vibrancy of town. They passed stately, lovely homes, all softly shaded in cool pastels and icy whites. Cole had mentioned to her that he had a home in Nassau, as this was one of his major ports for shipping, but she wasn't prepared for what she saw when he finally stopped.

The house was set away from the street by a small courtyard. An arbor covered in primroses framed the entryway; flat gray stones set a meandering path through garden to front door. The house itself had a limestone front, its outer walls washed in a pale pink. The veranda wrapped around the home was set off by an intricate fretwork balcony of shining white that matched the louvered shutters on the windows and doors. Devon fell in love with it on sight. It looked like something she'd seen in a book of fairy tales. Never what she'd expected Cole's home would look like, yet it fit perfectly in the quaint, charming neighborhood.

Cole assisted her from the wagon, watching her reaction but saying nothing as he took her hand and led her inside. She found the interior of his home a stark contrast to the exterior, but more in line with what she'd expected to see. It was strikingly masculine, filled with large, oversized pieces of furniture. The walls were painted white, the dark wood floors polished to a high gleam. All the home lacked was a woman's touch to bring it together. She made a mental inventory as she moved through the house. Soft cushions for the chairs in the front parlor, a lace tablecloth for the dining room, curtains for the kitchen, a few rugs scattered about, flowers from the garden brought indoors—

Devon stopped herself abruptly. She wouldn't be here long enough to effect any of those changes. It wasn't her place, in any case. Aware that Cole was waiting for her response, she turned to him and smiled. "It's lovely," she said sincerely.

"It will do nicely, Captain," Monty pronounced as he dropped into a chair. He lumbered back to his feet as a dark-skinned woman entered the room.

Devon judged her to be in her early forties, and by her attire, a native of the island. Only the hints of gray in her hair gave her age away, for her complexion was nearly flawless. The woman had a solid build, with a large bosom and broad hips. She moved gracefully despite her girth, her brightly colored skirts flowing smoothly behind her as she entered the room. "Welcome back, Mr. Cole," she said, her voice deep and rich, flavored with the same soft accent Devon had heard in the speech of other natives.

Cole made the introductions. "Devon, Monty, I'd like you to meet Elize. She and her husband, John, run the place for me while I'm gone." The woman smiled and politely inclined her head. "Elize, this is my wife, Devon, and her uncle, Montgomery Persons."

"A pleasure, madame," Monty said, beaming, as Devon murmured a polite greeting of her own. She glanced at Cole, stunned by the way he'd introduced her. *This is my wife, Devon.* She hadn't expected him to mention their relationship at all. She'd assumed he'd just call her and Uncle Monty guests and leave it at that.

Elize gave him a dark frown, her fists propped on her hips. She looked from Devon to Cole and demanded, "What dis you say?"

Cole draped his arm around Devon's shoulder in an offhand embrace, looking as though deliberately provoking the woman was one of life's finest pleasures. "I said my wife, Devon."

Elize lifted her brows. "Your wife, mister? You tell me you go off to fight de war. Instead you go off finally find de wife."

"Finally?" Cole repeated with a grin. "I wasn't aware I was supposed to be looking for one."

His servant sniffed in disapproval. "Dis house need a wife. *You* need a wife." She turned to Devon, her eyes glowing with warm approval despite the gruffness of her words. "How dis boy trick you into marrying him?"

"Blackmail," Cole answered for Devon, making it sound as if he were the one who blackmailed her, and not the other way around.

"Hmph," said Elize. "Now there is something I believe. Come, mistress, I show you upstairs."

Devon followed her obediently, leaving Cole and Monty behind as the two men poured drinks and settled in the parlor to talk. The upstairs was much like the lower level of the house, with airy, spacious rooms, filled with solid, masculine pieces of furniture. Cole's bedchamber was the largest. The focus of the room was a large mahogany four-poster bed, draped on all sides with a gauzy mosquito netting. The crisp white linens looked unbearably cool and inviting. A blush rose to her cheeks as her mind instantly conjured up visions of her and Cole making love beneath them.

A brief tap sounded on the door. Elize opened it and admitted her husband, who brought in Devon's things from the buggy. The man greeted her warmly, then left the two women alone. Elize opened the first bag, chattering softly as she started to unpack. She pulled out the pink silk dress Devon had been married in. Devon stared at the gown, a funny twist in her heart. "Elize," she said, "thank you, but it won't be necessary to unpack."

The woman paused in her task and looked at Devon. "Silk wrinkle very fast in de islands. It best if we—"

"Thank you, but I'll see to it later," Devon managed. She wasn't staying. Unpacking and settling in would only make it that much harder when the time came for her to leave.

Elize set down the items she'd been pulling from the bag, studying Devon with dark eyes that seemed to hold the wisdom of the ages. "I see," she said simply, then moved toward the door.

Devon spun away, feeling as though she'd just bitterly insulted the woman. And worse than that, as if she'd betrayed Cole in the process. She gazed blindly around the room, then her eyes lit upon three silver-framed portraits lined neatly on the bureau. She moved toward them, more from a desire to take her mind off the impending end of her marriage than out of any real interest.

The first showed an older couple. They were richly dressed and perfectly starched, their spines stiffer than the backs of the chairs in which they sat. So stiff and formal, they almost looked angry as they glared into the camera. Attractive perhaps, but grim. Cole's parents, she assumed. The second portrait showed another couple almost identical in pose, attire, and attitude, only about twenty years younger. His brother, Richard, and Richard's wife, Sarah.

She glanced at the third, smiling as she realized it was a picture of Cole. Obviously it had been taken years ago, for he looked much younger. She picked it up and studied it carefully, recognizing as she did that the photograph wasn't of Cole at all. It was Gideon who stared out at her, she realized with a shock. The resemblance was amazing. He had the same thick blond hair, the same strong, chiseled features. He was tall, but with a boyish leanness, though his frame promised he would one day have the same powerful physique as Cole.

Unlike the other photographs, this one hadn't been posed in a studio. Gideon stood outside, dressed in a navy uniform, the helm of a ship faintly visible behind him. His stance conveyed restlessness, an impatience to be back aboard. A hint of a smile played about his lips, as though he was preparing to make a randy comment to either the photographer or someone standing beside him.

He looked strong and alive, bursting with energy and vitality. Just as she'd pictured him: reckless and wild, a young god gifted with beauty and youth and immortality, ready to spring from the frame and bound through the room. She could readily imagine him coaxing kisses from his sweetheart, or showing his friends his "card tricks."

Devon set the portrait down, her heart aching as she sank into a chair beside the bed. She stared at the items Elize had emptied from her bag, each piece flooding her with memories: the tortoiseshell hairpins she'd confiscated from the train, the cockle pills, and the lacy pink corset. She looked at the pale blue calico gown Cole had given her in Virginia, the sheer chemise she'd worn on their wedding night, the boots he'd bought her in Fort Monroe.

Each item struck a different memory, strumming through her mind like strings on a harp. Producing a symphony that washed over her in waves, discordant and yet hauntingly beautiful. Everything she saw was so connected to her, to Cole, to what they'd shared together.

Finally Devon studied the wedding band she wore

on her finger. She remembered him standing before her as he gave it to her, so strong and proud, yet aching with regret and vulnerability, hurting as much as she was for the mistakes they'd made, for the past they hadn't quite learned to conquer or let go. Neither one willing to confront the future, but trying desperately to make the most of the present. Cole's voice echoed softly in her ears: *Let me love you, Devon* . . .

Without thinking any further about what she was doing, she stood and started to unpack.

Devon woke the next morning to the feel of a man's hand moving in playful circles across the top of her thigh. She snuggled up against him, her bottom pressed tightly against his groin. Without opening her eyes, she let out a sleepy sigh. "Hmmm, that feels lovely. Is that you, Sherman?"

Cole gave her a gentle swat. "Very funny."

Devon smiled and rolled over, staring up at her husband as he braced himself on one elbow above her. She loved the look of Cole in the morning, his golden hair slightly mussed and falling in tousled waves onto his forehead, his deep brown eyes hazy with sleep, a subtle shadow across his cheeks. His bronze skin was a vivid contrast to the stark white sheet that pooled about his waist. She traced her hand lightly over his chest and said, "You deserted me yesterday."

He lifted her hand and brushed her fingers softly across his lips. "I know. I'm sorry."

"Where did you go?"

"I had some business to take care of down at the docks."

A tremor of unease shot through Devon. When she'd finished her unpacking and returned downstairs, she'd found only her uncle. Cole had left without a word, not returning until the small hours of the morning. Devon remembered feeling the bed sink beneath his weight as he climbed in next to her, then sleepily rolling over on top of him as he settled in beneath the covers. Somewhere along the way, she'd acquired the habit of using Cole for her pillow, but fortunately he didn't seem to mind.

"Your business down at the docks had to do with Sharpe, didn't it?" she asked.

"Yes," he answered honestly.

She took a deep breath, pushing her feelings of dark foreboding away. "It's all happening so soon."

"Not soon enough. I want this resolved, Devon, so we can put Sharpe behind us and get on with our lives."

She forced herself to leave his statement alone and accept it at face value. But it took all her willpower not to twist it apart looking for hidden meanings and convoluted interpretations. He was referring to Jonas Sharpe, not the two of them. "What are you planning?" she asked.

He frowned. "I wish to hell I had a plan. At this point there's not a damned thing we can do but wait for Finch to report back to us. Until then . . ."

She studied him as his voice trailed off, sensing a tension deep within him that was caused by more than just the waiting. "What is it?" she asked.

Cole stared at her for a long moment, regret and worry etched deep in his features. He shook his head, as if dismissing her question, then startled her by asking, "Can I trust Monty? Really trust him?"

"I trust him with my life," she answered automatically.

A grim smile flashed across his face. "Let's hope it doesn't come down to that."

Devon frowned, not liking the direction the conversation had taken. "What do you need me to do?"

"Stay out of it."

"Cole—"

"I mean it, Devon. No matter what happens, I want you to let Monty and me handle it. Promise me you won't get in the way."

"That's very flattering," she snapped. "Maybe you should stay out of my way. I'm the professional, remember? You're the one who's too obtuse to know when your own wallet is being lifted, and you can't hang on to your watch to save your life—"

Cole rolled on top of her and pinned her wrists above her head, a reckless grin on his face as he said, "This brings back memories. It's been too long since we had a good fight." He leaned down, trailing soft kisses along the nape of her neck.

Trapped beneath him, Devon shivered as a tingle of pleasure raced down her spine. "Cole—"

"What?"

"This is supposed to be a fight, and you're not cooperating."

"I'm sorry, love, I'll try harder." He brought her nipple into his mouth, teasing the rosy peak with his tongue. Devon instinctively arched her back, offering herself up to him. He gave her other breast the same loving treatment, then reluctantly pulled away. "Is that better?"

"Yes. No—Cole, we can't."

"We are," he murmured, pausing at her navel as he continued to trail kisses down her body.

"Well, all right," she breathlessly agreed, "but only for a minute."

He looked up at her and arched a tawny brow. "Only a minute?" he repeated with mock offense. "Surely you have me confused with someone else's husband."

She smiled. "I'm sorry, Cole, but I just remembered, Uncle Monty is probably downstairs waiting for us. He wanted to take a riding tour of the island this morning and was determined to make an early start of it. I hope you don't mind."

Cole immediately rose to a sitting position and tugged his hands through his hair, their teasing banter forgotten. "I see."

Devon stared at him, stunned by the speed with which he abandoned their former pursuits. She'd fully expected him to tell her that Monty could go hang himself. Instead he turned toward her, his thoughts already focused elsewhere as he said, "You'd better get dressed then."

Miffed by his abrupt dismissal, she climbed out of bed and muttered under her breath, "We may have that fight yet, Cole McRae."

He gave no indication of having heard her. Instead he pulled on his clothes and left the room without a word. Devon stared after him, her irritation quickly turning to concern. Something was bothering Cole, and obviously that something had to do with Uncle Monty. She dressed as quickly as she could and followed him downstairs.

"There you are, my girl, looking lovely as ever," Monty boomed as she entered the front parlor.

"Good morning, Uncle." Devon brushed a quick kiss on his cheek and glanced around the room. "Where's Cole?"

"Out saddling the horses. Fine-looking animals they are too. I've already been out to see them myself."

She drew her brows together. "You have? Why?"

He shrugged. "Why not?"

"Uncle Monty, what are you up to?"

"Up to? My girl, absolutely nothing. Is this what marriage has done to you? Now you're suspicious of every move a man makes? If I'd known this, I never would have allowed—"

Devon drew in a deep breath, then slowly let it out. Though he was a decent rider, riding was definitely not something her uncle enjoyed. "Uncle Monty, you hate horses, remember? You refuse to travel anywhere unless it's by coach or train, and now suddenly you're aglow with excitement at the prospect of galloping around the island on horseback.''

Monty smiled. "Lovely day for it, isn't it?"

Dull panic took root inside her. In all the years she'd known him, not once had her uncle put her off when she asked a question, or talked to her the way he talked to his marks. Yet that was exactly what he was doing now. She reached into the pocket of her riding skirts and removed the slim linen card that he'd sent with her wedding-night flowers. *Trust me. I have a plan.* She'd completely forgotten about it until yesterday, when she found it while unpacking. "What are you planning?"

Monty turned over the card, read it, and crumpled it. "Ah, that's all irrelevant now, my girl. Everything's changed. Just trust your old uncle, and everything will be fine."

"I don't know if I can," Devon said softly. "I don't know what you're doing anymore, Uncle Monty, and it scares me."

Monty stared at her, his expression pained. "I'm doing what I've always done, my girl. I'm taking care of business. I'm taking care of you and me."

"What about Cole?"

"The captain can take care of himself."

Devon caught her uncle's sleeve as he started to turn away. "I love him."

Monty slowly smiled. "Do you think me blind, my girl? Anyone within ten feet of the two of you can see how you both feel about one another."

"Then what—"

"Trust me."

"Are we ready?" Cole called from the doorway.

Devon spun about, wondering how much he'd heard. It was impossible to tell from the closed expression on his face. She glanced from him to her uncle, then reluctantly nodded, knowing that she'd get no further answers. Cole tied the picnic lunch Elize had packed for them to the back of his saddle, then they mounted up. After a little while spent in the sunshine and fresh air, Devon began to feel remarkably better. She fell into the spirit of the outing, letting the natural beauty of the island soothe her worries away.

"I say, Captain, when did you last have this horse shod?" Monty asked as they reached the outskirts of the city.

Devon and Cole pulled up their reins and turned back to Monty. "John told me he had them all attended to last month," Cole answered. "Why?"

Monty shrugged and stroked his mount's neck. "He seems to be favoring his left a bit, doesn't he?" He nudged the horse forward, demonstrating as he spoke. The gelding pawed at the air, then moved in a halting, foundered step.

Cole frowned. "Probably picked up a rock."

"Quite so," Monty concurred. "Didn't I see a stable nearby?"

"About a mile back."

"Fine. I'll have the smith see to it. It shouldn't take more than an hour's time."

"We'll go with you, Uncle Monty," Devon volunteered.

"Nonsense, my girl. No sense in spoiling everybody's outing. You two go on ahead and I'll catch up."

Devon turned back, fighting her unease. "Uncle, are you sure—"

Monty laughed. "Go, my girl. Off with you both. Just see to it that you save me my lunch."

Monty dismounted and silently watched as Cole and Devon rode away. He crouched down and reached for his mount's afflicted hoof. A blacksmith wasn't necessary for what ailed the animal. All Monty had to do was unfasten the slim wire he'd attached around the fetlock earlier that morning. While not painful, the device was irritating to the horse and made it appear lame within a matter of minutes. He reached up and patted the gelding's smooth nose. "There now, my boy, that wasn't so bad, was it?"

The horse tossed its head and stomped its foot in response. Behind him, Monty heard the soft neigh of another horse. He turned, watching as a rider slowly emerged from within the shadows of the alley. "Nice work, Mr. Teller."

He glanced at Earl Finch and nodded. "You ready?"

Finch smiled. "Indeed I am."

The men rode the short distance required to bring them to the Grand Hotel. They dismounted and stepped inside, moving quietly through the crowded lobby. Finch led the way to a private parlor off the main floor. He tapped on the door, then ushered Monty inside.

The small room was richly furnished. A deep red velvet sofa and matching chairs sat in the center of the parlor, surrounded by a clutter of fringed lamps and china bric-a-brac. The walls were papered with a heavy gold and black pattern. Thick wool rugs lined the floor, and dark silk swags hung above the windows. The lush opulence was heavy and oppressive against the tropical island heat.

Monty took it all in at a glance, then his eyes moved to Jonas Sharpe. The man stood at the far end of the room, staring out the window at the activity in the street. He looked exactly as Monty had remembered him. Tall and fit, impeccably dressed in the finest-quality suit, as if anything less than perfection would not be tolerated. His dark hair was slicked back, his mustache perfectly groomed. The sweet, cloying scent of cloves emanated from him and drifted through the air.

"My time is limited, Mr. Teller," Sharpe said, barely glancing over his shoulder. "Mr. Finch told me you insisted on meeting with me before I arrange the transfer of my ship to your captain. Very well, you may speak your piece.'' He pulled a pocket watch from within his vest and clicked it open. "You have five minutes.''

Monty stepped from the shadows of the hallway and moved farther into the room. "My good friend,'' he said, "I may need a little more time than that.''

Sharpe froze, then turned slowly around. He stared at Monty for a long moment, then tucked away his watch. "Well. This is a surprise.''

Finch looked from one man to the next, his eyes wide with surprise. "You know Mr. Teller already—''

"His name's not Teller, you idiot,'' Sharpe hissed. "It's Persons, Montgomery Persons. The swindler I met in Liverpool.''

Monty clucked his tongue. "*Swindler* is such a vulgar term. I prefer the title *opportunist,* myself. Much more pleasant, is it not?''

"What do you want?''

"Exactly what I told your man Finch I wanted: a brief meeting with you, Mr. Sharpe. I believe you'll find what I have to say quite fascinating. If not . . .'' He paused, lifting his shoulders in an indolent shrug. "If not, I'll be on my way, and you'll have lost no more than five minutes of your valuable time.''

"I see.'' Sharpe stared at him for long, cool seconds. "Do have a seat, Mr. Persons,'' he said at last, gesturing to the plush velvet sofa.

"I find a touch of brandy always helps the words flow smoother,'' Monty said once they were both seated.

Sharpe glanced at Finch. "Two glasses.''

Finch jumped at the clipped command, rushing across the room to a tall cabinet. He removed a bottle from the shelf, splashed the amber liquid into thick tumblers, then set the drinks on a table between the two men.

Monty reached for his glass and took a deep swallow. "Privacy is also nice," he said.

Sharpe looked at Finch once more. "Get out."

Finch scurried to obey, rattling the door shut behind him.

"Quite an impressive economy with words you have there, Mr. Sharpe."

"What do you want?" Sharpe repeated curtly.

Monty smiled. "I believe you and I have some unfinished business to attend to. You remember my lovely niece, do you not?"

"Of course. According to my man Ogglesby, she found herself in a bit of trouble down in Charleston. Such a shame, really. She and Ogglesby would have been a good match." He paused to take a sip of his drink. "Certainly you realize that I had nothing to do with what happened."

"Of course, of course. How could I blame you? You weren't even in the country when it happened."

Sharpe's eyes narrowed. "That's quite magnanimous of you, Persons."

"Grudges are inappropriate in my line of business. Particularly when there are more important matters to settle."

"Such as?"

"As fate would have it, my niece was able to escape from her captors. She ended up marrying the captain of the blockade runner that Finch told you about." Monty paused, a slight frown on his face. "Unfortunately it's not a marriage that I approve of as I can't say that I truly like the man. Call me sentimental, but I've always had greater aspirations for the girl. I rather fancy Devon with an earl, or possibly even a duke. Someone who could give her lands and a title. Quite coincidentally, that would set me up as well. With the right amount of money, I believe an alliance of that sort would not be out of reach."

"Your niece and a duke," Sharpe sneered. "An alliance of that sort would take a prodigious amount of money."

Monty ignored the insult. "Yes, it will."

Jonas Sharpe rose to his feet. "As you promised, this has all been fascinating." He removed his watch and glanced at it once again. "You'll excuse me now if I have more important matters to attend to."

"You're the one who's going to give me the money."

Thick silence filled the space between them. Jonas Sharpe's face flushed with anger. "Why in hell would I give you a bloody cent?"

"Because I have information you need, sir. Information you desperately need. And I promise you it won't come cheap."

"I'm not interested."

"What a shame. Though I understand completely, of course. I suppose you're too busy preparing to hand that frigate over to my darling niece's husband, are you not?" He shook his head. "By the way, your man Finch—remarkably ineffective as an agent."

Sharpe glared at him. "If you have a point, Persons, I suggest you make it."

Monty leaned back against the sofa. He took a deep sip of brandy, then set the glass down, smiling broadly. "My good friend," he said, "let's talk about Captain Cole McRae."

Chapter 19

Devon ran her hands over Cole's shoulders as she helped him into his shirt. She frowned as she lightly traced the folds of the crisp white fabric. "Are you sure you've thought of everything?" she asked for the fifth time in as many minutes.

Cole caught her hands in his. "Sweetheart, there's nothing to worry about. Sharpe wants me to come aboard and give the frigate a test run, just to make sure I can handle her."

She nodded and glanced down at his hands, noting the thick ring he wore. "I've never seen that before," she murmured absently.

He glanced at the gold band and shrugged. "For luck," he replied, then resumed the task of buttoning his shirt.

They'd returned from their picnic a short while ago to find Sharpe's note waiting for them. The picnic, Devon admitted, had not been a sterling success. Monty had caught up with them, his horse no longer limping, but by then the outing seemed to have gone flat. The day had proved too warm to enjoy riding, and they were all too preoccupied with their own thoughts to truly enjoy the beauty of the island. The food Elize had packed for them went untouched.

Finally Devon suggested they return to the house. Monty and Cole both gratefully acquiesced, making it all too clear that they'd gone on the excursion just to please her. Devon shook her head. Had she known there would be a note from Sharpe waiting for them upon their return, she would have tried to delay them forever.

"But why now?" she pressed, fighting back her fear. "Why not tomorrow, or the next day? Why does he have to see you now?"

"I imagine he's anxious to have her leave port. According to Finch, the ship's been docked here in Nassau for over a week."

She glanced outside the window. "It's going to be dark soon."

"Not for a few hours. All Sharpe wants is for me to bring the ship out, execute a few maneuvers, then bring her back in. Besides, Monty's going with me. Nothing could possibly go wrong."

She watched as he checked his gun, then tucked it into the back of his boot. The steel grip of the pistol was barely visible between the edge of his boot and the deep gray of his pants leg. "Then what do you need that for?" she asked.

Cole straightened and sent her a lopsided grin. "In case something goes wrong."

Devon stared at him grimly. Cole sighed and pulled her into his arms. "Sharpe won't even be aboard," he said. "According to the note, he'll be watching the maneuvers from somewhere onshore. I couldn't get near the man right now even if I wanted to. It's just another test, Devon. One more hoop he wants me to jump through before he'll hand over his ship."

Cole brushed his lips lightly over hers. He pulled back and weaved his hand through her hair, staring at her intently. He shook his head and let out a deep sigh. "I've been meaning to tell you how much I love you, Devon. Will you forgive me for waiting until now to say it?"

Shock and disbelief coursed through her body. She

felt her mouth drop open as she stared at him, certain she'd heard him incorrectly. "You . . ."

"I love you."

"Oh, Cole . . ." Given that her heart was swelling to three times its normal size, taking up all the room in her chest and robbing her lungs of air, it was no wonder that her voice came out as little more than a breathy whisper. "When . . ."

"When did I finally realize it?" he completed for her, his grin broadening. "I think it all started that night I got you drunk on brandy. There was no turning back from there."

"And you waited until now to tell me?"

He shrugged. "You know what dreadful timing I have."

"The worst," she agreed vehemently, fighting back the tears that suddenly stung her eyes. "Not only that, you're stubborn, logical, opinionated, and I love you so much, Cole—" Her voice broke, and he gathered her into his arms. Devon squeezed him as hard as she could, willing every ounce of love and passion she possessed for him into the embrace. "Please don't go, Cole. Please don't go."

He pulled back and smiled softly. "I promise I'll be home in time for supper. Will you wait for me?"

Forever. Longer than that if I have to. Just come back to me, Cole. Come back to me. Devon nodded, not trusting her voice to speak. Rationally she knew that he was right, there was nothing to worry about. But deep inside it took every ounce of willpower she possessed to keep from grabbing him by the shirttail and begging him not to go. Something was wrong. She knew it in her heart, but was powerless to stop it.

She followed Cole downstairs. Monty was waiting in the kitchen. He sat at the table, sipping a cup of tea as he chatted with Elize, who stood at the stove stirring a pot of soup. Like Cole, Monty had changed his attire after their picnic. He looked fresh and ready to go, dressed in one of his newly laundered plaid suits.

"Well, Captain," he said brightly, "the show is on. Are you ready?"

Cole nodded. "Ready."

"Wait!" Devon cried. "Maybe I should come with you—"

"No," Cole and Monty answered in unison.

"But—"

"Devon," Cole said, placing his hands lightly on her upper arms, "everything's going to be fine. Just promise me you'll wait here until we return."

She shook her head. "This doesn't make any sense. Why are you taking this kind of risk? If Sharpe has set a trap, don't you see you'll be walking right into it? He's the one who needs a captain, let him come to you. You can meet him in town or here at the house. Anywhere would be safer than aboard his ship, surrounded by his men." She rattled off a list of possible scenarios and less risky courses for them to take. "Uncle Monty, surely you can see—"

"Now, now, my girl, no sense wasting any more time."

"But—"

"Promise me you'll wait here," Cole repeated.

Devon balled her fists against the fabric of her skirt. She looked from her uncle to her husband, feeling helpless and angry and worried all at once. She took a deep breath and reluctantly nodded. "I promise."

Cole smiled. "I love you," he whispered softly. "I'll be back soon to show you how much." He gave her a quick kiss, then walked out the door.

"Trust me, my girl," Monty said as he followed. "I've never let you down yet, have I?"

Devon watched in dismay as they mounted and took off at a full gallop, disregarding every one of her more sensible suggestions. She turned to Elize. "Why wouldn't they listen to me? Can't they see how fool-hardy this is?''

Elize shook her head. She let out a heartfelt sigh and wiped her hands on her apron. ''Men smart. Women smarter.''

Devon forced a tight smile. ''I'll be upstairs.''

She left the kitchen and took the steps slowly, her thoughts in jumbled turmoil. She could understand why Cole was so anxious to capture Jonas Sharpe. His own personal vendetta, combined with his sense of duty and honor, were making him race forward. Clouding his thoughts to the point where cool reason could no longer penetrate. But that was a dangerous way to operate.

Uncle Monty had taught her that. He constantly stressed the need for cool thought and analytical reasoning. Normally he had an elaborate plan, one with every contingency covered. Yet her uncle himself was rushing into this, with nothing but vague assurances that every-thing would be all right. It was not like him at all.

She stood in Cole's room, randomly picking up items, then setting them down. *Something's wrong, something's wrong*—the thought pounded away at her brain, making her head ache and twisting her stomach into knots. The vision she'd had the first night they'd docked in Wilmington loomed over her like a dark specter. But the more she tried to pinpoint what was wrong, the more hazy everything became. A desperate sense of urgency swept through her. She should move, take action, but she didn't know what to do.

She left the room and walked down the hall, hesitat-ing outside Uncle Monty's room. Fighting back feelings of disloyalty, she pushed open the door and glanced inside, unsure for what she was looking. Nothing was amiss. Devon sighed with regret for having invaded his privacy. The room was a little sloppy perhaps, but that was all. Monty had changed and tossed the suit he'd been wearing haphazardly across his bed. She went automatically to pick it up and hang it in the wardrobe for him.

She lifted the jacket and smoothed it out, trying to ease away the wrinkles, when she felt something sharp sting her palm. Frowning, she reached inside the pocket and removed a long, slim wire. Devon stared at it in uneasy bewilderment, then suddenly remembered a trick Monty had shown her years ago: when fastened around a horse's fetlock, it made the animal appear lame. Sick dread gathered in the pit of her stomach. He'd left them that afternoon on purpose, but why? As she pondered the question, a familiar scent drifted up to her from the jacket she held. She wrinkled her nose in distaste. Sweet, heavy, cloying . . . *cloves*.

Jonas Sharpe.

Devon let the jacket slip from her hands and fall to the floor. She closed her eyes, absorbing the shock and pain. "Oh, Uncle Monty," she whispered hoarsely, "what have you done? What have you done?"

Can I trust Monty? Cole had asked her only that morning. Her reply had been unequivocal, recklessly certain. *I trust him with my life.* But it wasn't her life that was at stake now. It was Cole's.

Devon tore downstairs and raced into the kitchen, her promise to wait for him at the house instantly abandoned. "Elize, I have to get to Cole, I have to warn him—"

"What is it, mistress?"

Her voice came out choked and hoarse. "I don't have time to explain. Cole's in trouble. I have to warn him, stop him before it's too late."

Elize straightened, her face creased with worry. "You know where—"

"Yes, yes I saw the note! Someplace called Green Turtle Quay. How do I get there?"

"John take you."

The two women raced into the yard, shouting for Elize's husband. Fortunately they caught him just before he left for town. Though they moved with speed and efficiency as they saddled the horses, to Devon's strained nerves it seemed to take forever. Nor did John ride as well as she did. She found herself holding back to keep from speeding ahead of him.

As they crested the top of a hill, she saw a glittering teal bay spread out beneath her. The small cove was banked by a treacherous reef on two sides, with a narrow channel that opened out to sea. The remote bay was the perfect hiding spot for the frigate, as the warship would not be seen by anyone approaching from sea. Devon's gaze focused on the party of five men who set off from the beach, pushing a small boat through the waves. She recognized Cole and her uncle immediately. "Cole!" she screamed, "Cole, don't!" The wind carried her words away and the men set off, rowing toward the frigate.

Devon dug her heels into her mount, intending to race down to the beach, but John shouldered his horse in front of her, stopping the movement. "Too late," he said. "This way."

She opened her mouth to protest, then immediately saw that he was right. They'd taken the only boat on the beach. By the time she reached the shoreline, not only would she be too late to warn Cole, but her only way to reach the warship would be to swim. Her terror increased as she watched the small boat bob toward the frigate.

John took off at a gallop moving east, away from the bay. Devon had no choice but to follow. They crested a higher ridge and tore down the steep slope on the other side. Grounded on the beach was a group of fishing boats that had been pulled ashore. A cluster of men worked inland spreading out nets to dry. Devon's heart slammed against her chest as hope surged anew. *Please,* she silently prayed, *let there be enough time. Let me reach them in time.*

She and John raced to the shore and leaped from their mounts, quickly commandeering the largest boat. The crashing waves nearly dragged her under as they fought against the current to push the boat out to sea. The fishermen raced toward them, screaming in protest, but they didn't stop to explain. They pushed the boat into the water, then climbed aboard and raised the sail, ignoring the clamor of the men who watched from the beach. John tilted the rudder and directed them out to sea, intending to go around the bay and back into the cove through the channel, but Devon stopped him. "The reef! Go over the reef."

"Too dangerous."

She gripped his wrist in dull panic, aware that she was not only risking her own life, but asking him to risk his as well. "John, we don't have a choice. We don't have time. There's no other way."

He studied her intently, then brought the small boat around. They entered the reef, tossed about by the savage currents and random winds. Devon's heart pounded furiously as she stared through the crystal waters at the deadly, jagged coral directly beneath them. The coral was sharper than glass, and far more dangerous. One strong gust of wind and the hull would be torn off the boat. If they capsized, it would slice through their skin.

Fortunately John sailed better than he rode. They made it through the violent, swirling currents and out into the calm water of the bay. They were beside the frigate almost immediately, their small boat gently bumping up against the massive hull.

Devon reached for the knotted rope that was flung over the side and climbed up, John directly behind her. The coarse rope burned into her palms as the weight of her sodden riding skirt threatened to drag her down, but she made it. She reached the deck, gasping and out of breath. She ducked beneath the ship's rail, amazed to find that none of Sharpe's men was there to stop her. Glancing around, she thought that the deck was deserted, until the sound of men's voices raised in anger drifted toward her from the aft section.

Devon lifted her drenched skirts and raced in that direction as John clambered on board behind her. "Wait," she heard him call, but she couldn't listen. She was operating on pure terror now. She understood immediately why no one had seen their approach. The crewmen were all clustered aft. Uncle Monty, Jonas Sharpe, and Earl Finch stood with their backs to her. She looked beyond them and drew up short, choked with horror. Two of Sharpe's crewmen pinned back Cole's arms; his lip was cut and bleeding.

Uncle Monty's words slowly penetrated her brain. "Nothing personal, my good friend," he said to Cole, "surely you of all people can see that Devon deserves better. I'm only trying to do what's best for her."

Cole's face went dark with fury as he struggled against the men who held him. "You son-of-a-bitch!" he roared. "You set me up!"

Devon froze, feeling as though she were trapped in a nightmare in which she could neither move nor speak. She watched as Jonas Sharpe raised his pistol, but Monty immediately caught his arm, lowering it. Devon nearly collapsed in relief. Then her uncle's words reached her.

"Please," he said to Sharpe, "allow me."

Monty raised his hand and pointed a pistol directly at Cole's chest. "No," she screamed, but the word scarcely came out. It was rough and raw and weak, a choked plea she could barely get through her throat.

The sound was enough to carry to Cole. In a split-second of time, she saw his gaze shift, his eyes widening in horror as he saw her.

Monty fired.

"No!" This time the scream was torn from her throat, a primitive sound of pain she hadn't known she was capable of making. Her uncle, Sharpe, and the rest of the men spun toward her in surprise, but her eyes were focused only on Cole.

He jerked his head toward Monty as he staggered back, then brought his hand up against his chest, staring down in stunned disbelief as blood poured through his fingers. He swayed, shock etched clearly on his features as he collapsed against the rough wooden deck.

"No! No!" Devon couldn't stop screaming. She rushed toward Cole, vaguely aware of Monty yelling for her, of hands reaching out to stop her. John lunged forward but was abruptly brought down by three crewmen who tackled him and held him still. Devon fought off the men who tried to stop her and threw herself down beside Cole.

He lay absolutely still, a pool of crimson blood seeping from his body. She touched his face, then brought her fingers down to his chest. The shirt, which only an hour ago had been a cool white linen, was now soaked with blood. She lifted her hands. Cole's blood dripped from her fingers.

"No ... No ... No!" It started as a whisper and escalated into a scream. She rocked back and forth over his body. Cole couldn't be dead. He couldn't be dead. The vision she'd had in Wilmington clouded her brain like a red, hazy hell: the gun, the blood, Cole was there ... but not there. "No!" she screamed, willing it not to be true, refusing to accept it. Tears streamed down her cheeks. She was still screaming as Sharpe's men grabbed her by the arms and pulled her away from Cole's body. "No! No! Let me stay with him. Please, let me stay with him! He needs me! I have to be here when he wakes up—"

The men dragged her away. Monty's face swam into

focus before her. "My girl," he said, "it'll be all right. I promise, it'll be all right."

"No! No! Cole needs me—"

"For God's sake, someone shut her up!" Jonas Sharpe growled.

A crewman stepped forward and slapped her hard across the face. Devon was knocked backward, remaining standing only by virtue of the two men who held fast to her upper arms. She felt a sharp stinging sensation in her cheek and heard a roar in her ears, but she was strangely removed from it, as if she was very far away. The world was no longer anything but echoes and shadows. She felt no pain, no horror, nothing at all. A numbing, freezing fog settled over her. She welcomed it, embraced it.

Dimly she was aware of her Uncle Monty surging forward, his face crimson with fury as he lunged for the man who'd hit her. But Monty was no match for the four crewmen who leaped to restrain him. The pistol he'd used to shoot Cole fell from his grasp. It skid across the deck and flew overboard.

"Pity," said Jonas Sharpe, "that was a fine piece. And I rather liked the thought of killing you with the same gun you used to kill McRae."

Monty struggled furiously against the men who held him. "We had a deal, Sharpe!"

"The deal's off," Sharpe bit out. He turned and motioned to his crewmen. "Start the engines and bring them all to the bow. I want to be further out to sea before we throw them overboard. We can't have their bodies washing ashore too soon, now can we?"

Devon watched indifferently as Monty and John put up a vicious struggle as the crewmen dragged them behind Sharpe. She followed without resistance, neither fighting nor helping, simply letting the crewmen pull her along. She realized with a sharp tug that they were leaving Cole behind, then just as quickly realized that it no longer mattered. He lay just a few feet away, motionless in a pool of blood. She faded once again into blank nothingness.

The wind whipped her sodden skirts around her legs as the engine rumbled to life. They finally reached the bow. Heated words about money and honor were tossed back and forth between Monty and Sharpe, but Devon paid them no attention. She stared at the sky instead. It was twilight, that glorious time of day when dusky shadows of lavender and sapphire filled the sky, when the clouds were edged with gold and the sun sank crimson into the sea. Cole's favorite time of day. She nodded approvingly. It was a good time to die.

The roar of an explosion suddenly shook them all. Devon stumbled as the ship lurched sideways, then a second explosion threw her forward. Released by the crewmen who'd been knocked off-balance as well, she stumbled onto her hands and knees. Jonas Sharpe grabbed her by the arm and yanked her roughly back up. "Go see what the hell that was," he yelled to the crewmen who'd held her. "It sounded like it came from the engine room." The crewmen raced off to obey.

Sharpe turned to Monty. "Looks like your precious niece won't get to marry that duke after all. Because you were so helpful, Persons, I'm going to let you watch her die."

Devon didn't flinch as the cold steel of his gun pressed into her neck. She was ready, but she had one final request to make. She closed her eyes and muttered a brief prayer.

"Drop the gun, Sharpe, or I'll blow your brains all over this deck."

Cole.

Devon's eyes flew open in disbelief. He stood just off to her left, his gun pressed against Jonas Sharpe's skull. His shirt was still caked with blood, his expression was grim, but he was alive. Absolutely, stunningly alive. More than that, he looked healthy—and more utterly furious than she'd ever seen a human being in her life.

Cole cocked back his gun. "Now, goddammit." Devon felt the steel pressure ease off her neck as Sharpe slowly pulled back. Cole reached for the man's pistol and removed it from his grasp. "Devon, are you all right?"

She opened her mouth, but no sound came out.

Cole flicked his gaze toward her, his eyes dark with worry. "Devon?"

She swallowed hard. "Yes," she finally managed.

Cole nodded tightly. "Tell your men to let them go," he said to Sharpe, gesturing toward Monty and John. Sharpe obeyed and his men backed off. Devon watched with stunned amazement as he passed Sharpe's weapon to Monty. "Watch them," he said curtly.

"You'll never get away with this," Sharpe hissed. "You try to make a run to sea without the proper signal from the port, and there'll be four Confederate warships roaring after you."

"I'm going to give you the same choice I'll give your men," Cole said, ignoring the threat. "You can surrender to me and I'll take you to prison alive, or you can drown in the wreck."

Sharpe seethed with fury. "You wouldn't wreck this ship, she's too valuable—even to the North."

"Wouldn't I?" Cole asked darkly. "Can't you feel it—we're drifting, Sharpe. When you failed to leave a guard to watch a dead man, I had enough time to sneak below and blow up your engines. In five minutes the hull is going to be sliced open by the coral reef."

Behind Cole, silhouetted in the fading twilight glow, Devon watched in awed disbelief as the *Ghost* entered the narrow channel of the bay and sailed cleanly toward them. A dull roar filled her ears once again, making her distinctly light-headed. Strange, but not at all unpleasant. She took a few steps backward, away from the group of men, suddenly needing more air than she was getting.

"You two had this planned all along, didn't you?" she asked, looking from Cole to Monty.

Her Uncle Monty grinned broadly. "Brilliant, wasn't it?"

"You never shot Cole."

Monty waved that away. "Fired way over his head."

She looked at Cole, who was staring back at her with the most peculiar expression on his face. "You really are alive then, aren't you," she said.

"Devon—"

"My. Isn't that wonderful." She gave him a wobbly smile. Her stomach flipped over, her knees turned to liquid, and the faces of the men spun around before her. Fortunately she didn't have far to fall. The rough wooden deck obligingly rushed up to meet her.

Chapter 20

Aboard the *Ghost*, the lights in the captain's cabin burned softly. Cole stared down at Devon, his eyes dark with worry. She was still and unmoving, her face deathly pale except for the ugly bluish-green swelling on her cheek. He reached for a cool, damp cloth and pressed it gently against the bruise. "She should be awake by now," he muttered, fighting back a rising sense of panic.

"Easy, my boy," Monty said from behind him, placing his hand lightly on Cole's shoulder. "She's had a bit of a shock, that's all. Give her a little more time."

A bit of a shock, Cole thought in disgust. According to John, Devon had risked her life sailing over a treacherous coral reef, only to have been betrayed by her uncle, slapped senseless by a hotheaded crewman, and had a gun held to her throat by Jonas Sharpe. She'd watched her husband die, then miraculously seen him come back to life. That qualified in Cole's book as more than "a bit of a shock."

She lay absolutely still, a posture that was completely unlike Devon. Even in sleep, she moved constantly, tossing and turning, cuddling against him one minute, rolling atop him the next—a pattern Cole had not only become adjusted to, but thoroughly enjoyed. Devon was a bundle of vibrant feminine energy, of life, of love, of everything he could have wished for in the world.

Cole studied her in grim silence. He could see that

she was breathing, but that was about it. He wet the cloth and returned it to her cheek, reviewing in his mind what had happened, wishing there'd been some way for him to stop it. He'd seen Devon only a fraction of a second before Monty had fired the shot. At that point, there'd been no way for him to stop their plan, or to react differently. Having been forced to lie there immobile while Devon touched him, to hear the naked anguish in her voice and not be able to reach for her, to comfort her, had been sheer torture. But had he done anything else, it likely would have cost them all their lives.

Still it had taken every ounce of strength he possessed not to move as the crewmen dragged her away from him. After that, from where he lay on deck, he'd been able to make out nothing but a muffled flurry of shouts and footsteps, all indistinct. The noise was buffered by the group of men who stood between him and Sharpe. It wasn't until Cole had seen the nasty swelling on her cheek and Monty informed him that she'd been struck by one of the crewmen that he was aware of what had transpired. Had he known, or seen it happen, there wouldn't have been a force on earth that would have kept him from leaping up and ripping the man apart.

He heard a gentle moan and returned his gaze immediately to her face, watching her thick, sooty lashes flicker open. Her beautiful eyes were cloudy and dull, her brows drawn together in silent confusion. He lifted her hand and gave it a gentle squeeze. "Devon," he said softly. "Devon, you're safe now, everything's all right." She studied him blankly, as though his words were nothing but gibberish uttered in a foreign tongue. Her gaze moved past him, fixing on a spot just over his shoulder.

"Welcome back, my girl," Cole heard Monty say.

"You're aboard the *Ghost* now, and we're here with you. It's all over."

Devon's gaze moved slowly around the room as comprehension slowly dawned on her features. Her eyes snapped back to Cole, no longer blank and frightened, but full of hope and disbelief. "Cole?" she said.

He smiled softly and lifted her hand to touch his face. "I'm right here, love. I'm not going anywhere."

"Oh, Cole . . ." Her voice came out a choked whisper that tore through his soul. She reached for him and he leaned down, gathering her into his embrace. He felt her shudder, then her tears trickled down and soaked his shoulder through his shirt. He cradled her against him and softly stroked her back, doing everything he could to ease away her fear, her pain.

"That's enough of that," Monty interrupted gruffly. "It's my turn, Captain."

Cole reluctantly let go and turned her into her uncle's embrace. Monty hugged her solidly. "Didn't I tell you to trust your old uncle?"

Devon pulled back. She sniffed and wiped away her tears. "Trust you? Never. You're horrible, horrible men, and I hate you both," she declared weakly, a shaky smile on her face. "I'm never going to forgive either one of you."

She struggled to sit up. Cole immediately reached to assist her, but she slapped away his hands. "Don't you dare try to act all tender and concerned, Cole McRae. You put me through hell and you know it."

"Now, now, my girl," interjected Monty, "it wasn't your captain's fault. You weren't supposed to be there, remember?" He frowned. "By the way, what tipped you off and made you come after us?"

Guilt flashed across her face as she met her uncle's eyes. "I found that piece of wire in your pocket, and your coat reeked of Jonas Sharpe's cologne. The only explanation I could find was that you were double-crossing Cole. I'm so sorry, Uncle Monty, I should have known better.''

"No, my girl, I'm quite proud of you," Monty soothed. "It just goes to prove that I didn't raise a fool. There's no pulling the wool over your eyes." He stroked his beard, a thoughtful frown on his face. "But you actually believed I'd work with Jonas Sharpe? Come now, my girl, you know me better than that. I wouldn't let that man lick the soles of my boots clean even if he paid for the honor."

Devon drew her brows together. "I don't understand—"

"We had to come up with a plan fast," Cole explained, "one that would give us both Sharpe and the frigate. Sharpe was right in saying there was no way we could smuggle the vessel out to sea, not from this port. Our only hope was to wreck it with Sharpe aboard. But up until that point, Sharpe had been staying as far away from his ship as possible, letting men like Finch do all his dirty work."

"There was also the risk of Sharpe finding out that Cole was actually working for the Union," Monty continued, "particularly here in Nassau where so many people know him. So we set up a double-cross to make him feel totally in control. Knowing the man's taste for blood, we knew there was no chance he'd stay away."

"Why did you trick us with your horse?" Devon asked.

"I only fooled you, my girl, and not for very long. Your captain was fully aware of what I was planning. Finch was standing nearby, and I needed a witness to report back to Sharpe that I truly was betraying you both."

Devon absorbed that, then her gaze moved back to Cole. "Where did you go last night?"

"Down to the docks," he answered. "You'd already told me how Sharpe handled his crew. I figured it wouldn't take much to bribe the ones I could find into not reporting back to the ship, and I was right. His men detest him almost as much as we do. That's why the vessel was so nearly deserted today.''

He watched her eyes as they traced back over his chest, painfully aware of what she was remembering. He'd stripped out of the clothing he'd worn earlier and washed all traces of blood from his body, wanting to spare her the shock of seeing him that way again. He now wore a light blue shirt and tan trousers that were neat and clean. He'd removed Devon's gown as well, for it too had been soaked in blood. Since her uncle was in the room, he'd left her in her slim cotton shift and tucked the blankets around her.

"There was so much blood . . .'' she said softly.

"Monty made a trip to the butcher's shop early this morning,'' Cole said. "I had a sheep's bladder filled with blood strapped beneath my shirt.''

"Disgusting bit of business,'' Monty said, "but effective.''

Cole showed Devon the ring he'd been wearing. The side that faced his palm had a jagged metal protrusion. "All I had to was slap my hand against my chest and jerk it upward.'' The blood had gushed out thick and heavy, just as Monty had promised it would.

"But I helped you dress,'' Devon protested, "there was nothing—''

"I didn't put it on until just before we met with Finch.''

Devon's face changed, and the pain of betrayal flashed through her eyes. "Why didn't you tell me?''

Cole sighed. "We didn't want you involved, Devon. I didn't want you to worry, and I was terrified that if you knew what we were up to, you would find a way to put yourself at risk. I tried to do whatever I could to keep that from happening. It was selfish, and I know you deserve better, but I was trying my damnedest to protect you. Obviously I failed miserably, didn't I?''

Devon considered his answer, then seemed to put the matter from her mind. Though Cole sensed clearly that within the next few days he would doubtless be treated to a stinging lecture on the subjects of trust and honesty.

"What happens now?" she asked, sounding tired.

"Now I do what I was ordered to do nearly a month ago: bring my prisoner to Old Capitol."

Monty's brows snapped together, and Devon gave a soft gasp. "I'm speaking of Jonas Sharpe, of course," Cole immediately clarified. "His men will be traded for Union prisoners of war. Last I heard, Lincoln and Davis were still swapping men. As long as they swear an oath never to lift arms against the Union again, there shouldn't be a problem."

"What about the ships that are being built in Liverpool?" Devon asked. "Do you have to stop those too?"

Cole shook his head. "Word is out that Lee was stopped in his invasion of the North. As long as the Union is winning, England won't dare release them."

Devon's eyes glowed. "You did it, Cole," she said, her voice filled with pride. "You won—you got everything you wanted."

"We won," he amended, gently brushing her hair back away from her face.

"Speaking of winning," Monty boomed out, "I must congratulate you on that swoon, my girl. First-class all the way. Your skin turned the most magnificent shade of green—it nearly matched your eyes! Fabulous! Now if you can remember that when we go back into business—"

"She's not going back into business," Cole announced firmly.

"What?" Monty frowned as he looked from Devon

to Cole, then he slowly stroked his beard. "Now that you mention it, Captain, perhaps this would be a good time to retire. Look at the profit we just made: we bought the cotton for six cents a pound in Wilmington, we'll sell it for sixty cents a pound in England . . . now how many tons did we have aboard?"

"You're right, the profit was extraordinary," Cole replied. "The people who run the Fund for Widows and Orphans of the War were quite astounded to receive it. They were so grateful, in fact, that I took the liberty of donating your half as well."

Monty's face slowly changed from red to crimson to purple. "You did what?!" he roared. "My half?! Did you say you my half?! Why you no good son-of-a—"

"Later," Cole said, rising to his feet. He slid a glance at Devon, who was looking pale and fatigued, as though the shock was finally setting in, and, taking the hint, Monty nodded and left the room without another word.

After seeing Monty out, Cole crossed the cabin and sat down beside her. Their eyes locked for a long, silent minute, then he reached out and gently touched her cheek. "Does it hurt very much?"

She shook her head, just as he knew she would. The bruise was probably throbbing. She frowned, glancing at his knuckles as he drew his hand away. "That looks painful," she said, referring to his swollen, torn skin.

"You should see the face of the man who gave you that bruise." Cole shrugged. "For that matter, Jonas Sharpe doesn't look very healthy either."

"Hmmm."

"Do you want to sleep?"

"No."

Another long silence fell between them. Finally Cole drew in a deep breath and slowly let it out. He glanced down at his hands, amazed to find that they were actu-

ally shaking. "Devon, when I came up from the engine
room and saw Sharpe's gun pointed at your neck . . ."

She gazed solemnly into his eyes. "Did you know I
was making my last wish?"

Cole thought about it and remembered her lips moving in fervent prayer. Gently he asked, "Will you tell
me what you wished for?"

Devon took a deep breath and gave him a trembling
smile. "I was begging God not to send me to heaven
if I died."

He stared at her in silent confusion. "Why?"

Her smile wavered as tears once again flooded her
eyes. "Because I knew that couldn't possibly be where
He'd have sent you."

Cole gave a choked laugh as his heart exploded in
his chest. He wrapped her tightly in his arms, squeezing
her against him. "I love you, Devon. God, how I
love you."

Devon let out a blissful sigh and rolled over onto
Cole's chest. There was something almost sinful about
being indoors, making love in the middle of the day.
She smiled to herself, wondering if that added touch of
"sin" was what had made the experience so wonderful,
or if it was merely the fact that she hadn't seen Cole
for two whole weeks.

He'd left the day after they'd captured Sharpe, heading back to Fort Monroe to see to the exchange of
prisoners. Jonas Sharpe was shackled and bound, then
placed on a heavily guarded barge sailing up the Potomac toward Old Capitol Prison. From what he'd told
her, the mood at Fort Monroe was one of determined
optimism after Lee's defeat at Antietam and the reduced
threat of England's interference. With any luck, the war
would be ending swiftly. Devon prayed that it was so.

For now, she fully intended to enjoy the fact that her
husband was with her once again, and had earned two

weeks of leave before he had to return to blockade duty. Cole lifted a finger and traced it over her mouth. "That smile is not only beautiful and enticing," he said, "but it looks to be a cover for some gloriously wicked thought. Tell me."

She laughed and gazed down into his eyes from her perch atop his chest. "Doesn't this seem . . . decadent, in the middle of the day?"

He grinned. "Absolutely. That's why we're doing it."

"What if someone catches us?"

"Who?"

"Well, Elize could just walk in . . ."

"Elize is not about to just walk into my bedroom. Besides, she and John are in town." He thought for a moment. "Where's Monty?"

Devon ran her fingers over his chest. "He said something about going down to the docks and teaching your crew a new card game."

Cole groaned.

"Oh, I got your watch back, by the way," she continued brightly.

He let out a sigh and rubbed his hand over his eyes. "I didn't realize it was missing again."

"I hope you understand, Cole. It's nothing personal; Uncle Monty just likes to keep in practice." She gave him a stern frown. "But you do make it awfully tempting for him. You should be more careful with your things."

"My apologies. In the future, I'll try bonding my watch and wallet to my skin. Though I suspect he'll find a way to pry them loose no matter what I do."

"True." Devon sighed contentedly. "This is nice."

"What?"

"This. Just lying here, doing absolutely nothing."

"Nothing?" Cole smiled and ran his hands lightly over her body. "You have a awfully short memory. It seems to me we were quite busy not more than ten minutes ago.''

Devon squirmed on top of him. "Maybe it's time for you to remind me.''

He laughed. "I've been meaning to ask you, my love, where do you sleep when I'm not around for you to climb on top of?''

She gave him a suggestive smile. "I don't. I stay up all night, yearning for you.''

Cole let out a long breath. "Thank you very much. That image is going to cost me at least one night's sleep while I'm away.''

Devon instantly sobered. "Please, let's not talk about that now. We have two whole weeks left.''

"You're right, I'm sorry.'' He brushed a light kiss over her lips and traced his hands soothingly over her back. Then he lifted her off him and moved to stand. She watched his gloriously naked body as he crossed the room.

"Where are you going?''

He didn't answer, but went to rummage through the bag he'd brought back from his ship. He returned and handed her a gaily wrapped package. "This is for you.''

"What is it?''

"A wedding gift.''

Devon arched a dark brow.

Cole grinned. "A little late, I know. We've already established what a horrid sense of timing I have, so there's no need to go into that again.''

She smiled and removed the wrappings to reveal an intricately carved gold box, the lid studded with pearls and semiprecious stones. "Oh, Cole,'' she said, "the jewelry box is lovely—''

"It's not for jewelry.''

She gazed up at him, surprised by his somber tone. "Then what—''

"It's a memory box, Devon. Something in which to

store all those memories you collect, so you'll never lose a single one." He paused, looking both tender and serious at once. "Unlike the wedding gift you gave me, this one comes with strings attached. If you accept it, I expect the next fifty years of your life in return to help fill it up."

Devon bit her lip to hide a wayward, trembling smile. "Only the next fifty?"

He shrugged. "We can negotiate after that."

She nodded, swallowing past the tight knot in her throat. "That sounds like a pretty fair deal to me."

She let her body melt against his as his hands drifted in random, loving strokes over her skin. "You know," she said, "I still can't believe that you let Uncle Monty talk you into that wild scheme of his."

Cole frowned as he searched her eyes, clearly puzzled. "What scheme?"

"His plan to capture Sharpe, of course."

"I'll have you know that entire scheme was my idea."

"No," she gasped.

"Every last detail," he smugly informed her.

Devon studied him in an altogether new light. "Cole McRae, I've come to the conclusion that you were corrupted long before I ever met you. You're nothing but a thief at heart."

Cole smiled and tightened his arms around her. "And you, my darling wife, are such a lady."

Avon Romances—
the best in exceptional authors and unforgettable novels!

MONTANA ANGEL **Kathleen Harrington**
77059-8/ $4.50 US/ $5.50 Can

EMBRACE THE WILD DAWN **Selina MacPherson**
77251-5/ $4.50 US/ $5.50 Can

MIDNIGHT RAIN **Elizabeth Turner**
77371-6/ $4.50 US/ $5.50 Can

SWEET SPANISH BRIDE **Donna Whitfield**
77626-X/ $4.50 US/ $5.50 Can

THE SAVAGE **Nicole Jordan**
77280-9/ $4.50 US/ $5.50 Can

NIGHT SONG **Beverly Jenkins**
77658-8/ $4.50 US/ $5.50 Can

MY LADY PIRATE **Danelle Harmon**
77228-0/ $4.50 US/ $5.50 Can

THE HEART AND THE HEATHER **Nancy Richards-Akers**
77519-0/ $4.50 US/ $5.50 Can

DEVIL'S ANGEL **Marlene Suson**
77613-8/ $4.50 US/ $5.50 Can

WILD FLOWER **Donna Stephens**
77577-8/ $4.50 US/ $5.50 Can

Avon Romantic Treasures

Unforgettable, enthralling love stories,
sparkling with passion and adventure
from Romance's bestselling authors

CAPTIVES OF THE NIGHT *by Loretta Chase*
76648-5/$4.99 US/$5.99 Can

CHEYENNE'S SHADOW *by Deborah Camp*
76739-2/$4.99 US/$5.99 Can

FORTUNE'S BRIDE *by Judith E. French*
76866-6/$4.99 US/$5.99 Can

GABRIEL'S BRIDE *by Samantha James*
77547-6/$4.99 US/$5.99 Can

COMANCHE FLAME *by Genell Dellin*
77524-7/ $4.99 US/ $5.99 Can

WITH ONE LOOK *by Jennifer Horsman*
77596-4/ $4.99 US/ $5.99 Can

LORD OF THUNDER *by Emma Merritt*
77290-6/ $4.99 US/ $5.99 Can

RUNAWAY BRIDE *by Deborah Gordon*
77758-4/$4.99 US/$5.99 Can